THE ETERNAL MASQUERADE

R.J. LEHNER

authorHOUSE®

AuthorHouse™
1663 Liberty Drive
Bloomington, IN 47403
www.authorhouse.com
Phone: 1 (800) 839-8640

Published by AuthorHouse 05/30/2018

ISBN: 978-1-5462-3771-6 (sc)
ISBN: 978-1-5462-3769-3 (hc)
ISBN: 978-1-5462-3770-9 (e)

Library of Congress Control Number: 2018904417

Print information available on the last page.

This book is printed on acid-free paper.

Acknowledgement

To everyone who has helped me with this book, thank you.

To my team at AuthorHouse Publishing, thank you, for without you and all of your hard work, this dream of mine would not be a reality.

To my family and friends, especially my mom, thank you for your unending support. You have all helped me grow as a person and encouraged me to follow my dreams, no matter how outrageous they may be.

And most importantly, thank you to my friend, mentor and teacher, Mrs. DeKoch. Thank you for fostering my love of writing, literature and learning in general. You have helped me through all of the hardest trials in my life, and I could never be more grateful. Without your love and support, I am afraid to imagine the path on which my life would have gone. I cannot say that I know where life will take me, but I can say for certain that I will never forget the lessons you taught me, the love, support and care that you have given me, and I will forever treasure our friendship. Thank you from the bottom of my heart!

It's dark, I can't see a thing. My heart races at a million miles per hour, and my breathing is ragged. I'm bleeding, I can feel the warmth oozing through my shirt, causing it to stick to my side. I'm going to die, *I think as I stumble through the pitch-black corridor. The stabbing pain in my side is agonizing. It calls my attention away from finding an escape from this black hell, but I keep moving forward.*

A freezing wind blows through and I stop, a cold presence sending chills down my spine. I feel as if someone has replaced my blood with ice water. I'm cold to the core.

"You can't run from me, Celia," he says. His voice is oddly soothing but with an undertone of malice. "I will always find you."

I wake up gasping. My sheets lay in a tangled mess at my feet, and the comforter is on the ground in a crumpled pile. I can feel my heart pounding away inside my chest, in time with my quick breathing. Slowly, I take deep breaths, calming my fried nerves. It's the third time this week that I've had this nightmare. It has always included the cold but lovely voice, promising to find me. I can't tell whether it's endearing or creepy, although based on my reaction, I'm leaning more towards the latter.

I roll out of my bed and onto the ground, hitting the carpet hard, momentarily forcing the wind from my lungs. I groan and roll onto my back, slowly regaining my ability to breathe.

"Damn dreams," I growl in frustration, climbing to my feet. I walk to my window and gaze out over the front lawn. The sun is barely rising, just coming over the peaks of the bluffs, bathing the city in a pale orange light. I rest my head against the window, the cold glass feels nice against my burning skin. It helps to soothe the nerves that were sent into overdrive.

"Celia, get your ass up!" There's a pounding on my door, shaking me out of the piece of calm and serenity I had found after my rattling nightmare.

"Step off, Amy. I'm up!" I yell back, irritation heavy in my voice.

"Then get the hell out here, we have to get to school."

"We have forty-five minutes," I say with exasperation as I open the door. My sister stands there with her arms crossed over her chest, a frustrated look adorning her face.

"Yeah but–" I hold up a hand, silencing her.

"Amy, we always get to school on time, there's no need to worry. I will get my little sister to where she needs to be in a timely manner, as I always do, okay?" I say reassuringly.

"Fine," she sighs in resignation, turning away and meandering down the stairs to the kitchen table.

I close my door and get dressed, putting on the outfit I had chosen the previous night, as I've always done. Today is nothing special, I've decided to go with a black miniskirt and a red and black plaid shirt with the sleeves rolled up. I've never thought of myself as the person who walks into school dressed as if I were heading to a job interview, but I've also never thought myself to be the person who comes into school looking like I rolled out of bed only seconds ago. I like to be in between the two extremes, looking nice, but also casual. Well, at least my opinion of casual.

I go through my morning routine. It's the exact same one I go through every morning, following each individual step as if it's the law. The only thing that ever changes is the way I do my hair, and today, I simply comb it and let it fall onto my shoulders as it naturally does.

I jog down the stairs to the kitchen table where my sister sits and grab the same Power Bar I've eaten every morning, quickly unwrapping it before wolfing it down and heading to my car.

Amy follows, quick on my heels, complaining about something which I neglect to pay attention to. Instead of listening to her, I focus on carrying out my morning routine the exact same way I have done every morning.

My sister and I pile into the flaming red Dodge Avenger that sits in the driveway, glistening in the light of the morning sun. I stop for a moment to admire my car before I climb inside and begin to drive away.

"Huh-uh, feet off the dash," I command, chastising my sister. "You know I don't like your dirty shoes on my clean dashboard."

She sighs and pulls her feet down, giving me the annoyed look she always does when I insist she keep my car as clean as it was when she entered it. I'm very affectionate towards my car, treating it better than I treat most people. I always make sure to keep the exterior and interior clean and pristine, careful so that my car is never scratched or damaged.

We pull into the parking lot with 15 minutes until class starts, snatching the same parking spot we do every other day.

"You have OCD," Amy declares as she closes her door and slings her backpack over her shoulder.

"Is that a problem?" I ask, doing the same as she had done. "My OCD and need to follow a routine are what get us to school on time every day."

"I guess you have a point," she says in defeat, wandering off to some place unknown, most likely in search of her friends.

I sigh, mentally preparing myself to deal with the idiots who infest Goodman High School, before locking the doors and heading inside.

If you've ever been in a high school parking lot, you know that it's a crazy mesh of speeding cars, frantic for a parking space, and reckless teenagers who believe they're invincible. Kids rush out in front of the cars, attempting to make it to the building before the warning bell goes off. This one is no exception. Impetuous students still sprint about, narrowly avoiding the speeding cars. Symphonies of honks and hollers can be heard from any and every point in the parking lot. If that isn't enough to wake you up, or drive you crazy, then there's obviously something wrong you.

With another sigh, I begin my journey through the treacherous high school parking lot. I only feel relatively safe once I'm in the building, and it's not because people are *that* bad at driving, but because I know that there are several people who would just love to run me over, simply for kicks. Because somewhere along the line, I really offended them, which happens a lot more than I'd like to admit.

As I enter the building, I'm immediately pulled into the slow meander of student traffic. It flows through the hallway at a speed that seems to crawl.

I push through the crowds of people. I just want to get to my locker so I can swap out my books and get to class.

Finally, I reach my locker and quickly spin in the combo, switching out my AP French and Culture book along with my AP Psychology book, for my College Calculus and AP Chemistry books. I grab my copy of *Paradise Lost*, by John Milton, from the top shelf of my locker before heading to class.

Almost instantly, I open the book to the page I had left off on, not that it really mattered. By this point, I've read the book so many times, I can open to a random page and know exactly what is going on.

Suddenly, I come to halt, running head on into someone in front of me.

"Oops, sorry," I say, lifting my gaze to see who it was that I had run into, and upon doing so, I almost drop my book. "You know what? I'm actually not sorry," I scowl, irritated at the sight before me.

"Watch where you're going," he growls. "Maybe if you didn't always have your head in a book you might be able to see where you're going."

"You know, this unfortunate predicament isn't just my fault. You could have used those athletic skills you pride yourself on and dodged me, but alas, you were too stupid to do that. But that doesn't really surprise me, considering you only have three brain cells. One to walk, one to breathe, and one to spout out stupid things," I retort.

"It's not possible for someone to live with only three brain cells," he tells me with a condescending voice.

"Well, Beckett, you are living proof that one can," I smile, a bitter mocking smile.

"God, you are such a bitch," he says.

"I never said I wasn't, but that doesn't change the fact that I *am* fantastically amazing."

"Does the word 'arrogant' mean anything to you?" Beckett asks irritably.

"Nope," I respond right away in a light tone. "Does the word 'stupid' mean anything to you?" I ask. "Because it should. Oh, and by the way, Calculus is down the hall, not the way you're heading."

"I was on my way to my locker," he scowls. "I forgot my textbook."

"Can't say I'm surprised," I mutter, as he storms off down the hall. "What a prick," I say to myself with a bitter laugh, turning and walking to my math class.

I enter the room to find a new seating arrangement displayed on the front board and sigh. I hate the momentary chaos of getting new seats.

"Nice of you to join us today, Ms. Walters."

"I always join you, Mr. Lawrence," I say drearily. I try not to scowl. I've been told that it's not good to scowl at your teachers, but it's hard *not* to with Mr. Lawrence. We disagree on everything other than one little fact, and that fact being that we both detest each other. He thinks that I'm a spoiled brat who happens to be a know-it-all. I think that he's an asshole who sucks at teaching, and that sums up our relationship.

Before I lose my self-control and allow a look of disdain to creep onto my face, I switch my gaze to the front board in search of my new spot, freezing as I do so.

"Are you kidding?" I practically shout, turning to my teacher in fury. "I have to sit by Beckett Halverson?"

"I'm not pleased about it either." There's a mutter from the doorway, a voice that sounds completely miserable.

I spin around to find Beckett standing there with a bitter look on his face, a look that matches mine.

I groan and move to my seat, dragging my feet along the way as if I were headed to my execution. I drop my bag and take my seat, letting my head fall onto the desk as I slump forward.

"Look, I don't like having to sit next to you either, but honestly, you're acting as if this is a death sentence," Beckett says.

"Ugh, don't talk, please," I say in as agonized voice. "Your voice gives me a headache."

"God, you are such a bitch." His voice sounds far away. I'm lost in my own world of thought.

Who is that person in my dreams? I wonder, staring absently at my desk while Mr. Lawrence rambles on about something I've deemed unimportant.

I can't forget the way my blood chilled at the sound of his voice. Although his words would be found touching under most circumstances, they made my hairs stand on end and put my senses into overdrive. They made me want to scratch my skin off, just so I didn't have to feel that cold feeling.

"Ms. Walters!" Mr. Lawrence shouts, jarring me from my thoughts, demanding my attention. "Can you tell us what the answer is?" He wears a smug smile, triumph shining in his eyes.

"Seven," I say, looking up at the board, solving the equation in less than a second.

"Correct," he says grimly, the triumph fading from his eyes, granting me an immense amount of joy.

I spend the entire class ignoring Beckett and Mr. Lawrence, burying myself in my thoughts. I wander into a world far away, a world almost forgotten.

I'm jarred from my thoughts once again as the bell rings. I leave as fast as I can, desperate to get to my next class and away from the two people I despise the most.

"Good morning, Celia!" Mr. Simons greets me as I enter my Chemistry class, his voice cheery and light like it normally is. "How are you doing today?"

"Good morning, Mr. Simons. I'm doing well, and how about yourself?" I ask.

"Not too bad, thank you for asking. Alright everyone, get to your seats, we've got an exciting day ahead of us!" he exclaims happily, clapping his hands together as he makes his way to the front of the room.

I do as he says and take my seat at the back of the room, watching the other students file in and slowly take their seats.

Despite the interesting lesson Mr. Simon has planned, I don't pay attention, and he has no problem with that, which is nice. I like that most people chose to ignore what I'm doing, most of the time, they just let me do my own thing.

No one glances back at me as I absently stare at my desk or start reading a book. Not even when I pull out a music score and begin reading it, hearing the music in my head as my eyes scan the notes on the page, creating a symphony held only for me, with music that only I can hear. Music that tugs at memories buried deep within the murky waters of my mind.

No one is bothered by me except for Beckett Halverson. His gaze periodically falls on me from the front of the room, disdain obvious in his face.

I sigh, using all my self-control in order not to throw my music score across the room at him. I think I might just hate him more than I hate Mr. Lawrence.

What the hell is she doing? I glance back to see Celia reading a music score. A freaking music score. I'm pretty sure it's Chopin. I've overheard her talking with Mr. Simons before about her love for Chopin several times.

I think it's rude the way she treats teachers, especially ones as nice and fun as Mr. Simons. I mean, she could at least pretend to pay attention instead of pulling out a damn music score. I honestly don't think she has a polite bone in her body.

She lifts her head from the score to survey her surroundings and our eyes meet. I turn my head away from her cold gaze, unable to bear the intensity of her eyes. I find them piercing and unnerving, maybe even scary. They hold an intensity that burns right through you. She looks at you with a predatory stare, like she's devising all the ways she could tear you apart, mentally and physically. It's something that makes you uncomfortable in your own skin, to the point where you want to take a bath in acid to get rid of the feeling her gaze leaves.

I can feel her eyes on my back, watching me, analyzing me. I can see her bitter scowl in my mind; it's a look that I've become very familiar with. She wore that same scowl the first time I met her, and it was at that moment that we started hating each other. You may not believe that it's possible for a six-year-old to hate someone, but I assure you, it *is* possible. That moment, almost twelve years ago, pure hatred was born, and I can feel it inside me as I hear her sigh and flip a page.

"Beck, chill man."

"Huh?" I turn my head towards the voice and my best friend, Ben Milton, is looking at me with a grin. "I can't help it," I tell him. "She just pisses me off. She does whatever the hell she wants and thinks that it's okay! How can you stand her?"

"Cause she's cool," he says simply. Unlike me, he and Celia were great friends from the start, in fact, I think he's her only friend. It's kind of sad if you think about it, but the truth is that she brings it on herself, and there's no point in feeling sorry for someone like that.

"I think you're into her," I say finally. I can't come up with any other explanation for why he tolerates her.

"Dude, that's gross," he says with a shocked and disgusted cough. "Besides, I think that *you're* into her. *You're* the one who's always watching her and brooding over her actions."

"Don't be ridiculous," I scoff. "That girl simply pisses me off. There's something about her that just rubs me the wrong way."

"Yeah, I'm sure it rubs something," he says quickly, his grin spreading across his face. I reach out and smack him hard in the arm and tell him to shut up. I look over at him, waiting for another smartass response, but it never comes. Ben just stares down at his desk with a sad and faraway look in his eyes. The look makes me wonder just how much pain the guy has been through.

When he was younger, his entire family was killed in a brutal homicide, and he was moved out here to live with his foster parents. He never talks about his past, the names of his family members, if he'd had siblings, or even where he used to live, but I had been able to figure out at least one thing about his past. He'd had a little sister. I could tell it by the way he treats Lily, *my* little sister. He treats her better than I do, to be honest.

"Ben, what's up?" I ask in concern upon seeing his sad expression.

"Huh?" his head snaps up and that forlorn look disappears. For a minute I think I might've imagined it, but I know I didn't.

"You had that look," I tell him.

"Oh, I was just doing some thinking," he says nonchalantly, but I can tell he's being guarded. I can hear the undertone in his voice.

He glances back at Celia and that look crosses his face once again, making me more worried that before.

Maybe he actually is *into her,* I think. *Maybe I just insulted one of the only people he loves who's still alive.*

"Earth to Celia Walters." I blink and snap my head up to see Ben Milton waving one of his hands in front of my face.

"What?" I ask, slapping his hand away.

"I asked you if you wanted to work on that English project," he says.

"Oh, no it's fine, we can do it tomorrow. I've got to get home and practice piano," I tell him. We sit at a table in the library with our textbooks spread out before us. "I've been working on a real tough piece."

"Aren't you always?" he asks jokingly. "It's more Chopin, isn't it?"

"Yeah..."

"What is it with you and Chopin?" Ben asks in exasperation.

"Hey! Don't dis on Frédéric, he is The Master," I say defensively.

"I would never consider such a dastardly, villainous act," he teases. "Honestly though, out of all the great composers, what draws you so close to Chopin?"

"I find him comforting. Even though a lot of his pieces are kind of melancholy, and on the sad side of the scale, his music really brings me a sense of peace and tranquility," I say sheepishly. Normally I wouldn't disclose this kind of information. Some people would consider it to be personal information, and I don't really like to hand that out; however, Ben has always had a way of getting me to open up. I really trust him. He's the only one that I truly trust, the only one I tell my thoughts and feelings to.

He looks at me, his stormy eyes sad and forlorn. He wears that look a lot when I share my emotions and how I truly feel about things. The look speaks of loss. It's as if I remind him of something he once had, but is now lost to him. It's like the look one wears when remembering a lost loved one.

It's at this moment that a group of girls walk by. They all smile and wave at Ben with deep red faces, squealing in delight when he waves back.

Ben happens to be somewhat of a heartthrob at Goodman High School. He's tall with dark brown hair. The front is spiked in an upward curl, and the sides are cut short with the top a mess of tight curls. His ever-changing eyes compliment his dark hair, drawing a rapturing contrast. His dark hair and inconstant eyes match his golden skin along with the mysterious aura he's draped in. The running theme of his looks, personality, clothes and everything else is that he is dark. He's always dressed in black skinny jeans and a band t-shirt, half obscured by his worn-out leather jacket. His sleeves are always rolled up to his elbow to show off the band bracelets and spikes that pile up to the middle of his muscled forearm. To top everything off, he always has a single earbud placed in his ears so he can he listen to music nonstop, completing the mysterious "bad boy" punk persona he has going on.

The girls all love him. They flock to him like bugs to a light, and it irritates me. They don't even know him, they only find his exterior alluring. Shallow people like that make me sick.

"You don't have to look so angry, you know," he says.

"Those girls are shallow leeches who just think you're hot. They aren't interested in *you*, they're interested in your *looks*," I scowl.

"You sound a little jealous," he says jokingly.

"Don't make me throw up," I say. "That's absolutely disgusting."

He simply laughs at the disturbed look on my face and slowly begins to pack up, his eyes now shining with joy.

"I'm glad you find my discomfort uplifting," I say sarcastically, shooting him a dirty glare.

"Yeah, me too," he says with glee.

I smack him in the arm and call him a jerk, along with an assortment of other names. He continues to laugh, which only increases my name calling and cursing.

"Excuse me, but things are getting a little loud." Mrs. O'Leary, the librarian, comes hobbling over to us, supporting herself on her cane.

"Oh, sorry, Mrs. O'Leary," I say politely. I always try my best to be polite and nice to her, simply because she's always been kind to me.

Mrs. O'Leary is your stereotypical librarian. She's short, with grey, curly hair and spectacles connected to her shirt with a small silver chain so as to make sure that she doesn't lose them. Every outfit she wears looks as if it came from a time long ago, a period of long-forgotten, simple times. It just makes it even harder to *not* like her.

"It's quite alright," she says sweetly. "I just thought I should let you know."

"Thanks, we were about to head out," Ben says, smiling at the old lady as he hoists his backpack onto his shoulders.

"Alrighty, well, I'll see you tomorrow." She waves goodbye as we exit the building and head for the parking lot, ending the long day.

"Hey, Celia, how was your day?" my mom asks as I walk through the door, dropping my backpack off by the stairs.

"Same as it always is," I say, going up and giving her a hug.

"Off to piano I take it?" she asks.

"No, I'm actually going to head to bed," I tell her. "I had planned to play piano, but on my way home I got this massive headache, so I think I should just sleep it out."

"That's unusual for you, you haven't felt even slightly under the weather in forever," she says, a perplexed look playing on her face. "Is everything okay?"

"Yeah, it's just school stress," I tell her as I head up the stairs to my room. I open the door and crash down on my bed, but not before choosing an outfit for the next day, so as not to screw up my schedule and keep up with my daily routine.

I curl up underneath my blankets. My body is racked with violent shivering and I can't stop my teeth from chattering. I don't know how I got this cold. I feel as if I'm lying out in snow in only my bra and underwear, even though it's barely fall, and I'm under three blankets.

My phone goes off, buzzing obnoxiously on my bedside table. I quickly roll over and snatch it up to see a new message from Ben.

Hey Celia, don't forget that you have to get to school early tomorrow to set up for our Psychology presentation. Sorry to break your routine, but I don't think we'll be able to set it up after third hour and start class on time. Lucky for us, Mr. Sharpe has a first hour prep, and then teaches

Sociology in the room next door, so no one will screw with our stuff. You're welcome :)

I give a hearty laugh and place the phone back beside my bed. "Does he really have to text me every time we have a project?" I ask aloud. "He knows I never show up to anything late, ever. But I do have to break my routine." I groan at that last part, already becoming unsettled at the prospect of not following my normal schedule, but at least that strange momentary chill is now gone.

Within minutes I'm whisked away into the world of dreams, a world of beautiful nightmares.

"Come with me, Princess, let us leave while the night covers us. Let us leave while we still can." His voice makes me feel warm, it causes butterflies to erupt in my stomach. It's a familiar voice, one I've heard many times before, but I can't place where. I can't decipher whose voice it is.

"I have a duty to fulfill, I cannot leave," I say sorrowfully, feeling my heat grow heavy with grief.

"You know this is our last chance. We can leave and live, we do not have to die," he says, his voice urgent and pained. "You know we cannot fight Mesmer, we cannot defeat him. At most, we could weaken him, but we cannot kill him, no one is strong enough to do so."

"I know, but we have to try. You know the alternative. I give up and submit myself to him," I say somewhat cautiously.

"As I told you before, I will die before I allow that to happen," he snarls, his hand gripping the hilt of his sword until his knuckles turn white.

"And you will, you will be one of the first he kills." My voice almost cracks at that thought, pain seizing my being.

"And you will be the last he kills. You know it will be torment. He will play with you until he is bored, or until he wins this sick game he has started. And then he will kill you, or worse." His voice is filled with anger and agony, and I can feel my heart breaking at the sorrowful sound.

"I know," I tell him, my voice quiet and calm. I take his face in my hands, and gently press my lips to his, savoring the feeling of his touch, drawing away after a few seconds. "But that is the price I'm willing to pay to be yours."

The scene changes and I'm in a dark throne room. The floor tiles are an obsidian black. The two thrones at the center of the room are made of bleach-white bones, the bones of his enemies.

I'm crying, I can feel the tears dripping down my cheeks and onto his dying body. He's bleeding badly, despite the amount of pressure I put on the wound.

"You could have saved him, Celia." It's that beautiful voice from my dream the night before. He stands a few feet away, watching the scene unravel in in front of him with a sadistic smile. The sword in his hands drips blood onto the ground.

I myself am covered in blood, but none of it is my own, it all belongs to the man dying in my arms.

"Run," he chokes. "Get out of here while you still can."

"I am not leaving," I say defiantly, tears choking my voice. "If I do, who will finish this catastrophic dance?"

"You cannot end it if you stay here," he says, pain evident in his voice. "Now run and do not look back. Use that brilliant mind of yours to find a way to bring this bastard down. Find a way to end this eternal masquerade." With those last words, he becomes still and cold, his once vibrant eyes now dull and lifeless. Carefully, I close them, and in that moment, I feel something inside of me snap. The tears and trembling stop, and I am still, like the calm before a storm. I caress his lifeless face and plant a gentle kiss on his forehead before rising to my feet, his sword held firmly in my hand. I glance down at the ring he gave me, remembering the night when he took me as his. Closing my eyes tightly, a single tear escapes and trails down my cheek.

I take a deep breath to gather every ounce of strength I have, and then let go.

Electricity shoots from my body. The room becomes charred as I thrust the sword into the obsidian floor, causing the marble to crack and shatter. The pillars that hold up the building grow fissures and crumble down. The planet shakes, I can feel it in my bones, as if I'm connected to it as it is slowly torn apart, along with our universe.

A bright light flashes, it's white-hot, blinding. It's the last thing I see.

I wake up breathless, and I don't know where I am, the only thing I know is that I'm not in my room. I'm lying on the ground, surrounded by trees, some fallen and others still barely standing. The air has an acrid smell and my hairs stand on end as if I had almost been struck by lightning.

I have no idea where I am.

I'm cold. My sweatpants keep my legs warm, but the wind and the cold of the night cut right through my tank top, chilling me completely.

I can tell that I'm on top of a hill by the way the ground beneath me slopes downward on one side and runs flat on the other, tapering off into an even plateau.

A light at the bottom of the hill catches my eye as I survey the landscape, and I make my way towards it, grateful that I'm not completely submerged in the wilderness.

I can't see for shit. I keep tripping over roots, through thorn bushes and every other pokey and spiking thing that hides in the woods. By the time I reach the light, I'm covered in cuts and sweat. My heart is pounding hard in my chest, stressed from the laborious journey down the hill.

The light belongs to a nice little farm house. It looks like it's painted a dull shade of yellow, with a deep brown porch looping around the front. About fifty yards away are two barns, and what looks like a shack. There's a man standing by the bigger barn and I run toward him, sure that I look like a maniac.

"Excuse me, sir, but could you tell me where I am?" I ask.

"About ten miles south of Rockford. How did you get here?" he asks suspiciously.

"I'm not sure," I tell him, deciding to be honest.

"You mean to tell me that you just popped up with no idea how you got here?" he asks, skepticism replacing his suspicion.

"Pretty much," I say. "I know it's not really believable, but that is exactly what happened."

"And how do I know you're not lying?" he says testily.

"Because if I were going to lie about how I got here, wouldn't it make a lot more sense to come up with a story that isn't completely ludicrous? My story's too absurd not to be the truth."

He pauses with a contemplative look, as if debating how valid my statement is. "What's your name?" he asks finally.

"Celia Walters," I state, matter-of-factly.

"I know that name," he says thoughtfully. I can see through his eyes that the gears in his mind are spinning, trying to place how he knows my name.

"You do? Well that's unfortunate. Normally when people know my name before I meet them, they hate me," I say. "You know, come to think of it, people who know my name in general hate me, whether they knew my name before meeting me or not."

"Alright then, Ms. Walters, let's get you home. I'm driving into town for work right now," he says with a sigh, walking over to the grey Chevy Silverado parked just outside the barn.

"Um, that's really okay, but I can run home, it's only about five in the morning. If I run the whole way I could probably get home by six thirty and get ready for school, I'm a pretty good runner," I say, now I'm the one who's cautious.

"How do you know what time it is?" the man asks with intrigue.

"The position of the stars," I say slowly. Something just doesn't feel right to me, who is this man?

"You really are as smart as they all say, aren't you?" he inquires.

"As smart as who says? Look, thanks for telling me where I am, I should probably go now," I tell him, preparing to haul ass away from this place.

"I can take you back into town, honestly, it's no problem," he says. His voice is warm and friendly, but I still feel unnerved.

"Yeah, but I'm not too keen on letting a stranger drive me anywhere." My voice is very guarded. I'm cautious of this man; he's nice which automatically makes me suspicious of him.

"What's the problem with it?" he asks innocently.

"Oh, you know, a young woman riding in a car with a grown man she's never met before, that doesn't spell rape or anything," I say sarcastically. "I mean, you could be a serial killer for all I know. I'd be walking right into your trap, and next thing you know, you'll be using my skin to create lampshades and other furniture."

"Well done," he says with a rich laugh. "I'm sure your parents would be very proud of you for that response. They certainly raised you right." His voice holds pride for some reason unknown to me. "I hope my kids would give that same answer if they ever found themselves in a situation like this."

"Thank you?" I say it more like a question.

"You're welcome, now come on, you're going to make me late for work."

"You're still a stranger," I tell him.

"Oh yeah, that's right. I'm Nick Mallard, the new head of the Board of Administration at Goodman High." He smiles at me with a warm and genuine smile.

"Ah, so that's how you know my name," I say, everything becoming abundantly clear. Over the last few years I've had a couple run-ins with the Board of Administration due to my issues with authority figures, i.e. Mr. Lawrence. The previous head of the Board quit because he got sick of having to deal with me. He said I was too smart for my own good, so I told him that he was too stupid for his own good, and that was the beginning of the end for our relationship. Several more incidents later he resigned, no longer able to tolerate my smart mouth.

"I'll take you home now," Nick Mallard says with a laugh, opening the passenger side door to his truck. He holds the door open for me, waiting for me to get in.

"Thanks for this, Mr. Mallard," I say, stepping up into his truck.

"It's no problem, Ms. Walters," he says kindly. After that it's all silence. The air is thick with an awkward feeling, as if it were trying to choke us.

"You have a really nice place," I tell him, saying the first thing that came to mind. "The land is really pretty."

"Thank you," he says. "I'm really going to miss it, so will the kids."

"What do you mean?" I ask.

"Well, I'm just not able to take care of the place or the animals anymore, not with my new job. I just haven't got the time, and neither does my wife. Besides, she shouldn't spend her weekends taking care of land and feeding animals, she's got other things to work on." His voice is heavy with sorrow, it's as if he's going to lose a part of himself. "I've asked for help, offered to pay, I even said they could use the house while we're out of town, which happens a lot, but no one would take me up on it. I've got no choice but to sell the place, I just can't keep up with it anymore."

"I'll take you up on it," I say suddenly. I feel the impulse to take him up on his deal, not because he sounds so sad, but because there's something strange about that place. I felt it the moment I woke up in those woods. Something is going on there, and I need to find out what it is.

"Are you sure?" Mr. Mallard asks. "You don't need to feel like you have to help us."

"Yeah, I'm sure. I'm a hard worker and I enjoy doing it. Besides, how hard can it be? You're lacking free time, and I've got too much of it. When you're here, you can feed the animals, when you're not, I can. And since I'll be working on keeping the land, you'll finally have the time to feed the animals. You get to keep your home and I get a job, we both win." Those aren't the only reasons I have to make this deal. I need to understand something, I need to figure it out. There's a reason my subconscious brought me there, and I need to find out what that reason is. Something is about to happen that will change my world forever, I can feel it in my bones.

I grab my jacket on my way out, rushing over to the black Volvo that's parked by the curb.

"Shit, I'm so late," I mutter as I toss my backpack into the back seat and jump into the car, peeling out and speed down the street.

I pull into the parking lot with three minutes to spare and rush into the building to my first class. I don't bother to stop at my locker and grab my textbooks, I just need to get to class.

When I enter the classroom, Mr. Lawrence is on one of his math rants directed at Celia, most likely because she asked something along the lines of "why do we have to know any of this? It's not actually useful," just to make the man angry. She doesn't care about whether it's useful or not, and everyone but Mr. Lawrence knows that.

I take my seat behind her, noticing her amused smile when the teacher begins to go red in the face.

She really enjoys riling people up, doesn't she? the voice in my head asks in an agitated tone.

After class, a man meets Celia outside the classroom. He wears a nice, pressed suit, and has a clean- shaven face with rusty colored hair. He's smiling brightly, shaking her hand enthusiastically.

"I'm so happy that you're willing to do this for me." His voice is excited and filled with joy.

"It's really no problem, Mr. Mallard," she says, giving him a hesitant smile. She looks nice when she isn't scowling, it makes her look almost approachable.

"Alright then, I'll see you tonight at six," he says.

"Sounds good, have a nice day, Mr. Mallard." With that she shoulders her backpack and heads to her next class.

I stand where I am for a second, thinking. I know that man's name, I've heard it before, and then it clicks. Nick Mallard is the new head of the Board of Administration.

What is the head of the Board of Administration doing talking to Celia? I thought they all hated her for causing so much trouble with Mr. Lawrence. And why is he making plans to meet up with her?

I shrug and make my way to my next class, taking my seat at the front of the room next to Ben. AP Chemistry, the most advanced science class offered at Goodman High, a college level class. I sometimes wonder how I got into this class, even though almost every class I'm taking is an AP class. All of my core classes are AP, only three of all my classes in total aren't, and those are PE and French 4 and Advanced Woods.

"And now for your lab partners!" Mr. Simons exclaims with a jolly clap of his hands. "You will all be working in trios, and I have already chosen your partners, yay! Group one is Ally Jenner, Garret Braddock, and Carry Maren. Group two," he pauses with a mischievous look on his face. "Is Beckett Halverson, Ben Milton." I rejoice inwardly. "And Celia Walters." My joy is dead, shot in the face.

"Shit." My voice echoes through the now silent room.

"I couldn't have said it better myself," Celia sighs, now standing next to me. I jump, I hadn't even seen her get up. I didn't know she was standing beside me until she had spoken.

"When did you get here?" I ask, startled by her sudden appearance.

"While you were too busy being stupid," she responds, her voice agitated and snarky. Mr. Simons is still naming off groups, but World War Three is about to go down between Celia and me.

"You're such a bitch!" I tell her, my hands curling into tight balls.

"And you're a dumbass," she says with a cold, harsh smile.

"Whoa, Mom and Dad, don't argue in front of the kids," Ben says playfully. Although his tone is light, he steps between us, his arms outstretched, pushing us away from each other.

"You wish!" she snarls at me.

"As if!" I growl, shoving Ben's arm aside as I lunge at her, rage taking over my being.

She's quick. She moves to the side, agile and nimble, stepping out of my way. I quickly spin around, anticipating some sort of retaliation, but there's none. Celia just stands where she is, looking shocked and dazed, like she wasn't expecting to dodge me.

"Let's do the damn lab," she says, her voice is calm and quiet, and it's threatening as hell. I had never thought of her as actually threatening or menacing, just mean and scary, but in this moment, I can see that there is a *very* dark side to her. The scariest part is, I have no idea what that side is capable of.

"Fine," I sigh in resignation, shouldering past her on my way to our lab station.

He lunged at me, he actually lunged *at me. What an idiot,* I think to myself. I sit alone at a table in the school library, reading Paradise Lost, completely neglecting to do research for the essay I was supposed to writing.

I hear a mix of low voices and a reluctant sigh, and then Beckett walks over to where I'm sitting and takes a seat across from me.

"What are you doing?" I ask in irritation.

"According to Mrs. Gibbs, I was abusing my research time, so she's punishing me by making me sit with you," he explains, looking bored and annoyed.

"Well this is great, maybe you should think about your actions and how they might negatively affect those around you before you do something," I say. I can't keep the snarky tone out of my voice, despite how hard I'm trying.

I stand up to leave. I don't care that the teacher wants me to babysit him, that's not the reason I come to school every day. If she wants Beckett to be supervised, she can come do it herself, at least she gets paid for it.

"Where are you going? Beckett asks.

"Wherever you're not," I respond.

"Why do you have to be such an insufferable bitch?" he asks, rising to his feet.

I hear someone clear their throat behind us and turn to see our principal, Mr. Sweeny, standing a few yards away, eyeing the two of us. I decide to ignore him.

"Because I can," I tell him. "In fact, I have the right to, because I'm a princess." *Where the hell is this coming from?* I ask myself. *A princess? Really? What are you, five? Where did you come up with that?*

"Ha, that's rich!" His voice rises with anger. "Princess of what? The 'I'm Better Than You' club?"

"Princess of Mercury," I correct him. The words just spill out of my mouth before I even know what I'm saying. *What the hell am I saying? Nothing lives on Mercury.*

"Great! You're the princess of a barren wasteland. Congratulations!" he says, his voice filled with malice and mockery.

"Who do you work for?" I yell, grabbing him by the collar of his shirt and slamming him into a bookcase, overcome with rage. "Where is he?!" *I sound like a raving lunatic. What the hell am I doing?* I wonder in awe and shock. *Why am I so angry?* I don't understand my rage.

"What the hell is your problem?" Beckett asks, slapping my hands from his shirt.

I can feel eyes staring at us, but there isn't a single part of me that cares.

"Answer me!" I shout, throwing my fist into the side of the bookcase right next to his head, leaving a hole in the wood.

"You are so crazy," he says, the panic in his eyes soon replaced by anger.

The fight everyone has been anticipating for the past twelve years breaks out, and it starts with me. I throw the first punch, something I've never done before.

My hand connects with his cheek, the force causing his head to roll with the hit.

He brings a hand up to his face, a surprised look in his eyes, and that's when all hell breaks loose.

He swings, and I dodge, ducking low and coming back up with an uppercut to his chin.

I have no idea where this is coming from. I've never been in a fight before, I've never even really watched people fight before, but I fight Beckett as if I've been fighting my whole life.

"Enough!" Mr. Sweeny all but pulls me off of Beckett. "My office, you two! The fighting ends now!" He grabs us both by the arm and hauls the two of us into his office where we are forced to take a seat.

"I have heard complaints and comments from staff and students alike about your constant bickering. So, as of now, you two are partners for everything. Your classes will be managed so that every class you have in common, you will share. You will be seated next to each other. You two will learn to get along or get expelled trying." His voice is stern. He's pissed.

I'm sore, my body hurts and my face is throbbing. I can't believe that I got my ass handed to me by Celia Walters.

The principal is talking, his words make me numb. *This cannot be happening*. The words echo through my skull.

I hear everything like I'm underwater. All sounds seem muffled and far away, until Celia stands up and slams her hands down onto the principal's desk, snapping me out of my daze.

"There is no way in hell that you actually have the authority to do that!" she shouts.

"Even if I don't, Jamie Goodman sure does. Do you want me to get him involved in this?" Mr. Sweeny tries to sound threatening, but everyone knows that no one can threaten Celia Walters. She lives without fear.

"Go ahead, give him a call. You know what? Give me his number and *I'll* call him and explain the whole situation to him myself. Just because some egotistical bastard builds a big building and names it after himself, does not mean he has the authority to dictate my life!" she yells. "You know what? Call the Board! I want every single one of them on the phone to bring validity to your claim!"

"That's not your call to make, Celia," Mr. Sweeny declares furiously.

"Then what do you want from me, damnit?!" she exclaims, bringing her fist down hard on the desk. I'm surprised for a moment that the desk didn't break beneath the weight of her rage.

Mr. Sweeny looks like he's about to respond, when the door bursts open and Ben comes rushing in.

"You can't be in here right now," Mr. Sweeny snaps, but Ben ignores him.

"Are you guys okay?" he asks, looking us both over to make sure we're alright. His eyes fall on Celia and he walks over to her, kneeling before her so their eyes are level.

"Ben," she breathes with a sigh of relief.

"I'm here, Cel, it's okay, calm down." His voice is gentle as his hands cup her face and force her to look into his eyes. I'm surprised by the amount of affection he's showing her. He holds her so close and tenderly, calling her by a nickname I've only ever heard him call her. I want to hit him for some reason, one unknown to me. *Why does this make me so angry?* I ask myself. I don't understand the way I'm feeling.

Celia's hands grip Ben's wrist, her eyes still trained on his. The anger slowly disappears from her gaze, melting away into misery. She's breathing heavily, and so is Ben, as if it had taken physical effort to get her to calm down. The scene only makes me more irritated.

"Now, what's going on?" Ben asks as Celia slowly lets go of him, leaving red rings around his wrists where she had been gripping him.

"Celia and I are going to be each other's new BFFs. Looks like you're out of a job, Ben, sorry man," I say. Upon hearing this, he looks relieved and like he's trying not to laugh.

"At least you two aren't getting expelled, because I totally thought you would be," he says, taking on a more serious face.

"At least? Ben, I have to kiss my four-point zero GPA goodbye, because I'm stuck with this troglodyte until we either get along or get expelled. That's my grade, Ben! It's going to affect the chances I have of getting into a good college! And all because I'm going be stuck with this idiot. Why can't people accept the fact that Beckett and I don't get along!?" She stands up and storms out of the office, slamming the door shut behind her, causing the pictures on the walls to shake and move out of place.

"Go talk to her, Beck," Ben sighs, leaning against the wall.

"Dude, she hates me, I'm not the right person to console her," I tell him.

"Just do it, Beck, she needs it to be *you.*"

I'm disappointed when I don't hear the sound of glass shattering after I slam the door. I was hoping that the force of it would cause at least one of the pictures on the wall to fall to the ground and shatter.

The door opens behind me and I expect to be yelled at by Mr. Sweeny, but that's not what happens.

"Celia, wait!" My hand is caught, and I'm spun around like I'm dancing.

I come to a halt a foot away from Beckett Halverson, my hand still in his.

I'm too shocked by his actions to think, to pull my hand away, to hit him. Too shocked to do anything really.

"Look, I'm sorry that you're stuck with me for all things academic, and that you have to sit by me in all our common classes, and that I annoy you. I'm not sure why I annoy you, but I'm sorry that I do. And I'm surprisingly not an idiot. I have a four-point zero GPA as well, so I won't bring yours down. I can promise that much, because my grades are very important to me, and I know I don't really show that, but it's the truth. Oh, and by the way, you pack a really nice punch." His words come out rushed. He's just as uncomfortable as I am.

"Yeah, sorry about that," I say with a somewhat flat voice, not knowing what else to say before I turn and walk away. I'm desperate to get away from him and that office.

I walk down the hall to the "hidden staircase." It's not actually hidden, but no one ever uses it, so it just adopted that name. I climb halfway up the stairs before I sit down with a heavy sigh.

"What the hell was that?" I ask myself. *Princess of Mercury? Who do you work for? Where was I coming up with all that?* My mind is racing, replaying what happened in the library. *Why did I get so pissed?* There's no reasonable explanation for any of it. None at all.

"What the hell is wrong with me?" I ask aloud, my voice echoing through the empty stairwell.

I get home later than normal. As soon as school had finished, I grabbed my running clothes from my trunk and ran until my body hurt and I couldn't breathe. Until I felt as if I would collapse at any moment.

The second I walk through the door Amy starts rattling on about something.

"Did you hear about the–"

"Yes, I heard about the fight at school," I say with bored exasperation, cutting her off.

"There was a fight at school?" she asks, eyebrows furrowed.

"Shit," I groan, scowling at the floor.

"Celia, what did you do? It was Beckett Halverson wasn't it?"

"Mind your own business, Amy," I say warningly.

"God you are *so* easy to read," she gloats "What'd you do to him?"

"Exactly what I'm about to do you if you don't drop this." My voice is cold, teeming with anger. I hate it when she inserts herself into my business.

"Whatever, I'll find out tomorrow. Anyway, did you hear about the murder in the valley?" she asks.

"Here's a better question, why do I care?" I respond. "Was it someone I know?"

"No," she says.

"Are any of the places I normally go to blocked off because of it?"

"No."

"Then I don't care."

"Humor me and listen," she says. "A body was discovered in the valley about ten miles south of here by some Mallard guy or something like that."

"Wait, Mallard? As in Nick Mallard, head of the Board of Administration at Goodman High?" I ask, suddenly very interested in what my sister is saying.

"Yeah! That's who it was. Do you know him?" she questions.

"I work for him," I say dazedly. "Amy, give me a minute okay?" I run out into the garage where I have privacy and pull out my phone, frantically searching through my contacts until I find the right one. I press the call button and hold the phone to my ear, anxiously awaiting a response and a reprieve from the static dial tone.

"Hello, this is Nick Mallard."

"Hey, it's Celia. I just heard about what happened, is everyone okay?" I ask.

"We're all pretty shaken to be honest," he answers.

"How are your wife and the kids?" I feel oddly compelled to make sure that everyone is alright. I find it befuddling, because normally, I couldn't care less.

"They're alright, they didn't see him. I was alone when I found the body, thank God for that, but they're all pretty scared."

"And how about you?" I ask with concern. "Finding a dead body has to be pretty traumatizing."

"I'm in a lot of shock," he says with a shaky voice. "I can't get the image out of my head."

"If it's not too much trouble, could you tell me where you found him?" I ask cautiously.

"I found him on the ridge. It was so strange. He looked like he had been electrocuted, or burned or something. His skin was charred, and so was everything around him. The police ruled it a homicide. Because there were no storms, accidental electrocution was ruled out, and no fires were reported, so the only thing left is foul play. You don't think the person who killed him could still be here do you?" he asks, panic thick in his voice.

"Are there any shoe prints you don't recognize around your house?" I ask.

"Other than yours, no," he responds.

"Is there anything different about your house or the barns? Objects out of place, doors that were locked now unlocked or vice versa? Missing items?"

"No," he says.

"Then the person is gone," I say with confidence. "You have three options after committing a murder. Number one, you can wait for the authorities to arrive and take you away. Number two, you can hide and lay low somewhere nearby. And number three, you can ditch the evidence, run, and act as if the murder never happened," I explain, using logic as my source. "Do you still want me to come over tonight and start working?"

"No, the police are here and are roping off the entire area, they're combing the woods for the murderer and any other evidence right now."

"Alright, then I'll be over there Saturday to start working and reshaping the landscape. I'll also clear the hiking trails in the woods and cut down the tall grass on top of the ridges. That way, once it dries out, you can bale it and feed your animals, or sell it to your neighbors or something. I'm pretty sure that they have horses," I say, recalling the flash of their eyes in the dark as we drove back into town this morning.

"You really are quite observant," he says. "But I can't ask you to do that, not with the murder and all. Besides, part of the woods is roped off because of the crime scene, and I'm not sure you should see it. A man lost his life there, it's even shaken me up, and I'm an adult. A teenager shouldn't see all of that."

"It's really not a problem for me. I'm not a very empathetic person, so crime scenes and dead people don't really bother me," I tell him. "I know that it makes me sound like a terrible person, but it really doesn't faze me."

"Thank you, Celia," he says, gratitude swelling in his voice. "You truly are a miracle. And it doesn't really make you sound like a bad person. It's a talent you have, to be able to distance yourself from those feelings. If there weren't people like you, we wouldn't have our homicide detectives, or an army, or anything like the others mentioned."

I let out a heavy sigh of relief, grateful that he doesn't see my unique trait as a bad thing, but as a gift.

"Well, I need to go, I'll see you Saturday, bye Mr. Mallard." I hang up the phone and walk back into the house to receive an odd look from my sister.

"What was that about?" she asks.

"I had to make sure that everyone at the Mallard house was alright," I say.

"Why?" she asks, looking at me as if I were sprouting new limbs from the side of my head.

"Because despite what everyone believes, I'm not a heartless bitch," I say in disbelief. "Man, you must have a really low opinion of me."

"You're the one who set it," she responds.

"You're obnoxious," I tell her. "I'm going to my room."

"Bye!" she exclaims, as I make my way towards my room to my piano.

I shuffle through piles of music before I find the song I'm suddenly itching to play. I place the music on the piano and take a seat as I begin to play Chopin's *Prelude No. 4 in E Minor.* My fingers grace over the keys, creating the beautiful and haunting chords that complement the melancholy tone of the melody.

My mind starts to wander as I play, the song seeming to flow out of my fingers as my mind flows down a river of thoughts, emptying out at Nick Mallard's house, tucked away in the valley.

Wasn't I on a ridge when I woke up? I ask myself. As I think more about it, I begin to feel cold, like my veins are freezing over.

When I blink, an image flashes across my mind's eye. A mask. A masquerade mask made with beautiful intricacy. It's a deep purple around the outside, and then washes out to a faded lavender towards the middle with black, vine-like swirls around the eyes.

My head is searing with pain, it feels like someone is stabbing white-hot needles into my brain. My fingers leave the piano keys and I clutch my head and grit my teeth, trying to fight off the agony assaulting my nerve.

My vision begins blurring and a high-pitched noise pierces my ears, causing me to collapse. I curl into a tight ball on the ground, my body riddled with pain.

I feel light, like I'm floating in water, and then the world grows dim, slowly fading into a deep black.

I'm on top of a building watching the scene play out before me.

A woman in a pair of ripped, black skinny jeans and a white tank top pulled down just past her waist stands brandishing a silver whip. A small leather jacket lays at her feet. I'm guessing it's hers, it can't belong to the man she's fighting. He's tall and stocky, but he looks sorely beaten. His face is swollen and bruised. He's bleeding from several deep gashes, presumably from the whip the woman holds so fiercely.

"Send Mesmer my regards," she snarls, planting a solid kick in the middle of his sternum. The kick sends the man tumbling over the side of the building.

She turns, enabling me to somewhat see her face. It looks familiar, but it's mostly obscured by a mask. The one I had seen before blacking out.

"You can't escape what's coming, Celia," she says. Her eyes pierce mine. I don't bother to ask what's coming, it's just a dream, none of it is real, and there is no real threat. But the question still lingers in the forefront of my mind. I'm curious as to what she means, even if it is the nonsensical craziness of my subconscious left unfiltered.

"You can't escape me," she says, as if reading the mind of my dream self. "Celia, awake, arise or be forever fallen." She quotes my favorite line from Paradise Lost before disappearing, melting into the shadows and becoming nothing.

What was that supposed to mean? *I wonder as I make my way to the edge of the building. I peer over the side to see where the man had fallen. It was a long way to the ground, probably about a 50-foot drop.*

It's dark, but I can still see the man's mangled body and the blood pooling around him. He lies on a pile of broken glass and plastic. He must've fallen onto the sign for the sports bar that resided at the bottom of the building.

I find myself somewhat disturbed by my lack of feeling upon seeing his abused corpse. But after all, it's only a dream.

I wake up slumped in the corner by the window, dazed and confused. *How did I get all the way over here?* I wonder, as I get to my feet.

My entire body hurts. It feels like I had been beaten with baseball bats. The worst part is the searing pain in my back, screaming for my attention, burning intensely each time I move.

I stumble over to the tall mirror on my dresser and pull my shirt off, cringing as I do so. I turn so my back is to the mirror and look over my shoulder. There's a gash on my back, starting at my shoulder blade, continuing across my back and wrapping around my ribs, ending just about at my right oblique. There's no blood, just the wound, and it isn't deep. I have no idea as to how, when, or where I got it.

I stand in front of the mirror, examining the cut in a daze until I catch the time displayed on my alarm clock.

"It's only four in the morning?" I ask with a groan, stretching out my sore body. "I hate not being able to go back to sleep."

I close my door and flick lights on, walking over to my closet to pick out an outfit for the day. I had forgotten to do so the night before, I had passed out before I'd gotten to that part of my routine. I choose something simple, dark grey jeans and a white V-neck that hugged my body. I'm too tired to bother being real fancy or sophisticated.

I pad downstairs and grab my backpack from beside the door. The sound of my feet against the hardwood floor is the only sound in the dark, silent house as I make my way back to my room. I plop down onto my bed and start doing whatever homework I hadn't finished at the library with Ben, unable to do it before, due to my passing out.

I'm finished around five in the morning, leaving me dressed and ready to go with too much time before I actually need to get to school.

"Well, I've already slaughtered my daily routine, why not keep going?" I ask, wandering down to the kitchen to make myself a nice breakfast consisting of bacon and strawberry pancakes.

I stop in the living room to turn the TV on so I can watch the news while I cook.

"There was another murder last night. This time, the body was discovered in town. The authorities have not yet linked this murder to the one in the valley, but Chief of Police, Brian Oswald, reports that instincts tell him that these two murders are indeed related, and that it's only a matter of time before the authorities figure out how. Citizens have also been asked to remain inside after daylight hours to avoid any more casualties," the reporter says. She looks exhausted, like she's been up for hours. The bags under her eyes are poorly hidden by too much makeup.

I switch the channel, disinterested in another murder, especially because it holds no immediate relevance to me.

"The body was found around three this morning, just outside *Scott's Sports Bar and Grill*," another correspondent reports. This time it's a man. He doesn't look nearly as tired as the lady on the other channel. He looks intrigued, excited almost, at the prospect of a new body and another lost life. "We will be displaying a clip caught by one of security cameras nearby, viewer discretion is greatly advised." And with that short warning, the clip is played. At first, nothing seems out of the ordinary, just a quiet street in the middle of the night, and then a man falls, like a comet from the sky, smashing onto the bar's sign. Now he lies on top of broken glass and plastic. His body is still, covered in cuts and purpling bruises as blood pools around him. The clip isn't extremely gruesome or anything of the sort, but I drop the plate I had just taken down from the cupboard.

"Shit!" I hiss, as the plate shatters on the ground.

My eyes are glued to the television, where I see the same scene as the one from my dream. It's like I'm back on top of that building, looking down upon the mutilated body of the newest murder victim.

The cut along my back starts burning with more intensity than before, searing my back. I grimace in pain, one hand shooting out to grab the sides of the counter to break my fall as I stumble, crippled by the pain rippling through me. The other hand goes up to my shoulder, trying to massage the tense muscles and ease the ache.

"What are you doing?" someone asks with a yawn.

"God! Don't sneak up on me like that, Amy!" I shriek, resuming a normal position. I grit my teeth and pull a piece of plate out of my foot, having stepped on it when Amy had scared me.

"It's not my fault you decided to be jumpy," she exclaims in defense.

"You're obnoxious. Now shut up, I'm watching the news," I tell her.

"Since when do you watch the news?" she asks, skipping around the broken plate to steal a piece of bacon from the still hot pan, burning her fingers.

"The pan's still hot," I tell her.

"Yeah, thanks for telling me," she says sarcastically. "Now answer my question, since when do you watch the news?"

"I've always watched the news," I say in an exasperated tone. "You should know that, considering the fact that you always complain when I do."

"Yeah, but you always watch it in the afternoon when you get home from school, not in the morning. I know how you are about your routine, so why are you watching the news?"

"Because there was another murder." My voice is grimmer than I had expected it to be.

"What!? Where?" Amy asks, her voice filled with excitement, her eyes sparkling with enthusiasm.

"Show some respect, Amy, someone just lost their life. It's not like you got invited to a major party or something, now stop acting like it is." I'm not sure why I'm chastising her for this, normally I couldn't care less about this sort of thing.

"Did you know the victim?" she asks timidly, sympathy lurking in her voice.

"No," I say.

"Then why the hell do *you* care?" she asks, confusion written on her features.

"Because, Amy, he probably had a family, like you and I do. Maybe an older sibling who felt responsible for him, or a younger sibling who looked up to him. Parents who loved him and who would've done anything for him. Maybe he even had kids and a wife, waiting for their husband and father to come home. All of them are now devastated by his death. Family is everything, don't you realize that? And I'm not just talking about blood ties, but the people you truly consider to be your family. They don't turn on you, even when the rest of the world does. No one should be excited over the loss of something like that. It's sick and it's cruel." The words spill out of my mouth like water from a broken faucet, uncontainable and uncontrollable.

"Who are you, and what have you done with my sister?" Amy asks suspiciously, her fingers creeping towards the butter knife on my pancake.

"What are you going to do, Amy, stab me with a butter knife? Really? God, are stupid," I sigh. "Now knock it off before I beat you and drag you out to the driveway so I can hit you with my car." My voice is back to its normal bored and snarky tone.

"You must have been tired," she says, shrugging her shoulders and munching on my bacon.

I don't understand why people think I have no emotions or respect for others. I especially don't understand why people act as if I've been abducted when I show that I really am human.

"Hey, stop eating my food and get ready for school!" I command, slapping my sister's hand away as she reaches for another piece of bacon.

"Fine," she sighs in defeat, heading up the stairs to her room.

I grab a broom and sweep up the broken plate, making sure that all the little pieces are in a pile, before sweeping them into the dust pan and tossing them into the garbage.

I take out a new plate and place my food on it, making sure that the bacon and pancakes don't touch. I hate it when my food touches, I find it disgusting.

I take my time and eat my food slowly. I appreciate every bite and explosion of flavor that coats my palate. When I'm done eating, I make sure to clean up the kitchen. I can't stand things that are messy. Cluttered counters and messes in general make me feel agitated and suffocated, as if the chaos around me is seeping into my lungs and blocking the passage of air. It drives me into panic.

"Alright, let's go!" Amy exclaims, standing at the top of the stairs with her coat in hand. She rushes to grab her backpack which lays just outside her bedroom door.

"Okay, let's go," I sigh. I don't want to go to school, I don't want to deal with Beckett.

"Shit!" I jump up and out of my bed. "I'm going to be so late." I rush to my dresser and pull out a pair of pants and a t-shirt, dressing myself quickly. *I only have ten minutes until school starts. If I rush, skip breakfast, and speed, I might be able to make it to class before the first bell.* I stop in the bathroom and quickly brush my teeth and gel my hair before I rush out to my car and almost forget my backpack.

I throw the backpack into the passenger seat and peel out of the driveway, just narrowly missing a mailbox.

"It'll be a miracle if I'm not late," I mutter. I can already tell that this is not going to be a good day. Waking up late is bad on its own, but now I have to deal with Celia. She's definitely going to notice that I'm late. She notices everything, and I'm sure she's going to give me hell for it.

I park about a block away from the school, knowing that all the spots in the school lot are taken. I've been through this rodeo several times before. I know when to cut my losses, and this is one of those times.

The moment I enter the building, the first bell goes off. It's a shrill sound, ringing throughout the now empty halls, signaling that class has begun.

I run to class, too absorbed in my thoughts of how completely screwed I am, until my body slams into another, and our textbooks go flying everywhere.

"Whoa there, Beck, watch out," Ben says, sitting on the floor with a dazed look in his eyes. "You should've gone out for football, running into you is like running into a wall."

"Sorry, man." I offer him my hand and pull him to his feet. "I'm late to class, and well, now I have to face the wrath of Celia," I explain.

"Oh yeah, that's right, you're stealing my best friend," he says jokingly.

"Honestly, you can have her, Ben, I want nothing to do with her." My voice comes out harsh and bitter to my own ears.

"Just a tip of advice, don't cross her," he says, pausing for a moment. "If you think she's mean now, you don't want to see her when she's pissed. What happened at the library was child's play compared to what she's really capable of. Be careful, Beckett." After giving me his cryptic warning, he walks off, disappearing around the corner.

His words hit me hard, rattle me even. If Ben is telling me to be careful, then the consequence of recklessness must be extremely severe.

No one pays me any attention when I enter the room, not even Mr. Lawrence, which is nice. I was expecting to get grilled by the teacher for being late.

I walk to the back of the room and hope that Celia will ignore me like everyone else. Of course, I'm not that lucky.

"Forget your textbook again?" she asks, her voice pure mockery.

"Do you actually care, or are you just looking for new ways to be a bitch? Like by trying to point out all my flaws?" I ask, not bothering to humor her, just cutting to the chase. In spite of what Ben said, I *really* want to piss her off.

"The latter," she says plainly. "I figured I couldn't point out all of them, so I decided to focus on a few. One of them being your timeliness, or lack thereof." She has the same growl in her voice as I do, she's trying to get a rise out of me as well.

"Well, it's a good thing we aren't focusing on *your* flaws," I tell her with a mocking smile, turning to face her. "Because then we'd never be leaving."

"What false claims," she says, adopting a hurt voice, bringing a hand to her heart. She drops the ruse and returns my smile of mockery. That predatory look comes back, accompanied by an intimidating lopsided grin. She looks like a killer who has just trapped their victim and is now circling in for the kill. "Don't question me," she commands suddenly. "Do as I say, and don't screw up my grades, think you can handle that?"

"What if I have conditions as well?" I ask, choosing not to answer her question.

"Then you can keep them to yourself, because I don't care. I follow no one's rules, but my own," she says. Her voice is cold enough to freeze a glass of water.

"Whatever," I snarl, turning my gaze back to the board, already done with her, and her bitchy attitude.

Class ends and I head off to Chemistry, where I've been moved to the back of the room in order to carry out my sentence of punishment. I can't understand why I got moved. They should move Celia up to the front, maybe then she would finally pay attention.

For some reason, teachers never put Celia anywhere near the front. It's like they're all afraid to do so, or maybe it's just because they don't want to deal with her.

Chemistry comes to an end quickly, and I'm grateful, because my next class is Advanced Woods. It's one of the only classes I don't have with Celia. She takes AP French Literature and Culture, AP Psychology and some other AP class for her electives. Thankfully, we share a grand total of none of those classes.

On my way to Woods I pass by Celia's locker and come to an abrupt stop at the scene before me. I don't know why I stop, or why it bothers me so much, but it does.

"You sure you don't want to?" Craig Collins asks her.

"Would you go away?" she asks with a bored look on her face. "No, I don't want to go to the movies with you, or go bowling, or jump your bones in the back of your car. Leave me alone now, or so help me God, I'm going to make you regret ever talking to me."

"Come at me, Baby." Craig's eyes gleam with a lecherous light.

"Yo, Craig, cool it man," I say, trying to sound casual. "I think she's had enough." Part of me intervenes because I don't want Craig to get his ass handed to him the way I did. My face is still sore from when she hit me, and I know that wasn't the worst she could do. I can only imagine what that is.

"Whoa, dude, are you tapping this?" he asks, eyebrows raised in surprise.

"No, man, no one's *tapping* her," I tell him.

"Then what's the big deal?" he asks, turning back to Celia.

I place my hand on his shoulder and spin him to face me, grabbing him by the lapels.

"The 'big deal' is that you're screwing with my Chemistry partner, and we have a big project coming up soon. I need her organized and focused, not plotting your murder. Now get lost," I growl, shoving him into the lockers, and then take my own advice and leave in haste.

"You didn't need to do that," Celia says, following me down the hall. "I can take care of myself."

"Normally, people say 'thank you' in these situations," I tell her, starting to become angry. I just saved her ass from that tool, Craig, and she's trying to chew my head off. Only *she* would have the nerve to be like this.

"Well I'm not thankful, I didn't need your help. Now everyone is going to think that I'm weak and that I have to rely on you for protection. So, you really only made the situation worse," she scowls, her eyes blazing with fury.

"You are so difficult!" I shout, dropping my backpack and spinning around. "I was trying to be nice to you, despite the fact that you've only ever been a bitch to me. Ben says that you can be cool, and that you're not just a psychotic woman who lives off intimidating other people. But Ben is obviously very wrong or has ulterior motives!"

"You *must* be the world's biggest idiot. Do you honestly think that just because I've been sentenced to deal with you, I'm going to open up and spill my heart to you? That I'm going to show you who I really am?" she asks in disbelief, looking at me as if I'm some crazy, two-headed sheep.

"You couldn't spill your heart to me even if you tried!" I yell, slamming my hand into the locker beside her. She doesn't jump at all, she just stares at me with cold eyes. "You can't spill something you don't have," I mutter, brushing past her. Our shoulders hit and she stumbles a bit, but quickly recovers herself. I hear her sigh and slam her locker, but I'm too far away to apologize. Even if I weren't already down the hall and almost to class, I wouldn't have gone back. I've always believed that you shouldn't say sorry when you didn't mean it, and there is no way in hell I would meant it.

Just who the hell does he think he is? I wonder, slamming my locker shut.

I storm down the hall to my next class, which, thankfully, is my favorite class, AP French Literature and Culture. If you asked me, I would tell you that French is the most beautiful language in the world. Forget about Spanish, Italian and Portuguese, because French is the only language worth learning. It's beautiful in every way. The words flow together to create a masterpiece of sound. It's a big part of art, music and history, all of which I greatly enjoy. It's simply amazing. It's also just the class I need to be in right now. My blood is still boiling,

Beckett does that to me. This class will soothe me and calm me down, it always does.

What the hell does he know? I ask myself as I set my bag down by my desk.

"Bonjour, Celia, comment allez-vous aujourd'hui?"

"Je vais ça va, et vous?" I ask, turning around to see Monsieur Pierre standing by my desk with a large smile.

"Je vais très bien," he says, ruffling my hair. I don't like being touched, and so my body goes rigid. It doesn't matter that I've known Monsieur Pierre since I was six, or that he's practically my uncle. I still don't like being touched.

"Sorry," he says sheepishly, switching to English, which is, in fact, his second language. "I forget that you don't like to be touched by anyone other than a very select few."

"It's alright," I tell him, my body slowly relaxing and returning to its normal state.

The bell goes off before I get the chance to say anything else. It rings shrill and high, cutting through the conversations and chatter of the room.

"I guess that's my cue to start teaching," he says, leaving my desk and taking his position at the front of the room. When class starts, I pay attention for once. Nothing is on my desk, Monsieur Pierre has my complete and undivided attention.

Even though I'm completely fluent in French, I still listen. I just like to hear the beautiful words flowing out of the teacher's mouth. The elegant sounds calm my agitated nerves, making me feel less like punching a wall. Soon, calm and serenity settle into my nerves.

I don't really participate in the class activity, or talk much, I just listen. Monsieur Pierre never calls on me, because he knows that I know the material, and that my speaking and comprehension skills are far beyond anyone else's in the class.

He knows all this because he comes over to my house to visit my dad all the time.

He and my dad have been like brothers since the ninth grade, when Monsieur Pierre stayed with my dad for a year as a foreign exchange student. The moment he had landed in America, he fell in love with the country, and afterwards, with a girl he had met in school. After his year spent with my dad, he came back every summer, and he continued to do so, until he was accepted to the university only an hour away, where he studied to become a French teacher.

He and my dad lost touch when they went to college, but when we moved back to Rockford, Monsieur Pierre visited us every weekend. He made sure that I knew how to speak French, and he tried teaching Amy, but she proved to be a lost cause.

He still comes over for dinner every now and then, to catch up with my family and make sure that my French is proper. I find his need to note my progress in the language pointless but endearing. He knows that I'm fluent in the language, and that I have been since I was fifteen. I personally believe that he enjoys being able to speak French with someone here, and also enjoys talking with me. It was something he did even when I was younger, talking with me as if I were another adult. That's something I've always liked about him. He's always seen me as the age I act and think, not by the amount of years I've been alive.

Class ends too soon, coming to a halt all too suddenly. The end bell cuts my joy short, ringing in my ears and clashing against Monsieur Pierre's voice and the beautiful words he speaks.

With a sigh, I grab my backpack and lumber out of the room, my footsteps heavy as I leave. I'm off to AP Government and back to the company of the one and only, Beckett Halverson.

Great, I have to deal with Celia for another forty-five minutes. I just want this day to end. It's only been about half the day, but I'm already done dealing with her. There's no way we're going to graduate from this school. We were told to get along or get expelled trying, and expulsion is the only probable outcome. I don't know if I can go to school on Monday and do this all over again. I'm so screwed.

"For the love of God, Craig, would you just leave me alone?" I know that voice, I would know it anywhere.

"Come on, Baby, you know you don't want that," Craig says. My teeth clench and my hands curl into tight fists. *Why won't he just leave her alone?* I ask myself irritably. I'm ready to keep walking, but suddenly I freeze, the air is cold and thick, something bad is about to happen.

"You have exactly five seconds to leave me alone, or I swear that you will be hurting for months," Celia growls. I can feel her anger, it's explosive and dangerous.

"Shit," I mutter, dropping my backpack and spinning around fast. "Celia, don't do it!" I shout, running in her direction. I get to her just as she starts her swing and jump between them. I duck under her fist and wrap my arms around her midsection, throwing her over my shoulder and pulling her away from the fight.

"Put me down!" she demands. I can tell she doesn't know it's me, she didn't end her sentence with "you asshole."

"No way in hell, Celia," I say, continuing to carry her away.

"Beckett, put me down, you asshole!" She kicks her legs in an attempt to shake me, but it doesn't work.

Everyone is staring as I haul her down the hall and through the "hidden stairwell," finally able to set her down.

"Would you just stop?" she asks in exasperation. "I don't need someone to save me. I could have taken him on just fine!"

"I'm not worried about you!" I shout. "I am very well aware that you can take care of yourself, and I honestly don't care about Craig. I stopped your damn tantrum because *my* grade depends on *you*, and vice versa. If you get yourself suspended, I'm kind of boned, don't you realize that? You'll fall behind on all of our projects and drag me down with you. And besides, something is going on with you." I add the last part with caution, not wanting to infuriate her further. "In my twelve years of knowing you, you've never been in a fistfight, you just outwit everyone before they even get a chance to hit you. But now you've started two fistfights in a matter of two days. What's going on?" I'm surprised by the sincere concern in my voice.

Celia sighs and runs a hand through her long hair. Her eyebrows are furrowed in thought, her eyes consumed by an intense, concentrated look.

She's pretty, *really* pretty, with that focused look in her eyes, and her hair falling over one shoulder leaving the side of her face clearly visible. Her hazel eyes are brought out by her dark brown hair and golden skin. Her cheeks bones are elegant and her full lips are a natural, deep red. She really does look like a princess. I can see why Ben is into her, and if I could tolerate her, I would probably be into her as well.

"What are you looking at?" she asks suddenly, snapping her head up, forcing our eyes to meet. Her gaze is piercing, but I refuse to break the stare. I refuse to be defeated, I'm not going to let her intimidate me.

"You. I'm waiting for you to give me an answer," I say, trying to sound plain. I can't let her know how nervous I am.

"Screw you," she spits, breaking the intense stare.

"What the hell?" I ask, astonished by her response. "What is your problem? I'm trying to be nice to you. I'm trying to help you!"

"Why? What do you have to gain? You wouldn't help me, someone you hate, unless you have a hidden motive," Celia says.

"Maybe that's the way *you* work, but it's not the way *I* work. Why would I help you? Because I'm not a horrible person. And the main reason I hate you is because you're always a bitch to me."

She says nothing, she only scowls at me. Her eyes analyze everything about me. Her brain goes over every word I just said, attempting to decode them, to find any hidden meaning. But that's just it, there is no hidden meaning. The only thing she'll find is disappointment and confusion.

"I'm not your enemy, Celia," I tell her, my voice filled with exhaustion.

"That may be true, but you aren't my ally either." She walks away, leaving me alone and feeling oddly hollow.

"Maybe I could be, if you just let me," I say, my frustration-filled voice reverberating off the walls of the empty staircase.

I sigh and sit down, my back sliding along the wall as I do so. I don't know why, but I feel sad. I want to believe Ben when he says that Celia really is a good person; I know she is when she's with him. I've watched them together, watched their interactions, and she seems like a normal human being. And for a reason unknown to me, I want her to act the same way with me. I want her to be able to let her walls down, I want her to be comfortable enough to lower her guard. I want her to trust me. Maybe it's because I like to help people, or maybe it's because I feel sorry for her. Maybe it's something else, I just don't know.

I decide not to go to the rest of my classes. I know I'll have hell to pay for it, but I can't pay attention, my emotions are ripping me apart. I'm angry, sad, frustrated and confused and it's causing a splitting headache.

I walk out to my car, slamming the door shut as I get in. I toss my backpack into the passenger seat and let my head fall onto the steering wheel, letting out a deeply agitated sigh.

"I need to go home."

I pull out from the curb, lazily turning the wheel to avoid the other parked cars. The streets are mostly empty. Everyone is either at work or in school, making the small city seem like a ghost town.

The house is empty when I arrive. It's earlier than when I normally come home, and my dog, Zeke, goes crazy when he sees me. He bounces around the house, tearing from room to room, wagging his tail furiously.

"Hey, buddy," I say, getting onto my knees, waving him towards me. He bounds across the room and into my arms, knocking me onto to the ground. His big paws pin me down as he relentlessly licks my face.

"Alright! That's enough, Zeke!" I gasp, pushing the golden retriever off of me.

I walk over to the couch and flop down, snatching the remote as I fall. Zeke follows me, curling up on my legs as I switch the TV on.

"Police have confirmed that the same person is responsible for the murder in the valley and the one here in town." My head snaps up, my interest piqued. To be honest, the murders really freak me out. Normally, this is a nice, quiet, little town, and with two murders in two days, people might start to think that there's a serial killer on the loose. "There are no suspects in the case yet, but we do have a description of the culprit, as well as more surveillance footage from the recent murder, that happened earlier this morning. We do not advise that children view this." With that, the screen no longer shows the reporter, but the top of a building and two people. One of them is a man who's cut up and bleeding badly, the other is a very intriguing sight. A woman stands a few feet from the man, wearing what looks like torn up skinny jeans and a white tank top. A leather jacket is discarded at her side, but none of that is what's really grabbing my attention. It's the mask she's wearing. It's a masquerade mask. It's hard to tell the color, but it looks like a swirl of purple.

I watch, somewhat in horror, as she lashes out with her leg and kicks the man off the roof.

"We don't know who this murderous masquerader is, but the authorities are advising citizens to stay indoors after dark and to stay away from the more vacant parts of the city." I switch the channel, I don't need to watch murders, or worry about them, I have enough to worry about.

I flip through all the channels, but nothing good is on, and so I switch the TV off with a bored groan.

"Ugh, I'm so stressed, Zeke. I don't know what to do," I complain, stretching out over my dog, scratching his soft body. He wags his tail happily and rolls onto his back, exposing his stomach.

"Good idea, Zeke, I'll go take a shower," I say, praising him for my good idea, scratching his belly. When I'm finished petting him, I get up and make my way to the bathroom, turning on the water in the shower.

I strip my clothes off and hop into the stream of hot water. Immediately, I feel myself relax. The hot water cascades down onto my body, forcing my muscles into a relaxed state. "Much better," I sigh contentedly. I grab the shampoo and scrub it into my hair, massaging my scalp. The water feels wonderful, drilling into my back as I rub the soap into my hair.

I go back under the jet of water and let the shampoo wash out of my hair, and stream down my body. I follow the same procedure with the conditioner and then finally wash my body down with a bar of soap. I use the bar to help message my muscles and scrub the stress from my body.

When I get out of the shower, the cool air hits my skin. It's not that intense cold that causes painful goosebumps, but the calming, soothing cool after too much heat. It feels nice.

I wrap a towel around my waist after drying myself off, and then take another towel to dry my hair. I rub my head frantically, I hate the feeling of sopping wet hair. When I'm done it sticks up at odd angles, and I look like a disheveled porcupine who just rolled out of bed. I grab a comb from one of the vanity drawers and comb it off to the side, letting it roll out into its waves.

My black hair is thick and naturally wavy, which I find strange, because no one else in my family has black hair. In fact, everyone in my family has thin, almost pencil straight blonde hair, Lily being the only exception. She has long brown hair that has a slight wave to it, but she's adopted, so that doesn't count.

I take a look in the mirror and sigh.

"The sides are getting a bit long," I say to myself. "I'll have to go get that fixed."

I sweep the top portion of my hair out of my face and off to one side, which is pretty cool with the natural wave, but I keep the sides short. It's a sweet hairstyle that looks great, especially with my kind of hair, but maintaining it is a pain. I feel like I'm going in to get my hair cut every other week.

I turn the lights off and exit the bathroom, taking my time on my way down to my room. I search haphazardly for something to wear when Zeke rushes down to my room, snatching one of my socks from the floor and running back up the stairs with his stolen treasure.

"Zeke! Get back here!" I shout, hurriedly putting my shorts on before chasing him to the main floor. The cold wooden floor is a shock to my bare feet. It makes me want to recoil and go back down to my room, but I can't let Zeke keep my sock, it'll be the fifth sock of mine that he's torn up this month. "Where'd you go, Zeke?" I ask, looking around for his shiny, golden coat.

I find him in the kitchen, facing the door with his hackles raised and a vicious, blood-thirsty look on his face.

"What's wrong, Zeke?" I ask, giving the dog a quizzical look. He continues to growl in response, now baring his sharp teeth.

"Zeke, you're freaking me out," I say, making my way to him, my heartbeat picking up. I can't see anyone at the door, but Zeke is going crazy. He barks and snarls, jumping at the door, snapping at the air.

I back away from the unexpectedly vicious dog, confused by his random aggression.

Suddenly, Zeke starts to whine and backs away from the door with his head and tail down. All his vicious energy from before is gone and he looks about as scared as I feel. He runs behind me, whimpering as if he had been badly injured. I'm completely unnerved.

I feel like a small dose of electricity has just been shot through me. All the tiny hairs on my body stand on end as apprehension washes over me.

"Shit," I growl, grabbing a kitchen knife, readying myself for someone to come out of nowhere and attack me.

There's a quiet knock on the door, and I walk to it. Hesitantly, I open the door with the knife raised in defense.

Celia Walters walks through the threshold with an armful of papers, her eyes widening when she sees me.

"Whoa! Calm down, it's only me!" she shouts, putting her hands up, holding the papers out like some sort of shield.

"Oh my God, you scared the shit out of me," I say breathlessly.

"*I* scared *you?*" she asks incredulously. "I've just got your homework, I didn't know that you found it *that* frightening."

"I thought you were someone else," I tell her, lowering the knife.

She cocks her head to the side, a quizzical look finding its way onto her face.

I'm ready for her to ask me just who I thought she was, but she doesn't, she just gives me that odd look until I speak.

"What?" I ask.

"Why aren't you wearing a shirt?" she asks suddenly. Immediately, I feel self-conscious, not that I need to. I'm a workout freak. With my defined stomach and pectoral muscles, I have every right to be secure about my body, but under her inquisitive stare I feel the urge to hide myself, to cover my skin from her gaze.

"Did you just get back from the gym or something? And who answers the door shirtless?" she asks at my silence.

"I just got out of the shower." I fumble over my words. I can feel my face growing red, and her stare only grows more intense. She's looking at me like I've got two heads again.

"Well aren't you bashful," she says with a small laugh. The corner of her mouth pulls into a half-sided smirk, but only for a second before returning to its normal state, giving nothing away. "Look, here's your homework, you're missing your afternoon classes and I figured that's because of me, so I got your homework for you," she says, handing me the few papers she holds in her arms.

"Thanks," I say timidly, taking the papers from her.

"Sure," she says, her voice filled with discomfort. I guess this situation is just as awkward for her as it is for me. "Well, I'm going to go, lunch will be ending soon and I have to get to class," she says after a long pause of awkward silence.

"Wait," I say, reaching to take her hand and stop her, but then I think better of it. I don't want her to steal my knife and stab me because I broke her touch boundary. It's not something I would put past Celia. If there's anything I've learned about her in these past few days, it's that I have no idea what she's capable of.

"What?" she asks, hesitantly coming to a stop.

"How did you know my schedule?" I ask.

"I asked Ben," she says plainly.

"Nice try, but Ben doesn't know my schedule, so how did you know?" I ask again.

"Because I memorized your schedule," she says with reluctance.

"Again, nice try, you haven't seen my schedule," I say. "What's the truth, Celia?"

She sighs and her eyes meet mine. For once they aren't filled with malice and irritation, they're normal, almost kind even.

"I checked the computer," she says finally. "I know it's illegal to break into school records and blah, blah, blah, but I figured I owe it to you. I don't want to get partnered up with Craig like I did with you because I punched him. He's a lot worse than you are. You're obnoxious, but he's nauseating. I guess this is my way of saying thanks. My number is on the rubric for your shop class-thing project, call me if you need help with anything." She walks out the door, softly closing it behind her.

"Ya know, she's really different outside of school. I thought she was always just inhumanly scary and mean, but she can almost be normal sometimes," I say quietly, as I turn to my dog. "And what the hell was that, Zeke? I almost stabbed her. You really freaked me out, buddy." I scratch his ears affectionately as I chastise him and then pause. I look at my dog curiously, and he returns my look, his head cocked to the side, mimicking mine.

"Zeke, where's my sock?"

"Celia, Celia!"

"Huh?" I turn my head to the voice.

"We're going to leave now," my dad says, grabbing his keys from the counter. "We won't be back until Monday night, are you sure you don't want to come?"

"Yeah, I'm sure. I don't really enjoy watching Amy's basketball tournaments, besides, I don't think I'm allowed at those anymore. I got 'escorted' out of the last three that I went to," I say, rolling off the couch and walking over to where my family is standing.

"That was all *your* fault, Celia," my mom says with a laugh.

"It's not my fault the refs sucked. Almost every call they made was wrong, someone had to let them know. And I was even polite the first two times," I say defensively.

"Honestly, before then, I didn't even know that you knew the rules to basketball, or any other sport for that matter," Amy says bluntly.

"I know the rules to everything," I tell her.

"Sure, you do," she responds.

"Whatever," I say as I pull her into a hug. "Good luck, Kid."

"Don't burn the house down," she teases.

"That was you, and the house didn't burn down, the kitchen stove caught on fire," I tell her in condescension.

"It was scary," Amy says before exiting through the back door.

I shake my head and give a small laugh as she leaves. The whole event wasn't nearly as frightening as she claims it was.

"Alright, we'll see you Monday," Dad says, planting a kiss on the top of my head. Mom does the same, and then they follow Amy's lead, exiting through the back door.

I watch them leave, my eyes following their car until it slips from my vision, disappearing into a hazy spot on the horizon.

"Well, let's go make dinner," I say to myself, sashaying into the kitchen. I love having the house to myself, there's no one to bother me or disrupt my thoughts.

The first thing I do is turn on the radio and switch it to the classical music station, and Debussy floats through the room.

I then take the bacon out of the fridge and cut it into little slices, frying it up in a pan as I boil the water for the pasta.

When the bacon is finished, I remove it from the pan and add minced garlic, browning it in a bit of the bacon grease. When the last part is finished, I add the pasta, bacon, a cup and a half of parmesan cheese and an egg to the garlic, creating one of my favorite dishes, pasta carbonara.

I dance around the kitchen to Beethoven's *Moonlight Sonata* as I search for a plate and silverware.

If I lived alone, this is probably what it would be like, which is a wonderful thought, but a lonely one as well.

Something is missing, I think. I'm startled by that thought; it's not one I normally think when daydreaming about my future.

As I stand there in the kitchen, the music slowly fades out, everything becomes silent and my surroundings change.

The sun is setting, casting an orange and red tint over the beautiful landscape before me. It's breathtaking. Lush, rolling hills covered in a variety of greens, spot the horizon, and a crystal blue stream cuts through it all.

I sit on a balcony. Gorgeous flowers I've never seen before spill over the balcony's ledge and climb down the stone building. I turn to survey my surroundings and my eyes are greeted by elegant majesty.

A beautiful bed with vibrant purple sheets lays pushed up against the wall, small pillars holding up a top with curtain-like sheets draping over the sides. I run my hand along the fabric to find that it's made of silk. As I reach my hand out I catch a glimpse of my sleeve, which I find odd, because the shirt I was wearing before didn't have sleeves. I look down at my body, shocked when I find myself in an elegant, deep blue dress, dark at the top and washing out to white at the bottom. Everything about this place is ornate and elegant, from the paintings on the stone wall, to the carvings on the bed posts, right down to the beautiful stone tiles that make up the floor.

"Where am I?" I ask myself, spinning around, my eyes absorbing everything in sight.

Suddenly, there's a knock on the door. I answer it, although I'm unsure why, my body just moves on its own accord, as if I'm on autopilot.

A young man with dark brown hair stands at my door, slightly bouncing on the balls on his feet. He holds a violin in his hands and has an excited look on his face.

"I've finally got it, Celia!" he exclaims excitedly, rushing into the room. He raises his violin and rests it between his shoulder and chin. He brings the bow to the strings, takes a deep breath and then begins to play. His fingers fly with grace over the strings and he moves the bow as if it were made of lightning.

The song is amazing, it's unlike anything I've ever heard before. It's haunting and beautiful, sad but happy, all at the same time. Everything about it is captivating.

"Peter, that's amazing!" I say in awe, unaware of how I know his name when I've never seen him before. "You've been working so hard on this piece, and now you've finally found the missing part!" My voice is filled with pride and excitement.

He sets his violin on one of the desks and I run to him, falling into his arms and warm embrace. He lifts me up and into the air, spinning me in circles, planting a kiss on my forehead as he puts me down.

"Shall we celebrate?" I ask with glee.

"Indeed, we shall," he responds, making for the door.

"Excuse me, the Princess has a visitor. It's the Prince of Saturn." A man in servant's clothes appears in the doorway.

I sigh. "I guess we will have to celebrate later, my dear brother," I say. "I have matters to attend to."

"I will leave you to settle your affairs," Peter says. "Come see me when you are finished and we will have that celebration."

"I will. Let us go," I say to the other man. We leave the room I take to be mine and head to the Grand Staircase where I meet my visitor.

He's gorgeous. Tall, with pale wavy hair, cut just above his ears. His hair looks as fine as threads of silk and equally as soft. He's dressed from head to toe in elegant black clothes, matching his charcoal colored eyes. His face is angelic with a hint of his impish personality.

"Good evening, Princess Celia," he says, his voice is musical and soothing.

"Hello, Prince Mesmer." My voice is flat and there's a scowl on my face.

He smiles a confident lopsided smile, filling my blood with rage.

"Are you doing anything this evening?" he asks politely.

"Yes, I am celebrating with my brother. Peter has just finished composing the piece he has been working on for ages," I say, trying to match his polite tone, but failing miserably.

"Do you mind if I join you?" he asks, feigning interest.

"Yes," I say curtly. "It is supposed to be a celebration, where people have fun. I would be too busy dealing with your harassments to have fun."

"How unfortunate," he sighs. "Either way, I did not come here for your evening plans, I have something I wish to discuss with you." He turns to the servants and commands them to leave, and they obey, disappearing from the room in a hurry, just as I wish to do. "You know, my offer still stands," he says, making his way towards me. I feel the urge to run, to call the guards, but I stand my ground, refusing to let him see how uncomfortable he makes me.

"And my answer still stays the same," I respond. "I am engaged, Mesmer, how big of a 'no' do you need?"

"I believe that I could change your mind," he whispers into my ear.

"Back away from me now, or I will be forced to use my... talents against you," I warn.

He laughs, knowing full well that I can't really fight him, not without starting a universal incident or getting myself into heaps of trouble.

"I would like to see you try," his voice is filled with malice and lust.

My back hits the wall, sending pain through my muscles as Mesmer lays his hands are on my shoulders, holding me in place.

"There is nothing you can do to stop me," he murmurs with sick pleasure. "I want you to be mine. I want the best, the most beautiful, I want what only you can give me. Won't you grant me that satisfaction?"

"I would die before I gave myself to you," I snarl, pushing against him.

"Do not try and fight me, little princess, you know you can't," he says, pushing me with force back into the wall.

"Step away from her, Mesmer," a voice growls. The voice fills my stomach with relief and butterflies. I feel safe.

"You," Mesmer spits, spinning around angrily. I can't see the person who's come to my rescue, Mesmer is in my way.

"This will be the last insult I will take!" Mesmer exclaims unjustly, as if the situation were unfair. "I gave you a choice, Celia, you made the wrong decision by turning me down. If I cannot have you, then no one can. You could have stopped the coming destruction."

"Leave," I demand, shoving him hard, forcing him away from me.

"As you wish. I will leave you now," he pauses. "But I will be back for revenge." He mutters a few words under his breath in another language, and then pain rips through my body.

"This is only the beginning," Mesmer mutters to me.

I collapse onto the floor, pain stealing my breath away.

"What did you do to her?" the other man shouts, grabbing Mesmer by the collar and shoving him against the wall.

My vision is clouded, I still can't make out the other man's face.

"Let's just say that our dear princess is now cursed," Mesmer gloats. "Cursed to walk alone forever, cursed to lose. As long as this spell is bound, she cannot kill me." He pushes the other man away and calls to his servant, leaving me gasping for air on my knees as agony tears into all my nerves.

"Celia." The other man drops beside me, holding me against his chest. "Celia, you have to fight this, you have to fight the pain. Don't let that bastard win." His voice is full of concern and he holds me tighter, beginning to rock back and forth slightly.

I look at him, hoping to see his face, but all I see is black hair and a pair of bright blue eyes before my world turns to black.

I look around in a daze, I'm standing back in the kitchen, my plate still warm and sitting on the counter.

"What the hell just happened?" I ask myself, my voice echoing off the empty walls of the house. I shake my head, as if to shake the delirium from my mind. "Well, my sleep hasn't been that great as of late, so I guess it makes sense that I'm starting to hallucinate," I reason.

No, not hallucinating, remembering. The voice is in my head, but it feels like it was whispered through the walls, like it wasn't coming from me.

"Remembering what?" I ask myself quizzically.

The past. A long-forgotten past.

"Well that settles everything," I say with finality. "I'm going to bed." I eat my food quickly and clean up in the same manner, rushing to go to bed. I'm deeply disturbed by the hallucinations and the voice in my head.

I lay out my outfit for the next day and then crawl into bed, curling up on my side, easily falling into sleep.

I'm in that elegant room again, staring at myself in a large mirror. I remember the words spoken by the vengeful prince and they chill me to the bone. "Cursed to walk alone forever, cursed to lose."

"I will not lose," I say defiantly, staring at my reflection. The more I think on his words, the more I am filled with rage. It grows inside me at an explosive rate, and I throw my fist into the mirror. I'm showered with glass, my ears ringing with the sound of the shards clinking onto the stone floor. Blood drips from the cuts in my fist, but I can't feel anything, I am numb. "I will not lose," I repeat, my voice shaking with anger.

"Celia." Gentle hands pull me away from the broken glass. "You're not going to lose," he murmurs, wrapping me in his arms. "You never lose, Celia. You always find a way to win, no matter how long it takes you." His words give me strength, strength enough to regain my composure.

"I know that whatever Mesmer did to you, you can overcome it. You overcome everything." He plants a gentle kiss on my shoulder, nuzzling the curve of my neck.

"I overcome everything," I repeat, turning so I can look into his eyes, so I can see his face and finally figure out who this man is. Slowly, my eyes fall upon his face, and my breath catches. He's not at all who I had expected him to be, and I stand there frozen and shocked.

I wake up gasping for air, as if I had been holding my breath all night. My lungs fill with oxygen and my breathing slows, the light feeling in my head fading.

I immediately reflect on the dream, but I can barely remember it, or the face of the mysterious man who pulled me from the shattered glass. I remember being surprised, and staring into a pair of shockingly blue eyes, very beautiful blue eyes.

I groan in complaint at forgetting that face, scolding myself for not analyzing it and committing it to memory.

"I should probably get up," I say, reading my clock. It's seven in the morning, which is a little late for me. I have a strict schedule for waking up. It doesn't matter how late or how early I go to bed, I always get up between six thirty and seven thirty, seven thirty being more on the late side. If I don't wake up in that time frame, my whole schedule is thrown off, and for someone who relies heavily on routine and schedule, having it thrown off is horrible.

I sit up and stretch out. My body is sore again, but there are no more random gashes, and the one on my back is healing up nicely. Instead of being a red line across my back that burned with every movement, it has become only a thin white line where the cut used to be.

I put on a pair of jeans and a plain black t-shirt and grab a Power Bar on my way out to my car.

I stuff the trunk with things I might need, like a chainsaw, work gloves, shovels, a hedge trimmer and a big jug of water.

I pull my phone out of my pocket and dial up Mr. Mallard, just to make sure that it's okay if I come over.

"Hello, this is Nick Mallard," he says, picking up his phone.

"Hey, it's Celia. I was wondering if now would be a good time to come over. I want to get as much work done as possible," I tell him.

"Yeah, it's okay if you come over now, but you really don't have to," he says.

"That's alright, I'll be there soon." I hang up the phone and start the car, driving away to initiate my investigation.

The Mallard house is even more beautiful in the daylight. The bluffs and ridges are a dark, luscious green, while the fields contrast with their bright, vibrant, lemony-green color.

Horses and cows graze in the fields, while chickens and a few peacocks strut around the barns. I catch sight of a few cats darting around up by the house, chasing each other and small animals that grab their attention.

When I pull up to the second barn, I see Mr. Mallard leaning up against an ATV with a trailer attached to the back. Around his feet run three toddlers, chasing after each other with wide grins on their faces, followed around by a happy chocolate lab. I can't help but smile.

"Good morning, Celia!" he says happily, coming to meet me.

"Good morning, Mr. Mallard," I say, returning the enthusiasm in his voice.

"Please, just call me, Nick," he tells me, helping me move the equipment from the back of my car and into the trailer. "I take it you want to clean up what you can on the ridge? You seem to be intrigued by the happenings up there."

"I am indeed intrigued by the happenings on the ridge," I admit. "But I'd also like to check up there for evidence of my own, just to make sure the police haven't missed anything."

"You really think they missed something?" he asks quizzically.

"I think they don't know exactly what to look for," I tell him.

"And you do?"

"Nope, but I'm not looking for the same thing as the police. If I were, it'd be no use to go to the ridge because all of the evidence is at the police station. I'm looking for answers to a completely different question." A question that only I can find the answer to.

"I guess that makes sense," Nick says, leaving it at that.

"You aren't going to ask me what question I'm trying to answer?" I ask, confused by his actions.

"Nope," he responds. "I doubt you're going to do something illegal, so if there's a question you feel compelled to answer, then you feel free to answer it. And if you wanted me to know what you were trying to answer, then you would have told me."

He says nothing more and we head up to the ridge where he drops me off, leaving me with the ATV and the trailer, hurrying back the way we came. It's obvious that he doesn't want to stick around, and I don't blame him. I myself am frozen where I stand, but not because the sight before me is gruesome and halting. It's because the sight before me, the roped off murder scene, is exactly where I had woken up.

"Sorry, Nick," I say as I make my way to the scene, ducking under the crime scene tape, ignoring the fact that what I'm doing is highly illegal. "But I have to do this, I need answers."

The entire area is black and covered in soot. I'm standing in the middle of a charred bowl. Everything within a twenty-foot radius is burnt to a crisp. It explains the acrid smell I had discovered upon waking.

I crouch down and study the footprints closely, lightly tracing the treads. It looks like they belong to a boot, maybe a combat boot. I can tell that the person who wore them wasn't very heavy by how deep the tracks are. The strange thing about the footprints is that they suddenly stop at an imprint in the ground and don't pick up anywhere else. I know they don't belong to the victim, he would have left a deeper imprint in the charred ground. They couldn't have belonged to me, I wasn't wearing shoes when I had woken up, so whose were they?

There are two body imprints. One I know is from when I woke up, but I have no idea how I got there. Despite my memory loss, I know that somehow I was involved in this crime.

How can someone wake up next to a dead person, and not even know it? I ask myself. *Perhaps I experienced something traumatic, inducing a sort of amnesia. The brain tries to block out traumatizing experiences, so it makes sense,* I reason. If I could kick my brain, I would. I *want* to remember what happened, I *need* to remember what happened.

I walk to the body imprints and kneel down to examine them.

He was right next to me when he died. I wonder if I had held his hand as the life left his body, if I had held onto him, or if I had simply watched him die. My bet is on the latter.

"What happened here?" I ask the empty forest.

I reach my hand out to touch the ground where the man had died, and jump back in shock as small tendrils of electricity leap from the ground and to my fingers. I yelp in surprise, but not in pain. The electricity doesn't hurt me, my fingers don't tingle, there's no pain in my arm. I should be hurting, but I don't feel anything.

Remember. The whispered voice in my head sounds as if it's coming from all around me once again.

"What am I supposed to remember?" I ask quietly.

Remember who you are.

"I know who I am, I'm Celia Walters!" I exclaim with agitation.

Rid yourself of the mask that conceals you and remember who you are.

"Stop!" I shout, anger filling my blood. Electricity shoots out of my body, coiling around the nearest tree. It hums through the air and hangs around me like a patch of electric fog.

I scuffle backwards, dragging myself across the charred ground, desperate to get away from the newly blackened trees.

"This isn't happening," I tell myself, closing my eyes tightly.

My mind is racing. I rack my brain for anything I should remember, hoping to spark a memory of what happened the night I found myself in these woods, but all I see is a masquerade mask. It's the one I had seen before passing out. The one I had seen before waking up here.

"Celia!"

I snap my head around and see Nick standing by the police tape with a worried look on his face.

"I heard a shout and so I ran up here, are you okay?"

"Yeah, I just... This is where I woke up Thursday morning when you drove me to school. I woke up on the ridge, in the middle of all this," I gesture to the blackened woods around us. "But I can't remember anything."

"What?" he asks, confusion playing on his face.

"I was here when that man died, this is where I woke up. How can someone wake up next to a dead person and not even know it? It makes no sense. I can't remember anything from that night other than waking up here. I can't piece anything together. Damnit."

"You don't have to work today," he says kindly, his warm eyes meet mine and comfort me. He doesn't think I'm crazy, he doesn't think that I'm a murderer, it's all there in his green eyes. "This has to be really shocking to you."

"You're paying me to work, and that's exactly what I intend on doing," I say, getting to my feet and brushing the soot and ash off my clothes. "But there's not much for me to do here."

He smiles at me warmly. "Alright, I'll show you what things you can get started on."

I hop in the trailer and Nick takes the ATV, pulling me along behind him. He drives down to the large barn and then stops, walking toward the back of the barn, waving at me to follow him.

"Okay, so, if you want, you can work on cleaning up this mess in here, or you can start on the lawn," he says.

I look around to survey the barn. It really is a mess. There are multiple piles of wood, a dumpy car and a bunch of other random junk like old, dilapidated furniture, tables, tools, and just about everything else.

"What do you want me to with the lawn?" I ask.

"Well, it has to be mowed for starters, and the flowerbeds need to be weeded…" he pauses with a contemplative look. "You know what, Celia? You're smart, so you do whatever you think should be done. I trust your judgement."

"Alright, well I'll start in here. I'll clean this place up which will give you more storage room for stuff in your house and whatnot. It will also give me time to figure out what to do with the lawn. After this is done, I'll clean up the trails in the woods," I say, giving him a brief overview.

"You'll be able to do that all in one day?" Nick asks.

"You mean clean this place up and clear off the trails? Most likely. A lot of the stuff in here could easily be fixed up and sold, so I'll just put those items in a pile and work on them another day. The rest of this stuff you could probably burn. I'll work on the truck another time, so clearing the junk out of here won't be too hard. Once this is cleared out, I can take the ATV and the trailer and use the chainsaw to take care of fallen branches and trees, load it all into the trailer, and you guys can have a bonfire tonight."

"Sounds great," he says with a wide smile. "Nothing in here is of any importance to us, it's all a bunch of junk, so don't feel bad about burning anything."

"Alright, let me get my gloves and I'll get to work."

"I really appreciate this, Celia," Nick says as I walk to the trailer and grab my duffel bag. "It means a lot to all of us."

"It's no problem, Nick," I say. "I have too much free time, I enjoy working and I want to help." *And this place has answers, answers that*

I need. I don't add that last part. Nick doesn't need to know about the civil war going on inside my head.

I walk over to my duffel bag and grab my iPod, earbuds and work gloves. The moment the music turns on, my work begins.

I get home at 8:00, and I'm exhausted to the bone. I spent all day cleaning out the big barn and carting out all the junk, placing it in a pile outside the barn. Once I was finished with that, I mowed the lawn, cutting it to a golf-course-like length, and then used the weed whacker to reach the places I couldn't with the riding lawn mower. After that, I went back up into the woods and cleared the paths of all fallen trees and overgrown brush that crawled onto the trails. I left the landscaping work for another day. I came up with several of ideas for the landscaping bit while I worked, all of them including a lot of flowers. It's not a widely known fact, but I love flowers. Most people think that I'm too soulless to find beauty in anything, let alone flowers, but they couldn't be more wrong.

Before I left, I made sure to douse the junk pile in gasoline and light it on fire for the kids to play around while under the watchful gaze of their parents.

I still have a bunch more work to do in the barn. Fixing up the items that hadn't been burned, seeing if I could salvage the truck, there's still so much to do, but Nick told me to go home and rest on Sunday. He also told me to get my homework done, but I had done that the moment I had gotten home on Friday.

I pull into the garage and slowly unload my car. I bring my bag inside the house, dropping it off just inside the door, too tired to carry it any further.

I stumble up the stairs and into my room where I collapse onto my bed, quickly falling into the hands of sleep.

I wake up with one thought on my mind, *I don't want to go to school tomorrow.* I don't want to deal with Celia, and I don't want to deal with Craig and all the rumors that will be going around school. I also don't want to have to keep Celia in check. She seems explosive lately, it makes me curious as to why. It's not like we're friends now, and we still despise each other, but we aren't each other's biggest problem anymore.

I roll over in my bed and stretch out, groaning as I do so, slowly bringing myself into a sitting position with my feet hanging over the side of the bed.

"Don't go in there," I hear Mom say, probably scolding Lily.

I'm right.

"But I really want to, Mama," the little girl responds.

"Wait until he's up," Mom commands.

I smile a bit as I walk to my door, opening it with caution. A small body is hurled at mine as my little sister jumps into my arms.

"Happy birthday, Beckett!" she squeals, throwing her arms around my neck.

"Thanks, Lily," I say, hugging the little girl. She seems so small, wrapped in my arms with her tiny feet kicking in the air. Lily's only seven, my mom and dad adopted her when I was ten, but as far as I'm concerned, she might as well be my biological sister. I love her.

"Wanna see what we got you?" she asks me excitedly.

"Sure," I say, copying her excited tone, watching her bright green eyes light up with joy.

"Come on then!" I set her down and she grabs my hand, dragging me out to the garage, where I'm greeted by a jet-black Suzuki GSX-R750, with a basket of Twix and Kit Kats on the seat.

"You got me a motorcycle!" I say in disbelief. "This is amazing!" I run to the bike in awe and just stare at it, letting my eyes take in the beauty of the piece of machinery in front of me.

"I got you the candy!" Lily says proudly.

"Thank you, Lily," I say, giving her another hug. I pick up the basket from the seat and set it on top of the car, but not before taking out a Twix-mini.

I roll the motorcycle out into the driveway and throw my leg over its body, taking a seat on the bike, my feet resting nicely on the ground. I adjust the mirrors and play with the blinkers and lights with a big smile on my face. I can't believe my parents actually got me a motorcycle. I'll be the only one at school who owns a motorcycle.

I twist my grip and apply the throttle, hearing the sound of the engine revving to life, feeling it hum through my body.

"You need your helmet, Beck!" my mom says, suddenly running over to me and placing a sleek, black, biker's helmet over my head. I don't protest, I'm just glad that she isn't making me wrap my entire body in bubble wrap, allowing me to ride off in my joggers and a t-shirt.

"Thanks, Mom," I say, my voice muffled by my helmet. I flip the kill switch into the "off" position and turn the ignition key all the way, letting the engine idle for a minute. With excitement in my bones, I pull the clutch lever, pressing the shifter into first gear with my foot, slowly relaxing the clutch and then applying the throttle. I feel the bike move and my heart soars.

I pull out of the driveway and head down the road at a moderate speed, feeling the wind whipping at my clothes. I can't help but smile as I zip down the road on my new motorcycle. I never dreamed that my parents would buy me a motorcycle, it's so unexpected and wonderful.

As I ride around, I see a familiar figure and race towards it, squeezing the breaks as I pull up next to him and come to a stop, resting my feet on the ground.

"Hey, you brought my motorcycle back!" Ben says with a playful tone.

"Ha, you wish. This baby is all mine," I tell him as I pull off my helmet.

"You know you've got to be careful now, you're officially an adult, and your parents might want you to pay for all that bike's expenses. You might want me to help with that, I think I know how we could cut a deal," he teases.

"Keep trying," I say with a laugh.

"Yeah, I'm just messing with you, happy eighteenth, man, you're officially an adult," Ben says in a congratulatory manner. "I honestly never thought your folks would get you a motorcycle."

"Neither did I," I tell him. "It was a pleasant surprise."

"I bet it was."

"So, where are you headed?" I ask.

"I'm out to go annoy, Celia," he says casually. "Oh! Speaking of Celia and annoying her, how are things going with you two?"

"Well, I pulled her out of a fight and then sort of called her heartless," I admit.

"I don't know why you two hate each other," he says mystified.

"You know, people often say that the person of the opposite gender that you hate a lot for no reason is most likely the person you're going to marry."

"Yeah, that's just a myth," I tell him. "That doesn't really happen."

"Oh, I think you'd be surprised," Ben objects. "My parents hated each other when they first met, and they continued to until someone threatened them both along with their families. The urge to protect their loved ones brought them together, and they grew to like each other and then got married and had me."

"Oh," I say, shocked at hearing Ben talk about his family, it's not something he makes a habit of. "Well, I guess I should let you get back on your way to annoying Celia," I say.

"Alright, be careful on your bike, I'd really hate to see it wrecked." He laughs and continues walking, his shoulders moving up and down as he chuckles.

After he leaves, I drive around the neighborhood for a little while longer before turning around and heading back home.

"You didn't crash?" my mom asks as I pull into the garage.

"No, Mom," I say in exasperation. "Not everyone who rides a motorcycle crashes and dies."

"But a lot of them do," she insists. I roll my eyes at her and hop off my bike, setting my helmet on the seat. I pluck the candy basket from atop the car and take a Kit-Kat out, breaking it in half, giving one half to my little sister and eating the other.

"How was it?" my dad asks with a wide smile.

"It was awesome," I tell him, returning his smile. "Really awesome."

"I'm glad," he says. "It took a lot of convincing to get your mom to agree to this, don't make me regret it." His voice holds a warning tone to it, but his eyes betray nothing.

"I won't, I promise." I give my mom a big hug, and then my dad, thanking them both for the motorcycle.

"Alright, let's go eat breakfast," Mom says, herding us all inside.

"Is Ben going to come over today?" Lily asks, standing at the foot of my bed.

I put my comic book down and take off my reading glasses to see her better.

"I suppose he might come over and play video games with me like he normally does," I tell her.

"Yay! I want to show him my new dress." She twirls like a princess, her green dress flowing out and around her. *God, she's adorable,* I think to myself.

"Do you think he'll like it?" she asks.

"I'm sure Ben will love it," I say reassuringly. I find it both incredibly funny and incredibly cute that Lily has a huge crush on Ben. I find it even funnier that Ben goes along with it, treating her like a queen, doting on her constantly, it's adorable.

"Yay!" she squeals with delight, her eyes crinkling as she gives me a big smile.

I smile back at her and then shoo her out of my room, wanting to finish my comic book in peace and quiet.

She runs up the stairs squealing with joy, excitedly exclaiming to our parents that Ben would be coming over, and as if on cue, the doorbell rings and Zeke starts barking crazily.

I sigh, set my comic book down, and then race to the door, but my mom beats me to it, swinging the door wide open to reveal my best friend.

"Hi, Ben! How are you doing?" she asks with excitement. My mom gets excited about everything, especially when someone is at the door. She loves greeting visitors, it makes her feel happy and energetic, but I just think she's weird.

"I am doing quite well, Mrs. Halverson, how about yourself?" he says.

"I'm doing just fine, Ben, and how many times do I have to tell you that you can just call me Jessica?" she chastises.

"My parents would roll over in their graves if I were to not be a gentleman. Calling you by your proper title is a sign of respect," Ben explains. My mom just laughs and welcomes him inside.

The moment he walks through the threshold, my little sister flings herself at him.

"Hi, Ben!" she says, hugging him tightly around the waist.

"Hello there, Lily!" He picks the little girl up and twirls her in the air and then holds her against his body, resting her on his hip. "And how are you, my little princess?" he asks, staring into her big, green eyes.

"I'm really good!" she proclaims. "How are you?"

"I am doing spectacular," he says enthusiastically, causing her to squeal and wrap her little arms tightly around his neck.

"Hey man, you here to slay hordes of zombies in Black Ops?" I ask, walking to his side to pry my little sister off his body. She groans in protest, but I manage to peel her off my friend and set her on the floor.

"Nope, I just stopped by to give you your birthday present," he says, and then he shucks his leather jacket off and hands it to me. "Every biker needs a leather jacket, here's yours."

"Ben, I can't take this. This was your dad's, and it's your only leather jacket. You without a leather jacket is like a cowboy without his hat, it's just weird," I say, handing the jacket back to him.

"I bought myself a new one," he says, refusing to take the jacket back. "And yeah, it belonged to my dad, but it doesn't anymore. It belongs to me and I'm giving it to you, my best friend, who keeps me out of trouble and always has my back. The Meyers were awesome for taking me in after what happened to my parents, but they haven't been much of a family, you have. Beck, you've been really good to me. You're a brother, best friend and father all in one. You keep me out of trouble, as stated before, get me into trouble, as all best friends do, and you've always, always had my back, and isn't that what brothers do? You deserve a real present, something special and meaningful, not some store-bought junk. Besides, it makes you look like a badass," he says, grinning widely.

"Ben!" my sister scolds, slapping him in the leg with all of her might. "You shouldn't say words like that!"

"You have my most sincere apologies, milady," he says, getting onto his knees so that they're at the same eye level. "I beg your forgiveness."

I find it endlessly funny to see this wild, punkish boy begging for forgiveness from a seven-year-old girl, it isn't something one sees too often.

"I forgive you," Lily says graciously.

"Thank you, milady," he says, holding her face tenderly in his big hands. He gingerly places a kiss on the top of her head and she runs off, squealing in delight.

"Alright, well, I should be on my way home," he says suddenly. "Lily, I've gotta go!" he shouts through the house, making sure my sister hears him.

"Do you have to?" she asks with sad eyes, appearing at his side in a flash.

"Indeed, I do," he says.

"Okay," she says with disappointment. "Bye Ben, you have to come back and see me soon!" She gives him one last hug, holding him tightly.

"Will do," he says. "Bye, Lily. See ya, Beck." He slaps me on the back and walks out, making his way down to the road. Ben doesn't own a car, he just walks everywhere, and he refuses to find another method of transportation. I remember the time his foster parents bought him a car and he returned it to the dealer and gave the cash back to his parents. When asked why, he said because he had no use for a car, it cost money for gas, money for insurance, and he didn't want to have to deal with that.

I watch him until he disappears from my vision, wondering how he walked everywhere. For me, I can walk for a day or two, but not everywhere, all the time. Eventually my feet hurt and my body becomes sore. I don't know how he does it.

"Beckett?"

"Huh?" I ask, turning to my sister.

"Is Ben going to come over tomorrow?"

"Well, he said he'd come over to see you soon," I say.

"But is he going to come over tomorrow?" she asks.

I sigh and look at her, and then to my smiling parents. "Sure," I tell her, ruffling her hair. "But you'll have to call and ask him." My parents and I start laughing at her blushed face, watching her turn a bright, glowing red.

I smile contentedly, it had been a good day, a good way to spend my 18th birthday.

I sit on the piano bench, my eyes straining to read the notes on the page.

"Why did you decide to play Bach's *Aria* at three in the morning? You should have just gone to bed, what the hell were you thinking?" I ask myself, my voice clashing with the quiet sound of the piano. Even though I'm the only one at home, I still play quietly, I don't like the sound of a loud piano. It's such a gentle instrument, it should be played as such, with gentle elegance. I feel like the notes lose their tone and in turn, their beauty, once played loudly, which is another reason why I only ever play softly, to preserve the beauty of the instrument's sound. My eyes burn. *It's too late to be playing piano,* I think to myself. *I'm tired, I should really go to bed.* I pause and look at the music. *There's only a page left, I can do this.*

Even as I think the words, I can feel my body slowing down, my brain shutting off, overwhelmed by exhaustion. My eyes slowly close as I collapse over the piano with a clang of the keys, creating a disgusting sound. It's the last thing I hear before slipping beneath the surface of my mind and into my unconsciousness.

"Celia." A gentle voice calls to me. It's a beautiful voice, coaxing me to turn towards its owner but I refuse to, and I don't know why.

"Gaze upon me, Princess," he says, his hand cupping my cheek, forcing my eyes to meet his. "A beauty to behold," he whispers in my ear. I can feel his breath on me and my body becomes rigid.

"Unhand me," I growl. I don't know why I'm so cold to him, he's beautiful. He's tall, his body is slender like a dancer's, his face is angular and beautiful, with eyes the color of onyx. Everything about him is perfectly proportioned, right down to his pale blond hair that looks as fine as silk, gently ruffled by the wind.

"You cannot hate me forever," he murmurs into my neck, wrapping his arms around my body, sending a flare of rage through my blood at the violation.

"Indeed, I can," I proclaim defiantly, shoving him away from me, scowling at his amused smirk. "I have lost everything that I have ever loved because of you. My family, my friends, my home, my fiancé." I add the last one with sorrow instead of anger in my voice, twisting the ring on my finger. "So yes, Mesmer Amar, Prince of Saturn, I can, and I will *hate you forever."*

I hit the ground hard, gasping for air that's not coming. My eyes open to see my blank ceiling. I'm no longer with the beautiful man, I'm lying on the floor of my room. My body is burning, agony rips through my muscles and nerves. I clench my hands into tight fists, confused by the ring I find on my left hand. I don't wear rings, but that's the least of my worries. I. Can't. Breathe.

This can't be happening. My mind is spinning.

But it is happening, the pervasive voice speaks once again, sounding as if it's coming from the walls themselves. *Remember who you are, Princess, Avenging Angel, Lady of the Masquerade. Arise, Celia, and claim the night, avenge what was lost. Remember.*

I scream in agony, no longer able to contain it. My body is wrapped in coils of blue electricity, but my room isn't charred like it should be, it's as if the electricity is channeling through me, running through my blood. I should be dead.

Images of people and places flash through my mind and colors swirl together. Memories of balls and ballets, of festivals and joyous times dance across my mind's eye, leaving a heavy pain in my chest, pain for what was lost to me. The memories keep coming and I keep screaming. My head feels like it's going to split open, and then it stops, and I'm pulled into a new world, a world that I had lost.

"Be mine, Princess Celia, forever. I swear to protect you and love you to no end. And whether or not you will take me, I will always love you." His voice is warm and causes my heart to soar inside my chest. He's on one knee, the moon is reflecting off his black hair, and his blue eyes shine with sincerity as he brings out a ring, begging for me to stay by his side.

I fall to my own knees in front of him, taking his hands in mine, repeating the same word over and over again. "Yes."

Avenge what was lost. Remember. The voice in my head repeatedly screams that one word in my head as I go back to writhing on the floor, overtaken by pain.

Remember! Remember! Remember!

"Stop," I beg, my voice weak and miserable, pleading for the voice to be silent.

Remember! Remember! Remember!

My body starts to grow tense, and I think I'm finally going to die, but I'm wrong. I'm changing. My body goes through a metamorphosis, my clothes turn into what feels like molten lava, scorching my skin, as they begin to mold together and change. My joggers turn into black skinny jeans, ripping up and down the legs, and a leather jacket materializes onto my body over a white tank top. My vision grows darker and my face feels heavier, I'm wearing a mask.

The electricity stops, and I feel like I've been hit by a truck, but the screaming in my head is gone, and I'm still.

I rise to my feet, my body shaking slightly, and I let out a deep breath, taking in the oxygen my body has so desperately craved.

I stand before my window, looking out over the night, brandishing a whip made of fine silver chords, fused together.

I open the window, letting the breeze in and ruffle my hair. It's cold, and it feels nice, the night's air is running its fingers through my hair and cooling my scorching body.

Remember. The voice isn't screaming anymore, it's quiet, calming, beckoning the deep recesses of my mind to come to light.

"I remember," I say quietly, speaking to the empty night. "I am Celia Walters, the fallen Princess of Mercury. I must avenge what I have lost, what was taken from me. I made a promise to you, Mesmer Amar. I promised that I would hate you forever, and that I would not stop until you were dead, and I don't break my promises." Even though the night is empty and vacant, I know he can hear me. I know that he can feel the lost soul inside of me is now awake, that I have become my true self, and now, I am out for blood.

I roll over and let out a heavy sigh. *I can't sleep,* my voice reverberates off the walls of my mind.

I turn my head and check the small clock on my bedside table. *Three thirty?! Why can't I sleep?* I sit up and stretch out. *Maybe I should go for a walk and just clear my head,* I think, searching for my running shoes and pants.

I open up the window, letting the cool breeze in, taking a deep breath, filling my lungs with the crisp, clean, cool air.

Alright, I can go for a short walk, no one will even know that I was gone.

I hoist myself out of the window and onto the ground.

It's a good thing my window is at ground level, I think to myself. *Otherwise I might not be able to close it.* I push my window until it's just a crack open so I can get back in.

I begin to walk with nowhere particular in mind, just away, as if walking away from my house would allow me to walk away from my problems as well.

School is going to be a mess tomorrow, especially with Celia's new-found explosiveness. I don't know how many more fights I'll be able to pull her out of before we repeat what happened in the library. I don't know if I *want* to pull her out any more fights, especially when all she does is snap at me.

"That girl is a pain in the ass," I groan, scowling at the ground. The only nice thing about Celia Walters is the way she looks. The girl never slacks. Every day she looks as if she's got a business meeting or some equally important job right after school, resulting in her stunning appearance. Aside from that though, she has no redeeming qualities. She's mean, self-centered, cold, detached and guarded, so you never really know what's going on in her mind, or what she's truly feeling. But for some reason, I want Ben to be right about her. I desperately want to see the person that Ben does, I want to be someone she trusts, someone she would let her guard down around, someone she could call her friend, and I understand none of it.

I sigh in frustration, running a hand through my hair. "What is it about that girl?"

I continue walking, heading into the Warehouse District, passing abandoned, dilapidated buildings, one after another. I feel like I'm walking through a ghost town, each facility I pass is rundown and falling apart, crumbling beneath the weight of time and neglect. It makes me uneasy, yet calm, all at the same time.

I catch a movement out of the corner of my eye, and spin around quickly, only to find an empty, battered warehouse.

I'm just imagining things, I tell myself. *I must be really out of it.* I continue walking, watching the shadows me carefully, and then suddenly stop, frozen in my tracks as the cold barrel of a gun is pressed into the base of my skull.

"Don't you know it's not safe to be out so late?" A man's cold voice echoes through the abandoned buildings.

I don't say anything, I have nothing to say, and if I did, I doubt I'd be able to speak, I'm paralyzed by fear.

"Tell ya what, if you give me everything you've got on you, I'll get you home safely, if not, well, who knows what might happen to you," he says, his voice crackling with insanity.

"I don't have any money on me, I swear. You can check me if you want," I say, attempting to keep my composure.

"Well, I can't have you running off to the cops, so I guess this is where we part ways. Luckily for me, we've got that mystery killer out on the loose, your death will probably be attributed to her."

Shit, I'm boned.

"Whoa, whoa, whoa, wait!" I say, starting to panic. "Think about it, I haven't even seen your face, and I swear I won't go the cops. Even if I did, I'd have nothing to go off of." I try to keep the panic out of my voice, but I'm certain that it's a vain effort.

"You raise a good point, but I have no way of knowing if you're telling the truth or not, it'll just be easier if I kill you."

I hear the sound of a bullet clicking into the chamber. I close my eyes tightly and silently apologize to my family, begging for their forgiveness in my heart.

Suddenly, I hear a loud crack, but not the crack of the hammer of the gun firing a bullet from the chamber and letting it loose into the world. It's the crack of a whip.

She stands in the shadows, her long brown hair blowing in the wind, the silver whip she brandishes glinting in the moonlight. She wears ripped, black skinny jeans, a white tank top and a black leather jacket.

My eyes travel up from her boots all the way to her face, obscured by a masquerade mask, like the kind you would see at a fancy ball.

"Well, well, well, what have we here?" she asks. Her voice is smooth, musical and fierce, all at once. It holds power and authority and I can't help but to bend underneath the dominance in her voice like a sapling bending beneath the winds of a hurricane.

She steps out of the shadows and circles around the scene like a vulture who's just spotted its prey, electricity crackling around her body.

"What the hell?! Who are you? *What* are you?" the thug asks, fumbling over his words, fear numbing his tongue.

"What am I? Obviously not human," she states with a small smirk. Her smile is cold and mischievous, it reminds me of Celia. "As for who I am, well, I've been called by many names, but as of late, I've been dubbed The Masquerader, or simply 'crazy killer.'" She gives a small laugh at that last part, its terrifying confidence ringing through with slight insanity lingering beneath it. "Now, what do they call *you*?" she asks, ceasing her predatory circling for a moment to face the thug. "Pathetic? Weak? Disgusting? Not worthy of life? That's what I would call you." Her voice is pure poison. "Look at him," she commands, the authority in her growling voice forcing the thug to meet my eyes. "He's a kid, probably with a family and friends, and you were going to end his life. Perhaps we should do the same with you."

"No, I wasn't! I swear!" the man says desperately. "I was just going to scare him and knock him out maybe."

"Hm, I have no way of knowing if you're telling the truth or not, it'll just be easier if I kill you," she says, her malicious smile returning to her face.

Her whip crackles with electricity, her excitement is palpable as she resumes her predatory circling, flicking her whip menacingly.

I watch in horror and awe as she raises her whip, ready to strike. Everything around her is tinted blue from the intense electricity coiling around her.

She flicks her wrist and the whip cracks down, barely missing her prey as he jumps back and away from her attack.

I expect her to be angry, but she laughs and her eyes sparkle with glee.

Everything about her freezes me more, fear constricting around me the way electricity does around her. I understand why the police are trying to enforce a curfew, why they suggest you stay inside once it becomes dark, because this woman is the physical manifestation of fear.

"Back yourself up against a wall? That's not very smart," she laughs.

She moves quickly, grabbing something from inside her jacket and throwing it hard. All I catch is the glinting of metal in the moonlight as the man stumbles backward, falling hard against the wall with his arms pinned to the concrete building behind him.

She spins something between her forefinger and thumb, I assume it's what she had thrown his way. Slowly, the object stops spinning, and I can finally see what it is that she holds. It's a throwing star shaped like a rose head, oddly elegant and adding to her menace.

The man is now trapped against the wall by his clothes, the rose blades keeping him pinned to the concrete.

The corner of the girl's mouth tugs into a smile, a cold smile, as she closes in on the thug, like a beast closing in on its prey.

"Wait!" The words spill out of my mouth before I'm even aware that I'm talking. "Don't kill him!" I'm terrified as she stops and slowly turns toward me.

"And why not?" she asks. "You are aware that had I intervened, he would have killed you, right?"

"Yeah, but still, it doesn't sit right with me. I can't just stand here and watch someone murder another person, it's wrong, even if he was going to kill me. Spare him for the reasons he should've spared me. What if he has a family too? What if he's got a little boy or girl at home, waiting for their dad to come back?" I say urgently. "Please, I can't have his life on my conscience. I don't know anyone who could watch a man die and feel nothing, I doubt even Celia could." The last part is added as more of an afterthought, but the rest is spoken with confidence and conviction, earning a quizzical look from The Masquerader.

She sighs with reluctance, suddenly looking quite bored. "Fine, since he is not tonight's prey, merely a lowlife inconvenience, and it was your life at risk, I will let him live. This was not part of the hunt, it was only the saving of an innocent life." Her words are strange and they confuse me. What hunt?

I watch her carefully as her whip begins to fold in on itself, becoming a coil of metal that snakes up her arm, upper back and shoulder area, reminding me of vines climbing up the side of a castle. I can't believe what I'm seeing, things like this aren't possible. People don't radiate electricity and have whips that turn into vine-like cords that wind up their bodies, but she does. Who is this woman?

She's incredible, I think as I watch her, my eyes absorbing everything they can.

She slowly advances on the man with fierce and cold eyes, taking her time until she's standing a few feet away from him.

"You will be allowed to live, but you're going to be *very* sore," she growls, electricity shooting from her body into his. "Well, that is, once you've woken up." She grabs the rose blades embedded in the wall and pulls them out with ease, and his body drops, lying limply on the gravel.

"I thought you said you weren't going to kill him!" I say, rushing to where he lies.

"He's not dead, he's unconscious. You didn't think I'd let him go with only a warning, did you?" she asks, a teasing tone lingering beneath the bored sound of her voice.

I don't respond, I'm not quite sure what I thought she would do, I hadn't put much thought into what would happen after she decided not to kill him.

"You should go home, it's not safe to be out so late at night," she tells me, her voice now gentle, her eyes no longer holding malice or that predatory glint. "Here, you dropped this." She holds out her hand, holding a flat metal rectangle.

"My phone," I say startled, I didn't even know I had lost it. "Um, thank you." I reach for my phone and my fingers brush her palm. I jump back slightly, a small current of electricity shooting through me.

"Sorry," she says, "I'm a bit shocking."

I laugh a little at her joke and retrieve my phone, making sure not to accidently touch her again, and I notice a unique and rapturing ring.

"Are you engaged?" I ask, words once again spilling out of my mouth before I can stop them, unsure as to why I feel the need to ask.

Her mask can't hide her surprise as my words settle into her ears.

"I was," she says curtly. I can tell that I've crossed into dangerous territory, I should be treading these waters carefully. "Now go home Beckett Halverson, it's not safe here." She walks off into the shadows and I rush to follow her, but she's gone, she just disappeared.

I sigh, and begin to run, heading home in a daze. Once I get to my house, I pry my window open and crawl through, dropping onto the floor of my room. I collapse on my bed, breathing heavily. My heart is slamming against my ribs, the shock capturing my body as the night's events come crashing onto me. I had almost been killed by a thug, and then I was saved by The Masquerader, who is responsible for the murders of two people.

My hands shake as I realize how close to death I had come, but soon my mind is distracted by something else, pulling my attention away.

How did she know my name? I wonder. She had called me by my name when she had told me to go home. *Who is she?*

I wake with a start, my alarm clock screaming. I lift my head from the piano, running my hands along my face and through my hair, feeling the marks left indented on my cheek from the piano keys.

"Ugh," I groan as I lift myself off the piano bench and stretch out my back.

I stumble over to my alarm clock and silence it, letting a deep breath out as I look around my room. I didn't do a single part of my routine last night, instead I played piano until I passed out.

"Shit!" I shout, rushing frantically around the room, a sudden realization setting in. "I have to get ready for school!" I didn't pick out an outfit the night before as I usually do, so I now have to waste precious time to find clothes.

"Oh, this is not good," I groan, quickly putting on a pair of blue skinny jeans and a plain, white V-neck t-shirt.

I'm worried, it's not like me to neglect my routine, it's how I manage to stay sane. It's not unlike me to play piano for hours on end, but it is unlike me to blackout while playing and to break from my schedule. *What is going on with me?* I wonder.

I slip into my pair of black and white Converse and throw my hair into a messy bun, not bothering to try and work with it. I'm running low on time, if I'm lucky I'll be able to make it to class just before the last bell.

I don't stop in the kitchen to grab a Power Bar, I ignore breakfast completely and grab my backpack and dash out to my car.

I grab the wheel and throw the car into reverse, backing out of the driveway at a frightening speed, almost taking off my side mirror on the basketball hoop. I slam down on the breaks in order to shift the car in drive when a glimmer catches my eye. A beautiful, elegant engagement ring adorns my left hand, and everything stops. It's as if everything in the world is pushed away from me and I'm floating in a bubble of disbelief, until reality rushes back in on me, exploding my bubble, leaving me seated in my car, shocked to the core.

"Shit," I gasp in disbelief.

I pull up to school on my bike, feeling everyone's eyes and looks of envy and awe as I navigate my way through the parking lot. I find an empty space and kick down the kickstand, easily dismounting and strolling into the building, finally on time for once.

I take my seat at the back of the class and rest my head on my desk, I'm tired as hell from last night's ordeal. All I can think about is The Masquerader.

I lift my head to check the clock, it's almost time for class to start and Celia isn't here. It worries me for some reason, she's never late.

Just before the bell rings she walks in, looking tired and disheveled.

"You were almost late," I say, shifting my gaze to meet hers.

"Back off, Beckett," she snarls.

"I'm sorry, I didn't mean to upset you. It's just not like you to arrive at a different time than you usually do, let alone be almost late. It's out of character," I say, an apologetic tone to my voice.

"You're apologizing to me, what's gotten into you?" she asks, eyeing me suspiciously.

"And this is why I don't bother with trying to be nice to you. You're always suspecting something bad, like you only see the worst in people. Maybe I didn't have an agenda, maybe I believe that everyone deserves to be treated with a little bit of respect, you know, simple human decency and all that. And maybe I was just trying to be polite," I say, snapping at the infuriating girl.

He apologized, something is obviously wrong, he's never apologized to me in his life, and now he's freaking out at me because I noticed it. *What is this kid's problem?*

"This is why you piss me off. Talk about out of character! You were acting strange, and when I noticed it and asked about it, you freaked out! Maybe I thought something was wrong, huh? Maybe *this* is why I don't bother being considerate, because when I do, people freak out! Maybe I expect the worst from people because they expect the worst from me. Did you ever think about that?" I ask, frustration rising in my voice.

"God, you're a complete pain in my ass, Celia!" he shouts. "You're a total hypocrite! When I ask you what's wrong, you close off, but I'm supposed to open up to you? You're ridiculous! I don't care if you're such an egomaniac that you actually believe that you're a princess, rules still apply to you!"

"Talk about pain in the ass, Beckett, I cannot freaking believe you!"

"Excuse me, is my lesson interrupting your couple's argument?" Mr. Lawrence asks, anger flaring in his eyes.

"We're not a couple," Beckett says defensively.

"You want the truth, Mr. Lawrence?" I ask, reaching my limit. "Yes, your half-assed lesson, put together and taught by a shitty teacher, meaning you, is in fact, interrupting my argument, and yes, I know, I'm headed to the office, you don't need to tell me."

"Damn straight, you are," Mr. Lawrence growls.

"Wait! That's not fair, you can't send her to the office for being honest, especially when you asked for it! I mean sure, she could have phrased it better, but you *did* ask for it," Beckett says, standing up and slamming his hands down onto his desk, his voice filled with injustice.

"It's fine," I say, surprised by his actions. "I'd rather be there than here. There's no need to play the hero."

"Celia–"

"My God, I said it's fine! I don't need a hero, I can take care of myself, just back off!" I shout, ignoring all the strange looks from the students around me.

"I don't care what you said, it's not fine," Beckett says defiantly. "He asked you a question and then got pissed when you gave him a straight answer that he didn't like. He doesn't have the right to punish you for that." Beckett is fuming; I can almost see smoke coming out of his ears and nostrils.

"Since you've got such a strong opinion on this matter, you can go explain it to the people in the office with Celia," he says, ending the conversation. With a menacing look, Beckett grabs his backpack and storms out of the room, almost knocking me over on his way out.

"That wasn't necessary," I say angrily, following him out of the room and down the hall. "You should've kept quiet, but because you're incapable of staying out of other people's business, we both got screwed. Real brilliant, hero."

"Would you back off?!" he shouts, shoving me into the lockers, dropping his backpack. He uses his arms to create a cage around me, as if to keep me in place, but I can't move, I'm thrown into shock by his sudden change in behavior.

I can feel his breath on my neck, it's warm and quick, he's breathing heavily and strained.

His face is so close to mine, and I'm scared, I can't predict what he's going to do, not when he's acting this way.

His eyes are angry and conflicted, burning with emotions that make no sense coming from him. Longing, loss, confusion, they don't follow his actions.

His body shakes, his hands are clenched into fists, smashed up against the lockers on either side of my head.

I swallow hard and take a deep breath. I take in a lungful of Beckett's scent and I almost pass out, I'm so lightheaded. My heart is racing, hammering against my ribs, as if it might jump out of my chest at any moment.

"Beckett, please, back away from me," I say quietly, my voice just a breathless whisper. He's so near to me, I feel like I'm suffocating, like I'm going to drown in the scent of Axe Cool Metal and a hint of leather, the scent of Beckett.

I'm shaking, I don't like to be so near to anyone. I'm so close I can feel the heat rolling off his skin, I can feel his shallow breaths, see the rapid rise and fall of his chest as he keeps my body pinned between himself and the lockers.

I can't breathe, I try to, but I can't get my body to work. I'm surprised I could even get myself to talk, when I can't even get my hands to stop shaking.

"I'm sorry, Celia," he breathes, dropping his head down as if he were ashamed. We'd be staring into each other's eyes if his weren't closed. His face is beaded with sweat, his jaw is clenched and I can see his pulse pounding in his neck. He's working hard to fight something, I wonder what that is. "I didn't mean to." He shoves himself away from the lockers, turning his back to me, resting his hands on his knees and leaning over, as if in some kind of pain.

"It's fine," I say, sucking in air, slumping against the lockers, breathing heavily. I let out a deep breath, closing my eyes and focusing on my breathing to calm myself.

I turn my back and begin walking toward a small stairwell that leads to the roof, heading in the opposite direction of the office.

"You aren't going to the office?" Beckett asks.

"No, come on," I say, waving him toward me and pulling out my key lanyard, grabbing the only key with a square head.

"Where are you going?" he asks with a gentle voice.

"To the roof, care to join me?" I respond making my way up to the narrow staircase, stopping to turn around and look back at Beckett.

"This isn't where you kill me and hide my body, is it?" he asks cautiously.

"No," I say with a small laugh.

"Well, then why not?" he sighs in a defeated manner.

We climb to the top of the dark staircase, stopping when we reach the top, coming to a door. I take my key and slide it into the hole in the doorknob, twisting it and then shoving the door open.

We step out onto the roof. The sun has barely risen past the bluffs, but it's warm and beautiful.

I sit down, drawing my knees to my chest, wrapping my arms around them. I gaze out at the scenery before me, allowing the serene picture to calm my flaming nerves.

Beckett sits down beside me, resting his arms on his knees. He doesn't say anything, he just sits there in silence, watching the sun slowly rise higher into the sky.

I look over at him and find myself smiling, although I don't know why. I like him like this. He looks at peace, with his midnight-colored hair ruffled by the wind, his blue eyes clear and crisp, it's like looking at a glacier or crystalline pools of water.

"What?" he asks, turning his head to look at me.

"I was just thinking," I say dismissively. "So, what's got you all out of whack?" My voice is filled with concern and kindness, it almost surprises me.

He sighs in resignation, his clear eyes becoming clouded. "I couldn't sleep last night, so I went for a walk. It was pretty late and someone tried mugging me. When I told him that I didn't have any money, he tried to kill me, but I was saved... by The Masquerader," he says. I'm glad he's opening up to me, for some reason I want to be someone he trusts, but that good feeling disappears at the mention of his rescuer.

"What's wrong? You don't look too good." His voice breaks through the walls of thought in my head.

"Nothing, I was just thinking about how scary that must've been," I say, the lie slipping easily from my mouth.

"Alright, now what's up with you? You were almost late today, which is really out of character for you, and you've been explosively angry this past week, what's going on?" He looks at me with warm, caring eyes, desperately hoping that I'll reach out to him. His blue eyes shine with concern for me, with a deep and caring feeling.

No one's looked at me like that in a long time, I think to myself, unaware of where that thought came from. Something about him in this moment feels familiar, and I can't figure out what it is, or why.

"You must pay a lot of attention to me," I mutter.

"It wasn't too hard to notice, you've never punched me in the face before," he responds with a small laugh.

"True," I pause. "I guess you wouldn't believe me if I told you that school has me stressed and I overslept today," I ask rhetorically. I sigh. "I've been having nightmares for the past couple weeks. They've been putting me on edge, consuming my thoughts, they're haunting me," I tell him, running my hands through my hair in a stressed manner, clenching my jaw in anger. "I got distracted last night and I didn't do my nightly routine, and then I blacked out, so when I woke up this morning I wasn't prepared at all for school." It's easier to talk to him than I thought it would be, it almost feels natural. I don't understand where this newfound trust is coming from, I've never been able to stand him, but for some reason, in this moment, I do. I'm actually enjoying this moment on the roof with him. He's not too bad.

She just opened up, I think in disbelief. Now she just sits, staring off into space, most likely thinking. She seems different from every other time I've been around her. She's not hostile and venomous, she's just quiet and calm, lost deep in thought. She almost seems relaxed, but I know she's not, I can tell by the way her fists are clenched and the way her arms are still shaking.

"I'm sorry," I say hesitantly. "About the whole locker thing." I still feel bad about it, even though she had said it was fine, I can tell that I had rattled her pretty badly. I can't forget the trapped and scared look in her hazel eyes, or the way her voice quivered when she'd spoken. I don't know what had come over me in that moment.

"Honestly, it's okay," she says, jarring me from my thoughts. "I was incredibly surprised, that's all." She pauses with a contemplative look. "And I don't like being touched, or when people break my space barrier." She adds the last part in a timid voice.

"Is there a reason you don't like being touched, or do you just not like it?" I ask curiously.

She looks at me like she's about to give me a snarky, smartass response, but then her face softens, and she exhales slowly.

"Yeah, there's a reason I don't like being touched," she says with great hesitance. "I've simply been touched in a way that I really didn't like before."

"Were you..." my voice trails off, I'm too afraid to ask her the rest of my question. I fear her answer and reaction.

"No, I wasn't raped," she says with a somewhat bitter laugh. "Not touched like that, it's more like..." she pauses with a frown, obviously thinking about how to explain it. "It's difficult to explain. Okay, you know how you think that Natalie Fitz is really gross, but you're good friends with Samantha Peterson and you think she's totally fine?"

"Yeah," I say, not seeing where she's going with this.

"Alright, so, say that Natalie comes up to you and puts her hand on your shoulder, what's your reaction?"

I shiver at the thought, feeling the sudden urge to puke and punch something at the same time. "It makes my skin crawl," I tell her.

"Now, say Samantha does the same thing, your reaction is different because you guys are friends. So, imagine how you would feel if Natalie was always touching you and there was pretty much nothing you could do about it. Eventually, simply being touched in general would make you feel sick. It's kind of like that," she explains. "A while ago, I had to associate with someone who made my skin crawl just looking at him, someone I truly hated. But he didn't reciprocate my hatred. He was quite domineering and tried to push his dominance on me, but it didn't work. At all." Her expression has become hard, frozen almost.

"Did you get a restraining order?" I ask, hoping for a good ending to the story. I'm terrified to ask any real questions, like *who was he? How old was he? Why did you have to associate with him? Where were your parents? Did they know about this?* And just about every other question one could ask. I'm afraid that if I do, she might get angry and throw me off the roof.

"Something like that," she says with a cold smile. "It's the reason I came here, to get away from him." She blinks as if snapping out of a daze.

I feel bad for her, perhaps there's more to her than I had thought. Maybe she isn't the person I believed she was, maybe there's someone underneath the layer of ice that encases her.

She gets up suddenly, as if to leave.

"Celia, wait!" I jump up and reach out to grab her hand, and then think better of it, I don't want to freak her out again. "I think I'm wrong about you. I think I have the wrong impression of you, and I think I've had that wrong impression for the last twelve years. There's a lot more to you than I thought."

She turns around with a sly smile. "You mean you don't think I'm a heartless bitch anymore?" she asks.

"About that," I say apologetically. "I shouldn't have called you heartless."

"It's alright," she says with a hearty laugh. "I *have* been kind of heartless towards you. We probably got off on the wrong page." Her face becomes straight as she thinks. "Yep, we did," she says with certainty. "Let's start over. Hi, I'm Celia Walters." She extends her right hand.

"Hey, I'm Beckett Halverson," I say, hesitantly taking her hand in mine, aware of just how much of a discomfort this must be for her.

She shakes my hand with a firm grip and confidence, she's not scared, and when her eyes meet mine, the message is clear. We're equals now.

"You know, you're not bad company," I tell her. "You're surprisingly interesting."

The corner of her lips pulls up into a lopsided grin, and I can't help but admire her. Her hazel eyes shine with her smile, for once they're not frozen and venomous. The sun glimmers on her caramel hair and bronze skin, I wouldn't be surprised if it turned out that she actually is a princess.

"You're still a pain in the ass," she says with a grin. "But you're not too bad of company yourself."

"If we're going to talk about pains in the ass, you are a royal pain in the ass, Princess."

She laughs at me and then scoops up a small rock from the rooftop and throws it at me, nailing me right between my eyes.

"Ow!"

"Come on," she says, ignoring my cry of pain. "The next class will start soon." She heads to the door and pulls it open, pausing for a second. "You know, you'd probably be less of a pain in the ass if I just left you up here." Her eyes shine with friendly humor and I can't help but laugh.

"Yeah, I guess I would be."

He's not that bad, I think to myself. *He's surprisingly nice and kind of funny.*

"Celia."

"Hm?" I snap my head up. Monsieur Pierre looks at me with worried eyes.

"Are you okay?" he asks.

"Oh, yeah, I was just thinking," I say. It's my go-to excuse for spacing out, it's always true and so most people just nod and leave me alone after that.

Monsieur Pierre smiles at me and leans in closer so only I can hear him. "If you ever need to talk about those thoughts, know you can come to me, I'm always here for you." His voice is soft and kind, it makes me feel warm and cozy on the inside. It's nice to see that he cares, not just about me, but everyone. I know a lot of kids think that their teachers are demons who wish only to inflict pain and suffering upon them, but that isn't the case with Monsieur Pierre. He genuinely cares about all of his students, that's why the kids at Goodman High love him. He's funny and kind, but he does his job and manages to keep the kids under control, maintaining their respect and still creating that bond of friendship with each individual person.

"Merci, Monsieur," I say, smiling back at him.

"Pas de problem, Celia." He walks back to the front of the classroom and continues with his lesson like nothing had happened, leaving me to become absorbed in my thoughts once again.

When I get home from my run, Amy is on the couch, holding an icepack against her leg.

"What'd you do this time?" I ask, flopping down on the futon beside the couch.

"I tripped," she said with a reluctant sigh.

"Ha! I told you to tie your shoelaces," I say, chastising her.

"I did, and it had nothing to with my shoelaces, Celia! I haven't done that in years, you can't keep bringing that up every time I get hurt," she scowls.

"Yeah, I can," I laugh. "You are never going to live that one down, Amy." When we were younger, Amy and I used to play basketball together in the driveway all the time, well, it was more like my parents made me. One day when we were playing, her shoelaces came untied and I told her she should tie them before she tripped and got hurt. Naturally, she refused to listen and ended up stepping on them and tumbling onto the pavement where she landed on her arm and insisted it was broken. At worst, it was scraped and bruised, and despite how many times I told her that, she refused to believe me, and for the following three weeks she wore my old splint from when I sprained my wrist in a bicycle accident. I still tease her about it all it the time.

"You sure it's not broken?" I ask with false concern.

"Shut up, Celia!" She throws her icepack at me and I easily dodge it, throwing isn't really her forte.

"Alright, alright, I'm done," I say, giving her back her icepack. "Now, what actually happened?"

She turns her eyes from mine before she speaks. "I tripped when I was walking through the doorway and smacked my knee on the open dishwasher." I can barely see her face but I don't need to, I know she's bright red with embarrassment.

I burst into laughter, unable to contain it.

"Hey! It's not funny! I really bruised my knee," Amy protests, undignified by my laughter.

"It's hilarious," I say, continuing to laugh until my stomach hurts.

"You're a terrible sister," she says flatly, giving me a blank look.

"I'm about to get worse," I tell her, picking up the TV remote.

"No! Celia, no! Please don't make me watch the news," she begs, her brown eyes pleading with mine.

"Sorry, Sis, but we have to watch it. It's important that we know what's going on in our town and around the country," I say, switching on the TV.

"It seems that our mystery murderer, The Masquerader, has struck once again as a fifth body has shown up. Authorities believe we have a serial killer on the loose and are requesting help from outside sources such as the FBI and Behavioral Analysis Units," the reporter says. I immediately turn off the television, almost dropping the remote in my rush to do so.

"Hey! Why'd you turn that off? That was unexpectedly interesting!" Amy shouts in protest.

"I feel sick," I respond, tossing her the remote. "Watch what you want, I'm going to my room to lay down." I leave the living room and stumble up the stairs, suddenly feeling lightheaded and weak.

I fall through the threshold of my room, catching myself on the dresser. I can't navigate, the room is spinning. The shadows grow and stretch across the room and then retreat before they reach my feet, reminding me of waves, rising and receding with the tide.

I use the walls to keep myself upright as I make my way to the bathroom. I turn the sink on to full stream, cold water gushing out of the spout. I lean over the vanity in order to keep my balance and fill my hands with the cold water, splashing it onto my face, hoping the cold shock will snap me out of this feeling that has washed over me.

Images flash through my mind with a searing pain and I clutch my head, trying to make the pain subside, but it keeps coming, along with the images. The flick of a silver whip dancing in the black night, scared eyes, pleading voices and blood, lots of blood.

I bring my shaking hands down and grip the sides of the sink, keeping my body steady.

My breathing is ragged and labored, my heart is racing, and I feel like my head will split open at any second and paint the walls red.

I look up at the mirror and meet my reflection which stares down at me with a cool, calm expression.

"Oh my God, I'm going crazy," I whisper, my mind spinning frantically.

"No, you're not going crazy, you're merely remembering a long-forgotten past and the memories you try so hard to suppress," my reflection says calmly.

"What the hell? Who are you?" I ask in a strangled voice.

"I'm you, well, you're me. A reflection of me cast through the universe," the girl in the mirror responds.

"This is insane. I've got to be hallucinating," I mutter, desperate to find a logical explanation for all of this. "None of this is real."

"But it is. All of it is," my reflection says. "You've already regained some of your memories, you've had them since you were just a child. You don't like being touched because of what you remember from the beginning. You can't escape the cold that lingers inside of you, the disgust that was burned into your nerves."

"How do you know about that?" I ask, frozen with shock.

"You mean how do I know about Mesmer? Because I was there, it was me. I am the dormant part of your mind, sleeping, slowly waking and becoming conscious. Stop denying me, and let me rise, allow me to wake up. You're only half alive without me, half complete, half sane," she says, adding the last bit with a cold smile. "You can't be whole without me. You can't win this war unless you stop denying me. You won't be you until the two of us are one. You won't even be sane until you embrace me."

"Shut up!" I growl, gripping the sink even tighter than before, my knuckles now matching the white marble surface. "You aren't real. If you're real, then I'm a murderer. If you're real, then I have no idea who I am. Everything about my life would be part of a twisted game, and I can't accept that," I say defiantly.

"Celia, take my hand." I look up to find my reflection pressing her hand to the mirror, as if we were friends trying to hold hands through a window. She holds her hand against the mirror with a sad look, pain burning in her eyes. I realize that she needs me as much as I need her. "If you take my hand, I can help you. Help you remember who are, what your mission is. I can help you remember your curse and your cause, your vengeance. If you take my hand, you *won't* be a murderer, you'll remember why you fight. I can give you peace, I can give you your sanity. All you have to do is take my hand."

I sigh in resignation. "I'll remember everything?"

"Yes," she says. "But in order to remember, you must forget."

"What the hell do you mean? 'I must forget?' I barely remember anything as it is, and that's only because I'm not stupid and was able to piece things together, so no chance in hell," I say, astounded by what I've been asked to do.

"Do you trust me?"

"Not in the slightest."

"Do you trust yourself?"

I look into her eyes and I know I don't have any other choice. If I want to remember, I have to trust her, I have to trust myself.

"To the end of the universe," I respond slowly.

"Then take my hand," she commands. "You won't remember this conversation, or that you are the masked vigilante, until those memories are triggered, but you *will* remember who you are, who you were before the war."

"I'll get answers?" I ask hesitantly. I mull over everything I've been told and I feel reluctant, but I have to do this, I can't keep living this way.

"All the answers," she responds. "All you have to do is take my hand."

I take a deep breath and raise my shaking hand to the mirror, bringing my finger tips to those of my reflection. I don't feel the smooth texture of a mirror, I feel flesh and the warmth of skin. *Oh my God, she's real,* I think in disbelief.

"This is going to hurt a bit," she says quietly. "Close your eyes, Celia." I do as she says and my eyelids light up as the room is consumed in a bright flash and searing heat, and then I collapse, clutching my head.

I'm on my knees, my ears ring and my head is in agony. Blood drips onto the floor from my nose, ears, eyes, and mouth, trailing down my face like crimson tears. *I'm going to die,* I think with cold detachment. It feels like my head is being ripped to shreds, thread by thread, fiber by fiber and my brain is being pulled apart, nerve by nerve, and then it suddenly stops and I'm surrounded by blackness and silence.

I wake up, as if from a deep sleep, lying on the cold bathroom floor, my body throbbing with a dull ache.

"What am I doing here?" I ask myself, my voice scratchy in my sore throat.

I push myself into a sitting position and almost pass out. The pain pulsing through my head causes me to see spots and halts my motion. Slowly, I manage to stand up on wobbling legs, using the sink to help me stay up and keep my balance.

The water is running. It's ice cold and fills the sink bowl and pours over the edge, splashing onto the cold tile surface below, soaking my legs and feet. I go to turn the water off, but then freeze, horrified by my reflection. My face is covered with blood, some dried, some not. It's all I can taste, coppery and metallic. My hair is disheveled, my clothes are wet and I look like plain hell.

I cup my hands and fill them with water, scrubbing my face, trying to get the blood off so I can find the source and take care of it properly, but there's nothing. There's no cut, gash or wound, no place from which the blood could come.

"Celia, are you okay?" I hear my mom ask from the other side of the door.

"Yeah, I'm fine," I say in a daze. I quickly straighten up my appearance and step out, flashing a smile at my mom.

"Are you sure?" she asks, worriedly. "You look... exhausted. And why is there water all over the place?"

"I don't know. I think I was washing my hands or something, but then I got lost in thought and didn't notice when the water started overflowing. And yeah, I'm alright, but I *am* exhausted," I say with a yawn. "I think I should go to bed, my homework is finished so I should be good. I'll clean up in here and then crash."

"Celia, it's six," she says in a worried voice. "You'll be up at four if you go to bed now."

"I'll be fine," I say, placing my hand reassuringly on her shoulder.

"But you haven't even had dinner yet, you literally just got home, you probably haven't had anything to eat since noon."

"I stopped and got subs with Ben while studying," I tell her, glad that I didn't have to lie to her about that part. I really don't like to lie to my family, I feel somewhat sick when I do, but I have no problem concealing or stretching the truth.

"Alright then," my mom sighs in resignation. "There's really no changing your mind once it's been made up is there?"

"Hmh, not really," I say with a weak laugh. "Goodnight, Mom." I give her a hug and walk into my room and choose my outfit for the next day before crawling into bed.

"I think you were right," I say. "About Celia, I mean. She isn't that bad." Ben and I sit on the couch with game controllers in our hands, our eyes glued to the screen, even as we talk.

"Told you so," he says, shooting down digital aliens. "What made you change your mind?"

"I got to talk to her, like *actually* talk to her, without her being ultra-guarded," I say, trying to sound casual. The truth is, I still feel super awkward about the whole situation and everything that had happened, from the fight in math class, to slamming her into the lockers, to our conversation on the roof.

"Yeah, that can be hard to do, she's been through a lot." His eyes take on that sad, forlorn look once again as he speaks.

"I'm starting to understand that," I say quietly. I've realized that there is a *lot* more to her than I had previously believed. "She's got a dark past, doesn't she?" I ask the question with great hesitance and caution.

"You could say that," Ben says, pausing the game. "Do you have any chips?" he asks, changing the subject for both our sakes.

"Yeah, they're in the cabinet where they always are," I say. "You should know where they are, you're the only one who eats them." No one in my family eats chips, mainly because Ben devours them before any of us gets a chance to.

"I know where they are," he says indignantly. "But I didn't know if you had re-stocked since I was over last."

"Don't we always?" I ask. "And what is it with you and chips? You eat them like they're a life source."

"The Meyers don't buy them," he says with a shrug, chomping into a golden potato chip. "They have this thing about eating healthy and blah, blah, blah."

"That sounds miserable," I say. I get up and walk to fridge and grab a soda. "Ben, you want a Doctor Pepper?"

"Yeah, just give me a minute, I'm getting a call," he says, pulling his phone out of his pocket. "Hello, this is Ben Milton." His tone is suspicious and filled with caution. "Oh, hey!" His voice suddenly becomes light and a small smile plays on his lip. "How are you?... That's good, I'm not too bad myself... Well, I'm at a friend's house right now, but I can meet up with you around eight. Will that work?... Sweet, see you then." He hangs up his phone and grabs a soda from my hands.

"Who was that?" I ask in confusion, he doesn't normally get calls, and when he does, he usually doesn't pick them up.

"Oh, it was a friend of mine. I haven't seen her in a while, so I was a little cautious when I got her call," he explains after draining his soda. "Alright, let's play now, we have aliens to defeat and a world to save!" His eyes shine with a triumphant light as he valiantly marches to the couch and resumes his alien slaying.

The night comes quickly, and Ben leaves with the fading day, running off to his next adventure around eight, much to my little sister's dismay.

"Why did Ben have to leave so soon?" Lily asks.

"He was here for four hours," I say.

"He still had to leave too soon," she complains.

"I'm pretty sure he had to go meet up with his girlfriend," I tell her teasingly.

"Ben doesn't have a girlfriend!" she insists with desperation in her voice.

"It's true that he hasn't said he has a girlfriend, but he hasn't said that he doesn't either," I say, enjoying the rise I get out of my little sister.

"Stop it, Beckett! You're so mean!" She pounds her little fists into my thigh in her anger.

"Okay, okay, he doesn't have a girlfriend," I assure her. "But I think he's in love with Celia Walters." My voice has become quiet and serious, it bothers me and I don't know why.

"Who's Celia?" Lily asks in shock with wide eyes.

"Huh? Oh, she's a friend of ours," I say casually.

"Well, I don't like her," my sister says with an angry frown, crossing her arms across her chest.

"You're adorable," I tell her, ruffling her hair in an affectionate manner.

"Cut it out, Beckett," she says, shoving my hand off her head.

"What are you doing still awake?" I ask, turning my curious gaze to my little sister. "You were supposed to be in bed like fifteen minutes ago."

"I wanted to say goodbye to Ben," she says bashfully, turning her eyes to the floor.

"You should get to bed before Dad finds out that you're still up," I tell her.

"Lily! Get back in bed!" my father scolds, coming up the stairs as if on cue, to find my little sister.

"Ooh, you are busted," I say.

"Sorry, Daddy!" she squeaks. She smacks me in the stomach with the back of her hand before running back to her room, her small bare feet slapping against the hardwood floor.

I smile as I watch her run, grimacing slightly at the pain in my stomach, and then turn to go to my room when I'm stopped by my dad.

"Everything okay, Beck?" he asks, placing a gentle hand on my shoulder.

"Yeah, I've had a long day, that's all," I tell him, unsure as to why he asked how I was doing.

"You just look a little worn out," he tells me, clapping me on the back.

"Oh," is all I say, not knowing how else to bring this awkward conversation to an end.

I retreat to my room and fall into my swivel chair with a heavy sigh. Suddenly, I get an idea, and flip open the laptop on my desk, typing furiously. *Masquerader.* I press the search button, and pictures of people in elegant masks pop onto the screen, causing me to sigh in aggravation.

"No, not people dancing," I groan, burying my head in my hands. *The Masquerader, Rockford.* I hit the search button and wait, clicking on the first thing that pops up.

As each night goes by, the body count increases. Authorities still don't have any suspects as to who this murderous masquerader is. No one has established a pattern to her kills or her victimology, all that is known for certain is that she attacks at night, so we insist that you stay in your houses after dark. The Masquerader is dangerous and unpredictable, a crazy killer on the loose. I stop reading, none of this is right.

She's not a crazy killer, she saved my life, I think indignantly. *I wish I knew her identity.*

Something about her enraptures me and draws me into her web of mystery, and I am unable to escape it.

I have to know who she is.

In my head, I see her with electricity crackling around her body, her silver whip in hand, guarding me from the thug.

"She's not a criminal," I say quietly. "She's a hero."

The heavy drone of my alarm clock pulls me out of a black sleep, warning me of the coming day.

With a groan I roll over and silence the clock, stretching out my sore body. I feel like I was bulldozed and then trampled by elephants, and to top it off, my head is pounding and my skin is burning.

I stumble out of my room in a daze of pain, my body aching with every movement.

"Jeez, Celia, you look like the physical manifestation of death," Amy exclaims as I make my way downstairs, focusing very hard on not tripping and biting it all the way down to the main floor.

"Shut up, Amy," I growl, irritated by her comment.

"No, she's right, Celia," my dad says. "You don't look good at all. How are you feeling?"

"Peachy," I respond, my voice flat and void of everything.

"Come here, let me see if you've got a fever." He doesn't wait for me to say anything and marches up to me, placing a hand on my forehead. I don't recoil at his touch the way I do with others, I just stand there and roll my eyes at him.

"Dad, I'm fine, honestly," I tell him, swatting his hand away from my head.

"Celia, you've got a fever, sweetheart," he tells me with a worried look. "I think you should stay home today."

"No, Dad! I can go to school! I have a perfect attendance record, I can't screw that up because I *might* be sick," I protest, staring him down with defiant eyes.

"Yeah, you've got to stay home today," he says. "I'll call the school and drive Amy, you go back to bed, Celia. The best thing for you to do is get some rest."

I give a defeated sigh and turn around, slowly making my way to my room.

I shut the door and collapse onto my bed. I don't like that I'm missing school, especially since my attendance record is spotless, but has now been tainted.

I close my eyes and groan, rolling over in my bed, and when I open them, I'm in a new world.

I'm lying in the grass of an open field. The wind is gently blowing, it's a nice reprieve from the warm sun.

I wear a beautiful, deep blue gown that flows in the gentle breeze. It feels soft and almost silky, and very pleasant on my skin.

Where am I? I wonder, looking around in confusion, sitting up to get a better look at where I am.

Shh, don't say a word, just observe. You are a guest in this body, this is only a memory, the remnants of a time long since passed.

I whip my head around to see who had said that, but no one is there. The voice had spoken in my head, but it seemed to have come from all around me.

"What's wrong, Celia?" someone asks. I look down by my side to see another person. She too, wears a beautiful gown, but hers is an intense green.

"It's nothing, I was merely thinking," I say absently.

"That's what you say whenever you don't want people to bother you with questions," she says with a knowing look.

"So?" I say, trying to sound casual. "It's because I *am* thinking, I can't be bothered by external distractions."

"I bet you're thinking about The Celestial Warrior," she teases, her grin wide and full of glee.

"Shut up, Jade, you know I can't stand him. Father believes that there is some sort of hidden attraction between the two us," I say with an irritated voice. "He's ridiculous."

"You know, I was told as a child, that when you hate someone for no reason, it's because you are secretly in love with them," she tells me, her smile growing larger.

"If that were the case, I would be 'secretly in love' with our obnoxious Mesmer Amar, Prince of Saturn," I say with a dark tone.

"Well, you have a reason for hating him, but you *don't* have a reason for hating B–"

"Don't say his name," I tell her. "It makes me want to hit something."

Jade laughs and rolls her eyes, sitting up next to me. "You know, for a princess, you're kind of violent," she says.

"I don't think one's title should stop them from behaving like a normal person. Just because I was born into royalty doesn't make me better than anyone else. Princess or not, I'm still just a person."

"And this is why you are going to be the best Queen Mercury has ever seen," she says with pride.

"Ugh, don't remind me," I groan, falling back down onto the grass.

"People dream of ruling. They spend their whole lives trying to get even just a little bit of what you are going to have," she tells me, her voice heavy and serious.

"Well, I dream of travelling and seeing everything that the universe has to offer. I dream of watching Peter flourish as a composer and seeing his music go into the history books. I dream of falling in love and getting married, not getting pawned off to some man I can't stand because of 'royal obligations.' I dream of having a family and being happy, not ruling, someone else can rule," I say bitterly, my face contorting, becoming a bitter scowl.

"But you are the most qualified to rule. Celia, you are sharper than a knife, you are kind, compassionate, and most of all, you are humble and you understand normal people," she speaks with adoration, her eyes sparkling.

"Don't lecture me about why I should rule," I say. "You don't want to rule either."

"Yes, but my reasons for not wanting to rule, and your reasons, are very different. I don't want to rule because I am not qualified to, my brother is far more suited for the throne than I am. He is very much like you, to be honest," Jade says with a downcast face.

"I think you would be a remarkable ruler. You have wonderful instincts and you are very charismatic, it is easy for people to connect with you. You also have a wonderful and helpful husband, and if I am not mistaken, a child on the way." I look at her with a knowing grin, watching her face lose its color, paling in the yellow sunlight.

"H-how did you know? I only found out two days ago!" she exclaims, her eyes wide and wild.

"Do you even have to ask? I just know things," I say. "What do you plan for names?"

"Well, considering that we just found out a few days ago, we haven't thought of many names. I guess if I had to give a name now, I think Elizabeth would be the one I would choose for a girl."

"Don't name her Elizabeth," I say, chastising my best friend. "Elizabeth is such a common name, give her a name that is pretty and unique."

"Well, what would you suggest, oh Wise One?" she asks with a half mocking tone.

"Me? I would name her Corrine. It is an elegant name that is not too common. If I ever have a daughter, that's probably what I will name her. I've liked that name ever since I was a little girl," I say with a dreamy smile.

"What if you have a boy?" Jade asks.

"Well, then my husband can name him," I say simply, shrugging my shoulders. "But hopefully I will have both, a son and a daughter." I close my eyes and bask in the warm sunlight and when I open them, I'm back in my bed, but not for long. The scenery around me changes again and I'm in an ornately decorated hall, my father and mother standing before me with scolding looks. They're dressed nicely, my mother in an elegant purple dress made of velvet, my father dressed in a dashing black suit.

"Will you please behave yourself tonight?" my father asks. "You know this ball is very important for all of us, at least pretend that you do not hate the fact that you have to be here. You normally love balls and soirées, please do not hate them now that we have chosen you as Mercury's next leader. You need to earn the respect of the other rulers now, so you do not have to struggle to do so as Queen, it will be easier if you are your normal, happy self, not brooding and angry. Please, Celia, please behave," he begs.

"Yes, Father," I sigh, defeat residing in my voice. "I will do this for your sake, but know that this fight is not over. I do not want to become a queen, and I will fight to see that I do not." I turn to leave, when a warm hand on my shoulder stops me.

"Celia, dear, please, we are guests here."

"Meaning, do not throw someone through a door?" I ask with a devilish grin.

"Yes, let's not do that again," he says warily.

I nod, and then leave, exiting into the ballroom, finding myself in a sea of people dressed in regal clothes and masquerade masks, dancing and twirling in time with the sophisticated music, music composed by my little brother.

"Well, don't you look ravishing tonight?" A cold voice stops me in my tracks. "The things I would do to you."

"Watch what you say, Mesmer Amar," I growl. "I may have been told to behave, and that I cannot throw you through a door again, but that does not mean I won't find another way to beat you like a dog." I turn with a cool expression to face the angelic-looking prince with the soul of a demon.

"Your threats delight me." He grins at me with a lecherous smile. "Shall we dance?" He holds out his hand and I recoil, taking several steps back.

"I would much rather saw my hands off," I spit, spinning on my heel to leave.

"It wasn't really a suggestion, or a question," he snarls, grabbing me by the wrists and pulling me against his body. "It was more of a command."

"Well, that wasn't too polite." A new voice enters the conversation. "Please unhand my guest, for she owes me a dance." His voice is polite with an undertone of authority and menace, but Mesmer just smiles in contempt.

"You can have your dance when we are done," he says, arrogance filling his voice.

I hear the scrape of metal and then the smirk disappears, replaced by a bitter scowl.

"It wasn't really a suggestion or a question," the man growls, and the glint of his sword catches my eye. "It was more of a command, now let her go."

The restrictive grip around me loosens and I shove Saturn's Prince away, letting out a breath of relief.

"I didn't need your help," I scowl, turning to the man who rescued me. My eyes fall upon him and I stop, taking in a shocked breath. *He looks amazing,* I think with astonishment, immediately scolding myself for thinking such a ridiculous thing, but it's true, he does look amazing. He wears a black tuxedo and a bowtie, it isn't unlike what many of the other men are wearing, but he's somehow more elegant, prince-like and downright handsome than the rest of the men here. His wavy, midnight colored hair is pushed over to the side and out of his face instead of slicked back like most of the men's. On his face he wears a simple, black mask that brings out the shocking blue of his eyes, eyes that hold my gaze and take me hostage.

"Are you okay?" he asks gently, walking to me, tenderly examining my wrist where I had been grabbed.

"I'm fine," I say, pulling my arm away. "I can handle myself, you didn't need to get involved in my affairs." I step away from the man, irritation scratching at my skin.

"I know, but I do believe that you were told to behave." His eyes pierce mine, they see straight through me.

"You heard my argument with my parents, didn't you?" Panic freezes me in place.

"Let's dance, we look strange just standing in the midst of the partygoers." He takes my hand and spins me into his arms, our bodies swaying with the music.

"You didn't answer my question," I tell him, trying to sound stern.

"Yes," he sighed. "I heard your argument with your parents. I was surprised, to be honest, that you're so against being Queen. The job suits you, you would be very good at it."

I simply scowl, the prince of Jupiter has that effect on me.

"Why do you reject the crown?" he asks, dipping me back in time with the music.

"Because I hate politics," I say, clenching my jaw, angered at the mere topic of politics. "Politicians are liars, they are dishonest to the core of who they are."

"But your father isn't, he's a good man," the prince says.

"Yes, and he is the laughingstock of the universe for that," I tell him, my voice bitter and poisonous.

"I think your father is remarkable," he says quietly. "When I was a child, I would parade around the courtyards, pretending to be King Jasper of Mercury. My whole life I have wanted to be like him. I want to be honorable and kind, honest and yet cunning." His cheeks are red and I can't help but laugh at him, it's not often that you see The Celestial Warrior look so bashful. He begins to laugh with me, the red slowly leaving his cheeks, his face returning to its normal color.

We dance along the outside of the room, past the tall windows in which I catch our reflection and become stunned. The image is enchanting. Him in his suit and plain, but elegant mask, and me in my regal dress of black lace and my dark purple mask that slowly fades to a washed-out lavender with black swirls around the eyes.

"I know, we look like something out of a fairytale," he says, his voice capturing my attention.

"Can you read minds?" I ask in a surprised tone. I know that the Royal Families have abilities that others don't, but I'm almost certain his ability is not mind reading, and I am shocked by his ability to speak mine so accurately.

"No," he says with a gentle laugh. "I'm just good at reading people. Although, that would be useful in times like this, so I could know what you are thinking. You are very challenging to read, Celia," he tells me.

"Then how did you know what I was thinking?" I inquire.

"Because I was thinking the same thing." He says it so simply, as if he isn't worried about it, but for me it's the opposite. It makes me want to step away from him, but I can't leave his arms; when I do, I feel lost and empty. I want to put distance between the two of us, not because I'm disgusted, but because I'm afraid, afraid of what I feel, and simply to breathe, for I can't when I'm so close to him.

"You look wonderful tonight," he murmurs, stepping closer, his hand gently caressing my face. "You are stunningly beautiful. Celia, I–"

I knock his hand away from my face and back away from him.

"Celia, what's wrong?" he asks, sounding worried and confused.

"You're just like all the others," I breathe, shock filling my being. "You're after my position. You've never been kind to me, never uttered sweet words to me, not until now, now that you know for certain that I will be Mercury's Queen. You wish to sway and woo me now that my position is no longer uncertain. You're all disgusting," I spit. "You all wish to be King."

"What?" He looks genuinely shocked. "Is that what you honestly believe?"

"It's what I know!" I shout. I walk away, but he follows me, determined to show me a different view of the situation.

"If my objective was to capture your position as future Queen of Mercury, there would be many easier ways of doing so than getting you to like me. Your father loves me, I would have no problem obtaining his consent, I could just talk to him and have him arrange the marriage."

"And I suppose that this is the part where you tell me to make it easier for the both of us and not bring it to that," I growl, clenching my fists.

"No! I would never force anyone into a marriage! I want the person I marry to love me, and I want to love her as well, a forced marriage would give me none of that. Also, why would I want your position? I am the single heir to Jupiter's throne, by default I already have a crown, why would I want yours?"

"Because that's what power hungry people want, more power!" I yell, angered by his ignorance.

"I am *not* Mesmer Amar!" he growls, his voice low and menacing. "Stop treating me as such."

"When are you going to realize that all people who want power are the same to me? They are all disgusting, and after my crown," I tell him, irritation rising in my voice.

"I hate to break this to you, Princess, but the universe doesn't revolve around you!" he shouts.

"Of course, it does. Who else would it revolve around?" I ask.

"You are unbelievable," he whispers, pain swimming in his eyes. "You know what? Maybe you deserve Mesmer." It's evident on his face that he regrets what he said, but I'm dumfounded. I stare at him in astonishment, frozen by his callous words.

"What did you just say?" I ask, still in disbelief.

"Celia, I–"

"No," I cut him off, my voice quiet, calm, and full of hostility and menace. "There are some lines that you just do not cross, it is a shame that you are too stupid to see where those lines lay." I spin, ridden with fury, and storm down the hall to the balcony, feeling the cool breeze blowing against my face.

What is it about him that makes me behave like this? I ask myself, sighing into the cold night.

"She's not here," Ben says.

I'm surprised by the disappointment I feel, normally I would be relieved, but today, that's not the case.

"Well I gathered that," I say irritably. "Why though? She never misses school, it makes me worried."

"Me too, that's why I talked to Amy, her sister."

"And?"

"And she said that Celia was feeling sick when she woke up, so her dad made her stay home," he says.

"She's probably going out of her mind," I mutter. In my head I can see Celia pacing her house in agitation, grumbling in complaint to herself.

"I'd love to get that on video, her reaction when her father told her that she had to stay home. God, that would've been priceless," Ben says, laughing with pure glee at the thought.

"You know, you're kind of evil, Ben," I tell him, giving him a cautious look.

"I know," he says, a devilish grin making its way to his lips.

"Anyway, do you know what classes she has? I should get her homework for her," I say, desperate to change the subject. "She did it for me when I skipped for a mental break."

"What classes do you guys have together?" he asks.

"All of our core classes," I respond, writing the names of the classes down on an empty page.

"Okay, she's got AP French, AP Psych and then I think she's taking Music Theory 4. You can check in the office, I think if you told them it was for her homework, they'd tell you her schedule," he says in a nonchalant tone, shrugging his shoulders.

"I've seen enough of the office for a while," I say warily, packing up my bag, anticipating the final bell.

The day ends with the shrill tone of the bell ringing through the halls, telling us that we can finally go home. I make my way to the classes written down on the page, stuffing all the extra work in my backpack. By the time I've finished collecting Celia's homework, my backpack is considerably heavier than it was before. I wonder how heavy Celia's bag must be with this insane amount of homework on top of her textbooks as I walk to my motorcycle. I sigh when I see that my bike is surrounded by a group of people I know too well.

"What'd you want, Craig?" I ask, trying not to sound bored and tired of him.

"I've got a bone to pick with you, Halverson," he says menacingly, but he doesn't scare me, not after being beaten by Celia in the library. After that, I doubt anyone at this school could scare me.

"And you need five other people to do that? Or do they all have a bone to pick with me too?" I ask. "If that's the case, you can get in line and wait, because I've got better things to do." My voice is filled with irritation as I grip my backpack's straps, fighting the urge to run him over with my bike.

I brush past Craig, my shoulder hitting his, forcing him to stumble back. I set my backpack on the ground, knowing what's going to happen next.

"We're not done here, Beckett!" he yells, grabbing me by the shoulder. He spins me around and lands a punch on my jaw, but it doesn't faze me, I already knew it was coming.

"I don't like you hanging out with Celia and pulling her out of my fights. I would have dominated her," he spits, throwing another punch, but I catch this one in my hand and squeeze, using the anger caused by his words as strength to crush his fist in my hand.

"I didn't pull her out of that fight to protect *her*, I did it to protect *you*. She would've kicked your ass into next week you sick, perverted piece of shit," I snarl. I bring my knee up and into his gut, knocking the air out of his lungs. "Now, if you have a problem with me, I suggest that you stuff it up your ass and deal with it, because it's *your* problem, *not* mine." I grab him by the collar of his shirt and bring my fist down hard on his face, feeling the bones in his nose crunching under the force of the punch.

My hand is throbbing, but I ignore the pain and sling my backpack over my shoulder, hopping onto my bike and revving the engine. I zip past Craig, narrowly missing him, and peel out of the parking lot.

I speed down the highway, wind whipping at my clothes, chilling me in a nice way. I feel hot from the fight, I still feel like my blood is on fire.

I exit the highway and turn into the residential/suburb area of the city, not entirely sure of where I'm going. I don't know exactly where Celia lives, but I know it's somewhere by Ben's house.

I drive through the neighborhood, hopelessly searching for a house that looks even remotely familiar when I see a figure I easily recognize working out in the yard.

"Aren't you supposed to be sick?" I ask, bringing the motorcycle to a stop and hopping off.

"Yeah, according to my dad," Celia says with irritation. "I told him I was fine, but I was still forced to stay home, even when I started feeling better. When my dad dropped by to check on me around noon I told him that I was back to normal, but he still wouldn't let me go to school. I told him if he wasn't going to let me go back to school, I was going to do as much work around the house as I could. He protested of course, and I told him he'd have to tie me to a chair to stop me. After he tried and failed, he gave up and let me get to work." She wears a proud smile as she recounts the events of her day, and I can't help but laugh.

"Your dad actually tried to tie you to a chair?" I ask, almost in disbelief.

"Yep," she says casually. "It's not the weirdest thing that my family's done. One time my little sister was being obnoxious and she wouldn't shut up, so I duct taped her mouth shut and locked her in a closet."

"What did your parents do?" I ask, intrigued by her story.

"They laughed and told me to make sure she didn't suffocate. After a little while they made me let her out though. I think they thought I would let her out soon after they got home, but I had ultimately planned to leave her there indefinitely."

"Your parents sound pretty chill," I say, amazed by their reaction.

"They are," she says with a smile, grabbing a shovel and sending it through the ground. She continues the action for a few more minutes, digging in silence.

The air is filled with a thick, awkward presence and I can't help but speak, desperate to break the silence.

"Are you planting flowers?" I ask, immediately chastising myself for asking such a stupid question. I mean, why else would she be digging a hole?

I look around and notice for the first time that her yard is absolutely beautiful. Flowers of varying colors, predominantly roses, bloom all around the house. The grass is thick and lusciously green, and there's a small fountain in the middle of it all. Her yard looks like a picture from a fairytale cottage.

"Nope," she responds, with sarcasm dripping from her voice. "I'm digging a hole to hide a body."

"Well, I hope that hole's not for mine, because I come bearing gifts," I tell her, sliding my backpack off my shoulders.

"Gifts?" she asks, her face shocked and cautious.

"Here is your homework," I say, handing her a stack of papers.

"Beckett Halverson, I could kiss you! You are a life saver!" she squeals, eagerly taking the papers from my hands. "I thought it would be double trouble tomorrow, but now it won't be!"

"Uh, yeah, no problem," I say. I feel uncomfortable, she's never actually thanked me for anything, or said she could kiss me, and I'm not entirely sure what to do.

"We started a new unit in AP Gov and Mr. Bronson gave out a study guide for chapter eight, due tomorrow," I say.

"Ugh, I hate the study guides, I'd rather just read the damn chapter and take notes on what I need to," she groans, angrily kicking a clump of dirt.

"Wouldn't we all?" I say with a bitter laugh. "I doubt that anyone enjoys taking a page of notes for every paragraph in the chapter."

She laughs at that comment, a genuine laugh. Her eyes sparkle and her face is consumed by her smile, she's pretty when she's laughing. It's enchanting.

"Well, I should probably go home and stumble through my French homework," I say, nervously clenching my backpack strap.

"Having troubles in French?" she asks, furrowing her eyebrows with concern.

"Sort of," I say slowly. "I'm having a hard time getting everything to make sense."

"Well, I can help you with that," she says. "I'm in AP French and Culture. I'm also fluent."

"Are you sure?" I ask cautiously. "I don't want to bother you."

"It won't be a bother," she says. "Come on inside." She puts the shovel in the garage and opens the door to the house, waving me in.

The minute I walk through the door, three sets of curious eyes land on me, watching me like I'm some strange specimen.

"Who's this?" a younger girl asks. I think she's Celia's sister, Amy, she's maybe a year or two younger than me. She looks me over once, and then twice, needing a double take. When she's done analyzing me, she looks at Celia with surprise in her wide eyes.

"Everyone, this is a friend of mine, his name is Beckett, Beckett Halverson."

"Hey, isn't he that guy you–" Amy is cut off by a scolding look from her sister and she is silent.

"Beckett, this is my little sister, Amy, the one I locked in the closet. That's my mom, Tammy, and my dad, Jared," Celia says, introducing me to her family. "Mom, Dad, we're going to study, if you need me I'll be in my room."

"Door open," her dad says with caution.

"I know," she tells him, waltzing up to her room. "Come on, Beck."

I follow her as commanded, jogging up the stairs to catch up to her. *She's never called me 'Beck' before,* I think absently, taking the stairs two at a time.

When I get to her room, I come to a halt, waiting nervously just outside the door.

"You can come in," she says, giving me an odd look.

"Yeah, sorry," I stumble over my words as I stumble through the threshold and into her room. It's not small, or unreasonably large, it's just big enough to tuck a piano in the corner along with a desk and still appear to be the size of any normal teenager's room. Various books and sheets of music are sprawled across the piano top, and on the floor around it, but aside from that, her room is pristine. Everything is clean, neat, and organized, just like Celia.

"Sorry about the mess," she says apologetically.

"You're kidding right? You can hardly call this a mess," I tell her with a laugh, nervously playing with my keys. It's strange being in Celia's room, I don't know what to do or how to behave, so I just continue to occupy myself with my keys and the compass my dad gave me in case I ever got lost.

"Huh, that's weird," I say, suddenly noticing the strange behavior of my compass. The needle is spinning in frantic circles, clockwise and then counterclockwise, like the compass itself is lost. "What's up with my compass?"

"What do you mean?" Celia asks, walking over to me to examine the compass.

"I was just standing in the doorway when the needle started to spin like crazy," I tell her.

"Here, let me see it," she says, holding her hand out. I hand the small compass over to Celia and the needle goes insane, spinning all over the place, shaking in the small plastic capsule.

She drops the compass, almost throwing it to the ground as she jumps back. Her eyes are wide, filled with shock, almost resembling those of a cornered animal.

"Are you alright?" I ask, furrowing my eyebrows, mystified by her intense reaction.

"Yeah, there must be something in my room creating a strong EMF," she says, returning to her normal self.

"EMFs, aren't they those things that ghosts give off?" I ask, my face riddled with confusion.

"Um, first off, ghosts aren't real, and second, EMF stands for electromagnetic field. You should know this because we learned about it in physics last year," she says with a nervous look still in her eyes.

"What would be creating an electromagnetic field at this intensity?" I wonder aloud.

"No idea, let's do French. I mean, let me help you with your French homework," she stutters.

"Are you okay?" I ask, cocking my head to the side, giving her a curious look. "It not like you to stumble over your words."

"How do you know so much about my personality?" she asks, her eyes suddenly clouded and troubled.

"I don't know, to be honest. I just kind of observe people and realize what's normal and not normal for them," I say with a shrug.

"Hm," she says thoughtfully, cocking her head to the side. Her eyes lose that caged animal look and go back to their normal analytical glint. She eyes me that way for a moment, and then grabs my hand and holds it tightly, studying my reaction. I try not to wince as she grips my hand, still sore from punching Craig. I chew my gum nervously and try to think of anything other than the throbbing ache rippling up to my elbow.

Her hand is soft and warm, and once she sees my discomfort, she loosens her grip, caressing my hand almost tenderly.

"Who were you fighting?" she asks suddenly, stepping back and letting go of my hand.

"Huh?" I ask in confusion. *How did she know I had gotten into a fight?* I ask myself.

"I'm like you, good at observing and reading people," she states, beginning to walk in a slow circle around me. "Now, I was watching you chew your gum earlier, and I noticed that you were chewing it on the left side instead of the right, and when you accidently did chew it on the right, you winced. I figured you had either gotten hit in the face, or had a sore tooth, then I noticed that your knuckles were red and starting to bruise. Now, to test my theory of a fight, I decided to see if your hand was injured and sore, and it was."

"How did you know what hand I punch with?" I inquire, completely shocked at how she put all these seemingly insignificant pieces together to create a complete picture.

"Because I know you're right handed, I've seen you write before," she says casually. "Also, I did fight you. So who were you duking it out with?"

"Craig Collins," I sigh in defeat.

"Really? Why? I thought you guys were cool," she says, her eyebrows furrowing.

"I'm not quite sure, he kind of just punched me in the face and said something about me pulling you out of that almost-fight you got yourself into," I tell her.

"Oh, thanks for that by the way," she says with a timid voice and bashful look.

"Yeah, don't mention it," I tell her, smiling at her.

"Alright, back to homework!" she commands, snatching a pen from her desk and marching over to where I stand. "Now, what are you having troubles with?" she asks.

"All of it."

"Thanks for all the help with my homework," Beckett says as we walk out the front door.

"It was no problem," I say. "It was either help you or try to perfect Bach's *Aria*."

"You chose to help me with homework over playing piano?" he asks, stunned.

"Well sure, you needed help, and besides, I'm only going to frustrate myself if I obsess over perfecting that piece. It's not that it's super challenging or anything, I'm simply a perfectionist, and I'll go ballistic if it's not flawless," I explain casually.

"You're too hard on yourself," Beckett tells me. "Next time I come over, you'll have to play for me, I'm sure it'll sound great."

"Yeah, next time," I say with a small laugh. *It's weird, I kind of enjoy his company,* I think. *I guess I was wrong about him.*

"Earth to Celia." Beckett waves his hand in front of my face.

I instinctively grab his arm and twist it behind him, pushing him face first into the side of the house.

I shake my head, as if snapping out of a daze, slowly releasing Beckett and backing away.

"Sorry," I mutter, my cheeks turning red. *I guess my run-ins with Mesmer really took a toll on me.*

"No, I'm sorry, I didn't mean to invade your personal space," his voice is sincere, just like his deep blue eyes.

"Don't be, it's just old instinct," I tell him, waving my hand in dismissal. His eyes catch mine and they hold me, paralyzing me where I stand. They're so intense, filled with emotions that I can't read.

His eyes are gorgeous, I think to myself. *They're like little oceans, teeming with life.*

"Well, I should go," Beckett says, breaking his gaze. "I'll see you tomorrow!" He hops on his motorcycle, throwing on his leather jacket. He waves goodbye before revving the engine and peeling down the street.

"You know, he's kind of cute," I say to myself.

"Oh my God, he's dreamy!" Amy exclaims, seemingly coming out of nowhere. "He's so tall and handsome, and his voice is so smooth and he's so polite, and ugh!"

"Close your mouth, Amy, you look like an idiot. I think you're even drooling," I say in irritation.

"I can't believe you beat him up," she says. "Why would you want to? I mean gosh, just look at him! He's such a babe!"

"Well, you better believe it, and you better believe that I'll do the same to you if you don't shut the hell up," I growl.

"You sound kind of... covetous," Amy says, her eyes glittering with glee.

"Amy, you're stupid," I tell her, ending the conversation. *Covetous, as if.*

Beep! Beep! Beep!

I roll over and silence the alarm, sitting up and draping my legs over the side of my bed. I feel great, I haven't slept this well in a while.

I get dressed quickly and make my way to the kitchen, grabbing my usual Power Bar for breakfast.

"Come on, Celia, we gotta go!"

"Quit hounding me, Amy," I say, taking a bite from my Power Bar. "We'll get to school at the same time we always do."

Just as I had promised, we pull into the school parking lot with exactly fifteen minutes until classes start.

I make my way to my locker and run head on into someone.

"Watch where you're going, space case!"

"Shut up, Ben," I say, smacking him with the back of my hand. "I've got better places to be than here getting harassed by you."

"Yeah, don't we all?" Beckett laughs.

"Good point," I say, giving him a small smile.

"So, where are you headed?" Ben asks.

"To my locker to grab my books," I tell him.

"Well then, we shall accompany you!" he announces gallantly. "And by 'we' I mean 'Beckett' because I have to go talk to Mrs. Severson about switching up some of my classes." And with that, Ben disappears into the sea of students.

"He's so weird," I mutter, shaking my head slightly.

"Tell me about it," Beckett says in agreement. "So, I don't know if you know this, but we have a test in Calc tomorrow. Lawrence mentioned it yesterday, and I doubt he'll say anything about it today because you're back and he'll want the test to catch you off guard," he tells me, leaning up against the locker beside mine.

"Great, a Calculus and a French test," I grumble as I grab my books.

"Oh God, that's right, all French classes are testing tomorrow. There goes my four-point-o average," Beckett sighs, his head falling against my neighboring locker.

"I can come over today after school and help you study," I tell him, closing my locker and leaning against it so that I'm facing the miserable boy.

"You don't have to," he tells me. "You already sacrificed your time yesterday."

"Sweet, I'll come over at five," I smile.

"What? I just said you didn't have to." His face is riddled with confusion.

"I heard you, I simply chose not to listen to you. I'll be over at five. I'm going for a run after school, and then I have to stop at home and take a shower," I say, slinging my backpack over my shoulders.

"Um, okay, but can I ask you something?" He pauses, stopping in the middle of the hallway. I stop with him. "Why do you want to help me?"

"I'm not sure," I say, shifting my eyes to the floor. "I've realized that you aren't a bad person, and that, honestly, you're pretty cool, I would even consider you my friend. And when I see that a friend needs help, I feel inclined to help them." I can't meet his eyes, I'm afraid of what they might see. I have no idea what my own eyes might be saying, and the eyes truly are windows to the soul.

"Yeah, I guess I'd call you my friend too," he says with a laugh, placing his hand on the top of my head, slightly ruffling my hair.

I don't go rigid the way I normally do, I just swat his hand aside and playfully hit him in the gut with my textbook. "Don't touch my hair, you're gonna ruin it," I tell him.

"Too late," he says, cringing.

"You didn't," I gasp, my eyes widening.

"I didn't have to, it was ruined when you got here," he tells me.

"You're such a jerk!" I yell, hitting him with my textbook again.

He laughs as he tries to block my attack, putting his arms up in defense. His laughter is contagious, it's rich and deep, coming from his gut, and it spreads to me.

We're still laughing when we walk into Calculus, and the lively class goes dead silent. I can feel everyone's eyes focused on us, but I ignore them, I'm used to people looking at me like I'm a foreign species.

"This is awkward," Beckett mutters.

"Thank you, Captain Obvious," I sigh.

"Well, isn't this heartwarming?" The voice comes from the front of the class. "It's nice to see that you two are finally getting along," Mr. Lawrence says. He looks like he just bit into something sour, his face contorting in disgust.

"You know, my mom always told me not to say things I didn't mean, you should try to do the same," I say in a light tone, malice hiding just under the surface.

"Take your seat, Walters, you too, Halverson!" the teacher barks.

I take my seat with a teasing smile, enjoying the fury blazing in Mr. Lawrence's eyes.

"Is there a story behind why you two hate each other?" Beckett asks quietly once class begins.

"Not really," I say. "He's an awful teacher and person and I constantly remind him of that, so naturally, he hates me."

"That's it?" Beckett asks skeptically, his eyebrows raised.

"Well..." I hesitate, debating whether or not to share the story. "I did glue his desk drawers shut during summer school one year. I didn't get in trouble with the school because he couldn't prove that I did it, but he knew it was me."

Beckett stifles laughter upon hearing my story before going in for another question. "Why did you do that?"

"He was being an ass to a student who didn't deserve it," I say, leaving it at that.

"So, you're like The Punisher, punishing the evil for their crimes," he says, laughter in his voice.

"Something like that," I say, an impish grin creeping onto my lips.

"Why are you smiling, Walters?" a harsh voice asks. "Is something about my lesson funny?"

"Nah, it's not your lesson," I tell Mr. Lawrence with false assurance. "I just noticed that your hairline is really starting to recede, and *that's* what I found funny."

"What?!" he brings a panicked hand to his head just as the shrill sound of the bell pierces the room.

"Would you look at that, saved by the bell," I remark, jumping out of my seat, and snatching up my backpack. "Bye, Mr. Lawrence, have a terrific day!"

I skip out of the room with Beckett close behind me in a fit of hysterical laughter.

"Why'd you tell him his hairline was receding?" he asks as he catches his breath.

"Because he's terrified of aging," I say casually. "He tries way too hard to stay in style and seem young. I also found Botox and a Bosley prescription in one of his desk drawers when I glued them shut."

"Whoa, whoa, whoa, Mr. Lawrence uses Botox *and* Bosley?"

"Yep, the man uses Botox *and* Bosley."

The end of the day comes sooner than I thought it could, I'm grateful for the final bell that rings through the halls.

As I'm walking out with my sister, I see a figure and stop, my blood beginning to boil at the sight of him.

"Amy, hold my bag," I command, handing her the heavy backpack, my body moving on its own accord.

"Celia! Where the hell are you going?" she calls as I march down the hall. I don't answer, choosing to simply ignore her as I continue on my mission.

"Craig!" I call his name, and when he turns around I hit him square in the jaw.

"What the–" I cut him off with another punch, but from the other side this time.

He stumbles back, and I plant a kick firmly into his chest, sending him into the lockers. He doubles over and clutches his torso as he groans in pain and gasps for air.

I grab him by the neck, squeezing the pressure points on the side and bend over so my lips are almost touching his ear to deliver a single, menacing sentence.

"If you so much as touch one of my friends again, I will decimate you." My voice is a low growl, adding to the fear factor.

With my hands placed firmly on the back of his head and neck, I bring my knee up and into his nose, and then push him onto the hard tiles of the hallway.

Without another word I leave, returning to my sister's side.

"That was amazing!" she squeals when we get to the car. "Where the hell did you learn to do that?"

"Television," I say, not bothered by the blatant lie. "I'm going to drop you off at home and I won't be back until later, so let Mom and Dad know, okay?"

"Sure thing, just don't beat me senseless," she says, looking at me with admiring eyes.

I ignore her and her admiration and drive, focusing on the road and not the intense burning inside of me as anger wages war on all my senses.

My hands grip the steering wheel until my knuckles turn white, and still, it's not enough, I can't relieve the fire raging within me. I want to squeeze the wheel until it breaks and forces us to swerve off the road. Maybe then this anguish would be gone. The worst part is that I can't figure out why I'm so infuriated, I simply am and it's eating me up from the inside.

"Hey, Celia, what's wrong? You look really tense," Amy says, her voice filling with concern.

"Nothing, I just had a long day." My response is quick and short, ending this and all further conversation.

I drop her off at home and then hurry down to the park, ditching my car at the start of the trail. I slam the door shut and take off, barely remembering to lock the vehicle behind me as I lose myself in the run.

Thud, thud, thud, my feet hit the ground in quick succession. I focus on the sound of my breathing, concentrating on the even breaths going in and out of my lungs.

My mind races in time with my feet, haunted by a single image, a man in what looks like a long tailcoat with golden buttons and black pants. His hair is a pale white, like fine threads spun by a spider, and his eyes are obsidian black and endlessly haunting. He has high cheek bones, a high-bridge nose, and an angular face with a jawline that might as well have been cut from granite. He keeps repeating one sentence over and over again, the words forming on his lips and freezing my blood. *I will always find you.* The words echo through the walls of my skull, attacking my mind from every direction.

I want to scream, to yell at my brain to make it stop, but I can't, so I keep running, losing myself in the rhythm of my feet.

It doesn't matter how fast I run though, I can't escape the image that lingers in my mind. It stays like a shadow that neither night nor day can cast aside, like a ghost that resides inside my head, haunting me even once I've fallen asleep.

You can't run from something that's inside of you, I tell myself as I pick up more speed, sprinting down the path that cuts through the park. *That may be so, but I can still try like hell to.*

"Jeez, Celia, are you being chased by a bear or something? It looks like you're running for your life," a familiar voice asks.

I come to a halt, breathing heavily as I turn to the person addressing me.

"Nah... I just needed to blow off some steam," I say, bending forward to rest my hands on my knees.

"You must've had a lot of steam," Beckett says with a small laugh.

"Yeah, I guess you could say that," I say slowly, my breath finally starting to come back to me.

"Seriously though, I've never seen someone run like that, like they were running from imminent doom," he tells me, leaving the picnic table he had been sitting at to make his way to where I'm standing.

"Just trying to outrun my demons," I say trying to sound sarcastic and joking; I'm not sure if I'm successful. "Well, I should probably finish my run, if I don't, they might catch up to me."

"Um, yeah, sure, I'll see you later."

Man, she's fast, I think to myself. I had no idea that the smartest person in school was a speed demon. She ran like she was being chased by a pack of ravenous wolves, like her life depended on it. And her eyes, they were so intense. Fierce with cold determination and a twinge of fear.

"Uh-oh, Beckett's got his thinking face on, something earth-shattering must have happened."

"Shut up, Ben," I say.

"What? It's not a common occurrence," he says, laughter ringing throughout his voice.

"Yes, it is!" I protest with indignation. "I think all the time, and at the moment, I was thinking about Celia." I mentally kick myself the moment the words leave my mouth, realizing how it must sound to Ben. *You are a* complete *moron, Beckett Halverson!* I mentally scold myself as I inwardly groan, feeling the need to hang my head and bash it against the table under the impish grin Ben gives me.

"Well, I'll be damned," he says.

"It's not what it sounded like," I say quickly, trying to recover my dignity. "It's only because she ran by a couple seconds ago, and holy crap she's fast! But when she stopped to talk to me, she seemed extremely rushed."

"Celia's always rushed," Ben says, waving his hand dismissively. "She's always rushing to do the next thing or learn the next song or do whatever's on her day's agenda."

"This was different," I tell him. "She was running like it was do or die..." I pause, hesitant to say the rest. "She said she was trying to outrun her demons, and at first I thought she was joking, but when I looked in her eyes, they were wild, panicked and scared, almost like she was trapped."

"What?" The playful look in Ben's eyes is gone, and concern has taken its place. "Weird." And just like that he's back to his normal self. "Speaking of weird and Celia, did you hear about what happened to Craig?" he asks.

"No, what happened?"

"He was sent to the hospital right after school with a broken nose, jaw, and three damaged ribs. One broken and two cracked," he says, his eyes beaming with his smile.

"It wasn't me, I swear. I only hit him once, and in the face. I broke his nose but that's it," I say, raising my hands in a defensive manner.

"I know, it was Celia. At least, that's what I heard from one of his posse members."

"If Celia did it, he probably deserved it," I reason. "She usually isn't one to go around picking fights for fun, she normally has a good reason."

"Honestly, you'd be surprised," Ben says with a laugh. "Most of the time her reason is because they pissed her off. She actually picks a lot of fights, but she always beats her opponent mentally, before they can get physical, but there have been a couple times where that wasn't the case. Counting you and Craig, I would say she's gotten physical on maybe six different occasions. The only reason we haven't heard about other times is because she's never gotten into a fight with someone from school before. And even if she did, they'd never say anything, no one wants to admit that they got their ass handed to them by the scary, quiet girl."

"It *is* pretty embarrassing," I admit, bringing a hand to my jaw, rubbing the spot she had punched a few days ago. The bruising was pretty much gone now, but the soreness had started coming back after my fight with Craig.

"You know, you never explained why we went to the park today instead of chilling at your house and saving the world from hordes of aliens," Ben says suddenly, changing the subject.

"Oh, I'm just trying to kill time until Celia comes over." I start again with the mental kicking.

"So are you guys Facebook official now?" he asks curiously.

"What? No! We've only barely started to be able to tolerate each other."

"I was just wondering, there's no need to get so defensive," he says in a chastising tone.

"I wasn't being defensive, I was simply explaining where things are, and besides, I thought you had a thing with her," I say, turning the focus onto him. "What kind of friend moves in on his best friend's girl?"

"Why does everyone think that Celia and I are dating?" he asks with a sigh.

"Because it just makes sense. I mean, you're you and she's, well, she's Celia," I say.

"Wow. That actually made no sense. Have you always been this bad at explaining things?" he asks.

"Yeah, pretty much," I tell him.

"Weird, I never noticed until now," he says perplexedly.

"It's probably because I sounded especially stupid this time," I tell him. "I did an exceptionally horrible job explaining it to you."

"It's fine, I don't really want to know why everyone thinks Celia and I are a thing. It'll probably just gross me out and make me angry," Ben says, leaning back against the picnic table with a defeated sigh. "So why the park?" he asks again.

"Because Lily's at home and under the impression that Celia's your girlfriend, and since she's coming over tonight, I want the hostility level to be as low as it possibly can," I say slowly.

"Why does Lily think that Celia's my girlfriend?" Ben asks in bewilderment.

"I might have let it slip that you were meeting a girl a couple nights ago," I say slowly.

"You did what?!" Ben shrieks.

"She asked why you had left so soon, and it kind of slipped out... and then she heard me voicing my thoughts," I add hesitantly.

"Which were?"

"That I thought you were with Celia..." My voice trails off and I become quiet, watching him closely.

"You're going to be the end of me, Beckett Halverson," he groans. "Now I have to go grovel to your little sister."

"Just tell her that she looks pretty and all will be forgiven," I say nonchalantly. "You know she worships you."

"As all women should!" Ben exclaims.

"Well aren't you quite the egomaniac," I say.

"Indeed, I am," he says with a smug smile.

I laugh at him and nervously check my watch, wanting to make sure I'm not late to meet Celia.

"You seem anxious," Ben says, studying my face.

"Yeah, I'm a little nervous," I admit. "Celia's so unpredictable, it kind of scares me."

"Dude, is she all you think about? I'm honestly starting to think that you *do* have feelings for Celia. She's all you've talked about," Ben says. "Do you?"

"No! I just find her very interesting. I hated her for twelve years based on misconceptions, a bad first impression and a lot of unpleasant interactions. But I've realized that she's not that bad. It's like when you've gone your whole childhood hating a specific food, but then you get older and your taste buds change and you suddenly find it delicious," I explain, frantically scrambling around for words.

"So... you think Celia's delicious?" Ben asks with a confused look on his face.

"What? No, ugh. You know what? Never mind," I sigh. "It's four thirty, I should head home."

"Okie dokie. See ya tomorrow, Beck!" he calls, waving goodbye.

"Yeah, see ya!"

Bang! Bang!

"I got it!" I shout through the house, running to the door.

Celia stands in the doorway with her backpack slung over her shoulder and a spacey look on her face.

"Hey, come on in," I say, stepping aside to let her in.

"Who's here, Beckett? Is it Ben?" Lily asks, running to my side.

"No, this is my friend, Celia. Celia, this is my little sister, Lily," I say, introducing the two.

"Are you Ben's girlfriend?" Lily asks, wrinkling her nose in disdain.

"Ha ha, no. He's just a very good friend of mine, nothing more," she says, reassuring the little girl.

"Oh!" she exclaims gleefully.

"Who's here, Beck?" my dad asks.

"Oh, Mom, Dad, this is Celia Walters. Celia, these are my parents, Tyler and Jessica Halverson."

"Hello, I'm Celia," she says, extending her hand to shake theirs. I'm surprised by the action, remembering the way she feels about being touched.

"It's nice to meet you, Celia," my mom says, smiling at her.

"The pleasure is mine, Mrs. Halverson," Celia responds.

"So, Celia," my dad begins. I hold my breath, waiting for what's to come. "I hear you have quite the punch."

"Oh, yeah. Sorry about punching your son… in the face… multiple times," she says with a wince.

"Ha! Are you kidding? That boy needs to toughen up. I mean, I was in shock when the principal told us that Beck had gotten into a fistfight at school. When I saw him, I thought for sure some jock had finally gotten sick of his smartass comments and gave him a good beating. Man, was I impressed to hear that it was a girl who beat him so badly. And now you're here, in the flesh, standing in my kitchen! You keep doing your thing, Ms. Walters, you keep right on."

"Huh?" Celia looks at him with intense confusion.

"Okay, Dad, that's enough," I say, trying to diffuse the awkward air that fills the room. "We're going to go study."

"Okay, sweetie, behave," Mom tells me.

"Okay, Mom," I say. I just want to get out of the kitchen and away from the awkwardness. "Alright, let's go."

Celia follows me through the hall and down the stairs to my room and drops her bag beside my desk.

"So," Celia says, surveying my room. "Shall we get started?"

He's so concentrated, it makes me wonder what he's doing. We had studied French relentlessly for two hours and then he had started to lose focus, so had I suggested that we take a break. Now he's completely absorbed in something, but I can't see what it is. A stack of books on his desk obscures my vision.

I put my book down and study him, too interested to go back to reading. I watch curiously as his intense blue eyes sweep across whatever it is that he's doing.

He sits so quietly, his face so focused. I've never seen him like this.

I walk over to where he sits and rise on the balls of my feet, tilting my head slightly to get a better look at what Beckett's doing.

He's drawing, and he's good at it, at least he is from what I can see. I can only see the bottom of the page, but it looks great.

"I didn't know you could draw," I say, startling him.

"What? Oh, you never asked, so I never told you," he responds casually.

"What are you drawing?" I ask, raising myself onto the tips of my toes to see over his tower of books.

"N-nothing," Beckett says in a fluster. He closes his sketchbook in a hurry, but not before I catch a full glimpse of what he's drawing.

"The Masquerader, huh?" I say. With a quick movement, I snatch the book from his hands.

"Celia, wait!" Beckett cries, attempting to grab the book back.

"Calm down, I'm not going to snoop through your sketchbook, I'm sure it's full of drawings of me with horns and a pointed tail," I say with a laugh. "I just want to see your most recent drawing, there's something I need to check." Something that will confirm my fears but explain my recent blackouts. Explain the feelings of loss and rage I've been dealing with as of late. Something that will explain the magnetic field surrounding me, along with my new ability to fight and my crazy sharp reflexes. If my hunch is correct, I'll be able to make sense of my strange dreams and delusions. But if I'm right, the ground upon which I walk will be destroyed and my world will be flipped on its head.

"Wow," I breathe, opening to the picture. "You're quite good at this." He captured the life of The Masquerader perfectly, as if he had trapped her inside the page.

She brandishes her whip with a menacing look in her eyes and a smile of contempt playing on her lips.

I know that smile, I think to myself. *That's* my *smile of contempt. I wear it almost all the time at school, especially around Craig and other people who are just as stupid.*

I feel cold, like someone is filling my veins with ice. I force myself to look at her left hand that rests at her side and my heart stops. Her ring, how did he catch its design so well?

I slowly pull my own hand out of my pocket and study the mysterious ring. It's a perfect match to the one in the picture.

Shit.

"Hey, is everything okay?" Beckett asks, his voice pulling me out of my head and back into the real world.

"Huh? Yeah, I'm fine. I was just thinking." I hand him back his sketchbook and his hand catches mine, holding it firmly.

"That's what you say when you don't want anyone to ask you questions," Beckett tells me. His suspicion-filled eyes pierce mine, holding my gaze.

My skin feels warm where he touches me, leaving a slight tingle in my fingers.

"That's a nice ring," he says. His voice is quiet and gentle, yet a hidden emotion lurks beneath the surface of his voice. One I can't quite put my finger on. "Who gave it to you?" He steps closer, inspecting my ring carefully.

"My dad did," I stutter, freezing up. "Why do you ask?"

"It looks familiar. Wait, this is an engagement ring, Celia," he says condescendingly. "I may not be a jeweler, but I know what an engagement ring looks like. Fathers don't give their daughters engagement rings, that's weird. It feels creepy and incest-y, that stuff only happens in anime." He pauses for a moment, running his finger over the ring. For a second his eyes clear into a startling blue, like the ring shook something loose, but then it slips away. "I didn't know you were seeing someone," he says quietly. "What's his name?"

"I'm not engaged," I say with a laugh. "I decided to try on my mom's old engagement ring and it got stuck. No matter what I do, I can't get the damn thing off."

"Oh," he says. I can tell that he doesn't believe my elaborate story, but the undertone in his voice disappears. Was it jealousy? That thought makes me smile for some reason.

"Yeah, not my brightest idea," I say sheepishly.

"I can help you get it off," he tells me, taking another step closer. "I'm really good at that sort of thing. When I was younger, I would always play with the rings whenever I found them at a store and they always got stuck on my fingers. I would panic and furiously attempt to get the ring off before one of my parents found out. They would scold me because I was always getting rings stuck. Now, I am the master of getting rings off." He smiles at me, his deep blue eyes losing the suspicion they held earlier.

Looking at him like this, I find it hard to think. I just want to study his eyes that gaze so intensely into mine.

"I'm good, thanks though," I say after a moment of silence. "To be honest, I kind of like the ring. It kind of feels like a piece of my history, a part of who I am, you know?"

"I guess that makes sense," he says. He hasn't let go of my hand or stepped away from me, and I'm beginning to have trouble breathing.

"So, The Masquerader, huh? Are you on the man hunt for her now?" I ask. "Does she grind your gears?"

"Grind my what? No," he says defensively, stepping back in surprise. "I just… I want to say thank you. She saved my life. I don't think she's as bad as the media says, I think she's misunderstood and maybe a little misdirected."

"Ahh," I say thoughtfully. "She gets you hot and bothered, doesn't she?" I tease.

"What? No! I swear it's not like that either!"

"You're so defensive, Beckett, are you sure you aren't crushing on a certain vigilante?"

"Alright, alright, that's enough. You're very funny, Celia," he says, making a face at me.

"You know, I could probably find her and talk her into a secret rendezvous with you," I say.

"How do you plan on doing that?" Beckett asks skeptically. "No one knows who she is or how to contact her, not even the police."

"Good question. It's a secret," I tell him with a smile. I pick up my backpack and head out.

"You're leaving? You can't drop a bomb like that and just leave!" Beckett protests.

"It's like eight o'clock and I still have homework," I tell him. "I have to go home." I make my way to the front door, followed by a persistent Beckett, asking me a million questions at once.

"At least tell me who you think The Masquerader is," he insists. "Or how you got your information. Come on, Celia, give *something.*"

"Sorry, Beck, but I can't give up my sources," I tell him, stopping before I open the door. "Don't do anything stupid. Misunderstood or not, she's dangerous, Beckett."

"Are you concerned for my safety?" Beckett asks, only half joking.

"My grades rely on you, Halverson," I say. "Don't read too deeply into things."

"Uh-huh, sure."

I shake my head and smile as I walk to my car. I drive away and watch his house fade into the distance through my rearview mirror, disappearing into the night.

She told me not to do anything stupid, but that's like asking me not to breathe. Stupid has always had a way of finding me. I swear it put a tracking device in me when I was born.

I continue down the road, stopping under a street lamp to catch my breath and check my watch. It's 10:30.

I've only been running for twenty minutes? I haven't been out as long I thought, I think, taking in ragged breaths. I've already run two and a half miles, and still have to turn back and go home.

I'm running too hard. I had been strung out from testing all day and had needed to blow off some steam. Now I wonder if I'll have enough steam to get me home.

"Excuse me, young man," a woman says, her voice jarring me from my thoughts. I look up and see her making her way to me from across the street. Aside from her, there's almost no one around, and I wish there were. I get a bad feeling from her.

She has long red hair, and not like a dull red, or a carrot orange, but a blazing crimson. She's tall and slim with pale skin and harsh facial features. She looks like an angry Marylyn Manson fan.

"Can I help you?" I ask, trying to sound polite.

"Yes, I need you to come with me," she snarls,

grabbing me by the wrist. She pulls me into the dark alley and throws me up against a brick wall, still holding my wrists firmly.

"Do you have a death wish?" I hear a cold but musical voice.

"You," the redhead snarls.

"Me. I was wondering when you'd show up. You've been hiding from me, convincing humans to do your job for you." The Masquerader steps out of the shadows, the darkness falling away from her body as if she were shedding a blanket.

"We *will* figure out your identity, and when we do, we will come for you," the redhead says, as if she wanted to scare the vigilante.

"Awesome, I'll be waiting," she responds. It's dark, and she wears a mask, but I can still see the excited light glimmering in her eyes. "Now, let the boy with the death wish go, this fight is between you and me."

"I think I'll keep him," my captor says. "You seem to have a certain interest in him, rescuing him from crooks and now me. He might be useful as leverage."

"I've already ended enough lives, I'd like to avoid senseless slaughter," The Masquerader explains.

I knew she wasn't what the media says. There's a method behind her madness, it's not senseless, I think. I mentally beat myself for getting carried away by the vigilante and start thinking of a way I can get free.

Option one: I can try fighting, but if I can't hold my own against Celia, I doubt I can hold my own against this redheaded chick. Besides, I don't know what she's got on her, she could have a gun or something. Fighting isn't an option right now.

Option two: I can call for help. I immediately dismiss that thought. No one's around, so it would be pointless. It's also likely to either spook my captor or just piss her off, and then she'll probably kill me.

Option three: I can trust this seemingly crazy vigilante. She helped me out the last time I almost died, and she said she wanted to avoid senseless slaughter. I feel like my chances of seeing the sunrise are better with her.

"I'm giving you one last chance, Mesmeritus, which, by the way, is a stupid name. I can't understand why you chose that, it's like you wanted people to make fun of you, but that's beside the point," The Masquerader says in a light, playful tone. It reminds of Celia when she tries to get under Mr. Lawrence's skin. "Let the boy go." Her voice has become deadly serious. She brandishes her whip and her entire body crackles with electricity, she's ready to go.

"Come and take him from me," the redhead spits. She faces the vigilante, still holding my wrist while her free arm turns a metallic gray and morphs into a sword. The edges gleam in the moonlight. It looks like it's sharp enough to cut through steel.

"What the hell?!" I yelp.

"Be quiet, Beckett." The Masquerader lunges forward, flashing her whip. It wraps around the redhead's arm just above her wrist and sparks blue and purple. She screams and lets go of me, recoiling from the pain.

"Run," The Masquerader commands, turning to face me. "Get out of here before– shit!" She spins around with a wild look in her eyes as her opponent disappears in a bright flash.

"Damnit!" She throws her fist against the wall. Mortar and brick bits fall around her, but surprisingly, she seems uninjured. With a frustrated sigh, she turns and begins to run back towards the shadows.

"Wait!" I call grabbing her hand before she's out of reach. "Who are you? I won't tell, I promise. I just want to know," I plead.

"It doesn't matter," she says. Her voice is guarded.

I avert my eyes and focus on our hands and my attention is snagged by her ring. It's pretty. I feel like I've seen it before, I just can't recall where.

"Yes, it does," I say, my voice soft and sincere. "I just have this feeling that I know you."

"You may know my name, but you're nowhere near knowing me." She's angry, it's clear in her voice.

She pulls her hand away and takes off, disappearing into the night.

I stare up at the night sky, searching for a specific twinkling light, searching for my home. I'm tired and stressed after a long day of testing.

"I wish I could go back," I say with a sigh. The world I used to know flashes across my mind's eye.

"I can take you back." A seductive, velvety voice speaks from the shadows of the night.

"Even if that were true, I'd never go anywhere with you, Mesmer Amar," I growl. I turn around and meet his cold, black eyes with mine. "What do you want from me?" I ask, my voice full of hostility as I glare at Saturn's fallen prince.

"The same thing I always want, Celia. You," he says, striding to my side with long, graceful steps. He grabs me by the waist and pulls me into his body, bringing my hips flush against his. He leans into me so our faces are almost touching. "I want you, Celia," he says, his breath falling onto my lips. "Come with me and rule by my side, my princess."

"That's never going happen," I growl. I shove him away, but he pulls me back, wrapping his arms around my body.

"There's no need to be like that," he murmurs, his breath tickling my ear. "All I want is you."

I feel disgusting, tainted by his touch, by his breath on my skin. I want to strip the flesh off my bones and tear my skin apart, thread by thread, to rid myself of the feeling of his touch.

"Let me go, Mesmer," I snarl, trying to push him away. His arms only constrict around me, pulling me closer to him.

"Your attempts to be free of me are useless. I'll always find you, Celia, no matter where you are. When will you realize that you are mine?" He tucks a stray hair behind my ear and draws my face closer to his.

"I am *not* yours." I spit. "I belong to no one."

"For now, and you can thank me for

that. After all, I was the one who killed your fiancé." His black eyes gleam with a sadistic light.

I clench my jaw and bite back on my words of retaliation. I would only be adding to his sick glee.

"Aw, no fight from you? That's a shame, I always enjoy it when you try and put up a fight," he says, tenderly caressing my face.

It's strange how his actions are so different from his words. If someone were to walk by, they would think he was passionately in love with me. They wouldn't know that he's a sadistic psychopath gloating about how he's destroyed everything I've ever loved.

"I'm not going to add to your sadistic pleasure, Mesmer," I tell him.

"That's a shame, but if you won't protest or fight, I'll just do as I please."

He shoves me against the side of my house. His hands pin mine above my head as his lips crash down onto mine.

A cold, disgusted shock wave washes over me, stopping my heart with pure fury.

He bites down on my lip, not bothering to be gentle about it and my mouth is filled with the bitter, metallic taste of blood.

I don't fight him. I clench my jaw and glare at him, saying nothing.

"What do you know about The Masquerader?" Mesmer asks suddenly, drawing a line down my throat with his fingertips.

"Only that she's a sporadic killer with an edgy fashion sense," I respond.

"She's been interfering with my plans, and I get the feeling that you know more than you're letting on." His lips graze my jaw, making their way to my neck, sucking and biting my skin. His hips grind against mine in a slow rhythm and I feel sick. My mind is fuzzy, but not in the euphoric way. It's like the static that fills your mind before throwing up, and it takes everything I have not to do so.

I want to peel the skin off my body where he's touched me. I want to bathe in acid to erase every trace of him from my flesh.

"Who is she, Celia?" Mesmer asks, running his hands down my body to rest on my hips.

"I don't know. But when you find out, let me know so I can send her an Edible Arrangements basket and a *Thank You* card," I say. I shove him off me, unable to stand his touch any longer.

"You'll tell me. I'll make you," Mesmer growls, his voice becoming dark and menacing. Every ounce of the tenderness from before is gone as he shoves me face first into the side of my house, once again pinning my hands above my head. His free hand travels under the hem of my t-shirt and up my spine, exposing my skin to the chilled night air. He trails kisses down the nape of my neck, aggressively biting the junction of my shoulder and my neck.

"Screw complacency, you're disgusting," I growl. I slam my head back, sending the hard part into Mesmer's face. He lets go of my hands and clutches his nose as he stumbles backwards. I spin around and plant a side kick in his chest, forcing him further away from me.

"And here I thought you weren't going to put up a fight," Mesmer says with false disappointment.

"Well, I changed my mind," I tell him. I square up and set myself into a fight stance, preparing myself to go head to head with the sadistic man. "Game on, you bastard."

He smiles at me, amusement gleaming in his black, heartless eyes.

"As fun as it would be to.... wrestle things out with you, I must be going. I only wanted to drop by and give you my personal regards," he says, backing up towards the shadows in the street behind him. "I'll see you later, Celia." He turns and disappears, leaving no trace of him behind other than the defiled feeling on my skin.

"I need to take a shower," I say, running urgently into the house.

"How are the stars tonight?" my dad asks as I enter the house. "Your lip's bleeding, what'd you do?"

"The stars are great, I bit my lip, I'm taking a shower." My words are rushed and strung together as I b-line for the bathroom.

I turn on the water and move the dial to the hot side. The room slowly fills with steam, fogging the mirrors.

I peel my clothes off in a frantic rush and submerge myself in the warm water cascading from above. I grab the bar of soap and scrub my body until it hurts, desperate to rid myself of all traces of Mesmer.

"I cannot believe that demented creature had the nerve to show up at my house and molest me!" I growl. I go back to scrubbing my body, now massaging the stressed muscles with the bar of soap.

My hands shake as I run them through my hair, scrubbing masses of shampoo into my scalp.

"I'm going to kill him," I declare. "For everything he's taken from me. For everything he's done to me. I don't care what I have to do." My entire body is shaking now, uncontrollably.

I place my hands on the shower wall to steady myself. Water and soap stream down my body and onto the floor, slightly calming me down.

"I'm going to kill him."

Not if you can't face who you really are, a voice says. It sounds like it's coming from all over, like it's coming from the water itself.

When will you wake up and come to face reality? All the pieces lay before your eyes. You simply have to put them together and accept the image they create.

"Could you cut the crap and say what you want me to know? Because these cryptic messages are really starting to piss me off," I mutter to the empty room.

Don't fight your nature, Celia. Don't–

"Stop!" I growl, slamming the side of my fist into shower wall, cutting off the voice in my head. "I will do whatever the hell I want to. Nothing can change that."

I turn the water off and wrap myself in a towel, drying myself off.

"I need to go to bed," I sigh. "Thank God it's Friday."

I dress myself and curl up in my bed, sleep falling upon me with swift wings.

"You know, if the rulers had any brain cells, they would realize that the smartest thing to do is join forces. We won't be able to defeat the insurgents if we keep running around like headless chickens. If every planet were to cut their military in half, leaving one half to protect home, and the other to enter a joint army, not only would we defeat the insurgents faster, but with less casualties as well. We could start with Pluto since it's the smallest and work our way up by planet size. With the insurgents secured on Pluto, they will only need minimal forces to defend their home and can add the rest of their forces to the joint army. From that point, we could work to stabilize the next smallest planet and so on and so forth until universal peace is achieved!" I exclaim, ranting on to my little brother.

"See, Celia, this is why Mother and Father want you to rule once they step down. You're so brilliant, you could solve everyone's problems. I do not understand why you adamantly refuse the crown. You know that in the end, you will have no choice," Peter says.

"Because power corrupts, and I do not wish to be corrupted," I tell him.

"Nothing can corrupt you, Celia, you are too smart. The devil himself would not be able to corrupt you."

"You have too much faith in me, Peter," I tell my brother. "There is always something that can corrupt an individual. For some it is money, for others it is power. Even something as pure as love can cause someone to become corrupt."

"Right, but you don't believe in love," Peter states.

"I do too believe in love!" I say defensively. "I love you, Peter. And Mother, and Father, and Jade and–"

"And the Celestial Warrior–ow!"

I hit Peter hard, my hand smacking against his bicep.

"I do not love that arrogant prince," I say. "Despite what most people believe, love does not just fall from the sky and it is not found hidden under rocks. It is made, created through experiences and memories. It is forged through the good times as well as the bad. It is not some magical thing that appears out of nowhere," I explain, going on yet another rant.

"I know, I simply enjoy seeing you get all worked up about it," he says, laughing at my irritation.

"You are awful, Peter, I hope you know that," I say, getting up to leave.

"I know, but how else am I supposed to show my big sister that I love her?" He pulls me in for a hug and I wrap my arms around his body, holding him tightly.

I wake up around three to the sound of Lily screaming about something upstairs.

"Why are you screaming, Lily? It's too early for that," I tell her, slowly making my way up the stairs.

"The day's halfway over, Beckett," she tells me. "And I was screaming because the Falcons lost miserably. It was a massacre, and I was angry."

"Oh, that's unfortunate," I say. Lily is a hardcore Atlanta Falcons fan, which I find strange because she's never even been to Atlanta, or Georgia for that matter. I'm also shocked that a seven-year-old can follow football games the way she does. All the rules and terms leave me still trying to figure out exactly how the game works.

"I know. We really need to get our crap together and stop sucking!" she exclaims.

"Listen, Kiddo, I've gotta dash to a friend's house because last night I was attacked by a psychotic redhead whose arm turned into a sword. So, either I'm losing it or something else is going on," I tell her, patting my little sister on the head.

"You're losing it," she says in a flat tone.

"Wow, thanks for the support, Lily," I say sarcastically.

"You're welcome, Beckett!" She gives me a wide grin and hugs me around the legs.

I hug her back and then leave, heading to Ben's house first.

"You know, I think I understand why you and Beckett used fight so much," Amy says, sitting down next to me on the couch with a thoughtful look on her face. "Repressed sexual feelings."

I almost spit my water out, but I force it down, choking as it travels down my throat.

"What?"

"Repressed sexual feelings," she states again. "You two were always at it because you were both dying to get in each other's pants."

"Amy, you take stupidity to a new level," I tell her.

"Well, he obviously likes you, and you obviously like him, although I could be wrong. You kind of have the emotional capacity of a wall, so I could just be reading into things too deeply," she says, her face becoming perplexed.

"Um, I have more emotional capacity than a wall," I say in an offended tone. "I simply don't show it. And you're wrong by the way, about everything."

"No, I'm not, and you know it."

I begin to respond but then stop. I remember the way I felt the other day with the whole ring incident. The way I felt warm where his hand touched mine, and the way I couldn't breathe when he stood so close to me. Immediately I shut those thoughts down. *I can't be thinking about guys right now,* I remind myself. *I have a universe to save and a revenge to plot. Revenge for the person I gave my heart to.*

"Hey, are you still listening?" Amy asks with a frustrated look on her face.

"Nope," I tell her. "You were saying absurdly stupid things so I tuned you out."

"Whatevs," she says. She leans back against the couch and becomes absorbed in her phone. Eventually, she turns her phone off and tosses it across the couch with a sigh.

"Celia, I'm bored," she whines, burrowing herself deeper into the couch.

"That sounds like a *you* problem, Amy," I tell her, my eyes never leaving my book.

Suddenly there's a knock at the door and Amy perks up, her eyes locking mine. I know we're thinking the same thing.

"I've got it!" she announces gleefully, rushing for the door.

"No, you don't," I tell her, jumping over the couch.

She reaches out to grab the doorknob and I grab her by the back of her shirt and push her to the side. I set my hand on the doorknob and look over at my sister, my eyes conveying a silent message. *Try anything and I will kick your ass.*

Amy sighs in defeat and takes a seat at the table next to our parents who are absorbed in a deep discussion.

"Come on in," I say, opening the door and moving aside to let out visitor in.

"It's so nice to see you again, Beckett!" my mom squeals in delight.

Beckett stands in the doorway. His body is stiff and discomfort swims in his eyes. I know something happened, something bad.

"Why do you look so nervous and uncomfortable?" Mom asks worriedly.

"Because he's got the hots for your daughter," Amy says, sashaying to the fridge.

"Amy, have I ever told you that the things you say are so stupid that I can actually feel them killing my brain cells?" My voice is sharp and agitated, teeming with hostility.

"You should be nicer to your sister," Beckett says with a gentle voice.

"Shut up, Beckett, no one cares about what you think," I say, shoving him playfully. "Now let's go work on our English project."

"English project? We don't have one," he says, giving me an odd look.

"Yeah, we do," I say, shooting him a harsh glance. "You were asleep when it was assigned."

"Oh, oops."

"Yeah, oops," I say. I grab him by the hand and pull him up the stairs to my room, closing the door behind me as quietly as possible.

"What happened?" I ask.

"Huh?" His eyes are foggy, like he's off in a different world.

"What happened last night? I know something did, so spill it."

"Alright, you got me," he says reluctantly. "I may have done something stupid, which, in turn caused me to run into The Masquerader."

"Do you have a death wish?" Celia shrieks. That jars me, it's exactly what The Masquerader asked me last night.

"No!" I say defensively. "I wasn't even trying to, I swear. I was just out for a run and then some redheaded chick with a metal transforming arm attacked me."

Celia looks at me the way she looked at Amy earlier. As if I had just said the stupidest thing she's heard all night.

"What? You don't believe me, do you?" I ask.

"No, of course I believe you. You don't have any reason to lie. I simply can't believe you did the exact opposite of what I said only two days ago," she says irritably.

"I swear, I wasn't looking for trouble, it just found me," I say, desperation heavy in my voice.

"Do you know where the old abandoned bar on North Avenue is?" Celia asks.

"Yeah, why?" I ask with caution.

"Be there at eight tonight," she commands. "I'll arrange a meeting with The Masquerader."

"How, Celia? Nobody knows who she is, not even the cops," I say with exasperation.

"Just trust me okay?" I can tell she's on edge by the tone of her voice, so I don't push it.

"Okay. Eight o'clock at the old abandoned bar on North Avenue, I think I can do that."

8:00 pm.

"You really do have a death wish, don't you?" she asks. The shadows part like flowing curtains to reveal her perched on the corner of a low, crumbling wall.

"No, I don't," I say dejectedly, jumping at her voice and her sudden appearance. "I'm danger prone, that's all, but that's not why I'm here right now. I want to say thank you for saving my life, but whenever I try, you disappear before I can."

"That's because you always ask me who I am," she says matter-of-factly.

"I'm just curious," I say defensively.

"And I'm just cautious," she responds coldly

"There's something about you. It draws me in and captivates me. It's so familiar. I *do* know you, don't I?" I ask hesitantly.

"Now that you've said what you needed to say, stop trying to find me. You keep putting yourself in danger, a lot of danger. You worry those closest to you, so stop. Stop looking for me. Stop trying to solve this puzzle and stop trying to unmask me. You're in over your head, this goes beyond you," she says, jumping gracefully from the crumbling wall, landing on her nimble feet.

"Please, let me help you," I rush to her, trying to stop her from leaving. "I'm not going to stop. I will keep looking for you until I find out who you are. I can't let this go. I want to help you, so please, let me."

"Goodbye, Beckett," she says. Shadows rush in to surround her, and when they disperse, she's gone.

"Well, that didn't go as planned." I look at my phone, it's 8:07. I dial Celia's number as she had instructed me to.

"How'd it go?" she asks, her voice masking the concern I know is there.

"Not as I had hoped," I say. "What are you doing right now?"

"Um, nothing. Why?" Caution fills her voice.

"Meet me at the bowling alley on Main Street in ten minutes?" I ask.

"Sure, why not?" she says hesitantly.

"Cool, see you there." I hang up the phone and leave, heading to the bowling alley.

I pull into the parking lot of the bowling alley and find Beckett already there.

"You look out of it," I tell him, stepping out of my car. "Maybe you should go home and get some sleep."

"I'm alright," he says reassuringly, rising to his feet, "Come on, let's go inside."

We walk to the side door, but I stop before we reach it. The air around me seems to drop ten degrees, throwing my guard up.

"Shit. I really thought I was done with this for the night," I say, anger melting away my apprehension.

"I've been waiting for you, Celia," she hisses.

"Well it looks like you found me. Go away now? Besides, I already dealt with your little henchmen, like an hour ago. I'm getting bored of this game, *Mesmeritus*." I cringe slightly. *God, that name is stupid.*

"Then fight *me*!" she screams. She lunges at me and her metal arm morphs into a sword.

My whip materializes in my hand and electricity courses through my body. I jump out of her way and flash my whip at her, catching her side and drawing blood.

"Celia!?" It's Beckett's voice.

"Beckett, get behind me and stay out of my way," I command as I will myself to change form.

The transformation starts at my feet and slowly spreads up to the rest of my body.

I drop to my knees, my being consumed by pain. It feels like fire is crawling up my body, only coming to a stop once my face becomes heavy due to the mask that now adorns it.

I slowly rise, a menacing laugh emanating from my throat. Confidence and control seep into my skin, melting away the uncertainty that lingered in my mind. I've become a different person. I am no longer Celia Walters, I am The Masquerader.

"So, you're the one who's been interfering with our plans," the woman snarls.

"Indeed, I am, Sylvia Trunnel," I say, snapping my whip, laughing again as I do so. "I am the one who has been interfering. I am the shadow that you can't escape. It doesn't matter where you try to hide, the sun will still set and darkness will fall upon you. And even when the sun does cast its light, it still forms a shadow, and so I will be there, to haunt you the way you have haunted me. It's time for the tables to turn. I'm done being hunted, it's time you learn how it feels," I growl, beginning to advance on my enemy. My body crackles with electricity as I'm consumed by anger. "And now, I'm going to end you."

"Oh, I'd love to see you try," she snarls. She lunges at me once again, brandishing her sword.

I duck down, slipping under her attack and spin around, grabbing two of my rose head-shaped throwing stars and propelling them towards her.

The two blades are blocked by Sylvia's metallic arm and she advances.

I twirl around her blade and flash my whip. It wraps around her arm, channeling electricity into her body. I pull the whip, jerking her arm down and to the side, leaving her chest exposed and land a solid kick just below her sternum and she stumbles backwards, gasping for air.

"If you hope to defeat me, you're going to need more than a whip and a few blades," Sylvia growls.

What are you going on about? You're getting your ass kicked, I think to myself.

"They aren't all I've got," I tell her, my voice filled with menace. I pull two small blades from the inside of my coat and leap towards my opponent.

Sylvia brings her sword arm down and I block it with an x-catch, pushing her back, forcing her backwards.

She spins quickly, slashing the air at throat level.

I jump backward, the tip of her sword barely grazing my neck. I bring my hand up to my throat, slightly shocked that she had managed to scratch me. I didn't think she would do even that much damage.

I need to end this fight before I get seriously injured.

"Beckett, do you have a quarter?" I ask, turning my head towards him, keeping Sylvia in my peripheral vision.

"Um, yeah," he stutters, digging through his pockets. His shaking hands toss a single quarter my way and I catch it, holding it between my pointer and middle fingers.

"Thanks. I'll pay you back later," I tell him. I throw the coin, propelling it forward with electricity towards the psychotic redhead, with a railgun-like effect.

The coin hits her metal arm, sending fiery shrapnel everywhere. I tackle Beckett behind a car, getting him and myself out of the hail of flaming metal bits.

I sit there in a daze as the redhead screams and writhes in pain. The flashing of flaming metal momentarily blinds me, but that's not the main factor of my daze. I kneel on either side of Beckett, straddling his hips. It must've happened when I tackled him and shielded his body with mine so as to protect him. My hands rest palms down, flat on the ground on either side of his head, and I find it hard to move.

He raises one of his hands and his fingers brush across the light scratch on my throat. His eyes are deep with concern.

His lips form my name, almost as a question asking if I'm okay. I nod, my eyes never leaving Beckett's piercingly blue ones.

A blood curdling scream rips through my daze, shaking me to my senses.

"Are you hurt?" I ask, my voice sounding timid and quiet.

"No, I'm okay," he responds. His voice is shaky, along with his breaths.

"Okay, then let's go." I get up and grab him by the hand, running to my car.

I jump in, but Beckett stands there, stuck in complete shock.

"Beckett, get in the car!" I yell, snapping him out of his daze. He does as I had commanded and climbs hurriedly into the passenger seat.

I peel out of the parking lot and zoom onto an exit ramp, heading toward the valley. I floor it on my way to the only place I know for a fact is safe. A place that the ghosts of my past won't be able to link me to.

Once we're far enough away from the city for me to feel safe, I begin to calm down, and my appearance changes once again. My leather jacket and tank top meld back into my plain red t-shirt, and the ripped jeans and combat boots return to my regular skinny jeans and Converse. The only thing that doesn't change is my ring, it never does. It's the first time I've been fully conscious when the transformation happened, both into and out of The Masquerader.

I look over at Beckett. He's pale and rigid and he hasn't said a word since we got in the car.

"Hey, are you okay?" I ask. "You haven't said anything, it's making me worried."

"How long have you known that you're The Masquerader?" he asks, finally saying something.

"I've had my suspicions for a while, but I wasn't absolutely sure until now."

"Who was that woman?" he asks.

"Her name is Sylvia Trunnel. She's the ex-advisor to the Royal Family of Saturn. She changed her name to Mesmeritus when she vowed servitude to the Dark Prince, Mesmer Amar," I tell him.

"And... who's that?" Beckett's face is contorted with confusion as he looks at me.

"He was the prince of Saturn, but that was before he destroyed everything. Before he destroyed my world, my universe and everything I loved." My voice becomes dark. I grip the steering wheel until my knuckles turn white.

"So, who are you?" His eyes meet mine. They're warm and kind, melting the walls that guard me.

"I'm Celia Walters, Princess of Mercury," I tell him, looking him square in the eyes.

"Ha, ha, you're hilarious. Are you going to send me into another bookcase?" Beckett asks.

"I wasn't joking. It was back then that I started remembering," I say.

Beckett furrows his eyebrows, becoming consumed in a thoughtful look.

"So, you're an alien then? I guess that explains a lot."

I crack a smile at that, grateful that he has a sense of humor even at a time like this.

"No, I'm not an alien, but I'm not really human either. I'm from a completely different universe."

"What was it like?" Beckett questions. "Were there spaceships? What about lightsabers?"

"I'll show you when we get to a safe place," I say.

"Where are we going?" It's obvious in Beckett's eyes that he's nervous and I don't blame him. If I were in his place, I'd probably be equally as nervous, if not more. The lack of knowledge would make me want to crawl in a hole and disappear.

"We're going to a place in the country," I tell him. "It's somewhere no one would think to look for us, we'll be safe."

Beckett lets out a soft sigh of relief, but his blue eyes quickly fill with panic.

"It's alright, you don't need to worry about your family, they're safe. No one knows about your involvement in this, so they won't know to go after you. They don't even know who you are. They wouldn't know who to go after even if they knew how you've managed to get yourself involved in all this," I assure him, laughing slightly at my last comment. I reflect on the times I had saved his life as The Masquerader. He should've listened to my warnings, he'd be much safer if he had.

"And what about your family?" he asks.

"They'll be okay. Mesmer isn't focused on them, he's focused on me. He won't bother going after them, it would take up time that he could be spending on something more important. Besides, it would only make me hate him more, which, in turn, would only make me more insistent on not giving him what he wants," I explain, touched by his concern for my family.

"What does he want from you?"

"It's not really a 'thing' that he wants, but, well, me. He doesn't want anything I have, at least I don't think he does. I don't have all my memories back, but as far as I know, he wants me," I say, shivering at the thought.

"Why is that bad?" Beckett asks, looking very confused.

"Because it's covetous, possessive and sick. He doesn't want me because he loves me, but because he's enraptured by my appearance and he wants to *own* me. He wants me to give myself over to him completely. He wants to control me, and not just what I do but–"

"Okay, I get where you're going," Beckett says, cutting me off before I can fully explain the whole of Mesmer's sick mentality.

"He's the reason that you don't like being touched, isn't he?"

"You've got a lot of questions, Beckett," I tell him.

"A lot has happened," he responds.

"I know. When we get to Nick's, I'll show you what I can and then I'll explain the rest."

"Nick?" Beckett looks at me suspiciously.

"Nick Mallard. He's out of town for the weekend, and I take care of his house and animals. Cleaning, keeping the yard nice and tidying up the hiking trails. I'm working on fixing the old pickup truck in the barn at the moment," I say, glad for the change of subject.

"Oh. Why are we going to his house?"

"Because it's a safe place in the middle of nowhere that no one knows about."

"That makes me a little nervous," Beckett says, his face turning a rosy color.

"Don't be, I'm not going to hurt you," I tell him, meeting his eyes with mine, hoping that he can see that he can trust me.

"I'm not nervous because I think you might murder me. I'm nervous because you intimidate me, and the thought of being alone with you in the middle of nowhere just makes me nervous," he says.

"You're very honest. I like that." I stop the car and get out. "We're here."

We walk up to the house and stop at the front door so I can get my key out.

The house is dark and empty, it's lonely. I'm used to seeing it so full and alive with the Mallard children.

"Okay, take a seat," I command, switching on the lights.

Beckett takes a seat on the couch and I take one next to him, bringing my hand up to his face, placing my middle and forefinger on his temple.

"You may feel a slight tingle," I tell him. "I'm going to use the electric signals in your brain for a moment."

"Will it hurt?" Beckett asks cautiously.

"Nope, just tingle. Now close your eyes and clear your mind. I'm going to show you a world you never knew existed."

I gasp, a world of vibrant colors appearing before my eyes.

"Where are we?" I ask, my eyes wide with wonder.

"In my head," Celia answers. "I transported your consciousness into my mind. Everything you see is a memory."

"Wait, what?" I stare at her, wondering how Celia managed to do that transportation thing.

"Try not to think too much about it," she tells me. "If you do, you'll get really confused and develop a massive headache."

"So, what's going to happen now?" I ask.

"You're about to see me when I was a little girl, talking to my dad. You won't be able to touch them and vice versa, and they can't hear you. It's only a memory."

A little girl and an older man come into focus. They're in what looks like a courtyard with beautiful flowers spilling around them.

The child sits on the man's lap with her arms crossed and a pout on her lips. Her hazel eyes are focused deep in concentration as well as confusion, while the man looks on her with a warm smile.

"Daddy, why do I shock people when they touch me?" the little girl asks, absentmindedly kicking her feet as they dangle from the man's lap.

"Because you belong to a Royal Family. We're given special powers to protect the people we rule over, you simply haven't learned to control those powers yet," he explains.

"That's weird, Daddy. Peter doesn't have any powers, why doesn't Peter have powers?" she asks.

"Sweetheart, Peter is only a baby. He won't develop powers for a long time still."

"So that's why you can do inhuman things," I say, turning to the older Celia. "The Royal Families have special abilities."

"Yeah." Celia's voice is quiet as she stares at the man with sadness in her eyes.

"Celia, what happened to your family?" I ask hesitantly.

"They were killed by Mesmer, along with all my friends and my fiancé," she says.

"Fiancé?"

"Yeah. I chose him over Mesmer, and Mesmer got pissed and filled with jealousy. He destroyed everything I loved, simply to get back at me." Her fingers go to her ring, twisting it around the base of her ring finger.

"He was the one who gave you that ring, wasn't he?" I ask, taking her hand in mine. For some reason, I find it comforting to hold her hand and I think it makes her feel better too. Her warm hand in mine soothes me. I feel like my world is spinning around in mad circles and the ground beneath my feet is breaking and I'm sinking. But with her hand in mine, the world stops spinning crazily and I'm standing on solid ground. She never made me feel this way before, but she does now, and I don't know why.

Celia holds my hand tightly in hers. Her eyes burn as she watches her father, pain evident in her eyes and all over her face.

"Let's go. I can't watch this anymore."

I open my eyes and I'm back on the couch with Celia next to me. When I look down I see our hands, locked together.

"Sorry," I say, letting go of her hand.

"It's alright," she says, her face blushing.

I smile at her slightly red face, never having seen that sort of reaction from her. She's usually so calm and collected, it's funny to see her a little off her game.

"I hadn't anticipated that sharing my memories would be so painful; I had planned to show you everything, but I couldn't even make it past my childhood. And those memories don't explain much either," Celia says slowly. "Ask me whatever you want and I'll try my best to explain it."

"You can explain it some other time. Everything seems too fresh, and I don't like seeing you look so sad," I tell her. I lift my gaze and our eyes meet. I can't breathe and my heart is racing. I slowly lift my hand and gently cup her neck, my thumb running over the cut she received while fighting. "Are you okay?" I ask.

"This? Yeah, it's fine," she says breathlessly, resting her hand on mine, lacing our fingers.

"I mean emotionally as well," I say.

"Oh. I'll be okay," she tells me, giving me a warm smile. She's breathtakingly beautiful, it makes sense that she's royalty. Her caramel hair and hazel eyes can't help but demand one's attention, and she has mine. All of it. She draws me in like a magnet and I find myself leaning into her and resting my forehead against hers. I only realize that Celia had closed her eyes when they suddenly shoot open, wide and alarmed.

"I didn't lock the doors," Celia says suddenly.

"What?" I ask, recoiling with confusion.

"The doors to the house, I had to unlock them to get in. I forgot to lock them back up." She gets up and hurries to the door. "I'm a little paranoid," she says. "I don't think anyone will find us here, but you can never be too careful."

"I think if they really wanted to get you, they would just blast a hole in the side of the house," I reason. "I don't think locking the door is going to stop these people. Which reminds me, what's the game plan? What are we going to do about Mesmer?"

"*We?* Nothing. *I* am going to find a way to kill him and end this game of cat and mouse. I can't risk you getting caught in the middle of everything. Too many innocent people have been killed in this battle between him and me," Celia says stonily.

"There's no way in hell I'm letting you shoulder this on your own," I tell her. "Besides, I'm involved now. That creepy redhead saw my face, and she hunted me down last night. She obviously thinks I can help her get something from you."

"What Sylvia does isn't important, what Mesmer does in the background is. Unless Sylvia can convince Mesmer that you're an essential piece in his twisted game, he won't pay you much attention."

"I'm sorry, Celia, but I'm not letting you do this alone," I tell her. "I just can't do it. I know we aren't super close, but I still can't do it."

"Why?" Celia asks. "Why do you insist on helping me?"

"Because I feel the need to protect you," I say quietly. "I don't know why. Ever since that fight in the library, I've felt the urge to protect you. Maybe it's because I've realized that you're a person, just like me. Someone who struggles and does their best to overcome the monsters that follow them. Someone who has demons around every corner with no one to help face them. Maybe it's because I finally see who you really are. Maybe it's something else, I don't know. All I know is that I have to protect you, and that I will."

"You are the strangest guy I've ever met," Celia says, giving me an odd look. "But fine, if you want to help, I know there's really nothing I can do to stop you. You'll need to know your history first. You'll need to know my backstory as well as Mesmer's, and then it's show time."

"Beckett, where have you been?" my mother asks frantically as I walk through the door.

"I was at Ben's," I tell her, feeling instantly guilty about the lie. "I went bowling with him last night and then went to his house to play video games. By the time we got done, it was super late so I slept over. Sorry I didn't tell you, I kind of forgot."

"We thought you had been kidnapped! Your car and motorcycle were both here, and then Lily was going on about crazy redheads with swords. Your father and I were so worried." She pulls me into a big hug, squeezing me tightly, as if holding me against some wind trying to blow me away.

"I'm sorry, Mom," I whisper, hugging her back, holding the fragile woman in my arms.

I wish I didn't have to lie to you, I think as she steps away and commands me to my room. *But if I told you the truth, you would only worry more, and then send me in for a psych evaluation.*

I go to my room as commanded and close the door with a sigh, and then recoil in surprise and horror.

"Beckett Halverson!" she screams, rushing towards me.

I'm so screwed. I wonder if those will be the last words to ever flit through my mind as she tears across the room.

"Lily, don't kill me!" I shout, putting out my hands in a defensive manner.

"Did that redhead get to you? Are you a zombie? A clone? Who are you?" Her questions come out rapid fire, attacking me from all angles.

"No, the redhead didn't get to me, I was saved by a friend. And I'm still completely normal, well, as normal as I've always been. Please do not attack me," I say, hoping the child will find my story fit to believe.

She doesn't, and I end up getting a pink wand getting smashed into my head.

"Ow! Hey, cut that out, you little gremlin!" I growl, picking up the small child and tossing her onto my bed.

She squeals and giggles as she flies through the air, laughing when she finally lands on the bed.

"Okay, you're the real Beckett," she concludes with a large smile.

"You think?" I grumble, rubbing my head where she had hit me. "I could've told you that much, you didn't have to try and take my head off."

She shrugs. "Well, I've got better things to be doing," she says with a sigh.

"What, harassing me with a pink wand isn't on the top of that list?" I ask, mildly agitated. That thing must've been made with really hard plastic if it stings this much.

"Nope," she says, dashing out of my room.

"Crazy child," I mutter, flopping down onto my bed.

I sigh and think about recent events. The killings, the attacks, all of it. I'm still shocked that Celia's The Masquerader, but it does help to explain the changes in her behavior. I'm curious about the world she's from, but more than that, I'm concerned for her safety.

If you really want to know more, meet me at the park at six tomorrow. She had said those words as if her offer were something I could politely decline, but for me, there's only one thing to do. I was in too deep the moment The Masquerader first saved my life. There's no turning back for me.

The gentle clatter of plates and soft voices lulls me into my own world. It's such a comforting and familiar sound to me. There's something about cafés that puts my high-strung nerves to rest.

One of my favorite things to do is sit at a café and read and people-watch, it always has been. It's so peaceful. Just take a book and order a nice iced coffee and a cinnamon roll, and everything is golden. It's the perfect recipe for going off into your own world.

"So, when are you expecting?" I hear someone ask.

"Next month."

I lift my head and see two women sitting a few tables away. One is petite and quite excited, the other has a bulging stomach and looks tired as all get out.

"What will you name her?" the petite woman asks, her voice filling with unnecessary amounts of excitement and anticipation.

"Katie," the pregnant woman announces proudly.

"Oh, how wonderful!" the woman squeals.

"Really? Katie?" I mutter to myself. "How unoriginal. I would give my daughter a foreign name, not one that belongs to seemingly every American girl." I already know the name I would choose for my daughter. One of the most beautiful names I've ever heard. Corrine. Ever since I was a child, I've been captured by the beauty of that name. It sounds beautiful and elegant, as I know my daughter would be. It's a name fit for a princess.

I feel a twinge of pain upon thinking that word. *Princess.* I used to be one. I used to be engaged, but all of that was taken from me and it makes my blood boil.

Ding!

The sound of the door opening for a group of college kids snaps me out of my thoughts. The doorbell brings my attention to the door and the clock just above it that reads half past five.

"I should get going," I say to no one in particular. I close my book and throw my empty cup and paper plate into the garbage, making my way to the door, hearing the soft jingle of the doorbells on my way out.

I sigh gently, closing my eyes to let the sound of the café linger in my mind a little longer.

"Celia!"

I jump, spinning around with a confused look. It's not a voice I've ever heard before, and it belongs to a girl I've never met.

She's about my same height and age, with walnut colored hair that's cut short and messy, like she rolled out of bed only a few seconds ago. Her skin is devoid of blemishes, like it's made of porcelain, and her blue eyes sparkle as if she's always smiling.

The girl is dressed head to toe in black, only making her eyes more noticeable than they already are. Her black skinny jeans are torn and her V-neck shirt is tight and snug, showing off her hourglass figure.

I'm stunned. Looking at her is like looking at an edgier, blue-eyed version of myself.

"Who are you?" I ask in bewilderment.

"Isn't it obvious?" she asks in a sassy tone. "I'm your daughter."

"Ha, that's rich! I don't have a daughter," I tell her.

"Not in this life." She gives me a knowing grin that freezes me.

"Who are you?" I ask again, this time my voice is menacing. My eyes have become cautious and cold.

"Like I told you before, I'm your daughter," she says.

.

"Look, Kid, I'm a virgin. Now, I don't know if you understand the way things work, but in order to have a child, you kind of have to lose that status," I tell her with a voice full of agitation and condescension.

"Again, rephrasing what I said before, not in this life you haven't. Jeez, do you even listen?" she asks, becoming annoyed.

"I didn't sleep with anyone in my past lives either! I think I would remember something like that. Besides, I've been too busy in the past for anything of the sort."

"God," the girl sighs, rubbing her temples. "I guess I have to spell it out for you. I am from an alternate universe, where you had plenty of time, along with a daughter. That's me. And when shit hit the fan and everything blew up, I escaped instead of you." She says every word slowly and clearly, as if she were talking to a complete idiot.

"Do you honestly expect me to believe that?" I ask in astonishment.

"Yes. You act as if out of everything you've seen and heard that this takes the cake," she says.

She sighs and looks tired and unimpressed when she sees the disbelieving look on my face.

"Look, I can prove it."

"How?" I question suspiciously.

"You know what you're going to name your daughter if you ever have one, right?"

I nod.

"Okay. Now, I'm going to tell you my name, and it's going to be the same one as your future daughter's. The most beautiful name you can think of."

"Kid, I don't have time for a parlor trick," I say in agitation.

"Hey, shut up, it's not a parlor trick," the girl snaps. "This is something you've never told anyone, at least not in this world. So how the hell would I know it if I wasn't your daughter?"

"Fine. But do it quickly, I've got somewhere to be," I say.

The girl lets out a steady breath and draws another in, as if to give herself the strength and courage needed to pull this off.

"My name is Corinne."

I stop. Stop moving, stop breathing, stop everything. For a moment, my world goes black as shock smacks me into nothingness.

"Hey, are you okay?" someone asks. I can't identify the voice, I can't even tell up from down anymore.

I stumble, struggling to keep my balance.

"I think you should sit down."

Warm hands guide me down to the curb where I slowly regain my senses.

"How is this possible?" I ask in a half daze.

"You of all people should know how possible this is," a familiar voice says. The voice is warm and gentle, belonging to the one and only, Ben Milton.

"Ben!" Corinne squeals, throwing her arms around his neck.

"Cor," he says with a grin, hugging the girl. He must know her pretty well to look at her with such caring eyes.

"So, Celia, I see you've met Corrine," Ben says, taking a seat next to me.

"Ben, what are you– How do you–" I stop, unable to finish either of my questions, my brain at a loss for words.

"In order to keep things short and simple, I know everything. I know about your past lives, that you're The Masquerader, about your ongoing battle with Mesmer Amar and how you lost everything you loved, including your fiancé. How do I know about all of this? Well, let's just say that you and I knew each other a long time ago. Now that we've covered that, let's go meet up with Beckett, we have to talk about strategies," Ben says.

"Whoa, whoa, whoa. Wait a minute," I command. "I'm not getting you involved in this too. Beckett didn't really have much of a choice, but you two do, so walk away."

"Celia, we're like you," Ben says. "We're stuck in this never-ending battle too, forever dancing in this eternal masquerade. We don't have a choice either."

"This is a horrible idea," I mutter to myself. "But fine, let's go. I don't like being late."

I arrive at the park a few minutes early so as to make sure I'm not late.

I sit on the bench feeling nervous and high-strung. Every time I hear a twig snap I spin my head, expecting to find some psychotic, hell-bent alien.

Off in the distance I hear voices, one voice in particular. I hear Celia's voice.

"I said no! Call me by my name!" she says, her voice poisonous and furious.

"But it's what I've always called you!" a girl shrieks indignantly.

"Great, now ask me if I care!" Celia's voice drips with sarcasm, a tone I'm all too familiar with.

"Why are you so mean?" the girl asks. "I don't remember her being this mean, do you?"

"Yeah, I do." It's Ben's voice.

What is Ben doing here? I wonder.

"Really? Hmm, it must just be me then," the girl sighs in resignation.

The group comes into my line of vision and I'm stunned by what I see. The girl who was arguing with Celia looks exactly like her, aside from her sparkling blue eyes. It's uncanny how similar they look. It's like the other girl is a slightly younger, edgier version of Celia Walters.

"Hey, Beckett!" Ben says, greeting me with his normal smile.

"Um, hi?" My words come out more like a question. I'm confused as to why Ben, and Celia's doppelganger, are here.

"Sorry if we're late, Beckett," Celia says. "I was on my way to meet you when I ran into these two. Turns out they already know everything, because they're like me." For a minute the world seems to stop spinning. Ben Milton, the guy I've known almost my entire life, my best friend, is in fact, a time travelling, dimension jumping alien. I can't wrap my head around that.

"Whoa, take a seat, dude," Ben says. "You look as pale as Edward Cullen."

"You're an alien?" I ask dazedly.

"Ish," he replies. "That's why I decided to crash your meeting. And now for the introductions. Beckett, this is Corinne. Corinne, this is my best friend, Beckett Halverson."

"It's nice to meet you," Corrine says, shaking my hand.

"Yeah, you too. How do you know Ben and Celia?" I inquire.

"Ben and I go a long way back, I've known him all my life. And as for Celia, well, I'm her daughter."

Celia's eyes bulge as she chokes on nothing, giving the girl a deadly glare.

"I TOLD YOU TO STOP SAYING THAT!" she screams, wringing her hands. "I don't care what your name is! I am not your mother! I, me, Celia Walters, born 1998, did not give birth to a child! You are the daughter of a different Celia Walters!"

"Denial is the first stage," Corinne says to Ben and me, causing us to chuckle. I'm mostly confused so I simply go with it, not really knowing what else to do.

"Alright, everybody shut up!" Celia commands, and we obey. "We're here to explain things to Beckett, so someone start."

"I think if you just did the talking it would help to avoid one massive headache," I say to Celia, looking at her with pleading eyes

"Alright, then I'll start from the beginning." She goes on to tell me her story. It sounds like some sort of twisted fairytale, taking place in a faraway land.

"Thousands of years ago, I had my first life. I was born into a universe where all the planets contained intelligent life forms. The planets we call gas giants were solid, and the life on every planet was the same. Everyone looked like normal people, no slime and antennae. It was a completely different universe, yet one so similar.

"I was born into the Royal Family of Mercury, the daughter of King Jasper and Queen Theresa Walters, and the older sister of Prince Peter of Mercury.

"I grew up seeking knowledge and wisdom, that's all I wanted to do with my life, but my parents wanted me to rule. I despised the idea.

I hated politics, but my parents saw that I was the only one who was smart and cunning enough to beat the insurgents that were rising up on each planet. I knew as well as they did, that I was the only one who could basically save the universe, but I still refused the crown.

"It wasn't solely because of my hatred for politics, it was also because of Mesmer Amar, the Prince of Saturn. Even back then, Mesmer was lecherous, perverted, possessive, misogynistic, deceptive, and a downright creep. He loves only himself, he always has, but he was great at making people think otherwise.

"He was hypnotic, everything about him was mesmerizing, thus the name Mesmer. He drew people in like moths to a flame. Only myself and a handful of others saw him for what he really was, a monster.

"He wanted to rule in chaos, with absolute power, and me by his side, but not because he cared for me. It was because I was the one thing he couldn't have, the one thing out of his reach, and it drove him crazy. It only got worse when I refused his proposal and became engaged to the Prince of Jupiter.

"He was the finest warrior the universe had ever seen, he was a combat god. That's why the universe dubbed him The Celestial Warrior. Fighting was in his blood, it was part of his power. Everyone in the Royal Families had a gift that went beyond human boundaries in order to protect their people. My power is electricity manipulation. Now, there are certain things I can do, like phasing or teleporting through shadows, which everyone in the Royal Families could do.

"I used to think that it was the greatest gift, these special powers, but they turned out to be our biggest curse. No one could fathom that someone would betray their family, their people and their home, not until Mesmer Amar. His gift is what destroyed us.

"After I became engaged and word got out, Mesmer was furious. He came to see me one last time to try and change my mind, and when he couldn't, he cursed me using black magic. I'm physically unable to kill him, so there was almost nothing I could do when he rallied the insurgents in each planet.

"The easiest way to take out an army is to take out the leader, without whom it's just disorganized and chaotic, so that's exactly what he did. Mesmer was able to sweep across the universe, demolishing everything in his path to the Capitol Palace. It served as the universal embassy, where the rulers of the planets would gather to make big decisions and pass universal decrees. Mesmer destroyed the Capitol Palace, slaughtering everyone in it. He was unstoppable, because I could do nothing.

"For thousands of years I've been jumping from universe to universe, through different timelines, trying to find a way to solve this. The problem with jumping universes is that I have to start over as in infant each time I make the jump. My memories are lost until I'm about twenty. For some reason, they started coming back earlier this time. But no matter what, there's always one thing I can never remember. I can't remember anything about my fiancé, other than that-he was the Prince of Jupiter. I can't remember his name, what he looked like, or what he sounded like. Those memories never come back, but I always feel like something else is missing. Like there's a hole in my mind, but I can't even begin to think about what that might be. I think it's the only thing standing in the way of Mesmer's complete domination.

"If I don't stop him somehow, every parallel and alternate universe will be swallowed by the chaos of his reign. The problem is, I don't know how to stop him. The only leverage I have is that gap in my mind, I know that much. I'm the only person who knows where whatever Mesmer wants is. It's locked somewhere deep inside my head, so he needs me alive. And until I remember where it is, I won't be able to stop him. So, from my viewpoint, we're screwed."

She finishes her story with that dismal sentence, damning everything for the rest of eternity.

Everyone is quiet. The only noise is the sound of our breathing, even the crickets have stopped chirping, as if soaking in their impending doom.

"I know what he's after," Corrine says slowly, breaking the oppressive silence.

"What?" Celia looks at the girl with plain confusion.

"I know what Mesmer's after," she says. "He wants The Imperial Crystals."

"That makes so much sense." I can practically see the lightbulb turn on inside Celia's head as the gears start turning.

"Um, what are The Imperial Crystals?" I ask, feeling as lost as a child in a supermarket.

"The Imperial Crystals are the source of the Royal Families' powers," Celia explains. "If you were to combine all of the Crystals, you would create The Imperial Stone, the single most powerful object in the universe, in any universe. The Imperial Stone was broken into nine pieces which became the Imperial Crystals, and when put together, they create an unspeakable power. With The Imperial Stone, Mesmer would have the power to create and destroy worlds with a simple thought. He could re-write the very fabric of time itself, changing the past, present and future to fit his desires. It's too much power for one person to wield, that's why it was divided into nine pieces.

If Mesmer's after The Mercury Crystal, that means he has the other eight, and that's why he needs me. I'm the only one who knows where the Crystal is, I'm the one who hid it from him."

"So, where is it?" I ask with excitement.

"Beats me," she responds, shrugging her shoulders. "That information is locked away with those missing memories, and I have no idea how to get those back. So, like I said before, we're screwed."

"Looks like I know who to thank for pessimism," Corrine says sourly, earning a vicious glare from Celia.

"Wow, you two really *are* mother and daughter," I say. "You're just like Celia, right down to the bitter and angry part." Now I'm the one receiving the vicious look, and from both of them.

"I have my reasons for being bitter and angry," the two girls say in unison. They freeze with appalled looks and turn to each other.

"That never happens again," Celia commands.

"Agreed," Corrine says in response, still wearing a face of astonishment.

For a few moments, the two stay that way, staring at each other with unnerved looks until Ben finally speaks up.

"We need to find that Crystal," he says, staring at the boards of the table.

"We won't find it," Celia tells him. "I'm the one who hid it. It could be anywhere, on a different planet, in a different dimension even. Mesmer's been after it for thousands of years and he still hasn't found it. We won't find it either, not unless we somehow unlock that part of my mind and complete my fragmented being. That's the only way I'll remember where the Crystal is. That was my failsafe so Mesmer couldn't get it. As long as I'm stuck in this curse, I won't be able to get the Crystal for myself, or for him. If Mesmer wants the Crystal, he'll have to remove the spell, and if he does that, I'll be able to kill him."

Man, she's smart, I think while listening to her speak. I'm beginning to realize that Celia doesn't just plan a few steps ahead. She anticipates everything and plans at least ten steps ahead for each possible outcome. It's kind of scary how smart she is.

"Finding it may not be a guarantee, but we need to try. Otherwise we're just wasting time," Ben says, agitation growing in his voice.

"Fine, then I think I know where to start," Celia says, her eyes locking with Ben's. A silent understanding seems to pass between them and Ben nods solemnly.

"The first Masquerader crime scene."

"Whoa, crime scene?" I ask, stumbling over my words. "I'm not sure that's a good idea. Isn't that illegal? Won't it be guarded or something? They guard crime scenes, right?"

"No, you're a moron," Celia says plainly. "The police have taken everything of value from the place, why would they guard it? Besides, there are several other crime scenes the police are investigating, they won't be back at the first one for a while." There's a hint of pride in Celia's voice, and it unnerves me ever so slightly. "It happened on Nick Mallard's land, so it'll be no problem getting access to the scene. I'll be going over there sometime soon to start the landscaping, and I'll look for the Crystal then."

"When did you start working for Nick Mallard?" Ben asks with a puzzled look.

"When I killed a man in his backyard." That ends the conversation and no more questions are asked. The plan is set and we're all ready to carry it out.

"Well, as fun as this is, I have something I need to do," Celia says, suddenly getting up to leave. And just like that, the meeting over.

The air is cool. It's a pleasant night with a gentle breeze, the only disturbance is the spray of bullets and occasional release of electricity.

"Is this really the best you can do?" I ask, boredom finding its way to me. "This is pathetic." I step out of the shadows, my body crackling with electricity. I use the iron in the buildings around me to help me levitate, using the electricity to keep my body in the air.

"Line 'em up, boys! Let's take this bitch down!" a man yells, propping his gun up against a crumbling and charred wall, taking aim.

"Oh, do let's," I chuckle, and they open fire. Thousands of bullets part the air, making their way towards me.

The corner of my mouth tugs into an amused smile. I watch the bullets disintegrate before they can touch me, destroyed by the heat of the electricity coming off my body in waves.

"Well that was fun, but now it's my turn!" I drop to the ground, falling a few stories to a single knee. My fist pounds into the ground, sending out an electric shockwave to level everything in the area.

For a moment, all I see is blue and white, all I hear is the steady crackle of electricity, and then the buildings topple. The sounds of steel beams grinding together and mortar disintegrating, leaving bricks and stones to crumble, assault my ears.

I watch in awe as everything within a fifty-yard radius comes crumbling down, leaving nothing alive in the shock zone, nothing other than myself.

Maybe I went a little overboard, I think with a slight cringe.

"Well, aren't you impressive?" a cold hate-filled voice calls from a distance.

"Sylvia Trunnel, I was wondering when we'd meet on the field," I say, turning to face my old friend.

"I no longer go by that name, I am called Mesmeritus!" She lunges, brandishing her metal arm in the shape of a sword.

My whip uncoils from my arm and I use the grip to block her attack.

"I know, and I've already voiced my opinion about it. Honestly though, I don't think you could have chosen a name that screams 'desperate' more than that one."

She grabs a hidden blade and slashes it across my free arm, cutting through the leather jacket.

Blood oozes to the surface, warm and gooey, filling the air with a coppery scent.

"You cut my jacket. Now I'm *pissed*," I growl, stepping back. I flash my whip above my head, as if to strike, drawing her attention away from my other arm. I grab one of the rose-shaped throwing stars at my waist and throw it with expert skill.

The blade cuts through her side, blood spraying from the wound and spinning from the edges of the blade.

She howls in pain and then lunges once again, brandishing her sword and the dagger dripping with my blood.

I bend backward, my torso becoming almost parallel to the ground as I barely avoid getting my neck slashed.

As soon as the blades clear, I shoot upright with another throwing star attack. This one cuts the top of her shoulder.

Her eyes flick to the wound and then to me, her face a mix between a grimace and a snarl.

"You'll need more than a few small blades and a whip to walk out of here alive," Sylvia growls, readying her blades.

"I figured as much, you always say something like that," I say, allowing my whip to coil itself up my arm like the vines of a plant. I reach into the inner pockets of my jacket and pull out two daggers, each blade about ten inches. "That's why I brought these," I tell her, twirling the blades in my hands. "And what would Mesmer think of you giving me death threats? Last I checked, he still wants to rule happily ever after with me by his side. Looks like you've been friend-zoned." Those words paralyze her for a moment and I strike.

She barely dodges my attack, following it up with one of her own. I block the first blade, but the second cuts low, slashing across my upper thigh.

I grit my teeth and stumble backward. My body stings, blood dripping from my arm and now my leg. I try to use my injured limbs as little as possible, but that doesn't stop the throbbing pain caused by Sylvia's daggers. My thigh burns, like it was cut with acid instead of steel. I see spots for a second and then snap out of it. I need to pull myself together, my life is on the line here.

Sylvia attacks again, and I successfully block both her dagger and sword arm, shoving her back as I do so.

I hear an amused laugh and I stop cold.

"I do love a good cat fight, but don't be too hard on my dear princess. I don't want her too banged up, that part's for me."

"You bastard," I snarl, turning to face Mesmer Amar.

"I'll take the fight from here," he says, drawing his sword from his belt. His black eyes gleam with sadistic glee.

I don't say a word, I just charge.

He anticipates my attack and counters with one of his own. He slashes his sword through the air where I would have landed after my attack, but I drop to my knees and roll under his blade. I'm back on my feet in a flash and embed my knives into each of his shoulder blades.

Mesmer simply laughs as I pull the blades out and moves his shoulders in slow circles.

"You truly are sick and demented," I say watching blood dribble down the back of his black tailcoat.

"I find my sadomasochism to be a gift, not a sickness. Without it, I'd be racked only with pain, groaning face down in the dirt. But no, I find pleasure with the pain. It's the greatest gift I have." He smiles a wholly demented smile, a smile that belongs on Satan himself.

"You're sick like a dog. I'll do the humane thing and put you down!" I yell, going in for another attack.

"Come at me, Celia, and don't hold back," Mesmer murmurs.

"I won't."

He grins and tosses his sword aside, raising his arms as if he were basking in warm sunlight.

I tackle Mesmer, knowing that running him through will do no good. It would only give him pleasure and he would just heal the wound with black magic.

I kneel over his body, a dagger pressed against his paper-white throat.

Every cell in my body screams at me, telling me to slit his throat. To drag the blade across his skin, cutting through his flesh and windpipe, and watch him bleed, but my body won't respond to messages sent from my brain. It's as if something's intercepting and blocking those messages.

"What's the matter, Celia? I thought you said you wouldn't hold back?" Mesmer mocks, causing my blood to boil.

I grit my teeth and summon every ounce of willpower I have, but it's not enough. Pain ripples through my body like waves on a small pond, coating all my senses. My nerves are burning with agony, like every cell is on fire. I can't do it. I can't kill him, this curse is too strong.

"DAMNIT!" I shout, jumping to my feet. I throw my blade down beside his head, grazing his ear.

My breathing is heavy and labored from combating the spell over my body.

"Looks like you're all out of fight," Mesmer says, slowly rising to his feet, advancing on me.

I shake my head, trying to knock the fuzziness and black spots out of my vision.

"It's time you come back with me," Mesmer tells me, grabbing me by the lapels of my leather jacket and pulling me closer to him.

"Over my dead body," I snarl. I grab the side of his thumb and drop my elbow, locking his hand in place, so that when I take a quick step back, it jerks Mesmer along with me. As I lunge backward I thrust my hand upward, sending a firm palm strike to his nose. Blood splashes across his face, speckling his white skin with crimson flecks.

His hand lets go of me and clutches his nose as he stumbles backward. I reach down and pull my blades from the earth and run, bolting for the nearest shadow, and the moment my body is blanketed by darkness, I am gone.

I fall back against the side of my house. My body is racked with pain, turning my vision into a mix of red and black, blurring together.

How am I supposed to get to my room without someone noticing me? Amy's always up late, she's bound to see me. How am I going to pull this off? I ask myself.

I don't have an answer, I don't need one. All I need is one damn good lie. I have to get to my room. I'll be able to tend to my wounds there, and until then I'll just continue to bleed, and I'm losing too much blood. If I lose too much more, I'll be in a lot of trouble.

Let's get this over with, I think as I shove the door open.

No one is up, not even Amy. All the lights are out and the house is silent.

I let out a slow breath and my body is flooded with relief.

I stumble through the dark house, tripping up the stairs to my room, falling through the threshold. I barely manage to catch myself on my dresser, knocking everything off the top.

"Shit, that had to have woken someone up," I grumble.

I peel off my jacket, wincing as I do so. My arm is covered in blood, it drips down my forearm and hand. I turn on the lights and begin examining the wound. It starts at the top of my shoulder and slashes diagonally down to the middle of my bicep. It's deep, but not too deep, maybe a few millimeters into my arm, nothing I can't fix.

I use a belt to tourniquet my arm and sit down on my bed, planning my next move.

"Hey, Celia, where have you–" Amy stops mid-sentence, looking at me with horror. "What happened?" she shrieks.

"Amy, I need you to forget this okay?" I tell her. "I need you to pretend that you didn't see anything and walk away."

"Have you started street fighting?" Amy suddenly asks.

"What? No, where did you even come up with that?"

"Well, you've been out late a lot, and then suddenly developed badass fighting skills. It just kind of makes sense," she says.

"Amy, I wish I could tell you what happened, but I'm trying to keep you safe, and that's all you need to know. I'm trying to keep you safe, I'm trying to keep Mom and Dad safe, so please, forget this happened," I plead.

"Well, we don't have any real stitching material, so I'll go get fishing line, a needle, pliers to bend the needle some, and a few towels," Amy says, ticking the items off with her fingers.

"Amy, I said–"

"Yeah, I'm not listening, so stop talking," she tells me. "You obviously need help right now, so I'll help you with no questions asked. You said that you're trying to keep me safe, and I believe you, so I won't dig around. But I'm also not going to let you bleed in your room and half- ass stitch yourself together. So, stay here for a few minutes while I go get everything." With that she marches out of the room, closing the door gently on her way out.

I sigh, knowing that once Amy has decided to do something, there's no stopping her, but I can't let her get involved in this. It's bad enough that I got Beckett into this mess, I can't get my little sister into it as well.

"Here we are," Amy says, walking into my room, her arms filled with items to patch me up. "Okay, you're not going to enjoy this, but you're going to have to deal with it. After all, it was your decision to start street fighting, not mine." She laughs a little at her own comment and I smile, amused by her quirky personality.

"Let's get this over with," I say, preparing myself for the storm of pain that would soon be upon me.

I cringe as she presses a wet washcloth against the gash in my arm. Slowly, she sponges away most of the blood surrounding the wound, and then puts pressure on the actual cut itself.

"I brought you this," Amy says, handing me a pencil.

"What the hell do you want me to do with this?" I ask. "Draw you a picture?"

"No, dumbass, I want you to bite it," she tells me. "You're going to need it if you don't want to wake up Mom and Dad by yelling a stream of profanities at me."

"Point taken," I say, taking the pencil and putting it between my teeth, clamping them down on it, clenching my jaw. I let out a deep breath through my nose, ready for the stitching to begin.

I wince. My shoulder burns with a searing pain. The skin around the cut feels as if it were being washed in acid, the edges of the wound sizzling with pain.

My teeth dig into the pencil as I try not to scream, the pain breaking through all of my nerves. A flurry of curses spills into my mind, screaming inside the walls of my head.

The fishing line pulls through layers of skin led by the sharp needle. The tugging sensation is woven through my skin surrounding the wound, webbing a dull ache through my arm.

Black spots crowd my vision, my head feels light and fuzzy as I stumble into a pain-filled haze. I can't find it in myself to breathe, I'm slipping into a state of pain-induced shock. It's the only thing I can feel or think of, it overrides everything, including my instinct to survive.

"Breathe, Celia," Amy says, commanding me in a stern voice, but she sounds so distant, like a fading dream.

"Celia, snap out of it!" There's a loud crack as Amy's hand whips across my face.

I take in a shocked breath, sitting in disbelief at the fact that my sister just slapped me.

"Well, that worked," she says cheerily as she ties off the fishing line and cuts it, completing the sealing of the wound.

"Thanks," I say, breathing heavily. The light feeling slowly leaves my body as my breathing becomes more normal and consistent. "I can do the rest."

"Alright." Amy makes her way to the door, and then stops with her hand on the doorknob, turning to look at me. "Think about all of this before you get into another street fight. By the looks of you, whatever you're waist deep in is dangerous. The fact that you want to keep me as far away from it as you possibly can only proves that. But if this burden ever gets to be too much for you, know that you can always come to me. If you ever need my help, I'm here. Whether it's to stitch you up, cause some sort of distraction or fake an alibi, I'm here with no questions asked." With that she leaves, softly closing the door behind her.

"I'm not street fighting!" I shout as she leaves. I hear no response other than her laughter as it slowly grows further away. I smile, grateful for my obnoxious sister.

I stand in a pitch-black room, the only sound is the beating of my frantic heart.

"Calm down, Beck, it's just a dream," I tell myself as I take deep breaths, trying to bring my heartrate down to a normal level.

I hear a new sound. It's Celia's voice, and I can tell she's furious.

"I will die before I stand by your side! Don't you realize that you have taken everything from me?! My family, my friends, my fiancé, they're all gone! You've condemned me to misery and isolation, isn't that enough?" Her voice is torn between anguish and despair, and I hurt for her. I feel her pain as if it were my own, and it's crippling. It makes my body feel weak and like my vital organs are being crushed. I want to curl into a ball and stop existing.

"But don't you remember my promise?" Another voice speaks from the darkness. This voice is dark and smooth, like rich, black velvet. It's cold and seductive, enchanting me. I want to hear him speak more, mesmerized by the sound of his voice, yet I also want to rip my ears off of my skull. His voice conjures a drowsy haze, shattered by cold rage and hatred. It's the voice of Mesmer Amar, the man responsible for all of Celia's suffering, and it makes me sick.

"I promised that I would always find you. It doesn't matter where you hide, the tortured spirit inside you will always call to me. It is your curse, Celia, and so I will always find you." His words are cold, they freeze me, grasping me with a frosty hand.

"Are you so quick to forget my *promise?" Celia responds, her voice crackling with rage. "I promised that I would end you, and I* will. *I never break a promise."*

"We will see."

Light blazes, I can't see anything but white.

I'm awake, gasping for air, my breath coming out in ragged puffs.

"What was that?" I ask, my mind spinning from my dream. I sit in my confused haze for what seems like forever, unable to form a coherent thought until my alarm clock starts to scream, jarring me from my daze.

I sigh and roll out of bed, stumbling to my dresser. I pull out whatever I touch first, not ready for another day of school, not with that disturbing dream haunting my consciousness.

No matter what I do, I can't shake the sleep from my body, even as I stumble through the halls on my way to Calculus. I still feel like only half of my brain is on. My footsteps feel heavy and slow, bringing me at a crawling speed to the classroom.

If I'm half awake, Celia must be almost asleep. She's slumped over her desk with her head buried in her arms. The only thing signifying that she's awake is her fingers that drum on her desk.

"You look like shit," I say, collapsing into my seat.

"Mmm," is her only response, her voice scratchy and sleepy. She lifts her head, her eyes shying from the bright lights of the classroom. "Class hasn't started yet, has it?" she asks, blinking rapidly at the harsh light.

"No, we've got a few minutes left," I tell her. "You don't look so good, Celia, did you get any sleep at all last night?"

"I slept for about an hour," she says proudly, flashing me a tired smile.

"Vigorous piano playing?" I ask, hoping it was nothing bad.

"More like vigorous getting my ass cut into bits in a fight for my life," she says, rubbing her shoulder and then wincing.

"What's wrong with your shoulder?" I inquire, studying her face.

"Huh? Oh, I've just got a scratch," she says.

"Yeah, I'm not really buying that," I tell her.

"It irritates me that you can tell when I'm lying," she grumbles, her head dropping back into her arms.

"I can tell when anyone's lying, it's like my superpower," I say nonchalantly.

"It's still irritating," she says.

"So, what'd you do to your shoulder?"

"It got cut." Her response is curt, attempting to close the conversation.

"How'd you cut it?"

"With a knife."

"Why'd you do that?"

"I didn't."

"So, who cut you?"

"Some psychotic, ginger bitch."

"Why'd she do that?"

"God, Beckett, enough with the questions!" she says, covering her ears. "I'm too tired for this, ask me tomorrow."

"Head up, Walters! Class is starting," Mr. Lawrence barks, entering the room.

"Ugh, can I just go to the office?" Celia asks, giving him a bored look.

"If you want to go for bad behavior, be my guest," he says, his voice dripping with malice.

"Sweet. You're an awful teacher and I hate you. Bye!" She grabs her books and backpack and joyfully leaves the room.

And suddenly she's bursting with energy, I think, smiling to myself. *She really does enjoy pissing people off.*

"What are you smiling at, Halverson?" Lawrence snaps.

"Nothing," I say, but the smile still sticks on my face, only washing away once the lesson begins and my mind is dragged elsewhere.

"How was school, Beck?" my mom asks, coming up to hug me.

"Boring. Why can't it be Friday?" I ask with a sigh, wrapping my arms around my mother.

"At least you have a short week," she says cheerily. "You only have to go to school tomorrow and then you have off for parent teacher conferences."

"Oh yeah, that's right!" I say, perking up. "I forgot about that, thanks, Mom."

"You're welcome, now go get your homework done."

"Hello, this is Celia Walters," I say, picking up my phone.

"Hey, Celia, it's Nick. My family and I are going out of town tonight, are you able to stop by a couple times a day to keep things in check and feed the animals?"

"Yeah, if it's okay with you, I could just stay at your house until you get back. That way I could take care of the animals and finish working around the house."

"I'm fine with that," he says, his voice cheery. "Thank you, Celia."

"No problem, Nick. Have fun on your vacation." I hang up the phone and set it on my dresser, letting out a deep breath as I will the transformation to take place. It doesn't burn the way it did at first. Instead, it feels like I'm being encased in warm goo, my body relaxing as I melt into the monster created by pain and a promise I'm determined to keep.

I throw my notebook across the room, thoroughly aggravated. I can't think, not about school or homework. I'm worried. I know that Celia's out there right now, fighting a battle she feels she has to shoulder on her own, and she's injured. She tried to downplay it, but I could see that it was wearing her down.

"That's it, I've gotta do something," I say with determination. I grab my phone and shoot a text to Ben, telling him to get Corrine and meet me in the Warehouse District.

If there's anything I've learned about Celia, it's that she doesn't like to involve others in her affairs, especially when it gets dangerous. There's only one place that Celia can keep everyone safe and still fight her battles, and that's the Warehouse District, the place where I had first been saved by The Masquerader.

"Mom, I'm going out, I don't know when I'll be back," I yell through the house, dashing out the door before anyone can stop me.

The wind whips at my clothes as I speed through the night, my eyes straining in the darkness. The headlights from my motorcycle give me some light, although not that much, but that doesn't stop me from zipping down the road.

I hope Ben got my text and that he chose to act on it, but even if he didn't, I have to help Celia. Whether she wants me to or not, with or without backup, I have to go.

"Celia!" I shout as I run through the abandoned district. I don't hear or see anything out of the ordinary, and I stop, feeling perplexed. "Maybe I was wrong," I wonder aloud, making my way back to my motorcycle.

"Beckett, get the hell out of here!"

"Celia?" My voice rings through the empty warehouses. "Celia, where are you?"

"Behind you, and you need to leave."

I jump, spinning around to see Celia. She's a mess. She's bleeding all over, and there are other random blood spatters on her clothes.

"I'm not leaving," I tell her defiantly. "I told you that I wasn't going to let you do this alone, and that goes beyond planning. You're getting pulverized out here, you need help."

"That's touching, but you *really* need to get out of here. These wounds aren't as bad as they look, and I heal quickly, so it's okay. Now get out of here, it's not safe." As if on cue there's a flashing light and I'm thrown to the side, hitting the ground hard.

When I open my eyes, the first thing I see are two crossed swords, the second is Corrine with a Celia-esque snarl on her face. She pushes back with her blade and our assailant goes flying.

"I'd advise you not to cross swords with the daughter of a genius and a combat god, because I *will* kill you, you redheaded, psycho bitch," the young girl snarls. She spins her blades expertly, slicing the air in a menacing fashion.

I roll onto my side with a groan and am somewhat dismayed by what I see.

I wasn't the only one thrown to the side by the blast, but I was the only one to crash into the ground. Ben had caught Celia, and now he holds her close, their eyes locked and foreheads almost touching. Her arms are wrapped tightly around his neck, both are breathing hard.

"Beckett, get Celia out of here," Ben says, his eyes never leaving hers. "Take her somewhere safe and text me your location." He stands up and gingerly sets Celia on her feet.

"Alright, Ben, let's play." Corrine smiles at him, a gleeful, maniacal smile bordering on sadistic.

"Come on, Celia, let's go." I grab her by the hand and we run. "Take the helmet," I say, handing her my black motorcycle helmet.

"Why do I have to wear this?" Celia asks in an offended tone.

"Because if we crash, your brain is the one worth saving," I state simply, revving the engine and peeling away.

The sudden speed throws Celia off balance and her arms shoot around my torso, drawing herself closer to me. I grit my teeth, fighting the smile that wants to creep onto my lips.

I can't feel this way, I think, mentally scolding myself. *Celia belongs with my best friend, I know that now.* I think back to the image in my mind of Ben holding Celia in his arms. The way his eyes stuck to her, the worried and caring look on his face. I can't forget it. It's burned into my mind and it hurts my heart, but that's the way it has to be.

"Go to Nick Mallard's," Celia says suddenly, moving her lips close to my ear to avoid shouting. I clench my teeth harder to fight the shiver that threatens to run down my spine. "He lives just a few miles off County Road A. His address is two, six, four, nine, seven, Anderson Road."

I sigh in relief. I know how to get to Anderson Road, it's just going to be a matter of finding the right house.

It wasn't as hard as I thought it would be. Nick's house is the last one in the valley, tucked away in the woods. I hadn't noticed how secluded the house is when Celia had brought me here a few days ago, I was too focused on her. I remember the thought of even mild seclusion had scared me at first, but now I'm grateful for the house hidden in the trees, hiding us from our enemies.

I bring the bike to a stop, getting off first and then helping Celia do the same, her movements restricted by her wounds.

"No one's home. The family is on vacation, so you can go right on in," Celia tells me, handing me a small house key.

I take it and open the door, helping Celia inside. It seems like every time she moves it puts her in pain, her face contorting with every step.

"I texted Ben where we are, but I don't know when they'll rendezvous with us," I say, assisting her to the couch.

"They'll be here any minute," she says, leaning back and letting out a deep breath. As if on cue, the living room is swallowed in lines of blue light, weaving together to form an orb. When the light disperses, Ben and Corrine stand in the living room, breathless and beat up. Corrine looks like she's been through hell in just this single night. She looks more than physically hurt, she looks emotionally shaken and furious, like she's drowning in pain and is pissed about it.

"You two managed to survive, that's good." Celia's voice is tired and worn out, expressing nothing.

"Yeah, we almost had Sylvia, but then Mesmer got involved," Ben explains. Corrine merely stands there, shaking slightly, her face stony and cold.

"I thought the daughter of a combat god would have easily been able to defeat those two," Celia says, irritation strung in her voice.

"It's more complicated than you think," Corrine says quietly.

"Isn't it always?" Celia asks disgustedly. "I should have stayed. I could have fought him."

"Celia, not even Corrine could kill him, and she doesn't have your certain disadvantages," Ben says defensively, anger rising in his voice.

"No, but she does have her own disadvantages, doesn't she?" Celia snaps. "It's always a real bitch when your feelings get in the way, isn't it?"

"You would know," the young girl responds, rage blazing in her eyes.

"No matter how much it hurt, I've always done what I needed to do. So, no, I wouldn't know," Celia says, her voice dripping with hostility.

"Bullshit!" Corrine yells, electricity crackling around her body. "If you would have just gone with Mesmer to begin with, we wouldn't be in this mess! That was the logical solution. You could have protected everyone you cared about, but you couldn't do it, because you were in love with someone else. Your feelings got in the way of what was best for everyone else! You were selfish and now we're all paying for it!"

Celia just stares at the girl dumbfounded, shock in her wide eyes. I expect her to give a snarky response, but she doesn't, she continues to stare at the girl.

"How did you do that?" Celia asks suddenly. "How did you manipulate electricity? You shouldn't be able to do that. You've got your fathers inhuman speed and reflexes, his combat skills, you have *his* Royal Gift. Why do you have mine as well? That isn't possible."

"Well, obviously it is," Corrine snaps. "And your son has neither of your abilities, he's got one of his own. I guess your kids aren't what you expected, learn to live with it."

"I have a son?" Celia asks, shock becoming even more prominent than the anger on her face.

"Yeah, like I said, learn to live it." Corrine then storms outside, leaving the air behind her thick with tension.

"I'll go check on her," Ben says, starting to leave.

"No, take care of Celia's wounds," I tell him.

"But, Beck–"

"Ben, just do it," I say, somewhat in defeat. "Corrine needs some time to calm down, give her some space."

"Alright," he sighs, making his way to Celia. "Let's get you fixed up, huh?" He picks her up and carries her to the bathroom and then grabs several items from the closet across the hall. I'm not sure how he knows where things are, but I don't care. I have only one thought, I need to leave.

Quietly, I slip out the door and head for my motorcycle, when a small voice stops me.

"You're leaving, aren't you?" Corrine asks.

"Yeah, I don't really belong in your guys' world, I just kind of stumbled in by accident. I figured I should leave before I totally screw something up," I tell her.

"You're wrong," she tells me. "You're in this world for a reason, that reason is merely obscured from your sight at the moment."

"Well then, please enlighten me, because I don't know what to do," I admit miserably.

"It's not my place to so do." Her voice is resigned, and she looks worn out and sad. "Look, if you leave, at least say goodbye, especially to Celia. She's never gotten to say a proper goodbye to anyone she's cared about, and she doesn't need any more unspoken words."

"You've never gotten to say a proper goodbye either, have you?" I ask cautiously.

"No, I haven't. In my world, my family was killed and I was the one who got away, not Celia. I think that's why Mesmer's after me. I'm just like Celia, we think in the exact same way. Mesmer thinks I might know where the Crystal is, and me looking almost identical to my mom is only a bonus for him. He figured he couldn't seduce the Crystal out of her so he might as well try with me." Corrine's blue eyes are sad, heartbroken even.

"He hurt you pretty badly, didn't he? I mean beyond being oppressive in your life," I ask, studying the girl's face. The muscle in her jaw jumps at my words, her body beginning to shake once again.

"He was different when I met him, or at least he did a good job pretending to be. He was this strange, beautiful man from a different time and place. His beauty bewitched me. He was kind and caring, with a heart seemingly of gold, and I fell for him. I loved him and I trusted him, and then he destroyed everything I cared about. The bitch of it all is that no matter what I do, I can't forget him, who he was when we met. Even if that's never who he truly was, I can't forget it." She runs her hands through her hair in a stressed manner, clenching them at the nape of her neck.

"We don't really have much of a say in who we love," I say, my voice filled with compassion for the young girl. I strongly sympathize with her. "But we do have a say, however, in how we let it affect us. We can let it hurt and destroy us, we can rise above it and let it make us stronger, or we can suppress it and run from it."

"So, you choose the last option, huh?" Corrine asks, her eyes meeting mine.

"Yeah, I guess I do." I can't keep the shame out of my voice.

"Then I guess this is goodbye." Corrine pulls me into a hug, wrapping her arms around me in a strong embrace. She holds onto me tightly, sighing sadly into my shoulders and I find myself folding my arms around her. I rest my cheek on the top of her head and clench my eyes shut. It hurts, saying goodbye to this girl I've only briefly known, more than it makes sense to.

"Good luck, Corrine," I tell her as I pull away from the hug and take a step back.

"There's no such thing," she says bitterly, turning her back to me. She halts her movements for a moment and then looks back over her shoulder, her sparkling blue eyes locking with mine. *Her eyes are so blue, they kind of look like mine,* I think for moment before my attention is captured by her voice.

"You know, I'm not the only one who's never gotten a proper goodbye," she says thoughtfully. "You should give your parting words to the others as well before you leave." With saying that, she disappears into the same blue lights that brought her here.

I assume she's gone to hide somewhere inside, maybe to watch me and make sure I carry out her command.

With a sigh, I make my way back into the house.

Ben sits on the couch, staring at the floor with an intensely blank expression.

"Hey, Ben, I'm gonna head out," I tell him.

"What?" His head snaps up and his eyes pierce mine. "You can't leave, we need you!"

"You guys don't need me. I'm just an ordinary guy, I'm of no use to you. Besides, I have plenty of faith in the three of you. Oh, and here, this belongs to you." I slip my leather jacket off my back and hold it out to him.

"It's yours, Beck," he says, pushing my hand back towards my body. "I gave it to you because I wanted you to have it, that's not going to change. That jacket belongs to you."

I sigh softly and slide the jacket back on, my eyes never leaving those of my best friend.

"It's been fun," I say, extending my hand. "You're the best friend anyone could ask for."

Ben ditches the hand and goes for a hug with bone-crushing pressure.

"You too, Beck. And if I don't come back, tell Lily in a nice way. Tell her I went down fighting bad guys. I want her to remember me as a hero and not hate me for leaving her. Tell her that I'm sorry, and that no matter what, she'll always be my princess."

His words choke me up, making it hard to breathe in steady breaths.

"I will," I promise, holding my best friend tightly.

"Take care of yourself, Beckett."

"You too, Ben."

He lets me go and walks away, leaving me standing by the couch, trying to gather the courage for what I have to do next.

I don't know where Celia is, but I have a good guess. I hear soft piano music coming from the porch. Somehow, I know it's Chopin, and there's only one person I know who listens to Chopin religiously.

"So, is this your normal stargazing ritual?" I ask, coming up behind her.

"Hm? No, normally I like to watch the stars in silence, but I've been feeling real homesick lately," she responds, staring sadly at the stars.

Looking at the pain on her face breaks my heart. I want to make that pain disappear. I would do anything she asked me to do, simply to see her smile.

"Homesick, huh?" I ask, resting my elbows on the porch railing, mirroring the posture of the girl beside me. "Why are you feeling homesick?"

"It'll be my birthday soon," she says. "My father would always throw a huge masquerade ball to celebrate it. I've always loved dancing, as well as masquerades, my father only found it fitting to celebrate with both. They called it Mercury Ball. It was a widely celebrated event. People looked forward to it every year, and they would cross the universe to attend, rich and poor alike, it was wonderful. When my brother Peter started composing music, it was played at the Ball. I guess that's why I'm listening to Chopin, it reminds me of Peter's music." She smiles sadly, no doubt thinking of the younger brother she thought the world of and vice versa. "I miss the balls and masquerades. I miss dancing. I guess I'm just waiting for my partner to show up, I mean, what's a masquerader without someone to dance with?" Celia asks with a sarcastic grin.

"You have a partner, you simply have to ask him to dance," I tell her.

"What'd you mean?" she asks, turning to me with furrowed eyebrows, confusion riddling her face.

"Just say, 'Ben, come here, I want to dance with you,' or something like that. He's smart, he'll catch on. Corrine was asking him if he remembered you being so mean, so he obviously remembers you."

"What are you talking about? Why would I want to dance with Ben? It's not like that between him and me, we're like family."

"Look, you don't have to spare my feelings. I know that Ben is really important to you and that you're equally important to him. I can see it in the way that you look at each other."

"As I said before, we're like family, of course we're important to each other," she reiterates. "Beckett, what is this about?"

"Come on, Celia, you're too damn smart and observant to not know how I feel about you, but I can't let the way I feel screw things up. Ben is amazing, and you don't deserve anything less than that," I tell her, trying to keep the sadness out of my voice. "I have been a jerk to you for almost twelve years, and while I was being an asshole, Ben wasn't. He got to know you, he became your friend and someone you could trust. He saw through that cold wall you put up and saw you for who you truly are, whereas I couldn't. He's always been there for you, through everything. And I know that there are obstacles between you right now, but there always have been, and if you two managed to overcome them once, you can do it again. You two are kind of star-crossed lovers, it's been woven into the fabric of the universe itself.

"God, I wish I had even the slightest chance with you, but I don't," I sigh. "He's from your world, Celia, we all know that. You can't remember who he was to you, and I don't think it's a coincidence that you can't remember who your fiancé was, or what he even looked like. All the pieces are there, you simply have to put them together."

"Beckett–"

"It makes sense, Celia," I say, my voice soft and gentle. "Don't fight the one thing in all of this that makes sense.

"You know, truth be told, I'm not entirely happy about it, because I'm crazy about you. I'm always thinking about you, always hoping that in the end, you and I can be together, but I guess that's just not in the cards. And yeah, I guess it sucks, but I'll be damned if you lose your fiancé again, especially if it's because of me." The words come out of my mouth with more conviction than I thought they would, and I realize how deeply I feel for her. I realize how strong my feelings must be in order for me to let her go so that she can be happy. Even if it breaks my heart and fills my chest with blood, forcing my lungs to collapse. It may hurt just to breathe knowing she's with someone else, but I'll take each painful breath until my heart and lungs give out, knowing she's finally happy, because that's what love is.

"So, this is goodbye," I say sadly. "It was truly an honor knowing you, Celia Walters, Princess of Mercury." I take her hand and bring it to my lips, placing a gentle kiss on the back of her hand.

I turn and leave, walking away from her. Each step feels like I'm trudging through mud wearing lead shoes, but I take another step, and then another.

"Beckett, wait!" She reaches out to me, her soft hand clasping mine, and I can't help but turn around and pull her into my arms, wrapping one around her waist, leaving her hand clasped in the other.

Three words is all she says.

"Dance with me."

"Dance with me," I say, gripping him tightly, afraid that if I ease up he'll vanish.

"Celia–"

"I'm not doing this as some sort of consolation prize for your chivalry," I say, cutting Beckett off. "I'm doing this because of the way I feel.

"I know you're trying to be noble and whatnot, but just stop. I don't want to be with Ben. I've never thought of him that way, he's always been my best friend and nothing more. I don't care if he turns out to be my fiancé., none of that matters to me, because I don't have those feelings for him. But when I think of the way my fiancé made me feel, it's the same way *you* make me feel. I've never felt better than when I am with you. I feel warm and safe, and for once I don't feel empty and hollow. I feel like I'm starting to be my old self again.

"It may not be in the cards, but at this point, I don't care. I'll burn the whole deck if I have to," I tell him, gazing into his gentle blue eyes. "You may be damned if I lose my fiancé again, but I'll be damned if I lose the guy I love again. So, shut up please, and just dance with me."

Beckett steps and my foot instinctively follows. He's hesitant. His hand in mine is shaking slightly, it's comforting that he's as nervous as I am.

My heart pounds in my ears, like someone planted a kick drum in my brain as he takes a second step, and then a third, and then we're dancing.

Soft music filters through the night air, filling the still, quiet night with the gentle sound of piano.

We move to the gentle music, swaying back and forth like trees in the wind.

Our bodies are pressed together and I forget that I don't like being touched. Beckett's touch is warm and gentle, causing my heart to take flight inside my chest.

We dance the waltz. The steps are ingrained in my mind, but I let him lead. When his foot advances, mine retreats and we spin in a slow circle.

Beckett steps back and twirls me, pulling me back into his arms in a hurry as if it hurt while I was away.

Suddenly, we're not dancing. We're just standing on the porch beneath the light of the moon and stars.

Beckett places his hand on my cheek, tilting my gaze upward to meet his piercing blue eyes, and then suddenly catches my lips in a kiss that steals my breath away.

I stand there, wide-eyed for a second, shocked, but somewhere in my static-filled brain, the message is sent to kiss him back.

His lips are soft and warm, and I pull him closer, winding my fingers into his hair, desperate to close any space between us. I need him the way I need oxygen. I need his lips on mine, they melt away all the anger and pain I've felt for so long.

His arms encircle me, drawing my body against his, and I feel safe. Safe in his strong arms, surrounding me like a fortified wall, protecting me from the cold world around me.

My mouth opens to meet his and our tongues come together in a passionate kiss.

A new dance begins, the dance of a kiss. Our lips come together and then part, only to meet once again and repeat the cycle until the air has left our lungs and we're forced to take reluctant breaths.

We part for air, and in that moment, memories come flooding back, bursting forth in my mind like waters from a broken dam. Watching sunsets, going on daytrips and wild adventures. Cold nights and warm fires, jokes, dances, sweet words and passionate kisses.

"Beckett," I breathe in complete and utter shock. "It's you, it's always been you. My Celestial Warrior, my prince. You've come back to me!"

"Celia." The word comes out in a single breath.

I throw my arms around him and he holds me tightly, spinning me in circles.

"Celia, my princess, I've missed you so much!"

"You can't even begin to understand!" I tell him, burying my face in his chest. "I have searched for thousands of years across thousands of galaxies to find you." The words begin to choke me, and my throat constricts as tears sting my eyes.

Beckett caresses my face with both of his hands, his thumbs wiping away the tears that leak from my eyes.

"Please, don't ever leave me again," I whisper.

"I won't, I promise. Mesmer himself cannot tear me away from you now. He will have hell to pay for the damage he has done to your heart," he says, his voice slowly filling with rage. Both of his hands cup my face and his blue eyes pierce mine as he makes a solemn promise. "There is nowhere he can hide from me. I will not rest until I have his head." His voice is sharp and menacing, and if it were directed at me, I'd be terrified.

I don't have much time to dwell on the rage in his declaration of revenge, because he leans in and presses his lips to mine, gently pulling away after a few seconds.

"Celia, my sweet, Celia," Beckett murmurs, combing his fingers through my hair. His eyes pierce mine with clarity and recognition, but most of all, with burning love, a look I never thought I'd see again.

The reunion comes to a sudden halt by the squealing of door hinges and out comes Corrine.

"Hey, Mom," her voice falters when she sees the look on Beckett's face, a look I've never seen before. It's a look of wonderment and love, the look a father wears when he sees his daughter.

"Corrine." He breathes the word, staring at the girl with pride in his eyes.

"Dad?" she asks hesitantly, taking a cautious step towards the man. "Dad!" She runs to him, jumping into his open arms. "Do you remember me?" she asks in bewilderment.

"Well, where I come from, I never lived long enough to have you, but you're still my little girl," he says, holding her tightly, burying his face in her hair as he holds her.

"Daddy," she whispers, as if she's a little girl in the arms of the first man she's ever loved, the man she's known her whole life, and I guess, in a way she kind of is.

"Hey! What's with all the commotion?" Ben asks, with slight irritation in his voice as he makes his way outside. "I'm trying to think." He looks over at Beckett and Corrine and gives me a quizzical look. "I thought he was leaving. What's up with those two?"

"Milton," I scoff in amusement, shaking my head with a small laugh. "We should have named you Johnathan and called you John for short."

He breaks into a huge grin, lowering his head so I can't see his face.

"What can I say? My mom gave me her love of literature," he says, lifting his eyes to meet mine.

"I guess I did." I pull him into a hug, holding him tightly, never knowing how good it felt to hug my son. It's not like it's the first time I've hugged Ben, but this time feels different from all the others. It's strange. I never had a son in my first life, or in any other life I've lived for that matter. I have no memories of any children, but I still felt that maternal connection to the young man.

"If I had known I was taking classes with my son, I would have at least tried to appear studious," Beckett says, walking over to us with Corrine at his side.

"You wouldn't have fooled anyone," Ben tells him, pulling Beckett into his tight embrace.

Watching the two of them, I feel a surge of joy. We're a family. We found our way back to each other, and we're a family, something I never thought I'd be able to have.

"Corrine, are we good?" I ask, turning to my daughter.

"Yeah," she responds. "But I'm not hugging you."

"You know, surprisingly, I'm okay with that," I say, smiling at the girl.

"Good." She claps me on the back and turns to Ben. "Well, it's time to go on patrol."

"Corrine, we don't have a patrol system yet," Ben says, giving his sister a confused look.

"We do now, and we're going first, so let's go. Besides, I think Mom and Dad could use some time alone." She puts extra emphasis on the words 'mom' and 'dad,' winking before dragging Ben off by the hand. "Oh, and by the way, we won't be back for a while!"

"She is so strange," I say, watching the girl traipse off, pulling the poor boy behind her.

"She must have had wacky parents," Beckett says, wrapping his arms around me, drawing me against his body.

I take in a sharp breath, feeling like an electric current ran through me when he touched me.

"I'm sorry, did I startle you?" he asks gently, brushing my cheek with the back of his hand.

"No, I just, my heart is racing," I say, unable to form a complete, coherent sentence.

"It's okay, so is mine," he says, his voice quiet and shaky. He leans in slowly, almost hesitantly, and his lips descend onto mine. They're soft and warm, melding with my lips in a way that only his can.

My stomach erupts with butterflies and fireworks, my heart fluttering like the wings of a small bird.

"Shouldn't we be coming up with battle strategies, or planning our next move against Mesmer?" I ask, reluctantly breaking away from the gentle kiss.

"You haven't changed a bit," Beckett declares with a loving smile. "All that can wait, I just got you back. Mesmer has been an oppressive presence in your life for thousands of years, I think you deserve to be free of that for one night. I think we should enjoy ourselves. I think it's about damn time we forget about him and celebrate." His lips come down on mine once again, more forcefully this time, with more desperation behind the kiss, and I can't help but respond with the same urgency. My mouth opens under his, allowing his tongue access to mine as I hook my fingers through his belt loops and pull him closer to me.

His hands run down to my waist and lift me up to sit on the porch railing as his lips move to my neck, tenderly kissing the shocked nerves along my throat.

"Beckett," I sigh his name, running my hands through his hair, entangling them in his black locks.

"I forgot how sweet your voice sounds when you're seconds away from breaking that stoic sense of self control you have," he tells me, his warm breath sending chills throughout my body, causing a small sigh to escape my lips.

My hands find Beckett's face and bring his mouth to mine. All the tenderness from the kiss before is gone, as our lips come together in an urgent and desperate rhythm. Every thought leaves my mind, everything is overridden by passion until I have one thought, one desire. Him.

"Inside. Now," I command between frantic kisses.

I get to my feet and fall against the door, my hands haphazardly searching for the doorknob, my lips locked in Beckett's passionate kiss. I finally find it and turn it, and we stumble through the doorway and into a wall.

Beckett's hands find mine and pin them against the wall above my head, his lips relentless upon mine. He bites down, sucking on my bottom lip before letting it slip through his teeth, a sensation of pleasure tearing through my nerves.

I want to scream. His lips hover near mine, agonizingly close, but still so far away. I growl in frustration as I lean in to kiss him, only to have him pull back before our lips meet.

"I hate it when you do this," I say through grit teeth.

"But it makes you so feisty," Beckett tells me, moving in closer but still not allowing our lips to touch.

"Just shut up and kiss me." My hands break out of his hold and I grab a fistful of his shirt and pull him to me, pressing my lips urgently against his. He answers in a similar fashion, his lips meeting mine and matching their desperation.

His hands slip under my shirt, pulling it up and over my head, resting his hands on the now exposed sides of my stomach. My skin burns where he touches me. The feeling of his skin on mine makes my heart race faster than it ever has.

"Guestroom," I tell him, pushing him backward towards a room directly to our left. "Ben and Corrine cannot see this."

"Uh-oh," Beckett says, his voice dark and smooth, his words merely whispers falling onto my ear. "Nothing good happens behind closed doors."

"Damn straight, it doesn't." The door opens and I push him, forcing him onto the bed. I pull his shirt off, running my hands along his muscled chest as I straddle his hips.

I lean in and kiss his ear, tracing the cartilage with my tongue, nipping his earlobe and then moving to his neck, leaving a trail of kisses burning along his collar bone and down his chest, feeling the ridges of his muscled stomach underneath my lips.

"Celia." He sighs as my lips come back down onto his, and I melt completely, and fully give into the lust flooding my veins.

His skin is hot, burning with the same intensity as mine. It's as if we're going to combust at any moment and turn into a raging fire, devouring everything in its path. A fire of passion, unstoppable and untamable, burning hotter than the sun, reducing the world to ashes.

"Beckett, I love you," I breathe, breaking away only for a second to utter the words that so desperately needed to be said.

"I love you too, Celia," he tells me, his affectionate blue eyes gazing into mine. He kisses me again, this time slower, more tenderly, but still burning with love and passion. It's deeper than the other kisses, there's more feeling behind it, as if it were possible for us to pour our love into each other through our lips. The kiss doesn't change when his hands undo the button on my pants and then his, or when I find myself in my bra and underwear and him in his boxers. The kiss remains slow, tender and passionate.

Beckett breaks away eventually, his eyes meeting mine once again.

"I don't want to push things," he says, his hands cupping my face. "Celia, is this–" I silence him with a kiss, refusing to let him finish his question. He shouldn't even have to ask me this, the answer should already be obvious.

"I want this, Beckett, I want you. For so long I've been without you. I've ached for you, burned for your touch, and now that I've got you back, I need you. Does that answer your question?"

"I think it does," he says, nodding his head slowly.

He kisses me again, tenderly and sweetly, his lips perfectly matching mine, as if they were specifically designed to fit together. His hands caress my body and remove whatever clothing we had left as we begin to grind together and pull apart in a soothing rhythm.

At first, there's only pain, but the pain soon subsides into pleasure, into white-hot ecstasy, coiling in my stomach, ready to snap at any moment. The only thing I can feel is pleasure spinning through my nerves in a pulsating rhythm. I'm held between the grips of insanity and bliss, each one begging me to come undone, bribing me with the euphoric sense that ripples through my body.

Finally, he is mine, and I am his. There is not a force in the world that can change that now, nothing can tear us away from each other. After so many years, I am finally complete, something that cannot be undone ever again.

Sunlight filters through the windows, casting long shadows across the room.

"Good morning, Princess," Beckett murmurs, his warm breath tickling my ear.

"Good morning, Prince Beckett Halverson of Jupiter."

"God, it's been a while since I've been called that," he says, his voice scratchy from sleep.

"How are you feeling?" I ask, rolling over to look into his eyes. "When I started remembering things, I didn't feel too good at all."

"I actually feel really good. I don't think I've ever felt better," he says, smiling at me with tender eyes.

"I'm glad you're all feeling good, because we have a strategy to plan and carry out, so get dressed and put your game faces on." Corrine materializes at the end of the bed, perched on one of the bed posts.

"Oh my God! What are you doing?" I shriek, pulling the blanket up to my chin.

"You're so bashful, Mom," she says, waving her hand dismissively.

I growl in frustration and electricity manifests around me, shooting out at the girl. It doesn't even touch her, it dissipates before it hits her.

"Nice try, but I can also manipulate electricity," Corrine says with a smug smile.

"Manipulate this!" I say, grabbing a pillow and tossing it at her.

"Hey! What was that for?" the girl shrieks, as the pillow smacks her in the face.

"Don't play dumb, you know what that was for! Did it occur to you that we might be in the middle of something?"

"It did, but I knew you weren't, because I have ears, and I'm not deaf. Although you know, in some cases – like last night – I wish I was."

I think my heart stops and my face turns beet red.

Electricity surges around me, turning my vision blue. I don't think I've ever been more embarrassed.

"Shit, bye guys, love you!" Corrine says, disappearing in a mesh of blue streaks.

"Celia, calm down, don't–"

"She is so my daughter," I mutter, cutting Beckett of mid-sentence.

Beckett breathes out a sigh of relief, laughing at my reaction to the young girl.

I sit and think of all the things I've learned in the past few days. I have a daughter and a son, and my fiancé is alive and lying right beside me. For once, I stand a chance against Mesmer, I actually might be able to defeat him.

A thought hits me like a bus. *The failsafe.*

"Oh my God."

"What?" Beckett looks at me with a worried look.

"It all makes sense," I say, rushing around the room, frantically trying to find my clothes.

"Whoa, Celia, calm down," he says, confusion on his face.

"I can't, there's no time," I tell him. "Beckett, I know where the Crystal is."

"What?" He looks at me like I've gone crazy.

"The Imperial Crystal of Mercury, Beckett, I know where it is!" I say urgently. I find my clothes and put them on, only missing my shirt, which is still lying somewhere in the hall.

"I thought you said that part of you was locked away, the information sealed off within your mind," he says, but he follows my lead and puts his clothes on.

"There was another failsafe, you. I tied all those memories to you, knowing that Mesmer would do everything in his power to keep me away from you. With the knowledge I've acquired along with your combat skills, it's entirely possible that we could bring him down, unless he has the last Crystal. But for me to unlock the memories of where the Crystal is, I needed you, and so we've been stuck in this never-ending cycle. I always thought that it was Mesmer's doing, but it was mine! He hates this game as much as I do, making this far easier than I thought it would be!" I exclaim, pacing around the room in excitement, discovering just how brilliant I had been when this whole thing started. I had an endgame. I had always had one, I simply didn't know it.

"Oh my God, Celia, that was genius!" Beckett strides over to me, places his hands on my cheeks and kisses me.

"I know, what else is there to expect from me?" I ask, pulling away from the kiss. "Now come on, we have to get Ben and Corrine." I rush out of the room, dragging Beckett behind me. "Where's my shirt?" I ask, halting for a second.

"By the door," Ben tells me, appearing from around the corner.

"Oh, thanks," I say abashedly, scooping the item off the ground.

"So, tell me, when are you expecting Mini Me?" he asks, leaning up against the counter with a wide grin.

"Oh my God, would people stop bringing this up? Isn't it supposed to be like a personal and private thing? And how are you not embarrassed out of your mind, Beckett?" I ask, turning to the young man.

"Because I'm too busy laughing at your reaction," he says, his smile matching that of his son's. "I've never known you to be so bashful, Celia." His voice is a seductive murmur as he pulls me close, drawing me in by my waist. "It's really cute." His lips linger near mine, threatening to close the distance at any moment. "It makes me wish our son wasn't in the room. I'd never be able to wash those images out his head." If my face wasn't red before, it definitely is now. I can feel the heat rising in my cheeks and flooding down my neck, but Beckett doesn't seem to be bothered by it.

Before I have time to say anything, his lips descend onto mine, his passionate kiss consuming my thoughts.

"Ew. And just like that, I need to leave," Ben says, hurriedly leaving the room.

"Go get your sister, it's time to make battle plans," Beckett says, shouting through the house.

"Well that worked," I say slowly, the heat gradually leaving my face.

"Oh yeah, I guess it did," he says with a laugh, scratching the back of his head in an uncomfortable manner. "I was only acting on impulse."

"What?" The heat returns to my face instantly.

"I was simply speaking my mind, which happened to make Ben uncomfortable," he states matter-of-factly.

"I don't think that's what made Ben uncomfortable," I tell him.

"You're right, it was probably this." He cups my chin and draws my lips to his once again. His other arm is still wrapped around my waist and he pulls me flush against his body.

I wind my fingers into his hair, losing myself in the feeling of his lips, becoming completely absorbed in the kiss.

"Jeez, I thought you said battle strategies!" Ben says, re-entering the room with Corrine at his heels. "Unless your strategy is to gross Mesmer out to the point of suicide simply to escape the disturbing images you've burned into his mind, then carry on, but if not, ungluing yourselves would be pretty wonderful!"

"Calm down, Ben, they've still got a lot to get out of their systems," Corrine says.

"Oh, shut up, you just want something to tease Celia about. You enjoy making others uncomfortable more than she does," Ben responds.

"They don't need to know that," she says.

I break away from the kiss, although with much reluctance. Things need to be done in order to defeat Mesmer, things that only I can do.

I climb up the steep hill with Celia's hand intertwined with mine as we trudge through the thick canopy of the woods.

"Where are we going?" Corrine asks

from behind us.

"We're almost there," Celia responds.

Her voice is sweet to my ears, tempting me to let go of my self-control. All I want to do is draw her closer and let my lips find hers. I want to feel her body against mine, feel the touch that makes my heart race to no end. I need her in a way I didn't know was possible. Before I had regained my memories, I had been attracted to Celia. I was drawn to her and I had fought that for so long, put off by her cold exterior. But once I saw through that, I couldn't stop myself from falling for her. Now, with my memories back, I need her more than ever. Becoming complete after so long, knowing I owe it to her, simply wanting to feel the most complete I can, it burns through me like a fire.

"Alright, we're here," Celia stops walking, and so do I, stopping by her side. I look around in confusion, baffled by my surroundings.

"Celia, why are we at a crime scene?" I ask cautiously.

"This is a crime scene?" Corrine asks. "This looks like a crater from a bombing or something. Why is everything charred?"

"Because this is where things came back to me, where I became The Masquerader."

"That doesn't explain anything," Corrine says flatly.

"Yes, it does. Before Mesmer destroyed everything, I hid the Imperial Crystal of Mercury, and sent it into orbit in space. I knew that after so many years, the Crystal would come down and find me like I had commanded it to do. When that time came, I would either defeat Mesmer or be defeated by him. This is the end all, be all. We either live or we die.

"This Crystal is what Mesmer has been after for so long. I was merely an accessory that came with the Stone and complete domination. He wanted the best to rule beside him, not because he wanted the help, but simply to show that he could force the best into submission. It would be a symbol of his power.

"Mesmer figured he could seduce me, get the Mercury Crystal and then break me so I would fall under his dominant shadow. But when he realized that he couldn't sway me, he took a different angle and went after my family and the ones I loved. He believed that if I lost everything I held dear, I would give up, but instead I did the opposite. Losing everything pushed me on, fueling my desire for revenge."

"That still doesn't explain why this place looks like it was hit by a meteor," Corrine says, confusion and boredom seeping through her voice.

"Because it was!" Celia explains. "The Crystal fell out of orbit and landed here, that's why there was a murder. I went out that night in a trance-like state, the Crystal was calling out to me. I was followed by one of Mesmer's henchmen that night, and being so near to the Crystal, filled with rage and bloodlust, caused my mind split and The Masquerader was created and as a result, the man was killed."

"You're saying the Imperial Crystal of Mercury is here, in this charred crater?" Corrine asks doubtfully.

"Yes!" Celia responds, her voice light with enthusiasm.

"Then wouldn't the police have taken the crystal as evidence or something?"

"Not if they couldn't see it. Normally it's a rich violet, but that's because it's always been in the possession of the Royal Family of Mercury. The Crystal wants to protect itself and the Family it serves, so it camouflaged itself, but now that I'm here, it should come back to life. And even if it hadn't camouflaged itself, the police still wouldn't have found it, it's too far underground."

Celia jumps into the crater, landing gracefully as she studies her surroundings.

"Find it yet?" Ben asks, hollering down to the girl.

"She said it's underground, you idiot, of course she hasn't found it yet," Corrine says, shooting Ben an annoyed look.

"Hey, everyone shut up. I need to concentrate," Celia commands. "Oh, and, Beckett, get down here and stand behind me. I'm going to need your help, well, more like your strength, but whatever. The closer you are, the easier it'll be for me to channel you, so just sit tight okay?"

I do as Celia tells me to, jumping down into the crater and landing agilely, making almost no noise as my feet hit the ground. I'm not used to having this kind of grace. I rise to my feet and make my way to Celia, standing behind her as I was told to.

She gets down on her knees, bowing her head and closing her eyes. Her fingertips graze the ground and she takes a deep breath.

"It's time to start."

The ground shakes. I can hear the plates beneath us moving, I can feel the power surging through the ground.

Celia glows with a blue hue as electricity wraps around her body, making the ground around her even blacker.

There's a tearing sound, like the earth itself is being ripped apart. The ground beneath my feet starts to waver, attempting to throw me off balance.

What the hell is she doing? I ask myself, struggling to keep on my feet.

Celia's body is now completely covered in blue coils of electricity, but she doesn't seem to notice, she just continues to kneel in the dirt with her fingertips on the ground.

As I watch Celia, I notice that the waves are coming from her, rippling from her body like from a rock thrown into a pond.

Suddenly, the earth stops trembling and the blue coils die down, retracting back into her body.

I step to her side, watching her intently.

Slowly, Celia opens her eyes and I'm greeted by electric blue, like her eyes are made of electricity, swirling inside her irises, because they are. Gradually, the color transforms into a deep, rich purple, the purple of royalty.

The ground rips apart and I'm thrown off balance, hitting the ground and rolling into a cat-like stance, prepared to lunge.

It's good to know that I've still got my moves, I think, watching Celia with an intense stare, prepared to act at any moment.

Slowly, a stone rises from the hole in the ground, glimmering like dew drops in the morning sun. It radiates a purple light, bathing the charred woods in a lavender hue.

"She actually did it," Ben breathes, his voice a shocked whisper. "She got the Crystal."

"And now the game begins." Celia turns so she can see us, her eyes still glowing purple. "Corrine, I am going to ask you to do the hardest thing you will ever do. I'm going to ask you to kill Mesmer Amar."

Corrine pales slightly, her jaw clenching, her hands slowly balling into fists.

"I can't do it, there's only one thing I can think of and it'll probably kill me, but I'll do it if I have to. If you believe that you can kill Mesmer, then the Crystal is yours. It will give you immense power, you'll be virtually unstoppable, invincible. The power of the Royal Family will be at your disposal, not just the diluted abilities that you possess now. I'll give you time to think about it. For now, I want you to hold onto the Crystal, Beckett." Celia turns to me, in her outstretched hand is a beautiful stone. It shines with an almost blinding light, shimmering like the sun in the dark forest.

"Um, why?" I ask, confusion playing on my features.

"Because it won't be in the hands of Mercury's Royalty, which should make it a little harder to track down," Celia explains.

"Are you sure? I might lose it," I say, slightly embarrassed.

For a moment Celia's face betrays worry, but it quickly returns to its placid state.

"You'll be fine," she tells me, placing the Crystal in my hand, holding onto me for a second, giving my hand a gentle squeeze.

I squeeze her hand back, taking the Crystal and putting it in my pocket.

"So, what's next?" Ben asks, his light voice lifting the dark and gloom surrounding us in its cold embrace.

"We go back and make plans and preparations for war," Celia says.

"What about Nick Mallard? When will he get back?" Ben asks.

"He won't come home until all of this is over. I don't want to drag anyone innocent into this, it'll only make what we have to do harder. If we survive this and manage to defeat Mesmer, then we can find a way to go back to our worlds and no one here will remember us or that we even existed. Everything we've been through, every life we've lived will be lost to our memories. So, if you need any type of closure, now is the time to get that. And if we don't pull this off, we'll all be dead and it won't matter anymore. That's why we can't let anyone else get involved. If they haven't wormed their way in already, then they weren't meant to be a part of this." Celia looks directly at me, and I know what's going through her mind. Me. If things had gone the way she had planned, I never would have gotten involved, and she'd still be wandering around, missing part of her soul, with no idea as to how to destroy Mesmer.

"I'm gonna need some time then," Ben says, his voice shattering the silence looming over us. "There are some strings I need to tie up. Let's take this day to say goodbye to those we love. At least, that's what I'm going to do." His eyes are melancholic. I can almost feel the sadness rolling off of him, settling into my bones, but then I realize that it's my own sadness that wages war on my heart. My family. I have to say goodbye to them. The people who have loved me, raised me and helped me even when I didn't know I needed help. The people who were always there for me and supported me no matter what. I have to say goodbye to them.

The walk back to the house is quiet. I can feel all the pain in each person's heart. I'm glad to be alone now, sitting on the porch railing with my feet dangling over the edge.

The door creaks open and someone joins me, mimicking my posture, moving his legs in time with mine.

"Did you say goodbye to her?" I ask, turning my gaze to Ben.

"Yeah." His voice is heavy and sad. I know it's hard to say goodbye to someone you love. I know it all too well.

"Who is she, Ben?" I ask. "I don't know her, but you obviously do."

"She's my girl," he says. "Your daughter-in-law, Corrine's best friend, the daughter of *your* best friend."

"Jade... Lily... I guess they like to stick to shades of green, don't they? I'm glad Jade took my advice about names. Does she know who she is?"

"No, she hasn't got a clue, I think that might be the worst part. Such a strong woman and lively character, reduced to a clueless child with just a shadow of who she once was. She reminds me so much of the girl I lost, but I know she's not her."

"Shadow or not, she's still the same person, I can attest to that. Living as a shadow is miserable. My guess is that she can tell that she isn't one hundred percent herself. It'll haunt her until she regains her memories, but it won't come to that. We're going to end this before she can understand what's going on and send her back to the world in which she belongs."

"We *can't* lose this, Celia. We *have* to win this for everyone that we've loved, for everyone that ever believed in us. We *can't* let Mesmer claim this world. We've got to beat him." His hands clench the railing at his sides and his eyes burn with anger. I can see that Mesmer has hurt everyone I hold dear and it fills me with rage.

"I know, Ben. I know." I place my hand over his and squeeze it tightly.

"It's like you said, Celia, it's the end all, be all, and we have to end this, we have to end him."

Never before have I dreaded going home so much. I've said too many goodbyes in my life, and I don't want to say anymore.

I take a deep breath to ready myself for what I have to do.

"Hey guys, sorry I've been gone so long, I was working at Nick's," I say stepping through the threshold.

"Where the hell have you been?" Amy asks in an anguished voice.

"I just told you, I was working, you idiot. I stayed at Nick Mallard's house and took care of his place and animals," I respond, with slight irritation in my voice.

"We've all been worried sick about you. We thought you might've been killed by The Masquerader!" she exclaims.

"Well, obviously I wasn't, now where are Mom and Dad? There's something I need to tell all of you, something very important."

"Downstairs. Celia, what's going on?" Amy asks with concern.

"I'll tell you in a minute." I rush downstairs and rally my parents, sitting down in the living room with my family.

"Celia, sweetheart, what's wrong, you look worried," Mom says, reaching out for my hand. Hers are warm, gentle and familiar, soothing my nerves.

"You guys, there's something I need to tell you," I start.

"Are you coming out as a lesbian?" Amy asks suddenly.

"No! God, Amy, why are you such an idiot?" I ask irritably.

"Because I take after you, Celia," she responds with a smile.

"Shut up, this is serious," I say. "What I'm about to tell you is going to be very hard to take in, but I need you all to stay open-minded and do your best to understand."

My family stares at me, nodding their heads in affirmation.

"I'm not who you think I am at all," I say. I pause for a moment, trying to figure out how best to word this, but there is no good way that won't make me seem crazy. It leaves me with only one other choice. "I guess it'd be easier if I just showed you," I sigh, standing up and stepping back. I close my eyes and take a deep breath, letting it out slowly, concentrating. It's the first time I've tried to make the transformation without going into a fight.

I feel the slight tingle start at my feet, slowly travelling up my legs and then spreading throughout the rest of my body.

I close my eyes as it starts, not wanting to see the look on my family's face as a monster appears in their living room.

I hear a few startled gasps, but no horror lurks beneath them, only surprise. It reassures me enough to open my eyes and meet their gazes.

"I'm The Masquerader," I say finally.

"Awesome." Amy stares at me with admiration.

"I don't understand, Celia," my dad says. "Why are you telling us this? Why do you do it?"

"Because I have to. I'm not entirely human, at least, not anymore. I'm not from this world. I've been jumping around from universe to universe, fighting a war that's been going on for thousands of years." As I tell my family my story, I expect them to look at me like I'm crazy, but they don't. Their faces never change from that look of patient understanding.

"So, you're not human, you have super powers, some creepy blond dude wants to keep you chained up in the basement and destroy everything, you're engaged to Beckett Halverson – congrats by the way – and you like to kill people. Did I miss anything?" Amy asks once I'm finished with my story.

"No, I think you hit all the main points," Dad says, answering my sister's question.

"Awesome. That explains so much! Why'd it take you so long to tell us, Celia?" Amy questions, looking at me with curious eyes.

"Because once I've told you all of this, I have to leave. Me telling you this means that it's time for me to end this game, and that you all need to get out of here, because I don't want you guys getting hurt."

"No way, we're going to help you," Amy insists.

"No, you're not. None of you are getting involved in this, it's way too dangerous. Besides, there's nothing you can do to help me."

"Celia, you know you wouldn't be inconveniencing us," Mom tells me, giving my shoulder a comforting squeeze.

"I know, Mom, but that's not why I can't let you guys do this." I feel my throat starting to choke up. "I can't let you get involved in this, because if you do, you'll all die, and I can't have that. I've never been able to protect my family, or anyone else that I've loved, please, let me do it just this once." My voice is solemn and my heart is heavy. I can feel it webbing apart, the threads that once held my heart together becoming nothing but a bleeding mess of pain. "I have to do this on my own now, I have to say goodbye, forever."

I can feel the atmosphere grow thick with sorrow, dragging each of our hearts to the depths of despair.

"Celia–"

"Please, don't make this harder than it already is. Let me do this. I've never been able to say a real goodbye, it's fitting that I get this chance at the last leg of the race," I say, fighting the pain that threatens to constrict my throat.

Silence settles over my family as understanding passes through their eyes. It's settled.

"I'm glad you guys understand, thank you. Thank you for giving me closure, it's something I've never been given before." I bow my head slightly as a sign of gratitude and then turn to my parents, starting with them. "Mom, Dad, thank you everything. For taking care of me and encouraging my insane quest for knowledge. For always trying to understand me. I couldn't have asked for better parents. You've taught me so much about life and love, and what it truly looks like. You gave me a little sister that I've always adored. You learned to sleep through my piano playing in the middle of the night. You accepted me for who

I am, something no one else has done before, so thank you." My eyes burn as I choke out the words, watching my sadness reflected in my parents' eyes.

I'm sorry. I'm so sorry.

With heavy movements, I pull my parents in for a hug, clinging to them as if they were the last thing that was keeping me tethered to the earth. Reluctantly, we let go, separating ourselves, allowing me to turn to my sister.

"Amy," I sigh, placing my hand on her shoulder in an affectionate manner.

"Celia." She copies my tone of voice, mimicking my actions. She's trying so hard to keep things feeling normal, fighting past the pain so evident in her eyes, all for my sake. It slowly breaks my already broken heart.

"You are a pain in the ass, you always have been. You badger me in the mornings and take me to basketball tournaments for the sole purpose of watching me get kicked out of them. I have no idea why, but saying goodbye to you is the hardest." Despite my efforts, a single tear escapes from my eyes, burning a sorrowful trail down my cheek.

"Wow, Celia, that was touching," Amy says sarcastically.

"Shut up, I'm not done," I tell her in agitation. "You sometimes knew me better than I knew myself, you understood me even when I didn't. You challenged me, you didn't just go off my words. You questioned things and it always annoyed the hell out of me, but without that, I'd have gone crazy with boredom.

"I've always trusted you with things I've trusted no one else with, like driving my car so I could eat when we'd sneak out and go to Taco Bell or McDonalds at midnight. Or stitching me up on the pretense that I was street fighting.

"Where I come from, I had a brother, and I had never wanted a sister, not until I had you. You are the sister I wish I could be, and it has been one of the biggest honors of my life to say that you are my little sister."

"Shut up, you cliché smartass," Amy says, tears leaking from her eyes as she pulls me into a tight hug. Her shoulders shake gently as she holds back her sobs. "Go kick that blond bastard's ass," she commands, peeling herself off of me. She goes to stand by our parents and I step away, taking one last look at the people I had learned to call my family, committing their faces to memory. Even if they'll forget me, I won't forget them. Their voices, their smiles, everything they've done for me. The way they loved me and took care of me. I won't lose those memories, even if all they become are hazy dreams of a time long past.

"I love you guys," I tell them, stepping away and into the shadows. "Don't forget that, even if you forget me. Remember that you were ferociously loved." The words leave my mouth, my last words to them, and I fade into the night, the way I've faded from their lives, melting away with the shadows until I stand alone in the field outside Nick Mallard's house with the cool breeze rustling my clothes and blowing my hair about my face.

"At least I got to say goodbye," I tell myself, smiling sadly. For once, my eyes and mind are here on the earth instead of wandering the stars above me, content to have my feet planted on this planet. "I finally got to say goodbye."

I didn't know something could hurt so badly, but saying goodbye had broken me. My parent's confusion, Lily's tears soaking my shirt.

"Damnit," I growl, clenching my fists into my hair, pulling at it in stress. "Damnit!" I bring my fists down onto my knees with explosive anger.

"Hey." A gentle voice calls to me, distracting me from my anguish and pain. "How are you?"

"I'm not good, Cel," I respond, letting a sigh escape from my lungs.

"I'm sorry," Celia says, pulling me to my feet and hugging me tenderly. She holds me tightly, as if she were trying to keep me together and prevent me from falling apart. I've become shards of a broken glass, and in this moment, Celia is the glue that keeps my broken pieces together. I hold her in the same way, my arms wrapping around her, refusing to let her go. I feel like breaking apart. The pain in my chest is ripping me to shreds, it hurts so badly.

"Beck, where'd you go just now?" Celia asks, her curious eyes peering into mine.

"Somewhere I'd rather not be," I tell her, meeting her gaze. A gentle smile finds its way to my lips, her shining eyes giving me a strange sense of joy.

She doesn't say anything and looks into my eyes, reading them. I can almost see the gears in her head turning, trying to solve whatever puzzle she's seeing.

"It still makes me uncomfortable when you analyze me like this," I say, shifting my weight from foot to foot, trying to ignore the unsettled feeling sinking in my stomach.

"Sorry, it's kind of a habit," she says, turning her eyes from me. "It's strange to have my memories of you back. I'm remembering things that had been completely lost to me. Like the time we went to have a picnic at the river by the castle and–"

"The horse I was riding decided to take me for a surprise swim?" I ask, finishing her sentence for her.

"Yeah, that time," Celia says in confirmation, a smile playing on her lips.

"That water was so cold. I told you that horse hated me, and you thought I was just being ridiculous until he charged head first into the water, taking me along with him."

"The water *was* surprisingly cold for the summer, wasn't it?" Her eyes glass over as she thinks back to that day.

"You barely got in!" I tell her. "It was *extremely* cold for the summer."

"I went all the way in!" Celia protests. "You were not the only one who went for a surprise swim, Beckett Halverson. If I remember correctly, you dragged me into the water when I went to help you out."

"I did no such thing," I say with false hurt. "I can't believe that you think I'd do something so villainous. You simply slipped."

"No, I didn't, you pulled me in! I can't believe you're trying to play the chivalrous gentleman right now."

"I'm always a chivalrous gentleman, I'm a prince, don't you remember?" I smile, remembering the shocked look on Celia's face as the cold water registered in her nerves.

"It's for the memories like those that we had to say goodbye to our families," Celia says, sadness lingering in her voice. "If we succeed, then they won't be in danger anymore and they won't remember us, so they won't be sad. We'll still remember them, but as a dream, not as something that really happened. It all works out in the end."

"Since when do you believe in happy endings?" I ask skeptically, giving her a cautious look.

"I don't, to be honest," she says plainly. "I don't believe the universe allows happy endings, but I also don't believe that the laws of the universe apply to me."

I smile, gazing upon her lovingly.

She hasn't changed a bit, I think to myself with a small smile.

"What?" she asks, looking at me with confusion.

"Nothing," I tell her. "I was just noticing that you haven't changed at all. You're still the same insufferable, entitled, defiant princess with a heart the size of your ego. It's nice to see that some things never change."

"I'm not insufferable or entitled!" Celia protests.

"Oh no, not at all," I say sarcastically, getting a rise out of the girl.

"How am I insufferable?" she asks. "I can sort of see where you get the entitled part, although it isn't true, but I don't know where the insufferable part comes from."

"When I first met you, I thought you were the most insufferable person on the face of the planet," I explain.

"Oh, well, yeah, I guess I did seem that way at first. But I'm not insufferable," she demands.

My smile grows larger. *She's adorable when she protests so adamantly.*

"What?! Why are you looking at me like that?"

"Because you're unbearably adorable," I say, pulling her closer to me, wrapping my arms around her waist.

"That's not the way people normally describe me," she says quietly, her hands sliding up my chest, lacing together behind my neck.

"And how would that be?" I ask, leaning in so our foreheads are touching.

"Insufferable and entitled," she says with a grin. Her smile is brilliant. It's beautiful and warm, and it fills me with strength and hope. It's a contagious smile. It spreads to my lips and fills that hole that had taken residence in my chest.

"Do you really think we can win this battle?" I ask in a hushed voice.

"Yes," she says, with confidence and certainty blazing in her eyes. "We'll win because we finally have a reason to. Losing isn't an option. I lost you once and I can't lose you again, so I'll fight until we win, or I die, and I'm too stubborn to die, so my bet rests on the former." Her voice is gentle and reassuring, and I feel confident that we can win this battle. Her certainty is as contagious as her smile. I'm no longer filled with pain and worry, because she's here. Celia is here in my arms, not far away, the way she'd been for so long.

Giving into impulse I in lean in and kiss her, our lips brushing against each other's. Her lips are soft and gentle, like everything about her. I lose myself in the feeling of her mouth, and as I do so, my mind slips away to a world long past and a memory long-forgotten.

"Celia!" I call out to her, rushing into the Grand Hall. She stands against the piano, watching the young man seated beside her in awe.

I come to a halt, taken aback by the beautiful music that fills the room.

"He truly is quite the composer," I say quietly, coming to take a stand behind the boy. "I see why you spend so much time in here listening to his music." I direct my words at Celia, catching her eyes and smiling.

"I have you to thank for this, Beckett," the boy says, the music never halting, continuing with its flowing rhythm. "You managed to steal the heart of my sister. You gave her an ally, someone to trust when she attains the crown, and because she knows she has an ally, she no longer resists the position of Queen. Now I can spend my time focusing on music."

"You make it sound like a great feat, Peter," Celia says, leaving the spot at his side to stand by mine.

"It is," he responds with a laugh. "And since he bested such a feat, I can live my dream."

"Enough with this serious talking, our voices clash with the music around us," Celia says, silencing the conversation. "Prince Beckett, may I have this dance?"

"Indeed, you may, my princess," I say, taking her extended hand and pulling her into my arms where we begin to move in fast circles, our feet moving to the time of the waltz in expertise.

Celia's red-violet dress billows out and circles as she spins away from me, and then back into my arms, mimicking the elegant scenes from the images painted onto the walls of the Ballroom.

Slowly, the music fades until only a ghost of its beautiful melody lingers in my ears, and I'm once again standing in the home of Nick Mallard.

"You saw it too, didn't you?" Celia asks, peering into my eyes.

"I guess so, yeah," I say, shifting my gaze to the ground in thought. "Has this been happening to you a lot?" I ask.

"Not so much anymore," she responds. "I had flashbacks like that when I first got my memories back and The Masquerader started showing up. Do you remember the day I stayed home from school sick?"

"Yeah, Ben and I were a little worried when you didn't show up that day."

"Well, I spent that night and morning in a state of delirium, probably until around noon. Images and scenes from my past played across my mind, slowly coming back to me in dreams."

"That doesn't sound very pleasant at all," I say.

"It wasn't, but I doubt that will happen to you," she says reassuringly. "I had a block on my mind to keep me from remembering. You, on the other hand, don't have that mental block, or at least I don't think you do." Her eyebrows furrow as she begins to think, trying to figure out if I have a block or not.

"Are you sure?" I ask, wanting to be positive that I won't share Celia's miserable experience.

"Not at all. I guess we'll find out when you go to sleep, which should be relatively soon. Tomorrow we're making plans and preparations for war, you should get some rest." It seems to be a suggestion, but I know it's more of a command.

"What about you? Do you plan on going to sleep soon?" I ask, flopping down onto the bed.

"There are a few things I need to take care of before I go to sleep. I don't know how long it'll take, so don't wait up for me, okay?" She plants a chaste kiss on my lips and hurries out the door.

"Hey," I say, giving her some warning, not wanting to sneak up and startle the girl.

"Oh, hey, Mom," Corrine responds, turning around only slightly.

"I don't think I'll ever get used to being called that, especially since you're pretty much my age. It feels kind of strange," I tell her, taking a seat next to the girl gazing at the stars.

"It feels pretty normal to me," she says. "It's what I've always called you."

"Can you tell me more about your world?" I ask cautiously. "I need to know what happened. The more I know, the better strategy I can make."

"You don't need to beat around the bush, ask me your real question," she says, getting to the point immediately.

"Alright, can you do it?" I ask. "Can you kill him?"

"Am I physically capable of it? Yeah. Am I emotionally capable of it? I have no clue. I mean, would you be able to kill Dad? Could you look him in the eyes and watch the light drain from them as you drive the knife deeper into his chest?" Corrine asks. Her voice is heavy with sorrow and completely miserable.

"If I had to, yes. I could do it, and I would hate myself forever, but I could still do it. It wouldn't be the first time I've watched him die," I tell her, shifting my gaze to stare into her eyes.

"What?" Her eyes are clouded with confusion as she returns my stare.

"I've watched Beckett die before," I repeat. "When Mesmer stormed the Capitol Palace with his group of insurgents, Beckett and I met them for what we thought would be a final battle. Most of our generation was protecting the civilians that were still alive, we were the last defense. It was decided that if we lost the battle, I was to destroy the universe and send the Mercury Crystal into orbit in order to prevent Mesmer from obtaining all the Imperial Stone. Of course, this was after he had assassinated all the rulers, leaving the decisions up to their children, up to us.

"Beckett and I fought hard. We were able to greatly decrease the insurgents' numbers, but by then Mesmer was done playing around, and we were worn out.

"The insurgents focused on me while Beckett and Mesmer went head to head. Beckett was tired and worn out, and I was too swamped to help him, the outcome of their battle was already known when it started. By the time I had finished off the insurgents, Beckett was down and bleeding badly. I knew he'd die soon, so I held him tighter than I had ever done before, believing it'd be the last time I'd do so.

"I watched the light fade from his eyes, held him as the life drained from his body. I watched him die once before, and I'd watch him die again in order to save this world and right all of the wrongs." I grit my teeth, the memory of Beckett's death leaving a bitter taste in my mouth.

"What happened next?" Corrine asks. Her voice is soft, soothing almost.

"I shot the Crystal out into space, into a different universe, and then I destroyed mine. I brought the whole place down with electricity, shooting it through the ground and ripping it apart. The shockwave rippled through universe and demolished everything, yet somehow, Mesmer got out of the destruction.

"With the last bits of power I had, I sent myself into another world where I started out as an infant, trying to find a way to kill Mesmer."

"Why can't you kill him?" the young girl questions. "You hate him enough to take his life, you have the skill set to do it, but you haven't."

"It's because I physically can't," I tell her, "He used some form of black magic to bind me to him in a way. He took away my physical ability to kill him. I'm incapable of it. I've been trying to find a way to get around it, but the only way to get rid of it is to have the caster lift it."

"I don't understand," Corrine says. "You're physically strong and fast enough, not to mention smart enough to outwit him. How are you physically unable to kill him?"

"I can press the knife to his throat, but I can't slash it. I can hold a gun to his head, but no matter how badly I want to, I can't pull the trigger. I'd black out before I'd kill him, but not before going through worlds of pain. As soon as it comes down to the final act, it's like the intense pain that shoots through me blocks all the signals sent from my brain. My body won't move, and the pain gets more intense the harder I try to kill him, it cripples me and forces me out of consciousness.

"So I'm going to ask you once more, can you kill him? Because if you can't, I will fight to my last breath, but there is no guarantee that I will be able to end this. The most probable outcome is that I die, and Mesmer creates the Imperial Stone and the world falls into chaos, and not just this world. Every world, everywhere, will pay for what I couldn't do."

"You're really trying to lay this on thick, aren't you?" Corrine asks, skepticism hinting in her voice.

"I'm simply telling you how it is," I say coolly. "I don't sugarcoat things."

She says nothing to this, she merely stares at the rooftop, with eyes glazed over and far away. They take her to a place far from where we're sitting, into a time that has long since passed us by and a world that is no longer there.

"Alright," Corrine says finally, determination blazing in her eyes. "I can do it."

"Huh?" Her voice jars me, I stopped paying attention when Corrine went into her own world.

"I said that I can do it. I can kill this bastard. That's the best way to get rid of all this turmoil inside of me and around me."

I look at her and know she's playing tough. I can see her pain hiding behind the defiance and determination that sit aflame in her eyes. I can see that slowly, her heart is falling apart. Any hope that she'd held onto was gradually dissipating, being crushed by the cold hands of reality. But she's strong, as strong if not stronger than me. If anyone is capable of destroying their heart, their hope, and their love in order to save everyone else, it's her.

"Well then, let's strategize."

My head feels strange as I drift. I feel like I'm lying on my back, floating down a stream, my body is warm and light, weightless and untouched by time.

Colors swim all over my vision, spinning and swirling, forming into shapes and images only to melt away into nothing.

What's going on? *I ask myself, the thought reverberating around me, bouncing off invisible walls to surround me in a cocoon of thought.*

A figure appears before me, walking out of the blurred images that surround me. He's tall, with hair as black as night and eyes that shine like blue diamonds. He's me.

"Come with me," he says, his hand outstretched before me. "Let me show you your long-forgotten past."

I take his hand and he hoists me to my feet, his hand remaining clasped around mine. He places his free hand on my face with two fingers on my temple. He closes his eyes, and so do I, and when I open them I'm in a different world. A world I never thought I would return to. A world that I had lost long ago.

I stand in front of floor to ceiling windows, looking out over my future kingdom from the Ballroom.

I catch my reflection in the windows and stop, wondering how and who got me to look this nice. I'm in a tuxedo. The black causes my blue eyes to shine and adds an aura of mystery to me.

I take a seat, snatching the sketchbook and pencil off one of the small dining tables and begin to draw, becoming absorbed in the true mystery that adorns the page.

Celia Walters, her eyes are strong and intense, even when captured in black and white. The picture looks so lifelike, as if Celia herself were emerging from the page.

"What is it about her?" I ask aloud. She has a way of getting under my skin and making me lose my cool. When it comes to her, I almost lose my ability to think, and I'm starting to understand why now.

"What are you drawing?" a voice asks from behind me.

I quickly snap the book shut before the person can see the drawing on the page.

"It's nothing, just the musings of a young man's troubled mind." I turn around to see my mother in a beautiful dress, her matching masquerade mask hanging from her hand.

"I am beginning to understand why the entire universe finds you mysterious," she sighs, taking a seat at the table.

"Well then, please enlighten me, because I still have no idea," I admit, relieved that I might finally get to the bottom of this ridiculous misconception.

"Because at soirées and other social gatherings you are always so warm and friendly, but you rarely divulge anything personal, like explaining what it truly is that is on your mind. Instead, you deflect those questions with cryptic words. No one knows much about you, you always manage to keep anything remotely personal obscured. You have become a mystery even to me."

"There are some things that I wish not for others to know. And as for what is on my mind, what troubles it, I myself do not yet completely understand. Therefore, I cannot correctly convey it and I would rather not risk more ludicrous rumors flying around," I respond, realizing only now how cryptic I sound.

"And there's your deflection, spoken with sweet words and complex sentences to weave complacency into the minds of those around you. Beckett, if you need to spill your incoherent thoughts and troubled musings, do know that I am always ready to listen."

"Thank you, Mother. I shall keep your offer in the forefront of my mind," I tell her, rising to my feet and planting a kiss on her forehead. "I should probably go prepare myself for the ball, the guests will be arriving at any moment," I say to myself as I wander away. "I still have so much to do."

I run up the stairs to my chamber and grab the plain, black mask that I'll be wearing for the dance, and a single key I had hidden behind a painting. I jog out into the hall and down a small corridor to find the man I left to guard the room. I can't risk anyone trespassing and ruining the interior, not in this room, it's far too important.

"Is everything set?" I ask, beginning to feel anxious, worried that my plan won't work.

"Yes, sir," the guard responds. "The room is precisely as you left it."

I open the door and peek my head in, surveying the room one last time, making sure it's perfect. Those architects did a spectacular job, *I think to myself. Everything is beautiful and elegant, down to each individual bed.*

"The men know to set off the fireworks once the sun sets?" I ask, making sure nothing is left unverified.

"Yes, sir," the guard responds once again.

"The director knows that once the fireworks are almost over, he is to begin the song?"

"Indeed, sir."

"And the director knows which song to conduct?"

"Yes, Prince Beckett, everything is in order," the man says with exasperation.

"I'm sorry, Alaric," I say. "You have my most sincere apologies. My anxiety has probably gone far beyond obnoxious by now."

"It is quite alright, my lord," he says with a smile. "It is rare to see you so flustered."

"I'm very nervous, Alaric," I admit. "I've finally figured it out. I have to tell her."

"As you should, my lord," he says. "I do believe I hear company though, perhaps a quarrel. You should be on your way, sir."

"Indeed, I should. Farewell, Alaric, I leave the rest up to you!" I pocket the key and dash down the stairs to be greeted by very familiar voices. A beautiful voice that halts me in my tracks.

"Will you please behave yourself?" a man asks. It's the voice of my hero, Jasper Walters, King of Mercury. "You know this ball is very important for all of us, please at least pretend that you do not hate the fact that you have been chosen as our next ruler."

"Yes, Father," she sighs. Her voice sounds tired and defeated. I don't like hearing her voice this way, devoid of the life it normally holds.

"I will do this for your sake but know that this fight is not over. I do not want to be Queen, and I will fight to see that I do not."

I hear the squeal of the large oak doors and I run further up the stairs and out of sight. Celia's already agitated, seeing me won't help her, not when she's like this. Now isn't the time.

I stand at the top of the stairwell and watch as Celia's scowl deepens, the Prince of Saturn arriving on the scene. I can't hear what he's saying, but it's making her furious. Immediately, I make my way toward her. I know she can take care of herself, but she was told to behave, and Mesmer will push her past that.

"It wasn't a suggestion, or a question, it was more of a command," Mesmer snarls, grabbing Celia's wrist and pulling her against his body.

I'm not sure if I've ever seen Celia so disgusted, and I can't stand it, I have to do something.

"Well, that wasn't too polite," I say. "It's shameful for a prince to act in such a manner. Please, unhand my guest, for she owes me a dance." My voice is surprisingly polite, but authority and menace linger beneath that false layer. Celia may have been told to behave, but I wasn't, and so help me God, he will let go of her.

"You can have your dance when we're done," Mesmer responds, his voice dripping with malice and hatred.

I unsheathe my sword, pressing the blade to the arrogant prince's throat, ready to cut him open at any second. I don't care if it might cause a massive war, the universe would be better off without his filth.

"It wasn't a suggestion or a question," I growl. "It was more of a command, now let her go."

Mesmer does as I say, but not before giving threatening words, and then I'm left alone with Celia.

"I didn't need your help," she tells me, turning around to face me. Her eyes fall upon me, and she stops, her mouth slightly agape. I can't help but smile a little. I know what's going through her mind and it's probably driving her crazy.

"Are you okay?" I ask, gently examining her wrist. Her skin is warm to the touch, and my heart flutters a bit when I feel her skin on mine.

"I'm fine," Celia says, quickly pulling away from me, her cheeks flushing red. "I can handle myself, you didn't need to get involved in my affairs."

"I know," I say, stepping closer to her. "But I do believe you were told to behave."

She asks me something, I assume it has to do with me overhearing her argument with her parents, but I'm not paying attention to her words, I simply stare at her in awe.

She is absolutely stunning, I think. Her black lace dress contrasts with her purple mask, all added atop her natural, jaw-dropping features. It creates a breathtakingly beautiful picture in front of me.

"Let's dance," I say suddenly. The urge to be near her is overwhelming. "We look strange just standing in the midst of the partygoers." I take her hand in mine and spin her, pulling her flush against me. She places one hand on my shoulder, the other remains clasped in mine as our bodies begin to spin and sway to the light music surrounding us.

"You haven't answered my question," she says, trying to sound stern. It doesn't work, she only sounds breathless and flustered.

"Yes," I say with a sigh. "I'm surprised, to be honest, that you're so against being Queen. The job suits you, I think you would be very good at it. Why do you reject the crown?" I ask as I slowly dip her back. I hold her tightly, and when she comes back up, we're even closer. Our noses almost touch. I can feel her shallow breath on my lips and I wish to close that gap, but I know it will only startle her.

"Because I hate politics. Politicians are dishonest to the core. They are spineless and disgusting and I wish not to take part in that. I'd rather have nothing to do with them."

"But your father is none of those," I say. "Your father is a good man. When I was younger, I would parade around the courtyards pretending to be King Jasper of Mercury. My whole life I've wanted to be like him. I want to be honorable and kind, honest and yet cunning. I strive to be more like your father every day. To be a strong, compassionate leader, a loving husband and caring father, and an all-around good man."

Celia stares at me with an odd look and I become nervous and my face heats up, turning a rosy color. She begins to laugh a hearty laugh, her eyes lighting up and she becomes even more shockingly beautiful.

We stay on the outskirts of the room, dancing past the large windows when she falters, a hazy look in her eyes. She's thinking, and I bet I know what about.

"I know, we look like something out of a fairytale," I say. My voice is soft and I lean in closer to Celia so she can hear me better and so that I can be closer to her.

Her eyes shoot open with shock and meet mine, curiosity and surprise riddling them.

"Can you read minds?" Celia asks cautiously, paling slightly at the possibility that I could be aware of every thought that has flashed across her mind this evening.

I give a small laugh. "No, but it would be useful in situations like this. You are very difficult to read," I tell her.

"Then how did you know what I was thinking?" she asks skeptically.

"Because I was thinking the same thing," I admit, slowly bringing our dance to a stop and peering into her eyes.

We stand quite close to each other, partly to avoid being run into by the other dancers, and partly because we both burn to be near one another, despite how hard we fight to deny it.

Both of Celia's hands rest on my shoulders and mine on her waist, drawing us closer than before.

Soft music floats around us and colors dance on the outskirts of my vision as the dancers twirl and whirl about the room. It creates a surreal, dream-like effect, tossing Celia and myself into a moment so shockingly beautiful that words would do it no justice.

"You look wonderful tonight," I tell her, wrapping my arm around her waist, drawing her flush against me, grazing her cheek gently with the back of my hand. "You are stunningly beautiful. Celia, I–"

Something flashes across her eyes and she backs away suddenly.

"Celia, what's wrong?" I inquire worriedly.

"You're just like all the others," she breathes in disbelief. "You're after my position. You have never uttered sweet words to me, not until now, now that you know for certain that I will be Mercury's Queen. You wish to sway and woo me now that my position is no longer uncertain. You are all disgusting. You all wish to be King."

"What? Is that what you honestly believe?" I ask, completely shocked by her words.

"It's what I know!" Celia shouts, storming away.

"Celia, if my objective were to capture your position as future Queen, there would be many other ways of doing so than getting you to like me," I tell her, following her on swift feet. "Your father loves me, I would have no problem obtaining his consent, I could just talk to him and have him arrange the marriage."

"And I suppose that this is the part where you tell me to make it easier for the both of us and not bring it to that," Celia snarls.

"No! I would never force someone into a marriage! I want the person I marry to love me, and I them. A forced marriage would not give me that,

especially a forced marriage with you. You'd be so miserable, a state I wish not to see you in, ever," I exclaim. "Besides, I myself am next in line for the throne of Jupiter, I don't need yours as well, nor do I want it, why would I?"

"Because that's what power hungry people want!" she yells in anguish. "More power!"

"I am not *Mesmer Amar!" I growl, becoming furious that Celia would even think to compare me to that vile creature. "Stop treating me as such."*

"When are you going to realize that all people who want power are the same to me?" Celia asks. "They are all disgusting and after the crown."

"I hate to break this to you, Princess, but the universe doesn't revolve around you!"

"Well who else would it revolve around?" she asks, arrogance consuming her voice.

Now I'm the one who's taken aback, hurt because I truly believed she was more than a spoiled, conceited princess, but it appears that I was sorely wrong.

"You know what?" I ask in bitter annoyance. "Maybe you deserve Mesmer." I regret the words the moment I say them. If I live through this, I am going to have a lot of making up to do, *I think when I see the look on Celia's face. She's furious and heartbroken. It's in her eyes and I hate myself for making her feel such a way.*

"What did you just say?" Celia asks, somehow finding it in herself to speak.

"Celia, I'm–"

"No," she cuts me off, her voice filled with hostility and menace. "There are some lines that you just don't cross. It's a shame that you were too stupid to see where those lines lay."

"Celia, wait!" I reach out to grab her hand and pull her back to me, but she's gone before I can, slipping out of reach. "I'm sorry, Celia, I didn't mean that," I mutter to the now empty corridor. "But I'm going to make things right." I throw my dignity aside, it's either do that or lose her, and nothing is worth that price.

With a tired groan I awake, slowly collecting my consciousness from the realm of dreams.

I roll onto my side to find that the bed is empty and I'm alone. *Where's Celia?* I wonder as I bring myself into a sitting position.

Suddenly the bed creaks and feels warmer as Celia emerges from the shadows and lies next to me.

"What were you doing?" I ask curiously.

"I was watching you sleep," she says plainly. "What were you dreaming about?"

"I was dreaming about that ball held on Jupiter, where you and I got into that fight," I say slowly. "I can't believe some of the things I said."

"That's what I thought when the memory came back to me," she says, gazing up at the ceiling. "I was kind of a basket case."

"That really hasn't changed," I tell her with a quiet laugh.

"Thanks," she says sarcastically, hitting me in the arm with the back of her hand.

"So why aren't you asleep?" I ask, shifting my eyes down to her.

"I honestly don't know," she says, shrugging her shoulders, keeping her focus trained above her. "Maybe it's because I'm afraid of what might haunt my subconscious, maybe it's because I just don't feel like it. Or maybe it's because someone was tossing and turning like a madman all night." With that last comment Celia shoots me a playful look, smiling at me, her hazel eyes shining brightly, even in the dark room.

"I'm going to go with one of the first two, because I'm a prince, and princes don't toss and turn. We are always on our best behavior, even in our sleep," I say, returning her playfulness.

"Who says I was talking about you?" she asks mischievously.

"You better not be talking about another man," I say, finding myself immediately on top of her. "Because if you are, I'll have to fight him to the death, and we know who will win. And then I'll have to chain you to my side so that you can't leave me," I say, murmuring into her neck, my words merely shallow breaths, ghosting over her skin.

"That sounds somewhat exciting," she says, tugging at my earlobe with her teeth.

My fingers trail up her arms, pinning her hands above her head as I lean in and kiss her, catching her lower lip between my teeth.

"Perhaps this wasn't my best idea," Celia says suddenly. "You should be resting."

"You started this," I remind her, my hands slipping under the hem of her shirt, running my fingers over her body, my fingertips brushing her skin.

She breaks free of my grip and grabs me by the collar of my shirt and brings my mouth down onto hers in a needy kiss. Her hands follow the lead of mine and run up my chest from under my shirt, forcing the fabric up along with her hands.

There's only static in my head as she kisses me, her mouth desperate upon my mine. She tastes sweet, like sugar and vanilla, a taste that conjures feelings that had been lost for so long.

I lift her shirt up and over her head as she does the same with mine. This time, when I run my hands along her body, I use my whole hand, not just my fingertips, relishing the feeling of her skin beneath my hands. I run them down her torso, following down her legs and back up, resting at her hips, holding her firmly.

My lips leave hers and trail to her neck, forcing a sigh from her lips, turning into a shocked gasp as I begin to grind against her.

I go back to kiss her when the door creaks open, revealing a tired and disheveled-looking Corrine.

I freeze, straddling Celia, my lips hovering over hers, waiting for a reaction from the young girl in the doorway.

"Hey! Pipe down!" she commands. "I get that being reunited with your lover is great and all – not that I would actually know – but to be honest, I don't really care. What you guys do makes no difference to me, but, do it quietly!" Her voice raises at the end and she's shouting. "Because I am trying to sleep! Do you even know what time it is? It's like three in the morning. Three in the freaking morning, and this is what I get to wake up to! Shut the hell up!" She slams the door, leaving Celia and me utterly shocked.

"Did that really happen?" Celia asks in disbelief.

"Yep, I think it did," I respond, just as shocked as she is.

"She is *so* my daughter," Celia sighs. "Fearless and constantly agitated."

She reaches up and caresses my face, her thumb rubbing soothing strokes on my cheek. "She does have a point though. It's late, you should go back to bed," she says.

"And what about you?" I ask.

"Me? I'll find something to occupy myself with," she tries to roll off the bed, but my arms constrict around her, holding her tightly.

"Celia, you can either run from what's haunting you and keep yourself up all night, or you can stay here in my arms, and I'll keep you safe. I'll help you fight whatever demons are chasing after you. I'll take care of you, I promise."

She sighs, but stays where she is, wrapped tightly in my arms, and slowly, her breaths become even and she drifts off to sleep.

The time has come, Celia. *The voice echoes throughout the darkness that surrounds me. All I can see is black, all I can feel is cold. My heart races, a cold sweat beads my body, and I'm paralyzed by panic.*

It's time to end this.

I don't know why, but those words spread fear and apprehension throughout my body.

"Who are you?" I ask aloud.

I'm you, Celia.

"What do you want from me? Haven't we already done this?" I ask, becoming irritated. I should no longer be haunted by my subconscious, that should have ended by now.

You're right, we've already done this, but you keep hiding. You can't escape what you know will happen, what you know you'll have to do. There is only one way to finish this, you know that. The question is, will you be able to do it? Will you be able to finally end this eternal masquerade that you started?

"I'll do whatever I need to," I proclaim, my voice radiating with defiance.

I'll make sure to hold you to that.

The voice is now screaming in my ears and my breath leaves me as pain seizes my body. I gasp, but no air comes and I fall onto my hands and knees. My lungs burn, my skin stings, it's like I'm burning up from the inside.

I come to, gasping for the air I had so desperately fought for in my dream.

Beckett's fast asleep, lying on his back, a peaceful look on his handsome face.

I sigh, rolling onto my feet and put my shirt back on, padding through the quiet house.

"Why is this happening?" I ask, my soft voice dampened by the empty room.

I leave the house and go onto the porch only to start pacing from railing to railing.

"What the hell would I not be able to do?" I wonder. I run a hand through my hair, my muscles are stressed and sore. All I can think of is the way my body burned, surrounded by that blanket of darkness and emptiness. "I decided a long time ago that I would do anything I needed to in order to kill Mesmer, I'm not going to go back on that now."

"You and me both," a voice says.

My attention snaps up to the roof where I find my daughter sitting, looking up at the night sky with a conflicted look.

"I thought you went back to bed," I say.

"Looks like nightmares are a genetic thing in this family," she responds, keeping her eyes trained on the sky.

"Two questions," I say. "One, what are you doing out here? Two, what is it with you and roofs?"

"I'm not sure why I like roofs so much, I think it's because I'm so damn short and they make me feel tall. And as for what I'm doing out here, I'm doing the same thing as you, facing reality," Corrine says, her voice bleak and bitter.

"I'm not entirely sure what you're talking about," I tell her. "There's nothing I need to face."

"You know that's a lie," she says. "You know as well as I do that pulling a victory out of this hat is a longshot. We're most likely going to all end up dead."

"Man, you are morbid."

"Well, I *am* your child, so what can you expect?" she asks.

"What are you thinking of, Corrine?" I ask. "I'm not a morbid person. I'm a realist, not a pessimist, same goes for you. I know that I find myself lost in the stars when my mind is troubled, and since I've realized that you're basically a copy of myself, I'm going to guess that you do the same thing. So, what's troubling you?"

"Even if we do win this fight, and that's a big 'if,' things still won't be okay. Even if Mesmer is dead and gone, it won't heal the pain we all feel. It won't change the fact that you lost everything, that I lost everything. None of that will ever change," she says bitterly. "It's not going to change the fact that I fell in love with a psycho. Said psycho will just be dead."

I feel myself meld into the shadows and assemble next to the girl.

Her words move me, stirring something deep inside of me and I begin to understand what it is that I have to do.

"Corrine, look at me," I command. "I am going to make things right, I can fix this." My words demand the young girl's attention, and they receive it.

"How do you plan on doing that?" Corrine asks skeptically.

"I haven't got all the details put together, but I'm starting to figure it out," I say slowly.

"Well then tell me, maybe I can help!" she exclaims.

I give a soft laugh, turning my eyes away from the young girl and up to the sky.

"If I tell you, you won't let me do it."

"What do you mean?" she asks in bewilderment.

"I mean that what I'm going to do is dangerous, and if you, Ben, or Beckett found out, you'd all try to stop me."

"Mom–"

"Shh." I place my forefinger and my middle finger on her temple and close my eyes in concentration.

She can't remember this.

I do almost what I did with Beckett the night my identity was revealed, but reversed in a way. Instead of sharing a memory, I'm blocking one.

I focus on the electric signals in Corrine's brain, using my electricity manipulation abilities to control them. I use the signals to disrupt her memories, to block them off. I can't afford for her to remember this, she'd try to stop me and I have to do this.

Before she comes around I dissipate, melting into the shadows, leaving her staring down at the rooftop with a confused look.

"I'm sorry, Corrine, but I have to do this," I whisper, hoping that someday my family will be able to forgive me for what I have to do.

Slowly, my eyes open, only to wince at the bright light streaming into the room. I'm alone, Celia's gone.

I sit up and rub the sleep from my eyes, taking my time as I get to my feet and wander out into the living room.

"Where's Celia?" I ask, snatching the attention of the two teenagers sitting on the couch.

"I don't know, I thought she was with you," Corrine says.

"No, she wasn't with me when I woke up. Has anyone seen Celia since last night?"

Apprehension seeps into my skin. Celia's known for doing rash things to protect those she loves, she could've gone after Mesmer on her own.

Silence hangs in the air and we all exchange looks, reaching the same conclusion.

"Shit," Corrine says, jumping up and bolting to another room. "Search the house!" she commands as she bursts into yet another room.

We don't wait, Ben and I split instantly. He goes out the door to the porch and I rush downstairs, praying to whoever will listen that Celia is somewhere in this house.

I sigh in relief, I've found her. She's sitting on a piano bench, slumped over the keys, fast asleep.

"Leave it to Celia to find the one house in the middle of nowhere with a piano," I say with a small laugh.

I walk up the stairs, letting her sleep.

"I found Celia," I say to Ben and Corrine. "She's sleeping on the piano downstairs."

"There's a piano downstairs?" Ben asks.

"I guess so," I say with a shrug.

"Is something going on with Mom?" Corrine asks, her eyebrows furrowed in thought.

"Well, she's about to fight a battle she's been running from for thousands of years. She'd be even crazier than we think she is if there weren't," I say. "Why do you ask?"

"I don't know, but I've got this weird feeling. I think she's planning to do something… insane."

"She wouldn't be Celia Walters if she wasn't."

"Celia, hey, wake up." A soft voice calls me to consciousness and away from the empty blackness that surrounds me.

"Uhh," I groan, sitting upright and closing the keyboard.

"Leave it to you to find a safehouse with a piano in it," Beckett says with a small smile.

"What can I say, pianos seem to follow me," I say.

"As do several other things," he says softly.

"What'd you mean?" I inquire.

"Something is haunting you, Celia, we can all see it, let us help you. Tell us what's going on. We're a family, we face our demons together."

"It's me, Beck. I'm my own demon, I'm haunting myself," I say with exhausted anger. "I started this mess and now I have to end it, but the only thing I've managed to do is hurt the people I care about. I should've just let him win when this whole thing started; no one would be in this mess then. I could have hidden the last Crystal and gone out fighting that bastard to the death. At least that way the last laugh would have been guaranteed to be mine."

He sighs quietly and takes a seat next to me on the piano bench.

"Don't talk that way, Cel. If you had given up at the beginning, you never would've known the joy of having a family, the joy of living, or the taste of victory. Celia, you and I, we'd have no future. All we would be is a bitter taste left in Mesmer's mouth. You and I, what we have, the love we share, it wouldn't exist. No one would be around to remember it, it would only be another forgotten tale held by the universe.

"Yes, the people you love and care about have been hurt, but that's nothing compared to the joy that we've felt. Now that we're not alone, now that we're a family, now that we're going to win this war. Celia, if you had given up, we would have lost the war. It's true that you started this game of deadly hide-and-seek, but you did so in order to win the war that Mesmer Amar waged on us all.

"Stop tearing yourself apart because you had to choose the lesser of two evils. No decision you could've made was easy, but you chose the one you knew would be best. That's what a leader does."

I turn and smile at Beckett, grateful that he's here, grateful that I'm not alone. His words reassure me and give me a tiny bit of warmth to hold onto as a plan slowly formulates in my mind. A plan that, once it comes together, will leave me cold to my core.

"I'm going to go back upstairs, we're going to start preparations for tonight. Meet us in ten minutes?"

"Yeah, I'll see you up there," I say, placing a quick kiss on his lips and then he's gone, disappearing up the stairs.

I sigh, my eyes scanning the room, searching for anything to pull this budding plan together.

I get up from the piano bench, walking to the windows across the room, resting my head against the cool glass, gazing out at the landscape before me.

I have to do this, I tell myself. *To protect this world that I've come to love. To protect the beautiful places like the one before me. To protect wonderful families, like the one whose house in which I reside. Like my own family I left behind. I have to do this.*

I sigh and drop my gaze, my eyes now focused on the windowsill.

"What am I going to do?" I ask the dust covered surface, fully aware that it isn't able to answer me.

A tiny movement catches my attention, playing at the edge of my vision. A plastic flower, powered by the sun, dances up and down. The center of the flower wears a large smile and black sunglasses, with purple petals fanning out around it.

Suddenly, my thoughts come together, rushing to a formulated point from the scattered sections of my mind. And as predicted, my blood runs cold.

"Alright, are you guys ready?" Celia asks, coming up the stairs.

"Yeah, we've been waiting on you," Corrine responds, perched on the edge of the table.

"Sorry about that, I had to gather my thoughts," Celia says. She takes a seat on the edge of the counter, assuming almost the same stance as her daughter.

They're so incredibly similar, it's almost scary, I think as I watch the two of them. *Why aren't Ben and I that similar?*

"So, what's the plan?" Corrine asks, her eyes trained on Celia.

"Well, you and I are both flaming blips on Mesmer's radar, so you and I are going to be the first two on the field. Ben and Beckett will stay back until Mesmer shows up. Since he normally sends out Sylvia to do his dirty work, Corrine, you and I will fight her first. The quicker we get her on the ropes, the sooner Mesmer will show up, and once he does, the boys will join us on the field. Beckett and I will keep him distracted while Corrine and Ben take out Sylvia. When that's finished, I want you two to hold back." Celia makes eye contact with both of them so that she knows that they both understand what their roles are. "If at any point you two think that Beckett and I need help, Ben will jump in. Corrine, you're staying back until you are absolutely certain that Mesmer is completely focused on us, and then you'll attack from behind. He won't be able to keep up a four-fronted battle on his own, and when faced with repetitive attacks and no breaks, he won't be able to phase out. He'll be stuck in the fight. When he starts to tire out and get sloppy, I want everyone to back off and leave him with me. I started this and I have to end this."

Corrine opens her mouth to interject, but Celia holds up a hand and the girl stops.

"I know what I said before, but I've realized that this is the way it has to be. If I can't kill Mesmer, and he ends up killing me, then, and only then, will the rest of you engage him." Celia's voice is stern and strict, it's the voice of a commanding officer, a role Celia was born to play.

"I thought you said that you physically couldn't defeat him, that's why you've been stuck in this game for so long," Corrine says, completely ignoring the silencing hand Celia holds up.

"I've got a plan this time, one I know will work." She doesn't elaborate, leaving it that, staring down Corrine, daring her to speak.

She doesn't, she only glares back at Celia, her eyes trying to see through Celia and grab ahold of her hidden plan.

"Okay, so what then? What's this other plan you've got?" Ben asks, seemingly oblivious to the tension that fills the room.

"It's better if I'm the only one who knows what it entails," she says, her eyes growing dark.

No more questions are asked. We can all feel the apprehension looming above us. The final fight will happen tonight, a fight that will either save the world or damn it completely. It's no longer about the four of us settling the score, it's about much more now. The entire universe is at stake, resting on our shoulders, and the outcome of tonight's battle will be the determining factor of the world's fate. A war that has been raging for thousands of years will be coming to an end with this one, final battle. It all ends tonight.

The sound of gravel crunching beneath our feet echoes through the empty district. It's the only sound other than the wind blowing through the abandoned, dilapidated buildings and factories.

"Are you sure they're going to show?" Corrine asks, surveying our surroundings skeptically.

"Without a doubt. Mesmer knows that we've got the Crystal and that I've got my memories back. He can feel it in his bones. Chances are he's probably preparing for war, just like we already have. My guess is that he's planned some sort of long range attack to try to throw us off balance and then he'll come in and take us out quickly."

"I thought you said he'd send Sylvia out first," Corrine says.

"He will, but he won't be far off. He'll be watching the whole thing very closely, and that's why Beckett and Ben are going to phase in from Nick's," I say.

"Are you sure they'll know when to join us? They can see the signal?" Corrine asks.

"It's kind of hard to miss a huge lighting storm," I respond. "Besides, Beckett will be able to feel it when Mesmer shows up, it's not a feeling either of us could miss or mistake."

"You're positive?"

"Yes," I say, becoming irritated. "Nothing else can make someone's blood run so cold."

We continue walking, waiting for something to happen, when Corrine suddenly stops.

"Don't move," she says, putting an arm out to halt me.

"Corrine, what are you–"

"Sh." She cuts me off, holding her hand up in a quieting manner. Her fingers move slowly, as if she's feeling the air for something.

I feel it, the air, it's heavy and tingling. The hairs on the back of my neck stand up.

"Get down!" There's a flash of blinding light, and before I can react I'm tackled, landing hard.

I cringe and grab my side, gritting my teeth against the pain, hissing slightly.

"What'd you do to your side?" Corrine asks, taking note of my reaction.

"I hurt it," I groan, rolling onto all fours, coughing and clutching my side.

"How? I didn't tackle you *that* hard."

"Does it matter?" I ask as another bolt of blinding light blasts the ground beside me. I roll to avoid it, watching the spot where I had been only seconds ago turn into a hole filled with dirt and debris.

"Yes, it does," Corrine responds. "I know you've got something crazy planned, that's why you tried to get rid of my memories." Her body moves as fast as light, gracefully dodging the next blast while hauling me to my feet.

I stagger back a bit, gaining my balance.

"You weren't supposed to remember that. How did you get those memories back?" I ask, jumping out of the way of another attack. The blast burns through the steel beam skeleton of one of the buildings behind me, leaving the metal glowing red and dripping to the ground below. My skin is hot on the side that the spear of light passed.

"You used the electric signals in my brain to lock those memories away, and when I found myself on the roof, confused about the last ten minutes, I figured someone did something to my memories. So, I used those same electric signals and messages to get those memories back."

"Damnit," I growl, dodging another attack. "You weren't supposed to do that."

"Well, I did, and this isn't over, but for now, let's focus on the fight or we're going to get burnt to a crisp."

"Okay, you distract her, while I phase out and attack."

"Let's do this." The girl clenches her fist, dust and dirt clinging to her body and chest. Her blue eyes shine like gemstones, bursting with life, not a single ounce of fear dwelling within them. This is a child who lives for battle, nothing else could ever make her feel so alive.

When the next blast comes, I move barely enough to not be hit but still be thrown back by the force, letting the blast knock me aside into the shadows of a broken-down warehouse.

As I begin to dissipate, Corrine pulls two short swords out and charges her opponent, making her way across the battlefield with a ballerina's grace, dodging every attack as if it were some sort of dance.

I melt into the shadows, materializing a few yards behind our attacker, stepping out of the darkness to draw her attention.

Immediately, the blasts stop and I have exactly what I want. All of Sylvia Trunnel's focus is on me, it's time for one last fight.

She turns instantly and lunges, her arm morphing into a wicked, sharp blade, slashing at neck level. I move aside and find my whip in my hand, glinting in the moonlight and I flick it towards her.

Sylvia rolls under my attack, popping back up instantly, jabbing with her weaponized arm. I jump back, the tip of her blade slicing a thin line across my white tank top. The pain in my side slows my movements, it's putting me in a dangerous position. I can't even seem a little off balance or Sylvia will pounce on me.

"You're lucky you didn't cut my jacket again," I tell her, trying to keep my normal appearance and confident bravado. "Then I would have been really pissed."

"You're lucky I didn't cut your stomach open," she snarls in response. "Then you would've been really *screwed*.

"You don't honestly think you can win this fight, do you? Even if you manage to kill me, neither you, nor your daughter, have it in you to kill Mesmer."

"We'll see about that!" Two blades protrude from the redhead's chest, Corrine stands behind her, a scowl burning on her face. The wind whips at her hair, her eyes are fierce, it's like looking back through time to see myself in battle. If there was any question about her being my daughter, it was gone now. The deadly look on her face is one that could only ever belong to me, and now her.

Corrine plants her foot on Sylvia's back, shoving her off her twin blades, twirling them back into a grip she can fight with.

The redhead turns toward the girl and snarls, blood dripping down her chin and seeping through her clothes.

She jumps at Corrine, bringing her sword arm down hard and the girl blocks the attack with an upward x-catch, shoving her opponent back.

"How are you still living?" Corrine asks with bored irritation. "You should be dead already."

"The one I serve provides me with strength!"

"Well that's good, because fighting only you would be *totally boring*," Corrine snarls.

Sylvia lunges at her, becoming airborne with the intent to kill, but the girl just stands there with a contemptuous smile, twirling her blades menacingly.

She lowers her head slightly, gripping her blades until the veins in her hands show, and then she charges, half imitating a move I've only ever seen Beckett do.

She hits the ground, sliding onto her knees as she brings her swords up to block the attack, slipping in between her opponent's legs.

Sylvia lands facing the girl's back and slashes downward, but Corrine spins one hundred eighty degrees on her knees, catching the attack with perfect timing.

With her free hand, Sylvia grabs another blade and jabs at Corrine's chest and she drops down further, her back now touching the ground. She sweeps her legs and knocks Sylvia off her feet and rolls on top of her, plunging her twin blades into the woman's chest, pinning her to the ground.

The redhead lets out a shrill scream of agony and begins to thrash about in the gravel in an attempt to be free.

This is it.

Time slows to a crawl as I drop to one knee, my fist brushing the ground, my eyes closed in concentration. I take a deep breath and summon all of my strength, feeling the electricity surging through me. I keep the energy contained, allowing it to build up inside of me, aching to be released, burning to burst forth like frothy water from a broken dam.

I look up at the sky and watch the stars disappear as charcoal-colored clouds cover us like a black dome, trapping us in this battle arena. And then I let go.

Blue, so pure, so piercing, fused with a rich, royal purple. It's the only thing I can see.

Electricity rushes out from every pore in my skin, through my eyes and mouth. I've become a blazing pillar of electricity, charring everything around me to a black the color of death.

All I hear is static and the crackle of electricity. It rings in my ears and echoes within my mind.

I kneel in the center of the shockwave with gale force winds blowing around me, whipping at my clothes and kicking up dirt and dust. Everything within a ten-foot radius of me is ripped apart by the vicious winds.

When I look down, I see that my exposed body is webbed with blue and purple lines, swirling underneath my skin. It looks like someone poured a fluorescent liquid through my veins, causing them to be seen through my flesh.

It's inside of me. Electricity courses through me, replacing the blood in my veins.

And then it stops. The electricity, the winds, the power, it all implodes back into me, knocking me flat on my back. The force of the implosion drives the air from my lungs and places me several yards from where I was before.

My ears ring, almost painfully, and my vision is blurred. Everything I see is doubled and wobbling, as if the ground beneath me were still trembling.

I shake my head, as if to shake off my daze, but it only makes things worse. My skull throbs and I suddenly feel nauseous.

I lift my head and catch sight of Corrine, who stands not too far away, looming over Sylvia Trunnel, but, I can't decide which image is real and which image is the side effect of being blasted with lightning.

I try to roll onto my good side, or onto my hands and knees, but my body refuses to respond. The shock from all that power leaves my muscles stunned.

There's a flash of light. It's white-hot, causing me to see spots in my blurred, doubled vision. I can't see who's arrived on the scene, but I don't need to see him, I know he's here. No one else could ever make me feel this way. No one else could make my blood run so cold.

"You've really outdone yourself this time, Celia," Mesmer says. "I wasn't expecting a spectacular light show upon my arrival, or for you to incapacitate yourself for me. It makes my job a whole lot easier." I can hear the gravel crunching under his feet as he makes his way to me, taking his time.

Corrine, I think frantically. *I need to get up, I have to protect her. I made her a promise.*

I force myself into a sitting position, demanding that my body do as I command.

I slowly make it to my feet, gritting my teeth through the pain. I take deep breaths to try and stop the shaking that runs through me.

I glance at Corrine. She's still, poised over Sylvia, frozen like a statue.

Mesmer follows my gaze, a cold smile forming on his lips when he sees Corrine.

"And here I thought you were mucking about with another time travelling version of yourself. If I had known it was Corrine you were with, I would have shown up sooner," he says, making his way towards my daughter.

"You saw her, you bastard," I growl. "You fought her, how could you have *not* known it was her? She practically announced herself! Corrine, wake up!" It's useless. The girl stands frozen in her place as Mesmer takes a knee beside her.

"Go on, Corrine. Kill her, my love," he murmurs, his voice soft and gentle. He threads his fingers through her hair, trailing them down her spine. His touch is tender, a caress, causing more damage to the girl than if he were to cut her open.

"Don't touch my daughter," I growl, taking a step forward. My leg gives out and I drop to a knee. My breath hitches from the pain but I push myself back onto my feet again. "Corrine, snap out of it!" I plead. "Don't listen to him, he's not the person you remember, he's not the person you fell in love with. That person was fake, a shadow of who he truly is, the ghost of what could have been." As I speak, I can see clarity come back to the girl's eyes. "You can't let his ghost haunt you forever. I made you a promise, didn't I? I need you to trust me and wake up. Please."

Mesmer smirks and lets out a bemused laugh. "She's not the one I'm haunting," he says, turning to me for a moment. He smiles at me, a cruel and cold smile, before turning back to Corrine. "Go on, get rid of her," he says. "You know Sylvia would never let us be together. She would never allow us to be happy. Kill her and together, we will defeat our enemies and rule. You and I, side by side, for the rest of eternity." His lips graze her ear as he speaks, and then he buries his face in her shoulder, nuzzling the crook of her neck.

I feel sick, but more than that, I feel furious. Slowly, I feel the strength come back to my bones. My body, now filled with rage, acts on its own accord, but not as quickly as Corrine's does.

In a flash, she rips the blades from Sylvia's chest and spins on the balls of her feet, slashing Mesmer across the chest.

He stumbles back, shock frozen on his face.

"Don't worry, Love, I'll kill her," Corrine snarls. "But not before I kill you!"

I sprint towards Corrine, desperate to stop her before she plays right into Mesmer's hands, before she falls into his trap, one I've fallen for many times due to my own rage.

"Corrine, stop!" I come to a sliding halt with my arms spread, my body blocking her path. Gravel flies around us and dust fills the air as I block the girl.

"Get out of my way, Celia," she growls through grit teeth.

"Calm down, Corrine," I command, refusing to move out of her way. "You may have surprised him with that attack, but if you'd stop and pay attention, you'd realize that he's only an image. He's not stupid enough to go up against someone as unpredictable as you if he hadn't already worked you into his plan. You being here took him by surprise and threw off his strategy. My guess is that as soon as he saw you, he cast his image and ducked into the shadows. He'll wait for you step in and kill what you think is him, and then he'll come out of seemingly nowhere and kill you."

"What makes you think that he's an image?" Corrine asks, the anger slowly filtering from her voice.

"He's not bleeding."

"How did I not see that?" she asks.

"Because you're angry and your judgement is clouded. Take care of Sylvia, she'll be up and ready to go. Mesmer's here now, she's channeling his power and she's not going to run. Everyone knows this is the fight to end it all. We fight to the death now, she knows that, and so does he. Mesmer will kill us both if given the chance, that's why you're not going to fight him. Let me take care of this."

She starts to respond, but I cut her off.

"Don't argue with me," I say sternly, then my voice softens. "Win, lose or draw, Kid, I'm proud of you. Now find Sylvia Trunnel and bury her!"

She clenches her jaw and nods. She looks just like me. Her eyes blaze with confidence and pride as she gives me a small smile.

"Ten bucks says I come out of this looking better than you."

"You're on." I clap her on the back before she darts off, engaging in deadly combat with the psychotic redhead.

I take a deep breath and turn my back to them, facing my old enemy.

"This reminds me of old times," Mesmer says. His voice is warm, as if he were reminiscing with an old friend about times long passed. "You refusing help in order to protect those you care about, look where it's gotten you. You don't ever learn from the past, do you?"

"You couldn't be more wrong," I growl, pulling out my dagger and tightening my grip on my whip.

I sigh. I can't rely on my sight, not when he's projecting his image. I'll have to take a different approach to this fight.

Slowly, I close my eyes. I'm forced to fight without sight, forced to fight as if I were blind. All my other senses go into overdrive. I can hear every movement on the battlefield, from the fight between Corrine and Sylvia, to every bug that lands on the gravel and takes flight again. I can feel the air surrounding me in currents of hot and cold, feel the pressure of the atmosphere. The air is filled with the scent of sweat and blood, leaving a salty, coppery tang in the air.

"Hm, you've got guts, Princess, I'll give you that. But guts won't save you, not now, not from me."

I feel a slight shift in the atmosphere, a change in pressure around me.

I bring my dagger up in time to parry his attack and flash my whip in his direction.

"You seem different," Mesmer says, his voice now coming from my left. "You're smarter, faster, calmer and more confident. It's as I thought, you've found it, haven't you? Oh well, it won't change the outcome of this battle." His voice is lazy, almost as if he's bored with the fight already. "You still don't have the power to kill me."

"She may not, but I do!" It's Beckett.

I open my eyes, sighing as relief floods through me.

Beckett stands behind the real Mesmer with his sword drawn, pricking the back of the dark prince's neck.

He wears a black t-shirt that fits snugly on his chest and his leather jacket that shines as it reflects the moon's light. The only color on him is his blue eyes that blaze with cold fury. He's never looked more like a prince and a warrior at a single moment.

"We don't have to do this, Mesmer, you can leave with your life. Stop this pursuit of power and leave us in peace, find peace of your own. I'm showing you mercy, Mesmer, you'd be wise to accept it." Beckett's voice is even and calm, but it's clear that this is Mesmer's last chance to back down.

"I don't want your mercy, Beckett Halverson, I want your head!" Mesmer spins faster than my eyes can track. He grabs the sword from his hip and knocks aside Beckett's blade.

Beckett ducks as Mesmer slashes where his head would have been and uses his legs to sweep Mesmer off his feet. He jabs down with his sword, narrowly missing Mesmer's chest as he rolls to the side.

The battle between the two rages on and Beckett is flawless. He moves like a dancing shadow, cast by a flame, flickering and darting across my vision. He twirls and slashes, thrusts and parries, ducks and spins, evading Mesmer's blade, attacking relentlessly with his own.

He truly is like a god in combat, I think in awe, watching him in a daze.

One minute I'm standing, watching Beckett in the heat of battle, and the next minute, I'm lying on my back in the gravel. Debris and bits of gravel lay around me. I cough up a lung full of dust and dirt and roll onto the ground beside me, slowly making it to my hands and knees.

What the hell was that? I wonder, trying to extricate all the junk from my lungs.

The left side of my body is searing, and my clothes are singed and coated in a layer of soot.

"Sylvia," I growl.

A pair of warm hands pulls me to my feet and Ben's eyes meet mine.

I start forward, but he puts his arm out and stops me.

"I'll take care of this," he tells me. "You need a breather, you look like hell."

"I'm fine, I can–"

"Save your strength," Ben commands. "You're going to need it."

Does he know?

Ben looks away, taking in a deep breath as he closes his eyes.

The ground begins to shake, and small bits of gravel, dirt and sand rise into the air, surrounding Ben in the swirling wind.

When he opens his eyes again, they're a dark, golden brown, like the color of sand in the hue of the setting sun.

Spears of sand shoot from his personal sand storm, rushing towards Sylvia Trunnel and she blows them away with ease, turning them to glass, causing them to crack and shatter from the heat of the blast.

Ben keeps up the attacks, occupying Sylvia as his sister sneaks up behind her.

Corrine jumps, almost knocking her opponent to the ground. She wraps her arms under Sylvia's and behind her head, struggling to subdue her opponent as she flails in the young girl's arms.

"Do it now, Ben!" Corrine yells from across the field.

He extends an arm and the sands obey, rushing out towards his sister and his enemy.

At the last second, Corrine jumps backward, out of the mass of sand swirling around them.

Ben closes his hand into a tight fist. Immediately, the sand hardens, condensing into an unbreakable shell.

"Finish this, Corrine," he growls.

The girl nods. She runs up the side of a rundown warehouse and pushes off the walls, projecting herself into the air. She raises her sword and brings it down onto the sand shell, bringing down a violent bolt of electricity.

The sand shell turns a honey color, crystalizing into a ball of glass, suspended in the air and then another lightning bolt comes down, shattering the glass into millions of pieces that sparkle like diamonds in the moonlight.

I jump as Mesmer drops down and swipes at my legs, landing quickly and stepping onto the flat of his sword, trapping his blade in place.

"You're getting sloppy," I growl, smashing the hilt of my sword into his nose.

Blood sprays out. It speckles my shirt and his face, dripping down his chin.

Mesmer loses his grip on his blade and stumbles backwards, his hands coming up to his face. I don't relent and I lunge.

He jumps to the side, spinning out of the reach of my attack. When I turn around, my blade is met once again with his own.

He attacks and now I'm the one playing the defensive, blocking and parrying, dodging out of danger. He keeps me at a distance, using long swipes and jabs to keep me from getting anywhere near him.

I need to get closer, I think desperately. *It'll be easier to end this in close combat.*

I step in and bring my sword down hard, meeting Mesmer's with force. He shoves me back and I let my body go with it, sliding a good distance from him. I seize my opportunity and run. When I near my opponent, I throw my sword up and over his head and drop down and slide feet first like a baseball player between his legs, coming out behind him, where I rise to a knee. My blade returns to my hand and I plunge it into his calf.

He falls, blocking my next attack as he does so, but barely. Mesmer struggles to his feet, rising slowly, making sure to keep the pressure off his injured leg.

"It's time to end this," I say, closing the distance between us.

"I couldn't agree more," Mesmer growls. He moves quickly, faster than my eyes can follow. Before I know what's happening, I'm lying on my back and Mesmer is standing over me, poised to attack.

A glint of silver zips through the night and Mesmer recoils, blood dripping from the back of his hand.

He turns to face Celia and all is quiet. You could hear a pin if it were to drop.

"How many times must we do this dance?" Mesmer asks, almost in exasperation.

"Once more," Celia responds coolly.

Wind blows around the two like a scene from an old Western movie. Everything seems to have become colder, it's as if the Earth itself can feel the tension between them.

"Hm, you seem to have forgotten that you can't kill me," Mesmer says, a sick smile forming on his lips.

"Things are different this time," Celia says, her grip on her weapons tightening. "Let's end this."

She makes the first move, sprinting at him with a blinding speed, a speed I've never seen from her before. My eyes catch the flash of her whip and the glint of her dagger, aside from that, she's just a blur, a tornado of color and electricity whirling around Mesmer Amar.

I can barely keep up with her, my eyes can't trace her movements. I catch a flash of what looks like a tornado kick as Mesmer flies backward, landing hard enough to create a crater.

Where is this insane power coming from? I wonder. I don't think more on it, the sight before me stunning enough to halt my thoughts.

Mesmer lies on his back with a dagger protruding from his chest, just above where his heart would be.

I look at Celia, and she looks terrible. She's bleeding as badly as Mesmer. She's pale and she looks exhausted, like she could pass out at any given moment. Her eyes shine with that fierce light that only she owns, but it's obvious that she can barely manage to stand. The only thing that keeps her on her feet is the sheer force of her will.

Slowly, Mesmer manages himself into a sitting position. He tugs the dagger out of his chest, grimacing from the pain.

"How did you do that? You shouldn't be able to do that!" he growls, tossing the dagger to the side.

"I said it before, things are different this time." Celia lifts up the side of her shirt, and every heart on the battlefield stops for a few seconds.

A purple light swirls beneath her skin in one tennis-ball-sized area, emitting a powerful light. It explains everything.

How did she do this? I ask myself in a daze. *I thought I had left it hidden at the Mallard house.*

"You didn't," Mesmer snarls.

"Celia, why would you do this?" I ask, stunned and angry at her actions.

"I didn't have any other choice, Beckett," she says solemnly. "I started this, and now I have to end it. I won't make the people I care about pay for my shortcomings, for what I couldn't do. Not anymore." Her eyes blaze with determination, God himself wouldn't be able to stop her now. "I love you, Beckett, hold onto that."

"Celia, no!" I go to run to her before she can do something stupid, but I can't, I'm held back. Ben and Corrine grab my arms firmly, restraining me.

"Let me go!" I yell, struggling to break their grip but it's to no avail, I can't get free.

"Dad, stop." It's Ben. Despite the calmness in his voice, I can feel the worry coming off of him in waves.

"Her mind is made. If you try to stop her, you'll only get yourself killed," Corrine says.

I'm frozen, paralyzed by fear. I can't stop her, I can't save her.

They bought it, I wasn't sure they would. I had only hoped that channeling electricity through the plastic flower petal embedded in my skin would create the desired effect.

I drop my shirt down and slowly make my way towards Mesmer, giving him time to get to his feet. I only have one chance to do this, I can't screw it up.

"You absorbed the Crystal," Mesmer says in disbelief, steadying himself, readying for battle.

"Damn straight," I growl, picking up my pace to a jog.

"Now you are completely of no use to me," he says. He looks almost sad as the realization sinks in.

"It ends now," I say, sprinting at full speed. I use electricity to propel me forward, creating the illusion of the Crystal's power.

I have to do this, the words echo through my tired mind. *I must end this.*

Mesmer meets me head on, his blade blocked by my whip. He steps in, scooping up the dagger I had stabbed him with earlier and brings it toward my chest. I jump to the side and flash my whip around his leg, pulling him off balance. He rolls with it, going down to his knees and swiping at my legs. I jump, managing to propel myself over him, landing in a cat-like stance behind my opponent. I quickly grab hold of two rose-shaped throwing stars, propelling them towards him which he easily blocks with his sword, laughing as he does so.

He advances once again, slashing with his sword, drawing my attention away from the dagger he then plunges into my leg. I go down, taken aback by the pain, no longer able to keep my battle-worn body going.

My leg is warm with blood. It seeps through my ripped jeans and turns the ground around me a dirty red. My body is throbbing, I'm bleeding all over. Every breath I take hurts, I've probably broken several ribs from the beatings I've taken these past few nights.

I kneel on the ground in too much pain to move. It's the moment of truth, my one chance to make things right. I have to do this.

Mesmer drops down to his knees in front of me with his sword poised.

I raise my head so our eyes can meet, so he can see the ferocity blazing within them. So he can see that I'm not afraid.

He betrays nothing. His eyes are cold and black, the way they always are, emotionless and void, like staring into a pair of black holes.

I glance over at Beckett and it breaks my heart. He's thrashing against Ben and Corrine who restrain him, holding him back by the arms. He's screaming. I can hear him, but I can't understand him. I can't make out any words, just the frantic sound of his voice.

I'm in a daze, a dream-like state, where sounds are muffled and distant, impossible to make out. Where everything is slow, like the world is moving through mud.

My name. I can understand what Beckett is saying now. It's my name. I can see it form on his lips with each anguished scream.

I'm so sorry, Beckett. I love you.

"You're right, Celia," Mesmer says, his voice chilled and vicious. "It ends now." He runs his sword through my body, thrusting the sharp blade through my solar plexus.

I gasp but I can't breathe. Blood clogs my throat and I cough it up, speckling the ground as I double over. Blood drips down my chin, it's all I taste, the salty, metallic taste that can only ever be described as "blood."

My vision is blurred and doubled. I can't make my body move, it won't listen to the electric signals sent from my brain. All I can hear is the frantic beating of my dying heart. I'm going to into shock.

Mesmer grabs the top shoulder part of my jacket, hauling me back to my knees, preparing for the final blow, but now it's my turn.

I muster every ounce of strength I have to manipulate the electric signals in my body, and by some miracle, I move. I grab the concealed blade from inside my coat and plunge it as far as I can into his chest, thrusting under his ribcage and up, piercing straight through his heart.

His eyes go wide with shock and his mouth hangs agape, surprise swimming across his face. Mesmer brings his hands up and finds the knife, slick with blood. He tries to pull it out, but his grip is too weak, and his hands shake as they become dark with blood, his own blood.

"How is this... possible?" he chokes, blood oozing from his mouth and down his chin, dripping onto the ground with slow drops.

"I realized that in order to kill you, I myself would have to die. Your curse can't affect me if I'm sitting on Death's doorstep. Besides, I'm no longer controlling my body, I'm just controlling electricity. The brain uses electric signals to command the body, all I'm doing is controlling those with electricity manipulation. Corrine gave me the idea when she manipulated the signals in her own body to get a few memories back," I manage. "It started with us, and it ends with us. I win."

I lean into his body and grip the knife, using everything I have to pull the blade out.

Mesmer falls onto his side, his hands clawing at his chest, trying to add pressure to his wound.

I watch as blood pours out of his body, leaking between his fingers, staining them red. Blood pools around him, soaking his clothes and the ground beneath him, turning his pale blond hair crimson.

His body is racked with miniature convulsions as he tries desperately to breathe, and then he stops. His lifeless, cold eyes, still ridden with shock, stare up at me in disbelief.

His chest no longer rises and falls, he no longer leaves a cold feeling in the air. He can no longer hurt us, for his heart no longer beats. He is still.

"It's over," I sigh in exhaustion, collapsing onto my back, ready for Death to take me.

I hear footsteps rushing towards me and suddenly, I'm no longer lying on the ground, but being held in a pair of strong arms.

"Celia, come on, stay with me," Beckett says desperately.

He's so warm, so much warmer than I am.

Why am I so cold? I wonder.

"I'm sorry, Beckett, I love you," I mumble haphazardly.

"Stop talking, you're going to be fine," he tells me. "You're going to get through this and we're going to go back home to our families. Amy's going to yell at you for being reckless, Lily is going to gush over Ben, and you, Corrine, and I are going to laugh at them. We're going to finish school, get married and go to college, and you're going to get a doctorate in everything because you're a genius and you can.

"We'll graduate and get jobs. We'll have kids and grow old together.

"Or we can forget about this world and we can find a way to go home, back to where we came from.

"Or we can do none of the above. We'll do whatever the hell you want, just stay with me." His voice cracks. I can see his blue eyes, now red around the rims, brimming with tears. "Please, Celia, I finally got you back, don't leave me again. I need you, I need you in my life. Please, I love you! Just stay with me."

"I can't," I say, my voice sounding raspy to my own ears.

"Don't go," Beckett pleads, holding onto me tightly.

"I have lived for so long, it's time I die. I couldn't have asked for more. I've got two amazing children and you. I have my family in the end, and that's the only thing I need. I love you all so much."

"Shut up!"

"Corrine, what–"

"I said, shut up!" she yells, cutting Ben off in the middle of his scolding. "You said that you would make things right! You told me on the rooftop that you were going to make things right, you promised me that! Don't you dare go back on your word. You're not making things right, you're making them worse! I get that you started this, and now you feel obligated to die alongside it, but in reality, you're just running away from what you've done, leaving the ones you love with the burden of your mistakes."

Her words cut deeper than any blade ever could, because she's right, and I know that as well as she does.

"Make things right," Corrine says. My hands grow warm as she grasps them, placing in them the Mercury Crystal. She must have realized that I gave it to her when she had tackled me earlier. "Make. Things. Right."

I understand where she's going with this.

I look to Ben, making sure I've got his attention.

"Ben, get the Crystals. Mesmer has them, he wouldn't go into a fight without them, and they would never leave his person, he's too paranoid."

He doesn't hesitate before doing as he's told, quickly returning, handing me a small brown sack.

I go to open the sack but pause. *What if this won't work?* The words nag at the back of my mind, holding my hands in place.

"If I do this, we might never be together," I say, looking at Beckett. "Our hatred for Mesmer brought us together, without that, we may live our lives hating each other."

"No. What we have is true and real, do not credit Mesmer for something so beautiful. I will always find a way to love you, Celia. I managed to do it this time, didn't I? Don't worry about it, and do it."

With a sigh, I un-rope the sack and empty its contents into my hands.

A blinding, white light, glows in my hands as the pieces of stone fuse together, creating the ultimate power. The Imperial Stone. It's hot, almost burning my hands, and yet freezing at the same time. I can feel the immense power radiating from it and burrowing inside my bones, filling my body with an overwhelming sensation.

The energy from the Imperial Stone has taken residence in every cell making up my body, becoming all of my genetic makeup. Every particle of my being now blazes with power, consuming me until it is all that I am.

I close my eyes and concentrate, focusing on the power that's coursing through me. I will myself back in time with the power of the Stone, erasing all traces of the evil of Mesmer Amar from every timeline, galaxy and alternate universe. I erase the pain, the chaos, the death and the destruction, washing the stain that he was from the fabric of time.

The light in my hand intensifies and spreads, consuming my vision and blinding me until I can see no more.

I blink, as if I had just woken up from a dream, staring dazedly out over the beautiful terrain of Jupiter.

Why does he make me feel this way? I ask myself.

A soft knock shakes me out of my ponderings, snatching my attention. I shift my gaze to the wide, oak doors that are swung open, with Beckett Halverson standing in the middle.

"You must be insane," I growl. "After everything you said, you have the nerve to come bother me."

"Celia, I'm sorry. I cannot verbally express how sorry I am," he says. "What I said was wrong and I meant none of it. You are not a disappointment to your people and you do not deserve to lose yourself and become what you hate. I know that with the suitors your father has had you interview, all you have seen are power hungry people, especially the Duke of Southern Saturn –who, I made very clear, was not invited to this ball– but I swear that I am not like them. I wish not to steal your power, that is not a goal of mine. When I look at you, I do not see your present or future title, I see only Celia Walters, the beautiful woman who mystifies me and drives me crazy."

"Why should I believe a thing you say?" I ask, trying to sound stern despite the way his words make my heart feel so light.

"Because, if you listen to your heart, you'll know that I am telling you the truth," he says, sincerity burning in his captivating blue eyes.

He's right. I know he's telling the truth, but I have to maintain my dignity. I can't let him know the intensity of what he makes me feel. I have to reveal it slowly, in order to keep his respect. I can't be the princess that swoons and falls into his arms simply because his words have made my heart take flight. I need to stay strong and composed and be the same Celia Walters I always am, for both our sakes.

"Give me one chance to make things right," he pleads. "Just one."

I'm scared. If I say no and let my anger win, I could lose him, and that would cripple me. It's time to put my pride aside and go with what my heart is screaming for.

"Fine," I sigh in defeat. "But if you make me regret this, I will make your life hell, Beckett Halverson."

"You won't be disappointed," he says, grinning widely, his eyes lighting up with excitement.

Beckett takes my hand and laces our fingers together. For a moment, I lose my breath, his touch sending a slight shock through me.

He suddenly takes off, running to The Grand Staircase, pulling me along with him.

"Where are we going?" I ask in breathless bewilderment.

"If I tell you that, it will ruin the surprise." He takes the stairs two at a time, leaving me to run up the stairs at a sprint to keep up with him, unable to skip steps in my dress.

We dash down the hall and veer off into a small, discrete corridor with a single door at the end.

"If you try anything funny, I will make what I did to the Duke of Southern Saturn look like child's play," I warn, as he leads me to the door.

"How many bones did he end up breaking when you threw him through a solid oak door?" Beckett inquires.

"I haven't the slightest clue," I respond. "I didn't care enough to find out."

We reach the end of the corridor and Beckett pulls a small key from his breast pocket and slides it into the lock, hesitating slightly. He turns around so that his back is to the door and he's facing me, and I suddenly find it hard to breathe. In this cramped corridor, we're only inches apart, and I'm burning to close the distance between us.

"Do you trust me?" Beckett asks. His voice is soft and sweet, and his warm breath falls onto my lips, causing anticipation to shimmer through me.

To the ends of the universe. Those words burn at the tip of my tongue, but I bite back on them, not wanting to seem easily won or too eager.

"Marginally," I tell him, trying to keep my voice flat so as to reveal nothing.

"Do you trust me enough to close your eyes?"

Hesitantly, my eyes close and I let out a deep breath to calm myself. My heart is beating erratically, thrumming in my ears, it's almost the only thing I can hear.

For a moment we stand just there. His hands rest on my shoulders, they're warm and shaking slightly, despite his efforts not to.

Is he going to kiss me? I wonder, my heart beating frantically at that thought. I'm surprised by how badly I want him to, by how badly I want to close the distance between us. I've never felt this way before.

His hands drop from my shoulders and I hear the sound of door hinges squealing, and then his hand finds mine and we begin to walk.

My steps are cautious and slow, I'm nervous. I have no idea where I am, but I trust Beckett, I know he won't hurt me.

We walk for what feels like forever, the more time that passes, the more nervous I get. My ears strain for anything that might help me decipher what lies before my closed eyes, but there's no sound other than that of our feet clicking on the stone floor.

We come to a halt and I let out a gentle sigh, glad to have made it to my destination.

The air is warm and it smells sweet, like a summer's evening spent in the courtyards.

"You can open your eyes now," Beckett murmurs. His breath tickles my ear, sending a pleasant shiver through my body.

I do as he says, and my breath is taken away by the sight before me.

It's so beautiful, in every sense of the word. Flowers, trees and plants, all of immense beauty, ornately arranged, fill the room with an intricate irrigation system running through it all. It's more beautiful than the Mercury Gardens, which are prided for being the most beautiful gardens in the universe. I didn't know it was possible to achieve this level of beauty, to surpass the gardens in which I grew up, but now I do. The room in which I stand is set up in such a way that could only leave a person in awe, shocked by the intense majesty surrounding them.

The room is filled with an array of colors that put a rainbow to shame. Various shades of luscious greens, vibrant pinks and reds, and deep blues and purples, weave their way in and out of each other, complementing and contrasting all at once.

It's as if I had stepped into a completely different world. A world that consists of only magic and breathtaking beauty.

Sunlight, red from the setting sun, pours in through the balcony, bathing the room in a warm, pale light. There are no torches, no sources of light other than the sun and the night flowers with their fluorescent buds, blooming as the day fades. Glowing orbs of blue, purple, white, red, pink, green and orange spot the room, while fireflies dance from flower to flower. Never before had I stepped into such a fairytale.

"How did you manage this?" I ask in awe.

"I had every Garden Master work together on this project. The famous ones, the ones no one has ever heard of before, the old ones, the young ones, as long as they were good. I wanted as many new ideas as possible, and all the man and mind power I could possibly get. I wanted to create the most beautiful garden this universe has ever seen, for the most beautiful woman this universe has ever seen. For you," Beckett says, his cheeks flushing to a deep red, almost matching the roses on the balcony.

"How did you know about my love for flowers?" I inquire. "That's something almost no one knows, I've only ever told my family and Jade."

"Because you're always in the gardens when I've seen you at the Palace. It's one of the only places you've looked relaxed and happy... and I may have sought help from Jade."

I smile despite my efforts not to, I can't help it.

I wander through the room in awe, taking in the sight of everything around me, making my way to the balcony with Beckett's hand held tightly in my own.

I can see for miles; my vision is only blocked by the mountains that burst forth from the ground.

"This is so beautiful, I don't know what else to say," I tell him, leaning against the balcony railing, inhaling the sweet scent of roses.

"Then say nothing," Beckett says, following my lead and leaning up against the railing. "And simply watch the sunset."

We stand together with our shoulders touching and fingers intertwined, watching as the sun dips below the mountains, leaving the sky an orange and pink color.

All of a sudden, there's an explosion, and then the dim sky lights up with sparkling colors. Fireworks.

I turn to Beckett with an astonished expression riddling my face. He looks back at me with a smile, amused by my reaction.

I'm about to say something, but he holds up a hand and points to the sky, indicating that I should just watch the fireworks.

I smile and turn back to the railing, leaning my head against his shoulder as I watch the sky light up with a beautiful display of colors. The show comes to an end with a gigantic boom and an almost blinding flash that lights up the grounds as if the sun were still out.

"Beckett–"

"Shh," he quiets me, turning so we face each other. "Listen."

I sigh. I have so many questions I want to ask him, but I do as he says, and I'm stunned.

"This is my song," I exclaim breathlessly.

"I know," Beckett responds. "Peter composed it for you." He steps in closer and wraps me in his arms as we begin to gently sway to the soft music.

"Why?" I ask. "Why did you do all of this? Why for me?"

"Because I... I couldn't think of a better way to tell you, to show you how I feel.

"I know that in the past, you and I have clashed, and I think I finally understand why.

"You and I are vastly different, and yet incredibly similar, we call to each other. The things we can't stand in ourselves, we see mirrored in the other, along with the things we love. On top of that, I always believed that you were merely arrogant because of your amazing intellect, and that made me angry. But I got to know you, at least a little bit, and I realized that I don't hate you, that's not the case at all. Celia Walters, I am in love with you."

My heart stops, my body stops, everything stops. We stand still, Beckett with his hands on my waist, and me with mine on his shoulder, poised like statues frozen in the middle of a dance.

"I'm sorry it took me so long to figure it out, and I know you have the right to hate me for the way I've treated you, and especially for some of the things I've said tonight. So, if you hate me, I don't blame you, but if you don't, I want to make you a promise.

"Celia, I want to be your ally, someone you know you can always depend on. I want to be the person that you can always trust, the person who will never turn on you and will have your back no matter what. I want to protect you and keep you safe. I want to help you shoulder your pain and overcome the things you fear. I want to be there for you when you are happy, sad, angry, scared and whatever else you're capable of feeling. I want to spend every day for the rest of my life showing you exactly how much you mean to me, and if you don't hate me, I promise to do all of those." Beckett's blue eyes burn with an intense passion, they pierce mine and hold me in place.

He brings his forehead to mine and closes his eyes, letting out a steady breath.

My heart is racing, pounding in my ears. I breathe fast, shallow breaths, anticipation coursing through me.

"Beckett, I-I love you too. You gave me a soliloquy, but I don't know what else to say," I breathe.

"Then say nothing," he murmurs, gently tilting my head up and closing the distance between us until his lips are on mine.

My heart hammers against my ribcage as if it were trying to escape from my chest and into his hands where it belongs.

I curl my fingers into his hair, bringing him closer, opening my mouth under his. He taste sweet, like sugar and honey, and it's intoxicating.

Beckett wraps one arm around me, pulling me flush against his body, while his other hand gently cups my face.

The kiss deepens, becoming passionate and desperate, and I become absorbed. I'm lost in a new world, a world that is solely Beckett Halverson, consisting of nothing else as his lips collide with mine in a frantic rhythm.

My head spins, my heart is racing as the kiss becomes slow and heated, the wildness from before dying down into a sensual passion.

His lips are soft, moving against mine in a slow, almost torturous rhythm. His hands slide down to the small of my back, holding me, and I feel safe. Here in his arms, with his sweet lips on mine, I feel safe and secure.

Too soon do we break the kiss, the need for air separating our lips.

Beckett wraps me in his arms, drawing me into his tight embrace.

I wrap my arms around his chest, resting my head above his heart, listening to the steady rise and fall of his breaths, sinking into the rhythm I will hear for the rest of my life.

Epilogue

"Ben! Corrine!" The two had been searching relentlessly for at least two hours now, scouring the woods for their children, but there was still no sign of them.

"Beckett, I can't find them," Celia said, worry leaking into her voice.

"They couldn't have gone far," Beckett said reassuringly, taking her hand in his. "We'll find them, don't worry."

The two continued to walk through the forest, scanning the land for their children when Celia came to an abrupt stop.

"Did you hear that?" she asked suddenly, perking up at the small noise she had just heard. "It's Corrine!" Celia took off in a sprint, running towards the sound. She ducked under tree branches, hurtling over rocks and fallen trees, navigating the rough terrain with nimble footwork.

She came to a stop only once she had reached a clearing divided by a small stream that wound its way through the meadow.

Ben stood in front of Corrine, looking off to the side with an irritated look, while his sister peered curiously out from behind him.

"What are you two doing? Your father and I have been looking all over for you!" Celia exclaimed. "I was worried sick."

"Mommy!" Corrine ran to her mother and Celia knelt down and caught the small child in a hug, holding the six-year-old tightly.

"You two shouldn't have run off like that," Beckett said, coming into the clearing. "You could have gotten lost or hurt."

"It's Corrine's fault," Ben said, turning towards his parents. "I was only going for a walk and she decided to follow me."

"You still ran off, Ben," Corrine refuted.

"Yeah, but I can," he responded.

"Just because you're ten doesn't mean you can do whatever you want," Corrine told him.

"I never said it did, but I'm certainly able to take a walk on my own."

"You're just angry because you couldn't kill that bird, it had nothing to do with me, so stop taking it out on me!" Corrine yelled, becoming angry at her brother's hostility.

"Yeah, I am, and it had everything to do with you! If you hadn't decided to tag along, we never would have run into that boy, and he never would have blocked that shot. I tracked that bird for an hour!"

"You didn't have to follow or stay with me when I saw him! You could have gone on with your little hunt!" his sister responded.

"Corrine, I'm your big brother, it's my job to take care of you and keep you safe. Leaving you alone in the woods with some random, strange boy is doing none of the above," Ben sighed in exasperation.

"What boy?" Celia asked, watching the two go back and forth in confusion.

"The one over there," Ben said, pointing towards the stream.

It was at that point that everyone's gaze fell onto the boy who sat in the sand by the riverbank, staring at his feet with a dazed expression.

He wore black from head to toe. Tight black pants and loose-fitting V-neck t-shirt.

His pale blond hair shimmered in the sunlight, tossed about by the gentle wind. He was an elegant figure, with high cheek bones and bright red lips that contrasted with his pale skin. He seemed as if he were from royal descent. He held himself in a regal manner, back straight and shoulders back, but none of that was his most shocking feature. His eyes were. It looked as if someone had melted gold and poured it into his irises. They were captivating, mesmerizing.

"Who is this boy?" Celia asked in wonder, cautious of the beautiful, angel-like child.

"I don't know," Ben answered. "Corrine and I were walking through the woods when she suddenly stopped, staring off at a boy wandering around looking lost. She ran to catch up to him and I followed her and then we ended up here. I tried to talk to him, but he'd only respond to Corrine. While they were talking that bird I had been tracking showed up and when I went to get it with my slingshot, this kid tackled me.

I shoved him off, and he's been sitting there, looking like that since," Ben explained.

"Did he say why he tackled you?" Beckett asked.

"Because he was going to kill it," the boy said, suddenly speaking up. "It never did anything wrong, so why would he kill it? Life is precious, no matter how small. It should be cherished, not wasted." His voice is soft and gentle, like velvet. One could not help but to sit and listen to every sweet word he spoke.

"What's your name?" Beckett asked gently, addressing the angelic child.

The boy cast his eyes down, becoming silent, resuming his previous state, lost in a daze.

Beckett looked up at Celia with confusion, bewildered by the child's actions.

"He'll only talk to Corrine, I already told you that," Ben said in irritation. "But after the kid freaked out, Corrine decided to be shy."

Celia looked down curiously at her daughter.

"Sweetie, can you do something for me?" she asked. "I need you to talk to this boy so we can help him and get him back home. Do you think you can do you that?"

"Will you come with me, Mommy?" the small girl asked, her electric blue eyes meeting Celia's.

"Of course, I will," Celia said, setting Corrine on the ground. "Come on, let's go." She took her daughter by the hand, and together they made their way to the river bank where the mysterious boy sat.

"Okay, Corrine, can you ask him where his parents are?" Celia asked.

"I don't know. I guess I don't have parents," the boy said.

"You'll talk to me?" Celia asked, slightly shocked.

"She trusts you," the boy said, pointing to Corrine. "If she can trust you, then I can too."

"Alright, how did you find yourself here?" Celia asked.

"I don't know that either," he responded quietly, casting his vision down so as to not meet anyone's eyes. "I don't know anything. All I remember is darkness, and cold misery, and then the forest. The soft ground beneath my feet, the warm sunlight all around me, and a pretty girl following me with curious eyes."

Corrine's face flushed to a deep shade of red as the boy explained the situation. Celia and Beckett exchanged a knowing look, Celia with a small smile, Beckett looking somewhat displeased.

"What are we going to do with him, Beck?" Celia asked. "We can't leave an eight-year-old with no memory wandering around in the woods alone."

"What makes you say he's eight?" Beckett asked, neglecting Celia's question.

"Because he looks older than Corrine and younger than Ben, but that's not the point, Beckett. What are we going to do with him?"

"I don't know. Can Jade take care of him until we sort things out?"

"No, she's got her hands full with Lily. That kid will tear the place down if not carefully supervised."

Now it was Ben's turn to blush, his face becoming a bright red at the mention of Lily's name.

"What about Peter and Amy?" Beckett asked.

"They just got married, they won't want to take in a kid right now," Celia reasoned.

"That's a good point."

"How about Ophelia?"

"Ophelia?" Beckett looked at her with confusion. "Who's Ophelia?"

"Ophelia Price, she's the Queen of Saturn. She and her husband Michael assumed the crown after Sylvia Trunnel assassinated the Royal Family of Saturn. Michael was the Duke of Northern Saturn and after the Insurgent War, he and Ophelia united the Northern and Southern regions of their planet," Celia explained.

"Oh, that Ophelia!" Beckett exclaimed. "Michael told me they were thinking of having a child, but they didn't want to deal with the baby stages. I said I didn't blame him."

"Beckett, get to the point," Celia said, demanding that he stay focused.

"Right. Well they don't want to deal with a newborn, so perhaps they would greatly enjoy the company of this child."

"Alright then, we'll take him to Ophelia," Celia said, matter-off-factly.

"Mommy, can I talk to him now?" Corrine asked impatiently, injecting herself into her parent's discussion.

"Of course, you can," Celia responded, smiling down at her daughter.

Slowly, Corrine let go of her mother's hand and took a seat in the sand in front of the golden-eyed boy.

"Can I ask you something?" she inquired.

"Anything," the boy responded with a warm smile.

"I didn't get the chance to ask you before, but what's your name?" she asked.

"It's Mesmer," he said. "Mesmer Amar."

Printed in the United States
By Bookmasters